D0114145

STRAND PRICE
$ 5.00

SPECIAL MESSAGE TO READERS

THE ULVERSCROFT FOUNDATION
(registered UK charity number 264873)
was established in 1972 to provide funds for research, diagnosis and treatment of eye diseases. Examples of major projects funded by the Ulverscroft Foundation are:-

- The Children's Eye Unit at Moorfields Eye Hospital, London
- The Ulverscroft Children's Eye Unit at Great Ormond Street Hospital for Sick Children
- Funding research into eye diseases and treatment at the Department of Ophthalmology, University of Leicester
- The Ulverscroft Vision Research Group, Institute of Child Health
- Twin operating theatres at the Western Ophthalmic Hospital, London
- The Chair of Ophthalmology at the Royal Australian College of Ophthalmologists

You can help further the work of the Foundation by making a donation or leaving a legacy. Every contribution is gratefully received. If you would like to help support the Foundation or require further information, please contact:

THE ULVERSCROFT FOUNDATION
The Green, Bradgate Road, Anstey
Leicester LE7 7FU, England
Tel: (0116) 236 4325

website: www.foundation.ulverscroft.com

SEARCHING FOR GRACE KELLY

1955: For a small-town girl with big-city dreams, there is no address more glamorous than New York's Barbizon Hotel — the place where Grace Kelly lived when she first came to the big city. Laura, an aristocratic beauty from Connecticut, comes to stay for a magazine internship, and dreams of becoming a writer. Her hopelessly romantic roommate, Dolly, is there to attend secretarial school, and is looking to be swept off her feet. Vivian, a brash British bombshell with a disregard for the hotel's rules, rounds out the trio of friends. Together they embark on a journey of discovery that will take them from the penthouse apartments of Park Avenue to the Beat scene of Greenwich Village to Atlantic City's Steel Pier — and into the arms of very different men who will alter their lives forever.

M. G. CALLAHAN

SEARCHING FOR GRACE KELLY

Complete and Unabridged

CHARNWOOD
Leicester

First published in Great Britain in 2015 by
Sphere
An imprint of Little, Brown Book Group
London

First Charnwood Edition
published 2016
by arrangement with
Little, Brown Book Group
An Hachette UK Company
London

A catalogue record for this book is available
from the British Library.

ISBN 978–1–4448–2777–4

Published by
F. A. Thorpe (Publishing)
Anstey, Leicestershire

Set by Words & Graphics Ltd.
Anstey, Leicestershire
Printed and bound in Great Britain by
T. J. International Ltd., Padstow, Cornwall

This book is printed on acid-free paper

For Philomena and Deegan

Prologue

December 1955

Good enough, she thinks, puckering one more time into a piece of tissue. She leans away a little from the dressing table, makes a final appraisal. Maybe a touchup with some light powder. She snaps the compact shut, stands, and steps back from the mirror. One last long view: tailored wool suit (fifteen dollars at Oppenheim Collins on West Thirty-Fourth Street), a single strand of pearls, gloves, and her hat. Since she was old enough to understand fashion, she has abided by one credo and one credo only, and that is from Edna Woolman Chase, the editor of *Vogue:* 'Fashion can be bought. Style one must possess.'

She slips her arms into her coat. She will not be outside long, but still, she will be outside. She takes a deep breath.

I'm ready.

Should she bring her bag? Yes, it will have her identification inside. She slides it onto her crooked forearm, then downs the final gulp of whiskey from the crystal tumbler on her dressing table, feels it barrel down her throat, warm and bitter. A small smile escapes as she glances at the suitcase and hatbox beside the door. Both are empty. Thank God, neither of the girls had the chance to pick them up before they'd left. She'd

1

have been found out. And then what would she have done?

She steps out into the hallway. Quiet. It is Friday, the last before Christmas. Most of the girls have left already. The lucky ones are sipping champagne, on dates at the Stork or the Harwyn, others already on trains or buses back home for the holidays, bags packed and brimming with lies about their fizzy days in the big city. Those left behind are scattered about the building, 'the Women,' as they are known but never called, each locked on the other side of her door, her only company tepid tea and crossword puzzles.

She passes the elevator bank. If she steps into the elevator, there will most certainly be questions from the operator, one always desperate for a story. Instead, she exits the door at the end of the hall that leads to the stairwell, beginning a slow, steady ascent up the steps.

It is fifteen minutes before she pushes the door out, feels the whoosh of crisp night air rush at her. She is winded from walking up so many flights in heels, but the biting chill feels good seizing her lungs. She steps onto the veranda, looks out onto New York — on beautiful, wonderful, dizzying New York, teeming with life, each tiny lit window a tale: of someone, of something, of heartbreak and triumph and joy and agony and stupidity and sorrow and sex and laughter and betrayal and loneliness.

She takes in another deep breath, places her hands on the balustrade. *It is*, she thinks, *a glorious night to die.*

1

June 1955

It was curious that a building so large, with so many people hurrying in so many different directions, could be so quiet. And yet the noise inside Grand Central was not so much cacophony, as one might expect from the 'train station of the world,' but rather a low, steady hum, like a running current of electricity, fed by hundreds and hundreds of people passing one another by.

Laura wanted to stay here. Just stay still and *be*. Stand invisible and safe by the elegant old clock in the middle of the terminal and study the faces of every single person coming and going. Imagine their back-stories, invent tales of long-lost lovers reunited, rushing to one another as the sun splashed, cathedral-like, down from the long, slender windows. It was at these moments when she felt her body tense with energy. She could write their stories. Would write them. It was, after all, why she had come.

She looked at the clock again. One.

I'd better call.

She lugged her suitcases over to a wall of phone booths and slipped into the last of them. 'Yes, operator?' she said. 'I'd like to place a collect call to Greenwich, Connecticut, please. Greenwich-1, 3453.'

3

David picked up. For an eleven-year-old, he had a strange obsession with the phone, always wanted to answer it, which no one could explain but everyone acquiesced to, grateful he didn't sport even more peculiar habits. His cousin Donald had occasionally been caught wearing his mother's jewelry, which everyone also knew but never acknowledged. Such things were not spoken of in the Dixon family.

'Hey, Bucko, it's Laura,' she said, enjoying the unvarnished glee in his voice as he unleashed an avalanche of questions about the train ride down, about the apartment — she'd stopped correcting him that it was just a room — that she actually had yet to step into. 'No, no, no,' she was saying, trying to cut him off. 'I'm still in the train station. I promise I will write you a long letter and tell you everything as soon as there is an everything to tell. But I *will* tell you I already bought you something.'

He sounded as if he might actually reach through the phone to get it. 'What?! What?!!'

'The latest Batman. I think they get them earlier here than they do at Carson's.' Now in a complete frenzy, he insisted on knowing what the cover looked like, what the story was about. She fumbled with her bag and extracted the July issue of *Detective Comics*. 'The Thousand-and-One Escapes of Batman and Robin,' she relayed, perusing the cover image of Batman and his trusty sidekick bound and about to drown. Marmy didn't like David reading comic books — 'Superman is not going to get him accepted at Yale' was a favorite axiom — but Laura's father pointed out that it was better than an addiction to television. 'I'll send it back with Marmy when she visits.'

'No, no!' the boy protested. 'She'll just throw it out.'

He had a point. 'Hmm. Okay, how about this: I'll hide it inside another gift for you. See how that works out? Now you'll get two things from New York.'

Mollified, he went to get his mother. Laura had pictured Marmy waiting by the phone for her call, but instead heard David yelling up the stairs, telling her to pick up. Perhaps she had one of her headaches.

The other line clicked alive. 'Hang up, David,' her mother said. The kitchen phone clicked off. 'Well, you arrived safe and sound, then? Are you at the hotel?'

'No, I'm still at Grand Central Station. It's — '

'Terminal, dear. It's Grand Central *Terminal*. Please be precise, Laura. Women of good breeding are always precise.'

Laura inhaled sharply. 'Of course,' she mumbled. She wanted to tell her mother that being precise wasn't what counted, what was important. Right now what was important was to be downstairs in the Oyster Bar, sipping a Tom Collins, making witty conversation with a traveling salesman from St. Louis who thought she was the most fascinating and sophisticated girl ever and had never heard of Greenwich, Connecticut, and never, ever wanted to go there.

But she couldn't and knew she wouldn't. One

wrong word and she'd be back in Greenwich overnight. And the next time she may never get out.

'Remember, Aunt Marjorie and I will be down in two weeks to take you shopping for the rest of your wardrobe,' Marmy was saying. 'We can't have you working on Lexington Avenue appearing anything less than your very best.'

'It's just for a month,' Laura reminded her.

'It's *Mademoiselle*, Laura. You cannot go into the most fashionable magazine for American college girls and not look the part.' A weary sigh escaped. 'We'll go to Bendel's and Bergdorf's, of course, and then perhaps pop over to Knox the Hatter if there's time. Aunt Marjorie will want to eat at the Colony Club, which will try me to the point of exasperation, but I suppose it can't be helped.' Laura's eyes had fixed on a woman wearing the new polka-dot dress from B. Altman and was about to remark on it when she heard her mother gently clear her throat, her effete signal that a conversation was ending. 'I'll let your father know you arrived safely. Go right to the hotel and call us tomorrow. I want to know how the accommodations are, that everything is in order.'

Ten minutes later, the city whizzed by as the taxi zoomed up Third Avenue toward East Sixty-Third Street. Laura wanted to take it all in but willed herself not to. *There'll be time for all of that*, she thought. *I am not a tourist. I live here now. Even if it is only for a month.*

The other girls — who, like her, had been named 'guest editors' at *Mademoiselle*, and who

6

would be putting out the magazine's annual college issue in August — would also be arriving this weekend. Laura had pleaded with Marmy and Dad that she should come a few days earlier, that getting settled first would leave her more refreshed, sharper than the other girls when they all walked into the Street & Smith offices for that first day of work. Marmy was nothing if not competitive, as her bridge partners could attest. But the Friday before was as early as they'd allow. At least they'd let her come alone.

The cab pulled over to the left, and the driver stopped the meter with a slap. 'Forty cents, sweetheart,' he said.

★ ★ ★

'What girl wouldn't want this marvelous location to live and study for her future?' the ad in the back of *Charm* had tantalizingly asked, and from the moment she'd read it, at the age of fifteen, Laura knew she would one day live in the Barbizon Hotel for Women.

'Name?' the dour-looking woman at the reception desk asked.

'Dixon. Laura Dixon,' she replied.

'Yes. You're part of the *Mademoiselle* group, correct?'

'Oh, yes. But I wanted to come a bit early to . . . ' Why was she so nervous? 'To get to know the city a bit. Get my bearings.' She sounded like an idiot.

The clerk, still peering over her glasses and never looking up, continued to scan the big black register on the desk. 'Yes, well. Normally you would sit for your interview with Mrs. Mayhew before seeing your room. Unfortunately, she is off premises today.' She began scribbling. 'You'll come down tomorrow morning at nine for the orientation tour to familiarize yourself with the amenities and procedures. Please be prompt.'

'Of course.' Laura nodded.

The clerk looked up, appraising. Despite the summer heat, Laura had worn her best pair of white kid gloves, feeling it would show her commitment to fitting in at the city's most desirable residence for young women. She had selected a canary-yellow linen dress with a cinched belt and a straw hat with a matching sash, hoping to broadcast a stylish contrast to her dark hair and eyes. But the cab had been stuffy and hot, and her nerves had exacerbated her perspiring. Her hair was matted underneath the hat, which now seemed pretentious and ridiculous. The palms of her gloves were almost soaked through. She had hoped to sweep through the doors of the Barbizon as Gene Tierney and had instead arrived as Gene Tunney.

'We would typically put you with another girl on the magazine apprenticeship program, but you've arrived early and those rooms are not yet available,' the woman was saying. 'So I've had to put you with one of the Katie Gibbs girls.' Laura had no idea who Katie Gibbs was but figured she must be important. 'This,' the clerk continued, thrusting a small pale blue handbook at Laura, 'is the Barbizon manual, with your rules and requirements for residency. Please read it thoroughly. Any violation of policy is grounds for immediate expulsion.' She lifted her eyes briefly, coolly surveying her as one would an unruly child on the first day of school. 'I would particularly draw your attention to page eight.'

Laura was about to start thumbing through to page eight when the clerk waved her away. 'Elevators around the corner,' she said, sliding a key over with her left hand. 'Twelfth floor.'

Five minutes later Laura was outside her room, fumbling to put the key properly in the lock, when the door suddenly opened, almost knocking her back on her heels. 'Oh, sorry! Sorry, sorry!' exclaimed a short, slightly stout girl — she couldn't have been more than five two — with curly black hair and a broad, heart-shaped face so kind that you almost couldn't imagine it dark or angry. She reached past Laura, grabbing her luggage. 'Here, let me help you!'

Laura protested but the girl was already ahead of her, two hands lifting the cumbersome suitcase and plopping it onto the single bed on the left. 'I'm so sorry,' Laura said, tossing her handbag, hat, and the Barbizon manual onto the bed with it. 'Packing lightly proved to be a challenge.'

'Well, you're here now,' the girl said brightly, taking a step closer and extending a hand. Laura wasn't sure why, but she suspected the girl was midwestern. 'I'm your roommate, Dolores Hickey. But everybody calls me Dolly. Except my grandmother, who is deeply religious and thinks

Dolores is much more suitable, but then Dolores means something like 'pain' in Latin — you know the Catholics — and who wants to be called 'pain,' anyway? So I'm glad to be Dolly.'

An almost maternal warmth radiated from Dolly, though Laura suspected she was probably a year or two younger than her own twenty years. For the next fifteen minutes, Dolly rambled on about anything and everything, from her studies at Katie Gibbs — a secretarial school, whose students all lived at the Barbizon, though most would be gone for the summer, but Dolly had landed a summer job working as a typist in a small publishing house, so no back to Utica for *her* — to how she had recently become addicted to whiskey sours at the Landmark Tavern, where she liked to go because even though it was a taproom, the hamburgers were to die for, even though she shouldn't really be eating hamburgers, of course, because, well, look at me, she said. She grabbed Laura's hotel manual, flopped onto her own bed as she kicked off her shoes. 'Have you read this yet?'

Laura was layering blouses into her tiny dresser. 'No, I just received it when I checked in,' she said. She took a step back, appraised the bureau closer. 'Oh my. Is this all the drawer space we have?'

'Yessiree,' Dolly said, thumbing through the booklet. 'The Ritz this ain't. No matter what the brochures say. Speaking of which, you don't have to read this. I can tell you anything you need to know about living here.'

'All right, then, Dolly Hickey of Utica, New

York. What's on page eight?'

Dolly laughed. 'Ha! You must have been checked in by Metzger. She's famous for trying to scare every girl who comes in the door with that.'

'With what?'

'Page eight. That's where they talk about male visitors.' Dolly looked over, wiggling her eyebrows. She flipped to the page, cleared her throat dramatically as if reciting *Macbeth*. ''The Barbizon understands . . . '' She glanced over at Laura. 'That's another thing: They always talk about 'the Barbizon' as if it's a person. Or God.' She resumed reading. ''The Barbizon understands that New York offers unlimited entertainment and diversion for today's accomplished young woman, and that dates with a suitor can enhance this experience. However, to ensure that the decorum and integrity of our residents is protected, no males other than fathers or physicians may be admitted into the personal domiciles of the Barbizon at any time. Residents who wish to entertain callers . . . '' Dolly looked over again, shrieking. '*Callers!* When was this written, 1890?' She shook her head, finished up. 'Okay, sorry. ' . . . callers may receive them in the public lounges on the mezzanine or on the outside veranda after obtaining a visitor's pass from the registration desk.''

Dolly tossed the book aside, laughing. 'I bet they lifted that entire paragraph right out of the handbook for the Carmelites.'

Laura had worried about what her roommate

11

would be like, expecting to be paired with another girl like herself, a college coed running around in new heels, aiming to impress the steely, impervious, and impeccable women who ran *Mademoiselle*. By coming early, she'd prevented that. Dolly was spunky, authentic. Laura could picture her married, ironing shirts and making endless meat loaves, and happy as could be doing it. What she herself would wind up doing, she had no idea. It didn't matter, as long as she didn't end up being Marmy.

Laura picked up a copy of *Movie Stars* magazine on top of the dresser. Jane Powell stared back from the cover, beaming under a straw hat not unlike the one she'd worn to arrive. Laura wondered if it was some sort of sign. She began fanning herself with it. 'It's awfully warm in here,' she said.

'Page ten,' Dolly replied drolly. ' 'No electrical appliances allowed.' '

'A fan isn't a waffle iron, for God's sake.'

'Mmmm . . . I would love to eat a waffle right now. With ice cream. On the boardwalk at Coney Island.' Dolly flopped onto her back and crossed her legs. 'Although I don't think Frank would like it.'

Laura stuffed the last of the blouses into the drawer and shoved it closed. How was she going to survive without an iron? She turned back to Dolly. 'Who's Frank?'

Dolly propped herself up on one elbow. 'My fella. Well, he *was* sorta my fella. But I think he'll be my fella again. He was always worried I was going to get fat. His sister Regina is *really* fat.'

'All of this talk of food has me starving,' Laura said, running her fingers through her damp hair. She'd only had fruit at breakfast — Marmy had insisted that bacon and eggs would make her nauseated on the train ride down. 'Want to go get a bite to eat?'

* * *

The Barbizon coffee shop was small and narrow: a long counter, stools, and a ring of leather booths that horseshoed around. It was also, mercifully, air-conditioned. Laura and Dolly slid into a booth, the cool leather a tonic on the skin. 'Ohhhhh, that feels nice,' Dolly said, looking around for a waitress.

Predictably, the place was littered with girls who lived at the hotel, though Laura noticed a few middle-aged types, each eating alone, engrossed in a book or magazine. Dolly followed her stare.

'They're the ones we're all afraid of turning into,' Dolly whispered.

'What do you mean?'

'The Women. They came here when they were our age, in the thirties and forties, and never left. They're the Barbizon spinsters.' Dolly dissolved into an exaggerated shudder. 'I'd rather *die* than be living here at twenty-five.'

Dolly ordered an egg salad sandwich and a Coke. Laura wanted a burger. Marmy would hate that.

Laura's eyes kept going back to the Women. There were three or four of them scattered about the coffee shop; Laura thought each had to be at least thirty-five. Maybe forty. What had happened to keep them here? Were these ladies as unhappy as they appeared, slurping as they sat reading *Ellery Queen*? Had they once been her, young and impatient and curious about the world, thrilled to have arrived in Manhattan, and then watched it all go horribly wrong? *Each one of them has a story*, she thought. *A love gone wrong, a promise unkept, a betrayal uncovered . . .*

'Hello? Hello? Are you still here?' Dolly was saying, waving her hands.

Laura snapped back into the present. 'Sorry. It's compulsive. I love watching people. It's the reason I want to be a writer.'

'I imagine being a writer would be fun. It gives you an excuse to snoop into other people's lives — Oh my. Don't look now, but look at who just walked in.'

Laura ignored the contradiction in Dolly's commandment and swiveled her head to catch a glimpse. A tall blond man in a sparkling white tennis shirt and draping linen slacks had come in. He had his elbows on the counter, ordering something from a girl who looked agog to be taking his order.

'Who is he?' Laura asked.

Dolly shot over a look of disbelief. 'And you're going to be working at a magazine? That's Box Barnes.'

Laura's eyes narrowed. He was impeccably groomed and unquestionably handsome in a country-club style she recognized from growing

14

up in Greenwich. He was clearly, if not an athlete, then at least supremely athletic, with a head of wavy, perfectly Brylcreemed hair and piercing pale blue eyes. In short, the kind of man women noticed and often dreamed of. But there was something else about him, a magnetism that seemed to emanate from him like aftershave. His gaze caught Laura's and he smiled. She whipped around in the booth, mortified.

'Did he just wink at you?' Dolly asked, suddenly aflutter.

'Don't be ridiculous,' Laura said. She could feel her cheeks beginning to flush. If she was going to act this embarrassed every time she locked eyes with a man in New York City, she was going to have a very short visit. 'So, who is Box Barnes?'

Dolly leaned across the table. 'Just one of the most eligible bachelors in the city, silly. He's the heir to Barnes & Foster, the Fifth Avenue department store. That's how he got the nickname: When he was a kid, he was always hanging around the store, playing in the empty boxes they delivered all the merchandise in. His real name is Benjamin. Or maybe it's Bobby. Anyway, he's always out at the most fabulous nightclubs and premieres.' She shook her head. 'You really need to start reading Cholly Knickerbocker.'

The waitress came, slid the sandwiches onto the table. Laura took the opportunity to ask her for mayonnaise, turning her head so that the end of the diner counter came into her peripheral vision. But Box Barnes was gone.

* ★ *

Back upstairs, Laura asked, 'So why would a guy like Box Barnes be in the Barbizon coffee shop? Does he live near here?'

'No idea,' Dolly replied. 'Probably meeting someone here. Boys from all over town come here to meet the Barbizon girls.' She looked over at Laura, who was now sitting on her bed, and added quietly, 'At least the ones who look like you.'

'Now, Dolly, I don't think — '

A frantic series of raps on the room door interrupted. 'Hurry! Hurry! Bloody hell, open up!' came the urgent stage whisper from the other side.

The two of them exchanged quizzical looks before Dolly walked over and opened the door. A tall girl with flaming red hair burst into the room, quickly moving Dolly aside and throwing her back against the door to slam it shut.

'Okay,' she said in an unmistakably British accent. 'If anyone asks, I was here with you two all afternoon.'

2

Laura froze, trying to will herself to move, to speak, *do* something. Anything. She was a good girl who had made a vocation, under the watchful eye and tutelage of a mother fully invested in that vocation's success, to be a proper girl, the girl who at the age of twelve already knew how to elegantly host a proper tea. She knew everything about the right thing to do. Unless she was in a situation where there was a very clear choice of the wrong thing to do.

The year before, she'd read an article in *Glamour* called 'The Girl Every Girl Wants to Be,' and looking at this red-haired creature splayed against the door in front of her, the only thought that crashed into her brain was, *I want to be her*. She wanted to be bold and British and have silky red hair pulled back into a tight bun with a crest of bangs and look elegant in a patterned shirtwaist dress while backed up against a door as if trying to prevent an invasion of creatures in a monster movie. She wanted to be dangerous and unpredictable.

'Look, I don't know what's — ' Dolly's protestation was cut off by another sharp rap at the door.

'Please open the door, ladies.' Laura instantly recognized the voice. Metzger.

Remember, the redhead silently mouthed to them, pointing to the floor a few times as she

17

gingerly stepped aside. Dolly walked haltingly to the door, still glancing over at the strange, glamorous invader, and opened it. Metzger stepped in.

'Ah, yes, Miss Windsor. I see you are indeed present. I was told you'd dashed in here.'

'Just visiting friends,' the girl replied, with the airiness of Princess Margaret casually reporting it had started to rain. She dropped into the small chair in the corner of the room, lazily turning an eye out the window.

'I see.' Metzger eyed Laura and Dolly. 'You two ladies know Miss Windsor well, do you?'

Dolly stammered out an answer. 'Oh, I wouldn't say — '

'No,' Laura interrupted, with more emphasis than she'd intended. 'As you know, ma'am, I've just arrived here. But Miss Hickey and Miss Windsor both stepped forward and introduced themselves and have been making me feel very at home. We've been together all afternoon.'

Why? she wondered. Why lie, protect a girl she'd never met, whose first name she didn't even know, who had been up to God knows what? She'd known the answer before she'd even posed the question. Because it was exciting. Because this was New York, the beginning of *her* New York, and because in New York you did crazy things you would never do in Greenwich, like making up stories about knowing people you actually didn't know at all.

'Is that so,' Metzger was saying. Laura caught Dolly's panicked eyes and willed some calm into the room. If Laura was caught lying, the consequences could be dire — what would Marmy say if she was kicked out of the Barbizon on her very first day? And yet the adrenaline now roaring through her body overruled everything.

'Yes,' Laura replied coolly. Out of the corner of her eye, she caught a glimpse of the redhead, still absently gazing out the window.

'Well, that is interesting,' Metzger said. 'Because not two hours ago Miss Windsor signed in a male guest . . . ' She pulled a piece of paper from her skirt pocket. 'A Mr. St. Marks. And obtained a pass for the fourth-floor lounge. And yet' — she looked directly at Laura — 'there is no record of the aforementioned Mr. St. Marks ever leaving the hotel. And, in fact, several girls reported to me directly' — she slowly turned her withering stare over to the redhead — 'that Miss Windsor and Mr. St. Marks were seen in a rather, shall we say, untoward position in the conservatory.' Her eyes, dark and harsh, shifted back first to Laura then to Dolly, who now appeared as if she might be sick.

'And yet you two insist that Miss Windsor has been with you all afternoon. My, my, such intrigue! How *shall* we sort it all out?' She leveled her gaze back on Laura. 'Now, Miss Dixon, perhaps you would like to recount exactly how you three spent your afternoon, specifically. I would love to be able to give your mother a full report.'

The mention of Marmy struck like an elbow to the ribs. What if she truly was forced out for some breach of Barbizon ethics? Her behavior would be reported to *Mademoiselle*; she'd lose her job before she'd even started. Her parents would have to come and retrieve her, escort her like a murder suspect through the lobby as the other girls stood in clusters, each looking over in whispering disgust. Laura felt her courage slowly dissipating, like the air seeping out of a child's birthday party balloon.

'Well, I — ' she began.

'I think it's time to tell the truth,' Dolly interjected, coming to her side and sliding her arm in Laura's. 'You see, Mrs. Metzger, it's all quite . . . delicate, as I am sure you'll see. We're all just trying to protect . . . Miss Windsor. I mean, what girl doesn't occasionally get her head turned by a handsome guy? And, of course, you no doubt saw Mr. Sinmarks for yourself — he's quite dreamy, wouldn't you say? — and Miss Windsor had no intention of leaving the lounge, of course, but then Mr. Sinmarks — '

'Yes, Mr. St. Marks,' Laura interjected.

' . . . Of course. Mr. *St. Marks* had heard so much about the conservatory, which is lovely, after all, and so she thought, 'Well, I guess a little pop-in wouldn't hurt, right?' and then the next thing you know, Mr. St. Marks was a bit too, well, friendly, you might say, and luckily that's when Miss Dixon and I happened to be passing by, and so we were able to intervene and convince him that it was best that his visit be cut short, and he was just so horribly embarrassed by the whole episode that he decided to leave by the back stairs, and that seemed like a good idea for everyone to avoid any more fuss, and so . . . yeah. That's . . . everything. That's what

20

happened, plain and simple.' Her eyes were positively shining, as if she'd just finished some bravura performance on the stage.

Laura looked again at the redhead, who by her measure hadn't moved an inch from her spot in the corner, content to remain securely in the wings as this melodrama of her own creation played out. Her dress fanned out to drape artfully over both sides of the chair, and her legs were crossed daintily at the ankles, as if she were sitting for a portrait by Horst. If she appeared the least bit worried, she betrayed no sign of it.

'Fascinating,' Mrs. Metzger said, a weariness in her voice that signaled that this was not the first time someone had offered a barely plausible, if inane, version of events centered on the comings and goings of the unpredictable Miss Windsor and one of what was surely her many male visitors. She eyed the still-stoic girl evenly. 'Miss Windsor, please make sure in the future that no more of your guests are given unauthorized 'tours' within the building and that they leave through the *front* door. Are we understood?'

The girl turned her head slowly. 'Of course,' she said, producing a smile suitable for a winning hand of bridge. 'Always glad to be of service. Good afternoon.'

'Please don't forget your appointment with Mrs. Mayhew tomorrow morning, Miss Dixon,' Metzger added as she walked to the door. 'Good day, ladies.'

No sooner had the door closed when Dolly flopped onto her bed. 'Oh, good Lord!'

'Where *on earth* did you come up with that?' Laura asked.

'Hell if I know,' Dolly mumbled into the pillow. She turned her head, smiled. 'Actually, I'm a little unsettled at my ability to lie that easily. I'm afraid it says something very terrible about me.'

'Nonsense,' Laura replied. 'The only thing it tells me is that if I ever get in a jam, I want you there to get me out.'

Dolly giggled, sat upright. 'Well, I guess this is as good a time as any for introductions,' she said, looking over at their guest. 'I'm Dolly, this is Laura. Otherwise known as the girls who just saved your heinie.'

'Indeed,' the girl replied brightly, rising out of her chair. 'Vivian Windsor, proud subject of the queen. Bravo. I knew I'd knocked on the right door. Christ, I need a fag.' She pulled a pack of cigarettes out of her pocket and lit one. She offered one to Dolly, who readily accepted.

Laura declined. 'So, what really happened with Mr. St. Marks? I certainly hope he was worth the trouble.'

'Good girls don't kiss and tell. Which is, of course, precisely why I do. Despite Miss Dolly's colorful rendition, alas the real story rather pales in comparison, I'm afraid. So I think I'm going to adopt hers and have the lasting image be one of an absolute rat scurrying down the back staircase.'

Laura loved the girl's faintly aristocratic bearing, her stylish wit. She longed to hear her talk further. 'I get the feeling this is not exactly a new experience for you.'

'You mean old Metzger? Oh, bosh no. We understand one another by now. She wags her finger and threatens to send me to the reformatory for bad girls, I say nothing, implying some form of contrition, and then we all happily move on. I must say that I'm not usually forced into such dramatics as intruding into the rooms of girls I haven't yet met. Terribly rude. So sorry. But any port in a storm and all that, you know? And look at it this way: If there's one thing the British know something about, it's good manners. So in order to show my gratitude for saving my lovely 'heinie' today, I'd like to invite you girls out tonight, as my guests at the Stork.'

Dolly looked like she might faint. 'The Stork Club!' she exclaimed. 'Jeez! Are you serious?'

'It's just a nightclub, darling, not a date with Rock Hudson, but I'm nevertheless glad to note your enthusiasm. I start work at ten, so come anytime after that and I'll get you all squared away.'

Laura knew the Stork. It was a nightclub famous for its glittering roster of Broadway and Hollywood celebrities, who came there to dance and sip champagne. To imagine that she'd be in such a place on her first night in New York was almost unfathomable. 'What do you do there?' Laura asked.

'Cigarette girl,' Vivian replied matter-of-factly. 'One day I'll be singing with the band, mind you, but for now, it's strictly selling smokes and avoiding wandering hands.'

'You're a singer!' Dolly said, as if amazed that

anything could prove more interesting than working at the Stork.

'Only for money,' Vivian replied. 'Well, I must run. See you girls later. Toodles.' And with that she floated out the door, in a strikingly different manner than she'd come in.

As Laura contemplated the whirlwind that was Vivian Windsor — and how many more surprises lay within the walls of the baroque Barbizon Hotel for Women — Dolly had more pressing concerns. 'Laura!' she wailed. 'What in God's name are we going to *wear*?'

★　★　★

They should have hailed a taxi. But in all of the things she had quickly learned about Dolly, her frugality had been one of the first. Dolly had convinced her that since the Stork Club was only ten blocks away (a lie; that didn't count the cross blocks from Lexington to Fifth), and since it was also such a nice evening, it was best if they simply sauntered their way to the club.

It was when they reached Fifty-Third Street that Laura realized the magnitude of their mistake. She'd decided to wear her new black peeptoe heels, which were now pinching; she could already feel the beginnings of a blister on the back of her left foot. To make it all worse, the night had turned unexpectedly humid; her hair, carefully combed down to her shoulders in shiny waves, now felt like a Brillo pad.

By the time they reached the red awning stretching across the sidewalk, STORK CLUB

24

blazoned in big, bold letters across it, she felt her spirits lifting. 'Hi, we're friends of Vivian Windsor,' Dolly chirped to the dour doorman. He continued looking down at his clipboard, occasionally barking a terse order to a passing page or busboy. Dolly tried again. 'I said, we're friends — '

'I heard you the first time, dear. I don't know any Vivian . . . '

'Windsor. She's a cigarette girl here,' Laura said. 'She invited us.'

He looked up briefly, with an expression that conveyed that the only bigger waste of time than explaining to him that they'd been invited was telling him they'd been invited by the cigarette girl. 'Oh, did she? Well, how kind of her majesty. I'm afraid you've come for nothing, ladies. The Stork Club does not admit unescorted women. Club policy, strictly enforced. Enjoy the rest of your evening.'

Her feet were killing her and her blood simmered from the rudeness of the rejection, yet the only thing Laura could think of was how her mother would have handled the situation. How she would have demanded to see owner Sherman Billingsley himself, then whipped up such a maelstrom that she would have ended up seated in a booth with Bing Crosby. But Laura was too sore and too tired from all of the earlier drama with Vivian to channel Marmy. 'Come on, we'll take a taxi back,' she said.

Dolly pulled her away from the entrance. 'Are you *crazy*?' she said. 'We were invited to the Stork, and we are going into the Stork.' She grabbed Laura's hand, began yanking her down the block. 'C'mon.'

For ten minutes they stood at the corner of Fifty-Third and Fifth, watching New Yorkers whir by in cabs, buses, the occasional DeSoto. Laura rested against a building and fantasized about soaking her feet, while Dolly stalked the intersection like a panther. Laura was just about to declare mutiny and announce that she was pouring herself into the next Checker cab no matter what when Dolly hustled over. 'Okay, two o'clock. There's our ticket.'

Laura followed her eyes and spotted two men in their thirties — possibly forties — ambling down the street, smoking. One was bald and fat. The other was wiry and better dressed, but with narrow eyes that gave him the appearance of a henchman in a Jimmy Cagney movie. The men crossed the middle of Fifty-Third and fell into line behind a collection of couples entering the Stork. 'You can't be serious.'

'Look, we only need two warm bodies to get us inside. Then we can do whatever we want.'

'Dolly, they're old enough to be my father!'

'Oh, c'mon, Laura! It's your first night in New York! It's the *Stork Club*! I thought you said you'd come here for adventure. Well, here it is!'

Before Laura could reply, Dolly was chugging back down the sidewalk, smiling at the approaching duo. 'Excuse me, gentlemen, might I trouble either of you for a cigarette?'

'What's your name, cutie?' the skinny one asked Dolly. He fumbled in his jacket pocket for his cigarette case. *Oh, even better*, Laura

26

thought. *I get the fat one.*

Hasty introductions and several puffs on a Camel later, Dolly had successfully smiled winsomely enough to get them escorted in. The doorman looked up in mild surprise. 'You're lucky it's a slow night,' he muttered.

Laura found herself once again astonished by, and admiring of, Dolly's gumption. *I have to remember that this is how you do things in New York.*

She hadn't taken more than a dozen steps inside when the throbbing inside her shoe began to subside. Even the chubby hand on the small of her back, guiding her to a table, didn't register.

She was in the Stork Club.

Facing the dance floor, the female singer was midway through an up-tempo orchestration of 'My Secret Love,' all soft drumbeats and quietly shaking maracas, as couples gently swayed with the music, the men in dark suits, their damsels in tight-bodiced dresses. The air conditioning was at full tilt, but the air was thick with sweat and smoke and better perfume no doubt dispensed earlier in the evening from expensive cut-glass bottles on dainty dressing tables. *What is it like*, Laura wondered, *to come to a place like this all the time? To have this be your normal routine, sitting at a small table in the company of a gentleman, a lamp-shaded candle between you, listening to the gentle clink of glasses and music that sounds like waves crashing upon sand?* She looked up at the plunging drapes on the windows, down to the gleaming wood of the dance floor, perked her ears to catch the echo of the loud, flirtatious laughter from the woman sipping champagne and sitting in the booth across the room, book-ended by two men in subtly striped suits. She fought to memorize the scene, every curve and bend and splash of light. *This is it. This is the beginning of my life.*

A strong hand on her wrist pulled her out of her thoughts. 'Laura, look — there's Tallulah Bankhead!' Dolly whispered a bit too loudly, her stare directing Laura to a corner banquette, where a stoic, bony woman with forbidding, deep-set eyes and meticulously arched brows smoked a long cigarette as she appeared to ignore the chattering of the man next to her. It certainly *looked* like Tallulah Bankhead.

Laura glanced around the table. 'Where did Mutt and Jeff go?'

'They got impatient for the waiter, so they went to get us drinks. I ordered you a brandy. It's what you drink here.'

'How would you know what you drink here?'

'I just know these things, Laura,' Dolly replied, scanning the crowd for the next Tallulah Bankhead.

'Well!' came a sardonic admonishment from their left, delivered with suitable English gusto. 'I see the maidens fair of the Barbizon have arrived.'

'We shouldn't even be speaking to you!' Dolly hissed. 'Do you have any idea what we had to do to get in here? They don't allow unescorted women, something you conveniently forgot to mention.'

'They also seem to have no idea who you are,' Laura chimed in.

'Oh, rubbish,' Vivian said dismissively. She carried a tray laden with packs of cigarettes and tins of mints and candies. Her pale skin positively glowed in the soft light of the club. Her flaming hair was parted on the side, draping down over one eye in soft waves, like Veronica Lake. Even in her nondescript black dress, with its demure white collar and short sleeves, she managed to look dangerous and sexual, her parted lips full and inviting, smeared with just a swipe of scarlet lipstick. Laura hated her envy, her own longing to be so effortlessly interesting and wicked. 'Those sad little men with their lists,' Vivian was saying. 'You'd think they were guarding the Café de Paris.'

A gentleman sitting a few tables away waved for cigarettes. 'Duty calls,' she said, drifting off to make the sale.

Laura hadn't even noticed the brandy sitting in front of her on the table. Fat One was now standing, hand extended. 'Care to dance, baby?'

The orchestra had struck up the first peppy chords of 'Amor.' *I'd rather do geometry*, Laura thought. But she knew Dolly was right: she was being foolish. She was in the Stork Club. *The* Stork Club, not walking through Chapin House at Smith.

'I'd love to,' she said.

He wasn't a bad dancer, really. It was sort of impressive how a man that large could be so dainty on his feet, directing her with an ease that would have shamed the boys at her coming out.

29

She had begged Marmy to allow her to skip the whole ritual of the white gloves and the gown and the Brenda Frazier — worthy descent down the stairs into 'society.' A major battle she'd lost. But she'd win the war. Now she had the home-court advantage.

'I'm in hosiery,' Fat One was saying.

'Sorry?'

'Hosiery. You know, ladies' personal garments,' he said conspiratorially. 'I sell wholesale to merchants. You could be wearing something of mine right now.' He winked, pulled her a bit closer.

Oh God. Laura looked around the dance floor. How long could a dance last, anyway? Her foot was aching again. She surveyed the slowly turning couples searching for Dolly. Maybe she could flag down Vivian, profess a sudden craving for a Lucky Strike. Or maybe she'd just tell her burly dancing partner she was a Communist.

Then he walked in.

His date was lithe and also blond and utterly predictable, in Laura's estimation, her hourglass shape poured into a tight-fitting mermaid gown on a Friday night when every other woman was in knee-length department-store issue. Box Barnes was in a tux — they'd obviously just come from somewhere, maybe dinner or the theater — and he was doing what heirs do, smiling and glad-handing and acting generally smarmy. He was no more than ten feet away when she realized she'd unconsciously steered Fat One toward the other end of the dance floor, where Box was now ushering his blonde into a banquette while ordering drinks.

There was no other truth: he was magnificent. His white teeth, his buffed fingernails, the way his tailored tux trousers crested just so onto the tops of his patent-leather shoes. He could be a murderer or a swindler or just your garden-variety cad with better tailoring, but there was no denying the power of his raw beauty. The term 'golden boy' had been invented for men like him.

Stop staring.

She pulled back to smile at Fat One just as the song wound down. 'What a lovely dancer you are,' she said brightly.

'Anytime, doll.'

Twenty minutes and another brandy later, she was on her way back from the ladies' lounge and feeling a bit woozy. She'd been able to rub her foot for only a few minutes before shoving it back into her shoe. She'd left Dolly parked on a striped chair, fussing with her curls and musing about whether her old boyfriend Frank would be jealous if he came in and saw her dancing with the Cagney henchman. Threading her way back to the table, Laura felt a slight headache coming on. The thought of more chitchat about ladies' undergarments seemed too awful to even contemplate.

She missed colliding with the busboy's tray by inches. In hindsight it was a miracle — either of gravity or circus acrobatics on his part — that kept the empty glasses from crashing in five different directions, but whatever the case, Laura found herself falling backward when she felt a strong hand at her back and another at her arm. 'Whoa, Nelly.'

31

She whirled around, directly into the gaze of Box Barnes.

'I'm afraid I'm going to have to have you cut off, young lady.'

She wanted to say something, but there was . . . nothing. Just an intense stare, the kind you gave a particularly exotic animal at the zoo. His face remained as ethereal as it had been from the safety of the dance floor. But up close there was something more discernible in his blue eyes, a hint of mockery that Laura tried to wish away so it wouldn't spoil the illusion.

'Pardon my manners. I'm — '

'I know who you are,' she blurted out.

'Hmm. I had a feeling you did.'

'You . . . you did?'

'Well, you were looking at me earlier today. That *was* you in the Barbizon coffee shop, right? And you've been staring at me all night.'

She took a slight step back, shrugged out of his arm. 'Yes . . . well, thank you. For the assistance. I . . . I'm wearing new shoes. And I haven't been staring.'

He leaned in, the mockery now stronger, more brilliant in his eyes, and flashed the smile that had no doubt dazzled dozens of girls. Perhaps hundreds. 'There's no need to be coy. You're in the Stork. You want a special night. It's nothing to be ashamed of. I can make that happen for you.'

'I watched you come in with someone.'

'There's more nights than just tonight, you know.'

Clarity seized her. 'I think there's been a misunderstanding.'

Box slipped his arm around her waist, pulled her closer. 'I doubt that.'

She pushed back, forcefully. 'You should.'

The mask dropped, just an inch. 'Are you really going to play hard to get, baby? I could have any woman in this place.'

'Except for one.'

He smiled. 'What's your name?'

She hesitated. *My God, he's good-looking.* 'Laura.'

'Laura what?'

'Why does it matter?'

'Because I want to know, and people tell me things I want to know.'

She deliberately looked over his shoulder. 'Maybe people give you too much of what you want.'

He sighed. 'I don't seem to be making a very good impression.'

'On the contrary,' she said. 'You're not making any impression at all.'

His brow furrowed, and Laura couldn't tell whether he was amused or insulted. His next words were more spat out than said. 'You're either a fake-out, stupid, or both.'

She tossed out her best look of nonchalance. 'You'll have to excuse me if I don't put a lot of weight in criticism from a man named for a cardboard container.'

She brushed past him and walked briskly back toward the entrance, her mind urging her to go faster, equally out of fear of reprisal and wanting to savor this, relish rising to the occasion in hand-to-hand combat with a lout who also happened to be one of Manhattan's most famous men about town. She felt a hand at her elbow. 'Let go of me!'

'Good grief, what is the matter with you?!' Dolly exclaimed. Two couples sipping martinis looked over. 'What's wrong? I saw you talking to Box Barnes! What did — '

Laura pulled her by the arm and hustled toward the doors, Dolly's protestations drowned out by the opening notes of another dance number. A few seconds later they were out on the sidewalk, rushing toward the beckoning roof light of a cab as Laura tried not to think about how badly the blister on the back of her foot hurt.

3

'I can't believe how stingy you're being.'

Dolly was pouting, or at least attempting a pout, a difficult maneuver when you had such a sunny face. She and Laura were in the back of a cab on their way downtown on a bright, beautiful late morning, the windows down. The oppressive humidity that had enveloped them leaving the Stork last night had broken, opening the door to a clear summer day.

It had been a day much like this that provided Laura with her earliest memory of New York. She had come in with Grandmother Dixon, on what would become a series of 'just us girls' visits to the city on the train, until the combination of her grandmother's worsening arthritis and the arrival of her younger brother led to their demise.

But, oh, those trips. Wonderful, sparkly, whimsical trips down Fifth Avenue, and clip-clopping in a carriage through Central Park in the heady years after the war, always ending at the Palm Court at the Plaza, where Laura would sit in her best dress and patent-leather shoes as Grandmother Dixon poured the tea and primly slid scones and tiny sandwiches with cucumbers onto her plate. And during every visit she would point out the people who served — the waiters and bellmen and hosts — and ask Laura to think about where they came from, what the lives were like for the people who were not sitting there enjoying the restaurant, but rather working in it. 'You always need to remember that there are many, many people less fortunate,' she would say. 'We all have an obligation to help those who need it.' Laura would dutifully relay all of this to her father on the evening of their return, resulting in his inevitable comment to Marmy, 'Mother's been playing Eleanor Roosevelt again.'

'Are you listening to a word I've been saying?' Dolly asked.

Laura jolted out of her reverie. 'I've told you, there isn't anything more to tell,' she said.

Dolly had been relentless. She'd spied the encounter with Box Barnes and had, from the moment they'd left the club, wanted to know everything: every word exchanged, how he'd looked up close, smelled up close, whether his mouth was truly as kissable as it looked in pictures. Laura had elected to take a name-rank-and-serial-number approach to parsing out details. The truth was she'd been embarrassed by the whole interlude: how he'd obviously caught her staring, but mostly how she had walked into the Stork Club feeling worldly and sophisticated and left feeling unmasked, the little girl caught prancing about in her mother's heels and pearls.

'You're being very circumspect about the whole business,' Dolly was saying. Laura arched an eyebrow. 'What? Don't look at me that way, Laura Dixon,' Dolly shot back. 'I'm in secretarial school, remember? I take dictation with big vocabulary words all the time. I'm not stupid.'

'I would never think you were stupid.'

Dolly shrugged. 'Just drop it. You'll tell me when you're ready. You just better be ready soon.' They both giggled. 'So, how was the tour?'

'Uneventful.' The tour. Still foggy from the brandy, Laura had dragged herself out of bed and gotten dressed just in time to make her nine a.m. appointment for the Barbizon orientation, once again finding Metzger behind the desk, pinched and vinegary. Did the woman ever go home? There was still no sign of the elusive Mrs. Mayhew, presumably still 'off premises,' and no explanation as to why she hadn't kept Laura's appointment. And so Laura and Metzger had spent the better part of an hour exploring the hotel, like Mrs. Danvers and Joan Fontaine death-marching through an all-female Manderley. Laura had received her 'Court Circular,' which listed that week's activities, from dramatic readings (this week, from the works of the ailing Wallace Stevens) to a backgammon tournament. The swimming pool had looked surprisingly inviting, if a tad over-chlorinated — the whole potted-ferned area reeked of bleach — and they'd briefly lingered to watch an aggressive badminton match between two ponytailed girls. After the sundeck, the solarium, the recital rooms, and the dining room, they'd finished on the mezzanine, where a latticed wooden railing overlooked the expansive lobby below.

'I noticed,' Laura had inquired of Mrs. Metzger, 'last night when I was leaving, that there were a few girls milling about here, all dressed up. Was there some special occasion?'

37

'That's the way it is every evening, most noticeably on Saturdays,' Metzger had replied, her raven-black eyes honing in on a group of girls sitting in the lobby lounge below. 'Rather than wait downstairs, many of the girls choose to stay up here, so they can survey their dates arriving. That way, if a gentleman doesn't appear as she'd hoped, a girl can simply not go down at all.' She'd turned to Laura, her face still as inscrutable as it had been yesterday behind the desk. 'It's discourteous and the kind of behavior we discourage here at the Barbizon, but we do not wield indiscriminate control over every young woman's manners. Or lack thereof.'

Dolly had taken in Laura's recounting with a gravity reserved for a pastor's sermon. 'Well, I can't believe I am saying this, but I think I'm warming up to Metzger,' she said. 'Her reputation may be as an old fuddy-duddy, but the lady has standards, and I admire that. Though I don't think she'd kick a girl out for a silly violation and leave her stranded on the sidewalk with her suitcases, like some of the others would. But if I'm being honest, I am one of the girls who would stand on the mezzanine to check out her date.' She glanced out the window, then added wistfully, 'If I ever had a date.'

Soon they were standing on MacDougal Street, two blocks south of Washington Square. 'Why, oh, why are we here again?' Dolly asked.

'I told you, I read about the most incredible bookstore that's somewhere right around here, and I've been dying to explore it.' Laura slowly circled as she meandered down the block, trying

38

to locate the shop's sign. 'It should be right here.'

'You're the only girl I know who would move to New York, meet the city's most eligible bachelor her first night, and then forget all about it to go hunting down some dusty old bookstore. You keep saying you want adventure, but you're quickly turning into a wet rag.'

'Oh, hush.' Laura's eyes zeroed in on a small basement window with BOOKS in arched gold letters across the middle. 'That's it!'

MacDougal Books & Letters was more like MacDougal Attic, three tiny cement steps that led down into a messy closet of books arranged . . . well, *arranged* wasn't really the word, Laura noted. While some genres had their own clearly labeled shelves — 'European History,' 'Plays and Playwrights,' 'Art,' and one in the back oddly declaring 'Medieval Rituals' — most of the books were tossed about haphazardly, as if some overly aggressive cleaning woman had come in and simply flung those laying in her path. Others stood in teetering piles, threatening to topple at the smallest wind gust. The shop had the stifling, musty feel of a trunk that hadn't been opened in quite some time, with a smell of cedar and pipe smoke that was aggressive yet not entirely unpleasant. 'Fantastic,' Laura whispered.

'What?' Dolly shook her head. She was already starting to perspire, and it wasn't even noon. 'You *like* this place? I will never understand rich girls.'

'Can I help you, ladies?'

They turned to see a slightly rumpled man

39

standing behind the well-worn mahogany counter. He wore a vest over a starched white oxford shirt and projected a faintly regal bearing, like a duke in an old oil painting. 'Are you looking for something in particular?'

Dolly answered, 'Oh, we're just brows — '

'I love your shop,' Laura interrupted.

'Thank you.' He lumbered out from behind the counter. 'You are a serious bookworm, I can tell.'

Laura beamed. It was one thing to be called pretty; it was a true compliment to be called smart. 'I'd like to be. I've just moved here. I want to be a writer myself.'

'I'd settle for having a nice lunch,' Dolly muttered from a row over.

'What kind of writer would you like to be?' the man asked.

'Honestly, I don't know. But the kind who writes things that change people's lives. Or . . . well, that sounds a bit egotistical, I think. Maybe just the kind who gets people to see things differently. Or perhaps one thing differently. To think about things. I think about things all the time.' She laughed. 'Perhaps too much. I just love stories that take you someplace else, that give you a glimpse into how people live who are different from you.'

'Hmm. I have a book you might like,' the man said. 'Wait here.'

Dolly weaved around to Laura's side. 'How long do we have to stay? I'm melting like the Wicked Witch in here.'

Laura laughed. 'Well, if the slipper fits — '

40

'That was too easy. C'mon, Laura, I want to go see pretty dresses and shoes. Do they even have those in Greenwich Village?'

'You've lived at the Barbizon since last September and you've never been down here? How is that possible?'

'Some of us find enough to do on the Upper East Side without having to come down with all the weirdoes.'

'They're not weirdoes. They're thinkers. They're *interesting*. And they're not big on rules. At all. Don't you ever just want to say, 'I want to do exactly what I want,' and have no one say, 'No, you can't do that'?'

'Only when it comes to Lindy's cheesecake.'

Laura watched the man walk back to the front of the shop; he had a slight hitch in his step, as if he was nursing a leg injury. 'I'm gonna run and do some window-shopping and leave you to play librarian. I'll meet you back at the room. We're still going to the movies tonight, right?'

'Right. You pick.'

'I hope I didn't scare your friend away,' the man said as he shuffled up to her and watched Dolly leave the shop.

'Oh, don't worry about her. She's more of a *Photoplay* kind of gal.'

'Ah, well. What was it Abbott Lowell said? 'Your aim will be knowledge and wisdom, not the reflected glamour of fame.''

'Who's Abbott Lowell?'

'Was. He was the president of Harvard.'

'Did you attend Harvard?'

'No. I came from far too modest a background

41

to aspire to the Ivy League.' He gave her an appraising look, took in her white sundress and ballet flats. 'You, on the other hand. Let me guess: Seven Sisters.'

She smiled. 'Oh, dear. Does it show that badly?'

'On the contrary, it shows beautifully. Now, don't tell me. I'm going to say . . . Vassar.'

'Smith.'

'Ah. The hair threw me. The Smith girls are almost always blondes.'

'What can I say?' Laura laughed. 'I'm an iconoclast.'

'You're far too young to be anything of the kind,' he replied gently. 'But you've got great spirit, I can tell. And, I suspect, a fair amount of verve. Qualities that will serve you well as a writer.' He reached behind him to the counter, extracted a card. 'My manners are deteriorating as quickly as my body. Allow me an introduction. Cornelius Offing, at your service.'

Laura returned the pleasantry. 'It's nice to meet you, Mr. Offing.'

'Connie, please. My family calls me Corny, which is not a name I wish to perpetuate to the grave. But they're set in their ways, so that battle's been lost. But you, you can call me Connie.'

For the next hour, he took her on a detailed tour of the tiny shop, dazzling her with his knowledge of writers, books, and publishing. The shop was stiflingly hot — Dolly had been right about that much — but it didn't seem to faze him. He showed off a limited edition of Keats and a set of Dickens bound volumes he said were rumored to have once been in the summer library of Queen Victoria. He inspected a copy of Steinbeck's *Sweet Thursday*. 'I don't keep a lot of the popular fiction in here. I don't think it's why folks come into this type of place. Did you read this?'

'No. I read *Cannery Row*, though.'

'And?'

'I enjoyed it.'

'Mmm. Yes, the first is always better than the sequel. Still, this one is probably still superior to most of the stuff they print nowadays. I worry about what people are reading. Or, rather, not reading. But, oh well. Man cannot live by Euripides alone, I suppose.'

'Or *Photoplay*.'

He smiled. 'You,' he said, 'are an old soul, fortunately housed in very lovely wrapping. Tell me: What was the last book you really loved?'

'That's easy. *The Town and the City*.'

'Kerouac. Interesting.'

'I just thought it was so incredibly . . . real, somehow. Like, it put you there, both in New York and in that small town in Massachusetts. You could really feel the main character's struggle to find his own life. Maybe I adored it because of where I grew up. Has he written anything new?'

'No, though I do hear he's working on something that's almost done and thought to be rather brilliant. But you could go ask him yourself. Chances are he's just down the street.' He looked at his watch. 'Though perhaps not quite this early. Probably still sleeping off last night's toot.'

She started. 'John Kerouac lives down the street?'

'In a manner of speaking.' Connie chuckled, ambling back toward the counter. 'And he goes by 'Jack' now. He and his crowd spend most of their time at the San Remo. Little bar not far from here, right on MacDougal. You should go in sometime. Most bars don't allow women by themselves, but they sort of make their own rules at the San Remo.' Connie shuffled back behind the counter, hopped onto a stool with a wince. 'Damn foot. Pardon my language.'

Her own foot was feeling much better than it had been last night, now that it was covered in a bandage. 'What happened?' The kind of personal question that Marmy would have been appalled at her asking.

For a moment he appeared embarrassed. 'Gout,' Connie replied. 'Now not only do I have a foot that's constantly giving me pain, but I can't eat anything that tastes good, either.'

'Well, at least you can *make* your own food. They don't allow cooking at the Barbizon.'

'The Barbizon. My, I am slow on the draw these days. Should have known that's where you lived. The most beautiful girls in New York in that place. I've always said if I wasn't running this shop, I'd be a doorman there. Men bribe them just to find a way in to meet the girls.' He slid the book he'd brought from the back across the counter. 'Here, I want you to read this.'

It was a slim volume, no more than two

hundred pages, with a plain cloth cover and a title that read, *Will the Girl and Other Stories*. She took in the author's name. 'Christopher Welsh,' she read aloud. 'I've never heard of him.'

'You will. A very exciting new voice. Mark my words. This is his first collection of short stories. If you want to be a writer, there are worse people to emulate.'

She tucked the book under her arm, reached for the coin purse in her pocket. 'Oh, no,' Connie said. 'Consider it a welcoming gift.'

'Oh, I don't feel right about that. I have to pay you something.'

'I'll tell you what. You read the book, and when you're done, come back to the shop and I'll make us some tea and we can talk about what you thought of it. That'll be payment enough.'

'Okay, Connie,' Laura said, shaking his hand. 'You have a deal.'

★ ★ ★

She fought the instinct to leave.

The interior of the San Remo was everything a literary bar should be: a light fog of cigarette smoke opening up to pressed tin ceilings, scarred wooden booths, a bar of old warped wood that curved seductively from front to back. Laura had walked up and down the block three times before mustering the courage to venture inside.

At midday on a Saturday in June it wasn't yet busy, which only made her feel more self-conscious: no crowd to thread through or to disappear into. A few wiry young men were at the far end of the bar gesturing wildly with their cigarettes and talking loudly over one another, all of them dressed almost identically in white T-shirts or short-sleeved oxfords, slim black trousers, and loafers. One in dark-rimmed glasses appeared to be making a particularly angry point to the others. Laura looked toward the rear and saw a back booth occupied by a white man and a Negro woman. She'd never seen people of different races sitting socially with one another, never mind a man and a woman. The man casually caught her eye and she looked away.

I'm not ready for this, she thought. *Maybe I can get Vivian to come back with me.* It seemed like the kind of place that an aspiring chanteuse would frequent. And the type of place that an ex-debutante from Greenwich, Connecticut, never, ever went to.

No.

She had faced down Box Barnes; she could face down her own fears about fitting in. She had to stop this, the second-guessing, the doubting, the unsteadiness. She knew she didn't belong in the patrician world of Greenwich. Why was it so hard to imagine that she could belong in a place like this?

'Hello.'

The bartender was no more than twenty-five, and maybe considerably younger; it was always harder to tell with men. Like the fellows at the end of the bar, he was slender, with rounded shoulders and a tapered waist. But his nose was too big for his face, giving him a slightly ethnic look, though what that ethnicity was exactly was hard to determine: Polish? Italian? He had short brown hair that seemed to go in eight different directions, ending in a small cowlick on the back of his head. Unlike the rest of the men in the bar, he wore blue jeans and a shirt in a bright shade of green, which accentuated his hazel eyes.

He smiled at her, tapped the bar. 'Come on over. We don't bite.'

She sauntered over — she felt that was how people moved inside a place like this — and slid her book onto the bar. He read the cover and seemed mildly surprised.

'Let me guess: You've been to see Connie.'

She laughed. 'Does he send all the wayward girls from the Upper East Side here?'

'I don't know,' he said. 'Are you wayward?'

She fought for a snappy reply, something worthy of Oscar Wilde, or at least Katharine Hepburn, but it wouldn't come. 'Just a girl who likes books, I guess. How did you know I'd seen Connie?'

He began picking up some wet glasses and drying them with a hand towel. 'He's the only guy who would sell a book like that.'

'Have you read it?'

'No.'

'Then how do you know what kind of book it is?'

'I know.'

She picked up the slim volume again, started paging through it. 'Didn't you ever hear the phrase 'Don't judge a book by its cover'?'

47

He laughed. 'You bartend long enough, you hear a lot of phrases.'

'I see. Do you read a lot?'

'Hardly ever. No time.'

'Everyone has time to read. Eisenhower reads. You can't be busier than Eisenhower.'

'Personally, I don't think Ike works too hard. Are you always like this?'

'Like what?'

'Sassy.'

'You think I'm being sassy?'

'I know girls, and I know a sassy one when I see one.'

'Hmmm,' she said. 'Maybe you need to know more girls.' *One for Hepburn!*

He laughed, threw the towel over his left shoulder. 'What's your name?'

The second time she'd been asked by a young man in the last day. 'Laura.'

'Well, hello, Laura, wayward girl from the Upper East Side. I'm Pete, slouchy bartender on the Lower West Side. Now, what can I get ya?'

'I wasn't sure you would serve a single woman at the bar.'

'Take a look around,' he said. 'We serve everybody.'

Upon closer inspection, each of his eyes had a slightly different hue — the left dark cocoa, the right milky coffee, both tinged with green. The result was that they gave his stare a slightly shape-shifting effect, as if his face were constantly moving. Studying him bought her time; she had no idea what a woman was supposed to order in a bar. Where she was from,

48

women weren't *in* bars. Where was Dolly when you needed her?

'Surprise me.' *Hepburn would have never said that*.

He pulled a draft beer from the tap. 'Try this,' he said, sliding it over. He walked down to the other end of the bar, presumably to pour another round for the angry guy in the black-rimmed glasses and his friends.

The beer was acid down her throat, and she gagged. Did people really think this tasted good? She couldn't ever remember beer once being served in her family's house. Or even knowing anyone who drank it. But the foam tickled her throat, and after a few sips she was able to get it down. 'Whaddya think?' Pete asked as he approached.

'Delicious,' she said, gulping hard.

She stayed for almost two hours. They talked about New York, then where she'd grown up, where he'd grown up (Philadelphia), her life at Smith, and in a testament to the bravura wrought by beer number two, his nose: 'Irish father and Polish mother, what can I say?' She met a poet and his girlfriend who walked in and sat nearby — from Pete's greeting and introduction, they were clearly San Remo regulars — and they regaled her with stories about their recent two months in Italy, where they sailed in Capri while also managing to picnic with a bunch of anarchists, among other pursuits. It was late afternoon by the time Laura strolled back into the Barbizon, where she passed Metzger leaving.

'Package came for you while you were out,' the older woman said, walking past her toward the door. Laura hiccupped, and Metzger whipped her head back. *Please don't let her smell the beer!* But a few seconds later, Metzger was out the door.

Laura went to the front desk to retrieve the package and was handed a long, slender white cardboard box. Undoing the shiny red ribbon, she lifted the lid and parted the tissue paper to find a dozen long-stemmed red roses inside. She extracted the card.

'THERE ARE FOUR LAURAS LIVING AT THE BARBIZON, AND I HAD TO SEND ROSES TO EACH OF THEM TO MAKE SURE I GOT THE RIGHT ONE,' it said. 'I'M SORRY ABOUT LAST NIGHT. THAT'S NOT WHO I AM. PERHAPS YOU'LL ALLOW ME TO SHOW YOU THE REAL ME.' The card was signed simply, 'B.'

4

'Nicola!!!'

The scream sent Vivian bolting up in bed.

'*Ni-coh-laaaaaaaaa!!!* Get up! You hear me? You're going to be late for Mass!'

Where am I?

Her temples were throbbing. Oh, the wine last night. She'd known it was a mistake. But he'd insisted, more than once. More than twice. 'C'mon,' he'd said, with those ridiculous dark eyes, 'just one more glass. What, you got a curfew?'

As a matter of fact, she did. God knows what Metzger's face would look like if she could see her now. Vivian would be not only out of the Barbizon, but probably out of the country, deported. Rubbing her head, she looked around the unfamiliar room, saw sunlight filtering in from around the edges of the pulled window shades. The room was small, plain, with an old but burnished highboy in the corner that had a small dressing mirror hung above it, a pair of black rosary beads dangling down from its corner. The top of the highboy was littered with bottles of half-filled cologne, along with a hairbrush. A faded photograph of three small boys in baseball uniforms was tucked in the lower right of the mirror, which with the rosary beads above it gave it the appearance of a tiny shrine.

His place? Yes, we came to his place after the bar. But where was his place?

'Nicola! If I have to come up those stairs — '

The reply, deep and masculine and slightly accented, boomed from the body next to her in the bed and catapulted her fully awake. 'Ma! Okay, okay, I'm up!' he yelled toward the closed skinny white door. 'Calm down! I'll be down in a minute!'

He turned toward her, his whisper sleepy and impossibly seductive. 'Hey, beautiful.'

'Your mother?' Vivian whispered, pulling the top sheet tighter around her bare breasts. 'You live with your *mother*?'

'My parents,' he corrected. 'Of course I do. Where else would I live?' He smiled, rose up on an elbow. 'Now I gotta get ready for church. Wait here till we leave, then slip out the back door. Don't go out the front. Mrs. Della Pietra next door, she sees everything.' He jumped out of the bed, naked except for his white T-shirt, and padded over to the highboy to retrieve a fresh pair of underwear and socks.

He had the lean, sinewy build of a boy, one augmented in strategic places — the shoulders, the calves, the ass — by the attributes of a mature, muscular man. His skin was a tawny olive, topped by a fulsome mane of black hair that normally curved back from his forehead, though which now, as she watched him rummage through his sock drawer, flopped down into his eyes. He was suave, but strictly in the context of the street. There was something impossibly feral that enveloped him like a fog.

She leaned back into the pillow, trying to decide what to do. Should she start getting dressed now, then perch herself on the end of the bed and wait for the proper clearance to escape the prying eyes of the nosy neighbor? What she wanted to do was laugh out loud and declare, in her drollest Kay Kendall, 'I cannot believe that a man who is still living with and going to church with his parents managed to seduce me last night.'

And yet he had. And that wasn't entirely her fault, because it was not simply his physical attributes that had contributed to her decision. Nicola Accardi had become something of a regular at the Stork over the last few months, though his entrance was guaranteed not by his charms but rather the company he kept, a legion of burly, impeccably coiffed men in bespoke suits who were always given if not the best tables, then decent ones. He was clearly a man of some influence, though how he had come by it remained a mystery. He had flirted with her from the start, which wasn't unusual from his sort, the dark and swarthys who were always employed in some vague and question-able business and answered any inquiries about same with Cheshire cat smiles and oily invitations to moonlit dinners. And he'd had money — a good deal of money — and wasn't shy about throwing it around: drinks for that table over there, Cuban cigars for my friends over here, and so on. She had flirted back — she knew her strengths — but kept it at that. Getting involved with customers was a blatant no-no at the Stork; Mr. Billingsley had been known to fire girls for less. And she needed the job. But then Nicola had come last night, and after his entourage had left he'd stayed. And stayed. Until closing. Then after closing. Which, by her estimation, had been about five hours ago.

The Stork had been quiet, the only sounds those of the mop on the dance floor and the dishwashers clitter-clattering plates in the back. Nicola had remained glued in his chair until she'd passed in front of him on her own way out, his hand shooting out from the table, grabbing her by the wrist.

'Give us a song,' he said, smiling up at her.

'What makes you think I sing?'

'I've heard you. I know you sing here sometimes.'

On occasion the boys in the band humored her, allowed her to sing a number after closing. Cesar, the trombonist, would pipe out a few notes, and then the pianist would kick in, and Vivian would slide behind the gleaming silver microphone and close her eyes and picture herself in front of a packed ballroom on a sultry Saturday night, wearing a strapless gown and gloves that snaked up past her elbows. And then, as she would belt out the first few bars of 'Night and Day' or 'Half as Much,' she was singing not for the old man swabbing the parquet floor, but for the ladies sitting erect in their best dresses and for the men in their suits, the ends of their cigarettes lit up like fireflies.

She was a star.

Vivian had looked around at the boys packing up. 'Too late for a private concert, I'm afraid. The guys have almost all left. Besides,' she said, turning back to Nicola, 'I'm exhausted.'

He'd kept his hand firmly around her wrist. 'You're going back on your word.' He had something, sweetness spiked with a dash of danger.

'How is it that I could have broken my word to a man I've never spoken to?'

'You've spoken to me with your eyes.'

She artfully shook her wrist free, bemused. 'That has to be the worst line I have ever heard. Do women actually respond to this kind of drivel?'

He threw his head back in laughter, and she liked it. 'You're makin' me work here!'

'Believe me, if you were working for me, love, you'd know it. Good night.'

He jumped up from behind the table and blocked her path. He was tall — at least six three, possibly taller — and his eyes bore into her. 'Please,' he said, arms extended. 'Just one song. I've had a terrible night. Just sing something for me. One song. And you know,' he said, slowly rubbing her hand in his with his thumb, 'I know all kinds of people. Including music people. Maybe I could introduce you.'

She smiled. Intellectually she took it all for what it was, a well-rehearsed empty promise with undoubtedly no basis in reality. But he did keep interesting company. More than that, he kept wealthy company. And even if he was bullshitting her, what the hell, she was English — she had a soft spot for thespians. 'One song,' she said. Cesar was still there, as was Joe, the pianist. Vivian tilted her head toward them. 'And you'll need to tip the boys.'

He nodded, sat back down. A few minutes later she was in front of the mic, checking to make sure Mr. Billingsley wasn't still around. The owner of the Stork, he was as famous as the patrons with whom he posed for the photographs that lined the walls. He would normally have already gone home, but sometimes he stayed in the back office to check on the night's receipts.

Joe tinkled the opening bars. Cesar softly joined in. Vivian sang.

> *'Meet me tonight in dreamland*
> *Under the silvery moon*
> *Meet me tonight in dreamland*
> *Where love's sweet roses bloom . . . '*

'Okay, Ruby. I'm going.'

Vivian whirled around to see Nicola's face come back into focus. His hair was slicked back again, and he was wearing his best Sunday clothes. She was still in his bed, the linens now twisted around her. She suddenly felt embarrassed. 'Oh, all right, then,' she said.

He leaned back, smiled. 'Do you even know where you are?'

'I'm going to say New York. Am I close?'

'Bensonhurst,' he said. 'Here's a token for the subway. Just go up the block, make a left, go down two blocks and catch the D back to

56

Manhattan.' He smiled, tousled her mop of red hair, and kissed her. 'I'll call you.'

* * *

Laura was halfway down the steps of St. Thomas Chapel on East Sixtieth when she spied her across the street, casually leaning against the pole of the traffic light smoking a cigarette, wearing dark sunglasses and the fitted black dress she donned every night for work at the Stork.

Laura nodded to a few of the other girls. 'Go on ahead, I'll catch up,' she said.

The light turned and Vivian walked over, falling in step with her as they made their way behind the pack back toward the Barbizon three blocks away. Before Laura had a chance to say a word, Vivian piped up. 'Don't ask,' she said.

'I don't have to. You're wearing the dress you went to work in last night. And you smell like a tobacco farm.'

'I'm a cigarette girl, remember? Comes with the territory.'

'It comes from staying out all night with God-Knows-Who.'

'Now, don't get all high and mighty, Miss Connecticut. We can't all be good girls from the country. And wouldn't life be boring if we were?'

One of the girls ahead looked back, quickly turning to her two walking mates and laughing. 'How did you even know where to find me?' Laura asked.

'Where else would you be on Sunday morning

if not the closest Episcopalian church? It's almost an annex of the Barbizon.' She peered up the block at the group in front of them. 'Where's Ethel?'

Laura rolled her eyes. This was her own fault. She'd made the mistake of sharing a belief that Dolly would one day end up like Ethel Mertz, and Vivian had howled in laughter, yelling, 'Perfect, bloody perfect!' Now she wouldn't let it go. 'You need to stop calling her that,' Laura said. 'And to answer your question, she's Catholic. She's at St. Vincent Ferrer.'

'Catholic? Oh, what a drag. I'd rather be a Druid. Though I must say, no one wears basic black better than the nuns. Always so drapey.'

'Are you always like this?'

'Like what?'

'Like . . . crazy. You talk like you're in a movie opposite Cary Grant.'

'Oh, don't be so flinty,' Vivian said, hooking her arm through Laura's as they made the turn onto Lexington. 'I'll tell you what, no one ever says, 'Gee, I wonder what Vivian thinks.' Because everyone always knows what Vivian thinks. I'm direct, perhaps to a fault, yes. But don't you agree that we'd all be better off if everyone was a bit more direct, rather than less? Wouldn't there be fewer problems, fewer misunderstandings? And I'll tell you another thing: I'm fun. I may not be the prettiest girl in the room, or the smartest, or God knows the richest. But I am very likely to be the most fun. There's merit in that.'

'I'm sure whoever's place you're slinking back

from would heartily agree.'

Vivian laughed. 'Oh, well done! See? That kind of reply shows you're already becoming a writer. A comeback worthy of Noël Coward!' She turned her head sharply as they passed a small bakery. 'Good God, those muffins smell heavenly.'

'The least he could have done is fed you.'

Glancing ahead, Vivian grabbed Laura by the hand. 'Hurry, we need to catch up to the rest.'

'Why?' Laura barked, holding her hat as they bolted across the street.

'Why? Why do you think? We need to walk in all together, a nice group of girls returning from Sunday services.'

Laura stopped dead on the sidewalk. 'You can't be serious,' she said. 'I know you think you have this down to an art form, but you can't honestly believe any of those women at the front desk are going to believe you went to church this morning dressed like that.'

Vivian yanked her back into a brisk pace. 'Still in mourning for my grandmother, for whom I dress in black every Sunday as a testament to my grief. At least that's what I tell them.'

'And they believe you?'

'They're bitter old women who live their lives through dime-store romance novels,' Vivian said as they caught up to the others, just as Oscar, the portly doorman, opened the entrance to the Barbizon. 'You'd be amazed at what they believe.'

5

The conservatory of the Barbizon was half full, good attendance for a summer Sunday. A girl with brittle shoulder-length hair fidgeted nervously at the front, occasionally dashing over to the pianist and flipping through pages, pointing to a particular chord or a key change she was mulling over. Every few seconds she looked anxiously to the door, willing more girls into the room.

Laura scanned the conservatory and spotted Dolly in the second row, her arm moving in a slightly frantic windshield-wiper wave.

'C'mon,' Laura said to Vivian, dawdling behind her.

'Must we sit in the queen's box?' Vivian asked as they sank down in two seats next to Dolly. Vivian was still wearing her enormous pair of dark oval sunglasses. 'We're not *playing* this concert, are we?'

'You don't have to stay,' Dolly said, shooting Laura a sideways glare. 'This is really important to Ruth, and I want to show my support. And why are you wearing those absurd sunglasses?'

'Sometimes a girl needs her privacy,' Vivian replied. 'Only Elizabeth Taylor could understand.'

Dolly looked back to Laura between them. 'Is she for real?'

'It appears so,' Laura said.

'Believe me,' Vivian said, 'I'd rather not be here, either.'

'Then why are you?' Dolly asked.

Vivian delivered her own sideways glance to Laura. 'Blackmail.'

Laura watched two more girls wander in, laughing. They took seats in the last row, where they began a spirited if hushed conversation that no doubt centered on some scoundrel they'd seen downstairs in the coffee shop. She thought of Box Barnes and his robust bouquet of roses, now stuffed into two Mason jars sitting on her night table.

Dolly seemed to be reading her thoughts. She'd been obsessing about the flowers since the moment Laura had brought them upstairs, reading and rereading Box's note as if deciphering the Rosetta stone. 'Did Laura tell you she got flowers from Box Barnes?' she asked Vivian. 'And not just any flowers: red roses.'

Vivian slid her glasses down slightly. 'Do tell.'

'They came yesterday,' Dolly gushed. 'We went down to the Village because Laura wanted to see some old bookstore, and I ditched, but then when she got home later' — she turned briefly to Laura — 'Where were you all day, anyway?' — 'well, she comes in and is carrying this *big* box of beautiful long-stem roses and a card that says he sent roses to every girl named Laura in the Barbizon because he didn't know her last name, and he wanted to apologize.'

Vivian was clearly curious, which excited Dolly. 'My, my, such high drama, Xtabay,' she said, glancing admiringly at Laura. 'Continue.'

'Well, we met — well, we didn't really meet him, we just saw him, well, really, Laura was the one who saw him, I mean, they made eye contact, in the coffee shop. Anyway, when we were at the Stork on Friday night, he ran right into Laura when she was coming out of the ladies' lounge, and he put the moves on her — '

'Dolly!' Laura interjected in an urgent whisper. 'Please! He did not 'put the moves' on me. We had a brief unpleasant chat. That's all.'

Dolly waved her off. 'It had to be more than that, though of course she won't tell me any of the details. But a man like that does not send roses and an apology unless he really screwed up.'

'This is fun,' Laura said. 'It's like I'm not here.'

Vivian shook her head. 'It's always the New England girls.'

Laura cocked an eye. 'Pardon?'

'Everyone thinks it's the southern girls or — pardon — the British girls who are the natural Venus flytraps for men. But in my experience, which is not inconsiderable, it's those steely New England roses who always manage to snag the most eligible men. There's something to be said for being slightly aloof and forbidden.'

'I am neither aloof nor forbidden.'

'No, darling. You're Grace Kelly.'

'Oh my God, I loooooove her!' Dolly squealed. 'Is it really true she lived here?'

'Yes,' Vivian said. 'In the late forties. While she was studying at the American Academy of Dramatic Arts.'

62

'Did you *know* her? And will you please take off those ridiculous glasses? It's like talking to Mata Hari!'

Vivian again lowered the glasses. 'Crikey, Dolly! How old do you think I am? I'm not one of the Women. I've only lived here a few months.'

'Grace Kelly is not a New Englander,' Laura interrupted.

'But she has that sort of New England breeding and reserve,' Vivian argued. 'It's like she's made of steel, yet the most lovely, beautiful steel ever crafted. There's something always lingering just beneath the surface when you look at her — a sense of mystery and sex, of all the weapons one can use to be a truly compelling woman.'

'I don't associate Grace Kelly with sex,' Dolly said. 'She's just . . . gorgeous. And elegant. A lady. I will never forget that scene in *Rear Window* when she walks into Jimmy Stewart's apartment wearing that fantastic green skirt suit.'

'I love the scene where she comes in and finds Jimmy Stewart sleeping,' Laura said, 'and the camera gets closer and closer, and her face gets bigger, and bigger, and it's almost like she's coming in to kiss the camera — '

'Ethereal,' Vivian agreed.

'It's *romantic*,' Dolly said with a sigh. 'But it's not about sex.'

'Well, it certainly was when she was living *here*.'

Both Laura's and Dolly's eyes widened. 'What do you mean?' Laura asked.

They were disrupted by Ruth at the front of

the room, still fidgeting, but now clearing her throat and asking for everyone's attention. She thanked them all for coming to this afternoon recital of selections from Rodgers and Hammerstein, announcing that for her first number she would be singing 'Hello, Young Lovers' from *The King and I*.

'Fitting,' Vivian said, patting Laura on the knee. 'Perhaps she can dedicate it to you and Box.'

'Stop it.'

'Hold it!' Dolly whispered urgently. 'You can't leave us hanging like that! What about Grace?'

'Oh, Grace, Grace, Grace.' Vivian sighed, theatrically putting her sunglasses back on. 'Still the face of the Barbizon, six years later. Well, from what I've heard she was more Marilyn Monroe than Grace Kelly back then. She had many gentlemen calling, and she knew where to hide them.'

Dolly looked positively stunned. 'No!'

'Oh, yes. There is a very often-told legend that one night she actually came out of her room and did the Dance of the Seven Veils *in the hallway*. I wish I could have seen Metzger's face for that. She was far more, shall we say, 'high-spirited' than the movie magazines would have you believe.'

'She was engaged to Oleg Cassini, which I do *not* understand,' Dolly said. 'He's awful!'

'He's rich, darling,' Vivian said. 'You'll come to appreciate that.'

'And this is who you're comparing me to,' Laura said, 'a girl who snuck men all around the

64

Barbizon and did the Dance of the Seven Veils and then hid it all behind some veneer of cold respectability? This is how you see me?'

'What I see,' Vivian said, 'is a girl very much like Grace Kelly in all the ways that count: beautiful, clever, and who doesn't show all of her cards. And who I suspect is far more adroit at keeping men off balance than she cares to admit.'

As Ruth began to warble the opening verse, Laura folded her arms, trying to concentrate on the music even as her mind flooded with conflicting images: feature stories from *Mademoiselle*, Box Barnes smiling at her in the coffee shop, Box Barnes demeaning her at the Stork, the dust particles flitting against the dirty windows inside Connie's bookstore in the Village, Pete the bartender's cocky smile, the roses sitting upstairs, demanding an answer.

She wondered if Grace Kelly had ever sat in this very room listening to another girl sing, and if her head had been similarly cluttered, wondering which door to choose, which road to go down. Which life would ultimately be her own.

* * *

Laura thought she would be more nervous, but perhaps being disorganized was actually helping. It would be enough just to accessorize the right shoes and belt. She wouldn't have time to worry about what came afterward.

She had fought for sleep and lost. After the

65

recital she and Dolly had gone down to the coffee shop for dinner, making sure to stop on the way out to tell Ruth what a lovely performance she'd given. It hadn't been true, of course — Ruth had sounded like a maiden aunt summoning the courage to sing at the family reunion after one too many brandies Alexander — but the Barbizon was about nothing if not civility.

Dolly had gone to the TV room to watch Milton Berle as Laura went upstairs and took a long bath, then returned to the room to rummage through her curated wardrobe and find the appropriate outfit for her first day at *Mademoiselle*, a maddening exercise that had her second-guessing everything she'd brought and doing something that a week ago would have seemed impossible: looking forward to Marmy's visit. At least it would result in something new to wear.

Dolly returned and sank into a deep and blissful sleep seemingly within minutes. Laura lay awake for hours, unable to shut down the traffic inside her head. She had considered writing Box a thank-you note but decided against it. He didn't deserve a response. A bouquet of flowers and some witty lines jotted down, all no doubt executed by some family servant, weren't enough to mitigate his behavior at the Stork.

Her thoughts had then settled on an unlikely subject: Vivian. Here was a girl she certainly had no faculty to understand and yet fascinated her. Some of it was her sheer exoticism — the red hair, the tweedy accent — but there was an intangible quality to Vivian, a whimsy that came easily to her that would appear odd and affected on someone else. Her carefree attitude and dramatic bearing were elixirs, perfumes that made you notice her when she walked into a room. There was a certain power, a seductiveness, to that, one that Laura hated herself for wanting. She had come to New York to forge a career as a writer, to be admired for her words, her intellect, and yet here she was, staring up at the ceiling at two in the morning, fantasizing about what it was like to be the vamp.

Her memory had drifted back to her coming-out party at the country club, which she'd begged Marmy to let her out of. There had been a part of her that was secretly happy she'd lost the argument, the part that had stood for the fitting in the tight-bodiced ball gown with the flowing skirt, the part that had mastered the rhythmic sway of the waltz. But standing upstairs on the landing with the other girls waiting to be announced and descend like swans down the winding staircase, she had felt like a fraud. She listened to the other girls' talk of the vacant boys who would serve as their escorts, about the extravagant gifts they'd extracted from their mothers for enduring this charade.

There had been one girl who had stood apart from the others. Laura had seen her at a few of the rehearsals but had never spoken to her. Tall and clumsy and swathed in filmy white, she seemed to stand out even more. Her long neck hooked back into her head like a question mark,

67

and her thin, bony arms seemed too frail for her opera gloves. Struck by the girl's obvious discomfort, Laura had walked over to her.

'Hi. I'm Laura.'

It seemed to take the girl a few seconds to realize someone was speaking to her. 'Oh, hi.'

'It's all a bit much, isn't it?'

'Yes.' The girl had looked at Laura intently. 'You're very pretty.'

'Thanks. So are you.'

'No, I'm not,' the girl replied matter-of-factly. 'But it's nice of you to say.' She hitched up her skirt. 'I feel like Mother Goose in this thing.' She walked away.

A few minutes later the nine girls descended the staircase in order, each announced to a ballroom packed with their families and their families' business acquaintances, distant relatives, and glommers-on. Halfway through the evening, Laura had sought out the odd girl but couldn't find her anywhere. Stepping out onto the veranda of the club, she'd caught the tail end of a discussion between the girl and her mother, a formidable-looking matron in the Marmy mold clutching a small beaded handbag in her gloved left hand and pointing accusatorily at the girl with her right. The mother was alternately pointing at the girl and then shaking her head. Laura slowly walked toward them.

'I just don't feel comfortable making all of this small talk,' the girl pleaded. 'I'm trying — '

'You're *not* trying, Mariclaire, and I for one — '

'Laura!' Mariclaire had caught her eye.

'Getting some fresh air?'

Mariclaire's mother turned around, her face softening in an instant as they were introduced. 'Of course, the Dixons' girl,' she'd said. 'How lovely you look, my dear.'

'Not as lovely as Mariclaire,' Laura said. 'We've all been so envious of her dress. It's definitely the prettiest one here.'

A few minutes later, Mariclaire's mother went back inside. 'You didn't have to say that. About the dress,' Mariclaire said.

'It's true.'

'It's bullshit.'

Laura had never heard a girl swear. Not even the 'bad girls' at her country day school would have said such a thing. 'I'm . . . I'm sorry. I was only trying to help.'

Mariclaire grabbed her arm. 'No, no . . . I'm sorry. That was rude. You seem like a nice girl. None of these others has ever said a word to me, and I took dance lessons at the same place as two of them. It's just . . . ' She looked around. 'All of this . . . I don't belong here. They want me to, but I don't. And I know it and they know it. And sooner or later, we're all going to have to face it. This kind of thing was made for girls like you, not me.'

'That's funny,' Laura said. 'Because I don't feel like this was made for me at all.'

'But you can *survive* in it. Maybe even thrive in it. I never will. I don't have the right smarts for this. And I really don't want to.'

'What do you want, then?'

Mariclaire smiled for a few seconds, as if she

knew the answer but was somehow afraid to share her joy in what it was. 'Freedom.' She took Laura by the hand. 'C'mon, let's take a walk.' She tugged, answering Laura's look of doubt. 'C'mon, just down to the marina for a minute, to look at the water. We'll come right back.'

They galloped down the path to the weathered gray dock, their respective white dresses fluttering in the night breeze. Several small boats bobbed in the water. Laura looked back up at the country club, its windows blazing with candlelight, the faint whisper of soft music echoing out onto the pier. The two girls walked down the catwalk that jutted out onto the lake until they got to the end, looking at the dusky night sky, streaked in shades of baby blue and purple and pink. 'It's so beautiful,' Laura said.

A mischievous look swept over Mariclaire's face. 'A perfect night for a moonlight swim,' she declared.

Laura laughed. 'Oh, yes! I'm sure that would go over well.'

Mariclaire stepped back, kicked off her satin shoes. 'C'mon. Live a little.'

For a few seconds Laura lost her bearings. 'Wait . . . You're . . . you're not serious. You can't do this! Are you insane?!'

'Maybe,' the other girl replied, shrugging. And with that she gathered up her ball skirt, turned, and leapt into the water.

Later, after all of the hullabaloo and the scandal and the tittering of the other girls watching from the windows, Mariclaire — still sopping wet and bundled in a fluffy beach towel

70

from the club — walked, head high, to the family car, trailing her parents, still tomato-faced with embarrassment and rage. Laura impulsively bolted from Marmy's side and hustled down the embankment to the parking lot, where it was now her turn to catch the other girl by the arm.

'I don't understand,' she said breathlessly. 'Why?'

Mariclaire smiled. 'Sometimes,' she said, 'you just have to save yourself and jump.'

6

Dolly was passing the window of the Barbizon coffee shop when she spied Laura inside sitting at the counter, reading a book. She stopped to hastily look at her watch, then hustled inside.

'I thought you'd already left for *Mademoiselle*,' she said, sliding onto a stool. 'You don't want to be late for your first day of work.'

Laura put down the book, took a sip of coffee. 'I have time. I didn't sleep well last night. And I don't have to be there until nine thirty. They start late in publishing.'

'That's because they're all out every night going to parties and generally being swell.' She waved off the counter guy approaching with the coffee pot. 'I wish I had time for coffee. I'm so bad in the mornings. I envy Vivian — she sleeps in every day.'

'Vivian is also on her feet every night, in heels, selling cigarettes to lecherous men.'

'Yes, but at least they're rich lecherous men.' Dolly picked up the book on the counter. '*Will the Girl and Other Stories*, by Christopher Welsh,' she read. 'What kind of title is that? And who's Christopher Welsh? I've never heard of him.'

'I haven't gotten to the title story yet. It's the book Connie gave me. You remember, the sweet man who runs the bookshop down in the Village? The shop you couldn't wait to run out of on Saturday?'

72

Dolly rolled her eyes.

'The writing is actually quite good,' Laura continued. 'Intimidating, really. I read stories like this and wonder if I can ever produce prose like that. Connie was right,' Laura said, pointing to the book, 'this guy is going to be a famous writer someday.'

Dolly patted Laura's arm. 'So will you.' She looked again at her watch. 'I'm going to be late. Gotta run.'

'You know, all this talk about my new job and all this time I've completely forgotten to ask anything about yours. Where it is it, again?'

'Julian Messner,' Dolly said, awkwardly sliding off the stool and almost tipping over. 'Damn, these stools are a pain to get off of in a fitted skirt.' As she adjusted herself, a look of panic swept across her face. 'Oh my God!'

Laura leapt up in alarm. 'What? What's wrong?'

'Did you just hear that?' Dolly whispered urgently. 'I think my skirt just ripped. Oh, Lord, don't tell me I just did that. God couldn't be that cruel, could he? To have me rip my skirt at a coffee shop when I *didn't* have the pie?'

Laura turned Dolly around, traced her hand over the back. 'I don't see anything,' she said. 'I think it's okay.'

Dolly smoothed down the front, grabbed her clutch off the counter. 'Oh, thank God. Anyway, what was your question? Oh, right. Messner. I started, what, last Tuesday? Right before you got here. So it's only been a few days. It's a small publishing house, but everyone seems nice. I just sort of float around between departments, filling in for girls on vacation. I was lucky to get it.'

'I'm sure you'll have all of the office gossip by the end of the week.'

'I hope so,' Dolly said, smiling as she headed toward the door. 'God knows I can't rely on *you* for any. Ta-ta!'

Going to work was Dolly's favorite part of the day. Other people complained, loudly and often, but to her each trip was a reminder that she was not buried in Utica but rather living in Manhattan, where anything could happen. Hadn't she just landed at the Stork Club? She didn't understand pessimism. Why look on the cloudy side when there was always a bright side? Her bright side was getting shinier every day. She'd made new, interesting friends, she was acing her classes at Katie Gibbs, and in no time she would be working in a big office packed with eligible men. *Or maybe*, she thought, *I've already found him*.

She was sitting at her desk an hour later when another girl brushed by. 'Mr. Shaw wants to see you in his office,' she said airily. 'He said to give him five minutes, then go in.'

Dolly felt her face go hot. Bertrand Shaw was the assistant director of accounting at Julian Messner, and from the moment she'd walked into the building, she'd had trouble getting him off her mind. He was hardly tall — maybe five eight — but incredibly dapper, and had movie-star presence in an environment that desperately needed it. Dolly had pictured a book publisher as an elegant spot brimming with men in tweed jackets (okay, maybe seersucker — it *was* summer) and women spewing Dorothy Parker one-liners but instead had found your standard-issue Manhattan office, with rows and rows of interchangeable faces typing, answering phones, picking up and dropping off files, clearing out twice a day — once for lunch, then for home. She had hoped that was because she had just gotten here and had yet to work on the publishing side, with the editors, artists, and designers whom she was sure had to be more interesting than the number crunchers and administrators.

Except for Bertrand Shaw, of course. With his starched shirts always rolled up at the sleeves, his bulky body taut in his signature suspenders, he was more than simply attractive — he was a dreamboat. In the way Box Barnes was, even if Laura was too stupid to see it. Laura still hadn't even acknowledged Box's flowers, despite Dolly's repeated protestations. How could you not acknowledge flowers sent to you by one of the biggest catches in New York City? Why were the pretty girls the ones who never knew how to handle men?

She, Dolly Hickey, had no such hesitations. From her first day last week, she had been making casual eye contact with Bertrand Shaw — at the water fountain, in the occasional hallway pass-by. On Friday she had been inside a deli ordering a sandwich when she caught sight of him walking by outside; she'd feigned sudden illness, shouted to the counterman that she was canceling her order, then bolted across the street, running down a block and then coming back up, so that she and Bertrand Shaw would 'happen' to enter the building right at the same moment. She'd prayed he hadn't seen her breathing heavily.

As she reached for her steno pad, she thought of Frank, still back in Utica. Did he miss her? Maybe, maybe not. It wasn't like there had ever been a promise or understanding between them. And there were always those rumors around, that he had been seen with another girl at the movies or driving back from Oneida Lake. He was a good guy deep down, she knew. They'd grown up in similar families, knew similar people, had lived similar lives in many ways. He was the kind of solid, dependable guy your mother was always telling you to marry. But he didn't call when he said he would, which had driven her to despair more than she'd ever cared to admit, and twice he'd actually stood her up, leaving her by the front door, powdered and perfect, looking out the window for a date that never materialized. She'd been thankful when her father had overruled her mother and allowed her to go to secretarial school in New York. When she'd told Frank she was going, that she would be living at the legendary Barbizon Hotel for Women, the only thing he could manage to say was, 'Honestly, Doll, I don't see you as a New York career girl.'

She'd show him. She'd show them all: her sister, her mother. She couldn't wait to go home for her next visit. She'd get a new hairdo. Maybe she'd ask Vivian for some makeup tips. And then

76

she'd make a date with Frank, and he would pick her up in his cousin's Olds and take her on a long, leisurely drive, and be so dazzled by her beauty and sophistication that he would realize he would be nuts not to scoop her up right then and there. And maybe she would accept his proposal and maybe she wouldn't. Because, what about Bertrand?

The intercom on her desk blared to life. 'Mr. Shaw is waiting, Miss Hickey.'

She pressed down on the button. 'Of course, sorry. Coming. Right away.'

Bertrand Shaw's office was near the far right corner and included a small anteroom where his secretary sat, which led to an oak door that had his name affixed in officious white block letters. A temp sat at the vacationing secretary's desk, answering phones and taking lunch orders, but Bertrand Shaw's typing and dictation had been farmed out to a bunch of the other girls, including Dolly, who had taken suitable pride in turning around two letters before any of the others had even finished her first. Now, as she nodded to the temp and quickly rapped three times on his office door, she wondered what task he needed her for now. Or could it just be an excuse to see her? No, that couldn't be.

Could it?

'Come in,' came a deep voice, and as she entered she took in the surroundings. The office itself was pro forma, a desk, two chairs in front of it, boxy windows to the right with blinds turned to block the midsummer sun, a tidy bookshelf stacked with accounting volumes. Dolly instantly noticed there were no photographs in the office. No silver-framed portrait of an adoring wife or towheaded children.

He was standing behind the desk. Blue suspenders today. They brought out his eyes. 'Please have a seat,' he said. As she complied, he thrust a raft of papers at her. 'I need these typed up. There's four letters here. Nothing terribly urgent, but if we could get them out this afternoon, that would be great.'

'Of course,' Dolly said, thumbing through them. 'You know, Mr. Shaw, I take excellent dictation. You don't have to write these out going forward.'

'I'm sure you do. Old school, I guess. Just easier for me to scribble them out.'

Dolly looked closer at the letters. 'Oh.'

Bertrand Shaw looked up from his desk. 'Problem?'

Dolly couldn't help but chuckle. 'Are you sure you're not a doctor? I'm not sure I recognize whatever language these are written in.'

He winced. 'That bad, huh?'

'I'm afraid I have yet to take the class in decoding hieroglyphics.'

His throaty laugh filled the room. 'You know, since you're being so honest, I have to admit I had an ulterior motive asking you in here today.'

I knew it! She tried to feign insouciance. 'Oh?'

'It's a little embarrassing.' He looked away for a brief second. 'May I ask you a rather direct question?'

'There's no better kind.'

'Well,' he said, settling into his chair, 'let's say a gentleman meets a young lady, and he wishes to convey his . . . ' He looked out the window. 'Interest.' He looked back at her. 'If a gentleman wanted to express that sort of interest to you, and he was, appearances to the contrary, rather shy in this realm, what would be the best way for him to go about it?'

She smiled. 'Flowers. Always, always flowers.'

'Really. I don't know, that seems so . . . expected.'

'May I ask, how well does this gentleman know this young lady?'

He smiled, shook his head. 'Not very.'

'Perfect. Flowers are personal, but not overly so. You can't send a woman you've just met jewelry — it's too much. Dropping a note is too impersonal and also implies he's tight with a buck, which no woman wants to know, trust me.'

'Roses, then?'

'No. Roses are too unimaginative. If a man wants to be truly noticed, truly send a message to a woman that he has noticed *her*, he needs to send something more original. Something novel. Like gardenias.'

'Gardenias,' he repeated. He scribbled it on a piece of paper.

'Classic, beautiful, slightly exotic, original. All the things she wants to believe about herself.'

'So if a man sent you a bouquet of gardenias, what would you do?'

Her smile, pleasant and restrained, blossomed into a toothsome grin. 'I guess I'll have to see when he does. But I guarantee you, it would be

79

the reaction he hoped for.'

He leaned forward, laced his fingers together on the desk. 'Well, thank you very much, Miss Hickey. It's been an education.'

She rose, sliding the steno pad on top of the papers. 'I'll have these typed by the end of the day.'

He looked slightly amused. 'What about the hieroglyphics?' he asked.

'Don't worry,' she said, backing toward the door. 'I'm a quick study.'

★　★　★

Don't panic, Laura told herself. *Play it cool.*

She had left the coffee shop and found her way to the offices of *Mademoiselle*, located in a nondescript prewar building on Lexington Avenue. She had come over with several other girls, part of the cadre of thirteen lucky 'college editors' who had been selected from hundreds of applicants (or so they were all told) to put out the magazine's annual college issue in August. Walking in, she recognized several other girls from the recital yesterday.

Herded into a conference room, they had all taken seats around a long mahogany table polished to a lustrous shine, each handed a packet outlining the duties and expectations of the college editors and spelling out each one's individual assignments. Laura felt her heart sink when she saw she had been relegated to the fashion department. A month of cataloging dresses, shoes, and handbags and mollifying difficult models was hardly going to do much for her writing career.

Standing in front of the conference room was a stern-looking young woman who couldn't have been much older than the collegians, but her demeanor was that of a strict librarian just waiting to shush the next chatty offender. Seated in the rear of the room, Laura had missed her name — Miss Kyle? Heil? Lyle? — but it was clear that whoever she was, she was going to be the Lady in Charge for the month they were here. She wore a fitted white blouse with brocaded trim on the sleeves and collar, a skirt without a single wrinkle, and efficient two-inch heels. Her hair was pulled back into a severe chignon, and she wore a pair of black-rimmed cat-eye glasses that made her appear perennially angry, even on the rare occasions when she was attempting to express gracious commentary on life 'at the premier magazine for the young American woman as interested in her mind as her makeup.'

'More like interested in how to land a rich husband,' a girl two seats down from Laura had muttered, causing a minor flutter.

'Is there a problem in the rear of the room? Because if there is, please do let me know,' Cat Eyes had announced, craning her neck to ID the offender. There was quick silence and she continued, explaining the various duties expected, the deadlines and editorial procedures for getting the college issue produced, and, most of all, the strict rules of conduct. '*Mademoiselle* is a magazine that represents refinement, poise, grace, and intelligence,' she said, 'and as such, we expect all of our editors, whether they be full-time or our college apprentices, to carry themselves with the utmost decorum and respect at all times, both inside the office and out. Upon being accepted, each of you was mailed a list of rules for your employment with the magazine, and if you haven't already, I strongly urge you to familiarize yourself with these. Any violation of the morals code will result in immediate termination.'

Laura had read the rules more than once and found that while they covered the expected territory — basically, a girl was expected to dress well, show up on time, know how to tell a soup spoon from a shrimp fork, and avoid going too heavy on the makeup — they were firmest on one point: No boys. While they could not prohibit dating, obviously, it was made very clear that there were to be no dates at magazine outings, no cancellations of such outings due to said dates, and absolutely no dates coming into the office, ever. While this was a given at the Barbizon — despite the seeming prowess of both Grace Kelly and Vivian, it was difficult to sneak a man past Mrs. Mayhew and the matrons — the *Mademoiselle* editors seemed positively apoplectic at the thought of a 'bad girl' infiltrating their lily-scented midst. Not unlike the Barbizon manual, the briefing materials had entire sections devoted to 'appropriate' social conduct. Reading it over in Laura and Dolly's room, Vivian had remarked, with suitable British pathos, 'Oh, blimey. Why don't they just hand you each a chastity belt and be done with it?'

Then there was the issue of Mrs. Blackwell.

Betsy Blackwell had briefly greeted the new girls when they had first come in, like a hostess at a grand lawn party, then quickly turned the meeting over to Cat Eyes and floated away. A trim, stylish woman in a tailored suit and delicate jewelry, she boasted a magnificent bouffant of jet-black hair that fell in soft waves to frame her delicate face, and her skin was as snowy and unlined as a Greek statue. She had been the editor in chief of *Mademoiselle* since 1937 and was known for being both gracious and as tough as Churchill. Her office was strictly off-limits unless you were specifically asked by a senior editor to take something to it or retrieve something from it. If you saw Mrs. Blackwell in the hallway, you were to politely smile and nod, then keep walking. Perhaps she would acknowledge you, but most likely she would not. She was extremely busy and was not to be bothered. Ever.

There had been just one more order of business. The one that had now left Laura with an alarm bell clanging in her ears.

'Today, to celebrate the beginning of your journey here at *Mademoiselle*, I am pleased to say that there will be a welcome luncheon at the Barnes & Foster department store on Fifth Avenue,' Cat Eyes declared, 'hosted by none other than Benjamin Barnes.'

Laura fought to keep her face expressionless, even as the girls around her quickly devolved into babbling wonder at this first step on the road to heady cosmopolitan travels. How had she not known who he was? Everyone else sure seemed to. And now she would have to face him again, just days after the disastrous night at the Stork.

The briefing lasted another ten minutes, and then the girls were again rounded up and led down the corridor toward the main editorial offices, walking in lockstep like a bunch of WACs on their way to the barracks, the sound of their collective heels reverberating through the halls. Laura fell in line and tried to stay calm. She hadn't acknowledged Box's flowers, a social faux pas that no doubt would have sent Marmy reaching for the smelling salts. But she had been unsure of just how to do it. Send a note to the store, thanking him? For what? Calling a florist? Trying to rehabilitate his playboy image? The one thing she knew she *couldn't* do was tell any of her fellow college editors about what had happened. All she needed was to become the object of idle office gossip on her first day, hauled into Cat Eyes' office, and sent back to Greenwich on the evening train.

There are thirteen of us, Laura told herself. *There will probably be more people there. He'll never even notice me.*

God, she was a terrible liar.

Barnes & Foster stood on the corner of Fifty-Third and Fifth Avenue, a Corinthian building that when lit up at night conjured images of something very stately and serious, like the Parthenon or the Supreme Court. On its north side it spelled out, in huge backlit wrought-iron Edwardian script, BARNES & FOSTER, while on the other three sides a simple B&F asserted its stature as a temple of Gotham style and good taste. Its elongated paned casement windows on the ground floor each sat above an English garden flower box overflowing with seasonal selections: hydrangeas in spring, tea roses in summer, holly, ivy, and tiny white lights at Christmas. Unlike Saks and Macy's, whose holiday window displays attracted a multitude of passersby at the yuletide, Barnes & Foster eschewed the theatrical, instead beckoning the curious not to stroll by, but to be piqued enough to enter a rarefied world of refined retail enchantment inside.

At noon Laura was walking toward the rear of the pack of girls up Fifth Avenue when she caught a glimpse of herself in a shop window. She wished she had dressed differently for her first day. She had selected a navy Anne Klein suit, which, while succeeding in telegraphing 'up-and-coming career girl,' came up rather short in telegraphing 'polished and sophisticated siren you mistreated at the Stork Club who is not simply mollified with flowers.' *You're being ridiculous*, she told herself as she and the flock of girls crossed the street. *It's ludicrous to think he's not going to say something. There may be some sort of receiving line! You need to be prepared. He says, 'Well, hello there. Nice to see you again.' And you say . . . What? 'Thank you for having us.' Idiotic. Okay, how about, 'Your store is lovely.'*

Even worse.

She saw the outline of the store, its front flags whipping in the summer breeze, come into view. *Come on! What are you going to say?*

She needed something with a little more snap. Hadn't she just channeled Hepburn with the bartender at the San Remo? She would show Box Barnes that she was cool, confident. She was living in the former home of Grace Kelly. Now she needed, for at least one afternoon, to *be* Grace Kelly, trading pithy bons mots with Jimmy Stewart as they watched Raymond Burr murder his wife.

'Are you coming, or are your deep thoughts simply far too compelling to abandon?' Cat Eyes was saying, holding open the door to the entrance. The others had already walked inside.

'Sorry,' Laura said, scurrying past.

The entrance led into an atrium that felt more like a cathedral than a store, with baronial white support columns that soared up to a rounded ceiling painted with frescoes of cherubs, clouds, suns, and moons. The marble floors shimmered. In the center of the store, there was a huge Grecian vase overflowing with wildflowers. Dueling white marble staircases swept up on either side, leading to a mezzanine that surrounded the entire floor, so you could stand by the stone railing and look down on the shoppers bustling below, like the girls inside the Barbizon peering down at their prospective dates. To the far left was a bank of elevators coated in gold leaf, which opened to expose men in tailored red uniforms and box hats declaring, 'Going up,' using their white-gloved hands to throw the lever and gently close the doors.

Founded by British cousins who had come to America in 1840, the store had begun as a small-scale emporium selling housewares, candy, and coffee. There was a silver-framed black-and-white photograph hanging inside the entrance that showed the store's centennial celebration in 1940, and Laura had instantly recognized Box, a handsome nine-year-old in a white tie who even then had exuded a certain mischievous charm.

Laura followed her fellow editors up the marble staircase and down the mezzanine, until they entered a small room with ornate double doors. The room was anchored by a three-tiered crystal chandelier hanging in its center, its soft glow a flattering compliment to the sunlight streaming in from the windows. Five tables of eight had been set with starched white tablecloths and fine bone china, an indication that there would be many guests at the luncheon other than the girls from *Mademoiselle*. Indeed, there were several businessman types engaged in conversation around the room, along with the occasional society matron sipping a glass of white Bordeaux. Mrs. Blackwell, having come separately by car, was already present, in the same cornflower-blue skirt suit and gold jewelry she had worn for the meet-and-greet this morning, her gloves in her right hand, her purse dangling daintily from her forearm. She was animatedly chatting with Box Barnes.

It had only been three days, but Laura had forgotten how commanding his presence was. He wore a khaki summer suit that hinted at a kind of relaxed refinement, like a Scottish land baron just back from a hunt on the moors, and a pair of brown-and-white spectators. When he moved, his cuff links caught the light from the chandelier, twinkling around his wrists like diamonds.

It wasn't more than three minutes — though it felt like years — before he spotted her. She kept her chin up and her gaze neutral, and to her surprise so did he, glancing at her for a few seconds, then just as quickly turning back to Mrs. Blackwell, who was now in animated discussion, her purse swinging slightly as she gestured for emphasis. Everyone was soon directed to take their seats, which had been marked by calligraphic place cards. Laura found herself next to a buyer from the store on one side and one of her fellow college editors on the other. Box was two tables away. Throughout the lunch, he never looked at her once.

Perhaps all of her self-remonstration had been for nothing. Maybe he didn't even recognize her. Was he angry she'd ignored his flowers? Oh, what did it matter, anyway? She took a deep breath, scooped a spoon into her fruit cup, and began lobbing a series of banal questions to the buyer about how he selected the garments sold at a department store.

As the coffee was being served, there was a gentle *tap-tap-tap* on a water glass. Box Barnes rose from his seat at the center table, where he had been seated to the left of Mrs. Blackwell.

'I am honored to have been chosen as the official welcoming host for the 1955 college editors of *Mademoiselle*,' he said, grabbing his wineglass and raising it. 'A toast to your collective creativity and success.' He went on for several minutes about the history of Barnes & Foster, about the importance of style and grace in a world too often without it, splicing in the occasional joke about bargain sales and the particularly smelly parts of the city. Laura found herself impressed with his effortless ease at public speaking. He occasionally glanced her way but again made no sign of recognition. *Just as well*, Laura thought.

As he went to wrap up, his tone became slightly more serious, as if he were delivering a closing argument at trial. 'This may come as a surprise to you,' he said, 'but I actually read *Mademoiselle*. I do because I appreciate who it is written for and who it is written by, smart girls who aren't afraid to dream big and dare to try and achieve those dreams. We men are always complaining that we can't understand women. But *Mademoiselle* helps me do just that.' His eyes suddenly shifted to the left, honing in on Laura's like lasers. 'In the end, I'm just like any other guy out there, trying to find a way to be a better man. One worthy of a *Mademoiselle* girl.'

She felt like her face had just burst into flames.

Had anyone noticed? She glanced around, panicked. But everyone at her table seemed thoroughly engrossed in Box, who was finishing to polite applause.

Before the luncheon ended, Mrs. Blackwell gathered all of the girls together for a group photograph with Box. Laura made certain to stay on the far right side, with six girls between her and him. The last flashbulb popped, and the editors filtered back to their respective tables to gather their things and head out to the mezzanine and then back to the office.

Laura had just grabbed her clutch from her seat when she felt a presence. 'Now, you *really* didn't think you were going to leave without talking to me, did you?'

She looked into his face and saw . . . something. Not mockery this time, but the childlike grin that sweeps a boy's face when he gets his first bicycle or baseball card. She felt her own expression slowly dawn into a smile. 'It was a lovely lunch.'

It was a lovely lunch? Oh, good God.

'Did you get my flowers?'

'I did. I apologize for not sending a note. It's been incredibly hectic.'

'A note? I only warrant a note?' She said nothing. 'You can make it up to me,' he continued.

She looked around, spied two of the other girls watching this little scene over their shoulders as they slowly — very, very slowly — sashayed out toward the doors. 'I really need to get back to my group. This is my first day and I don't want to get into any trouble.'

He folded his arms. 'You know, this is providence, us meeting again. I mean, you have to see that.'

She shook her head nervously. 'Oh, I don't know if I would call it that.'

'Well, I would. I will let you go. But before I do, I need two things. First, you need to tell me your last name. Because, appearances to the contrary,' he said, waving a hand around the room, 'I do not have the liberty of sending flowers to every Laura at the Barbizon indefinitely.'

'It's Dixon. Laura Dixon.'

'Very well, Laura Dixon,' he said. 'Let's try all of this again, okay? I am Benjamin Barnes, who is actually a hell of a lot nicer guy than the version you met Friday. And who would like to prove that to you. Say, Thursday night?'

Aside from the busboys clearing dishes, they were now completely alone. The other girls must all be downstairs by now. Cat Eyes would be wondering where she was. 'I really have to go. I'm sorry.'

He walked out alongside her. 'I'll escort you out. This way you won't be able to avoid my invitation.'

She turned to look at him as they moved out onto the mezzanine. 'Are you always this persistent?'

'Only when I want something badly. And you owe me, you know.'

'I owe you?'

'You called me out for being named for a cardboard box.'

Laura laughed, bemused while also quickly becoming unhinged. She looked over the railing and saw the *Mademoiselle* group below, gathering near the main exit. Cat Eyes was milling about. It looked like she was counting heads. Laura hustled toward the staircase, Box still beside her. She went down the first few steps and then turned back to him, started to say something.

He cut her off. 'Thursday,' he said. 'Just say yes. One little word. Yes.'

She let out a big exhale, smiled. 'I can't. I would love to, but I already have plans that I simply can't break.'

'Okay. Saturday, then.'

Her mind was whirling. Was he just going to keep throwing out dates until she relented? 'I don't know . . . '

'Of course you do. Saturday. Don't worry. You've played hard to get enough. You've turned down the first offer. But you really must take the second. It would be uncivilized not to.'

'I . . . ' She shrugged. 'Okay. Saturday.'

'Perfect. Saturday was my first choice anyway. I'll pick you up at nine.'

'Nine? Where are we going at nine?' she said.

'To dinner at El Morocco.'

El Morocco. The most fashionable nightclub in Manhattan, tucked away on East Fifty-Fourth Street. 'I don't have anything to wear to the El Morocco,' she said feebly.

'You're in luck,' he said, backing away on the landing, his face exploding into a cocky grin. He spread his arms wide. 'I know the guy who owns this place.'

7

Dolly nodded as Oscar the doorman opened the door to the Barbizon and wondered, as she did almost every time she saw him, how he kept cool wearing that ornate formal uniform in the middle of summer. She thought maybe that was part of the interview process: They forced you to put on this ridiculous outfit that made you look like you were a Napoleonic general, then asked you to stand in a ninety-five-degree room to see if you didn't sweat. She loved Oscar — all the girls did — because he was always jovial and kind, because he knew the art of a well-placed compliment when you needed it most, and because he was almost leonine in his protection of the young women whose residence he stood sentry for. He was constantly being offered bribes — for introductions or to assist slipping some cad upstairs when the desk matrons were occupied. But he never relented. Girls besieged by overly amorous suitors knew they could count on Oscar's protection.

If only I were one of them.

The late-day lobby was quiet, just a few girls taking refuge from the stuffy city streets. The lobby itself was a huge rectangle framed by a vast Oriental rug, on which was placed an imposing pocked leather couch and various tasteful upholstered side chairs, with a long mahogany coffee table in the middle. The lobby's focal

93

point was the curving staircase that led to the mezzanine, which for some reason always made Dolly think of the one that Clark Gable carried Vivien Leigh up in *Gone with the Wind*, though the Barbizon's was neither as wide nor as grand. But Dolly often mused that perhaps that was what the Barbizon did best — provide a tableau where girls got to indulge their romantic fantasies, to play Scarlett O'Hara, looking down amused at all of the boys of the county who had come courting.

She spied Laura, in a pale pink linen suit, sitting in the far side of the room, lazily flipping through a copy of *Vogue*. She'd taken off her fitted jacket and tossed it on the arm of the adjacent sofa, and her legs were crossed, as if she were waiting to be called into a doctor's office.

'Hey there,' Laura said as Dolly approached. 'Out early today?'

'Only a half-hour,' Dolly said, plopping down onto the sofa. 'What are you doing? Shouldn't you still be at *Mademoiselle*? Don't tell me they're tired of you after only three days.'

'I had to return a bunch of dresses they used in a shoot all over town, and they told me I didn't have to come back after I was done. So I had a little snack at Isle of Capri and then came home. But it's too stuffy to sit in the room.' She closed the magazine. 'I was going to treat myself to a milkshake in the coffee shop. Wanna come?'

Dolly took in Laura's figure, the way her bosom tapered to her narrow waist. She would love a milkshake. 'No, I ate late.'

'You seem distracted. What's going on?'

Plenty, Dolly wanted to say. This morning Bertrand Shaw had walked up to her desk as she was typing, perched himself on the edge, looked down at her, and said, 'Well, I took your advice.'

She'd almost lost her breath. 'What . . . Really? How so?'

'Well,' he said, smiling sheepishly, 'let's just say someone is going to be getting a very nice bouquet of white gardenias very soon.'

Dolly had silently thanked God she was sitting. She might have fainted right there on the spot if she'd been caught in the hallway having this conversation. 'Well, I'm sure she'll be thrilled.'

'I'm hopeful,' he said, sliding off and heading to his office.

Laura was looking at her expectantly, but Dolly couldn't risk jinxing it. No, better to wait. 'Nothing much,' she replied. 'Any news from Box? Are you guys still going to El Morocco Saturday night?'

It had been two days since the luncheon at Barnes & Foster, and Laura hadn't heard a word. She'd succumbed to love-story hysteria and come back and told Dolly and Vivian everything that had happened the first day at *Mademoiselle*, breezing past the intimidating welcome from Cat Eyes before settling into a blow-by-blow recitation of the next chapter in the Box Barnes saga, right up to its cinematic staircase crescendo. Their disparate reactions had been predictable: Vivian warned her that he was a cad who would never follow through and who was probably at that very moment in bed with a

Broadway dancer; Dolly already had Laura shopping for a trousseau at B. Altman. Laura hated being thrown off balance like this, of having her level of happiness so quickly altered by the affections of a man with whom she was barely acquainted and who she strongly suspected had the propensity to behave badly.

'I don't know,' she said with a heavy sigh. 'I mean, he hasn't officially canceled. But he hasn't confirmed, either. And it doesn't matter anyway. I still have nothing to wear.'

A clipped British voice behind her interrupted. 'I suspect, in fact, you do.'

Vivian circled around and took a seat in the chair next to Laura's, setting down a huge cardboard box onto the floor. A huge black B&F stared up at them in script, partially obscured by a wide green satin ribbon tied in a bow across the lid. 'This was at the front desk. Special delivery,' Vivian said.

Laura slid the card out from under the ribbon. FOR THE PRETTIEST GIRL AT THE BALL. I HAD TO GUESS THE SIZE, BUT THINK I GOT IT RIGHT. UNTIL SATURDAY — B.

Dolly practically ripped the card from her hands. 'I think it's safe to say your date is still on.'

A few of the other girls walking by had slowed down to glance over, and Laura suddenly felt self-conscious. 'Let's go upstairs. I feel like a mannequin in the Saks window.'

'Oh, bosh,' Vivian interjected. 'They're all going to see you in it soon enough, Cinderella. Might as well whet the appetite.' She pointed to

96

the box. 'Let's have at it, then.'

Dolly nodded eagerly in agreement, frantically clapping her hands and barely suppressing a squeal. Laura quickly untied the ribbon, lifted the lid, and delicately peeled back the reams of scented mint tissue paper. 'Oh my,' she whispered.

The dress was not a dress, but rather a work of art. A strapless tulle gown in a deep shade of jeweled purple, with a subtly patterned bodice flecked with silver and trimmed with silk cabbage roses, leading down to a flaring ball skirt. Underneath was a filmy stole in a pale shade of lavender and a pair of gray opera gloves. Laura stood, pressing the gown to her body. Never in her life had she seen anything so breathtaking.

Vivian checked out the label. 'Philip Hulitar,' she mused. 'Well, I've got to say, lout or no, he's got excellent taste. Or a secretary with excellent taste.' She took an appraising step back. 'My, my,' she said, 'something tells me you're going to be a popular lunch date at the office on Monday.'

Laura was elated. And frightened. And confused. She turned to Dolly, the dress still pressed against her bosom. 'What do you think, Dolly?'

Dolly was looking back toward the desk. 'Agnes Ford,' she said.

Laura and Vivian followed her gaze. 'What?' Laura said. 'Who's Agnes Ford?'

Across the lobby by the entrance, they could see a wispy young woman in a simple shift standing at the reception desk. Her hair was honey blond, her skin as white and flawless as fresh snow. She appeared to be fumbling with some sort of chunky charm bracelet, though it was hard to tell from this distance whether she was attempting to get it on or off.

'That's Agnes Ford,' Dolly said, in almost the identical conspiratorial whisper she'd announced the appearance of Box Barnes in the Barbizon coffee shop. 'She's a really famous model. The Ford agency stashes all of its top models here.'

Vivian knitted her eyebrows. 'She runs a modeling agency? She looks barely twenty.'

'No, no, no,' Dolly said. 'Her last name is Ford and the agency's name is also Ford. It's just a coincidence. But she's really famous. And very dramatic. She had a pale blue Thunderbird delivered to the door here. Oscar signed for it.'

'How do you know that?' Laura asked, still clutching the dress.

Dolly sighed, exasperated. 'How do I — Where do you two live, on some Indian reservation? It was all over the gossip columns! Sheesh!' She turned back to Laura. 'She's been on the cover of *Mademoiselle*.'

Dolly was about to offer more color commentary — such as the fact that Agnes Ford had grown up in Nebraska, though there were those who thought that had simply been invented to create a rags-to-riches mystique — when a delivery man walked into the lobby and headed toward the front desk. Dolly gasped.

A bouquet of white gardenias.

They'd come. He'd sent them.

Without a word she dashed over to the desk, sidling up next to Agnes Ford as Metzger absently signed for the flowers. 'Well, a case of perfect timing,' Metzger said. 'These are for you.'

She slid the bouquet over to Agnes Ford.

Agnes was still fumbling with her bracelet — definitely trying to get it off, Dolly could now see — and paid no attention to the bouquet. Her bouquet. Dolly knew she should walk away, back to Laura and Vivian. No one would be the wiser. But somehow she couldn't help herself. She couldn't stop herself from accepting the full, brutal force of the torture.

'Your flowers, they're . . . they're beautiful,' she said cheerily. 'Aren't you going to open the card? See who they're from?'

Agnes Ford thrust out her arm. 'Can you get this thing off?'

Dolly hesitated, felt Metzger's dead eyes flicker up from behind the desk, appraising. 'Uh, sure,' Dolly said, taking hold of the bracelet on the girl's left wrist. As she worked to unhook it — the clasp had gotten lodged in one of the bracelet's loops — she inquired again about the flowers. Agnes Ford reached over and plucked out the card, deftly removing it from the tiny white envelope with one hand. She shook her head.

'Wrong boyfriend?' Dolly asked, still fiddling with the bracelet. She'd figured out how to release the clasp but didn't want Agnes Ford to see her eyes welling up.

The model sighed deeply. 'No such luck. Just some drip I talked to for, oh, I don't know, two minutes one night at '21' who now seems to think we're the next Elizabeth Taylor and Michael Wilding.'

Dolly continued to play with the clasp, her heart heaving. Her voice was barely a whisper. 'So, not for you, is he?'

'That's an understatement. He works pushing papers at some publishing company. I've talked to more interesting statues.' She glanced over at the flowers. 'Who sends *gardenias*?'

Enough. 'There you go,' Dolly said, sliding off the bracelet and handing it to her.

For the first time, Agnes Ford smiled, the smile that had beckoned from the magazine rack, the smile that sold countless tubes of toothpaste and pillbox hats and silk stockings. 'You're an angel,' she said.

She slid Bertrand Shaw's white gardenias across the counter. 'Here, take these. It's the least I can do.'

★ ★ ★

'Marciano is going to kill him.'

The subject was boxing, specifically the upcoming fight in September between Rocky Marciano and Archie Moore, and Nicola Accardi was telling anyone — in this case, two similarly swarthy men and their dates sitting at a corner table at Antolotti's on East Forty-Ninth — that Marciano wouldn't let the bout go more than three rounds. A detailed analysis of the respective fighters' hooks and jabs and crosses had been going on for a good fifteen minutes;

100

Vivian had tuned out somewhere around the three-minute mark. She had never understood the fascination two men pummeling one another to a pulp had held for her father and uncles back in Surrey.

Of course, there's so much I've never understood about Dad, she thought. *Or he, me, for that matter. Which explains how I ended up in New York in the first place.*

Why *couldn't* she have been more like Mary and Emma? It certainly would have made life easier. Yes, her life would have turned out predictable and boring, but there was comfort in such things, she'd come to realize. But her sisters' lives were an argument she could never talk herself into making: the sacrifices too big, the payoffs too small. Security was for the timid and the weak.

She took another drag on her cigarette, looked around the room. There was the occasional couple engaged, laughing, clinking wineglasses over dinner, but for the most part the restaurant seemed stuffed with men like Nicky and his cohorts. *What the hell am I doing here?* she asked herself, not for the first time tonight. But then she glanced at Nicky's profile, his strong jawline and languid eyes and thick mane of silken black hair.

Carnality was a dangerous pastime. Not for some faux morality reason, the scorn of the sentries who ran the Barbizon or the Women, who looked at girls such as she as wanton harlots. But because in the end, indulging in it was invariably empty and fleeting. Wasn't what she was doing simply the sensual version of what the girls back at the hotel, watching telly while eating ice cream and trying to guess some contestant's hobby on *I've Got a Secret*, were doing? Passing time, trying to stay entertained, forgetting the drudgery of everyday life. She longed to be a singer but instead spent her nights passing out cigarettes. Laura wanted to be a writer but instead spent her days taping boxes of shoes. Dolly wanted — oh, who knew what Dolly wanted? A husband, that was for certain. Vivian flashed back to the episode in the lobby yesterday. *How very odd.* Dolly had rushed over to see the model and then after several minutes had walked out of the hotel, head down and clutching a single gardenia.

Vivian would never understand women.

She lifted her champagne coupe, silently toasting herself. Tuning in once again, she found the topic had now switched to the Brooklyn Dodgers and their odds of winning their first World Series. Boxing, baseball. What was it with American men and their sports? Not that the Brits were much better, she supposed: Dad was absolutely mad for golf, a sport so dull she couldn't fathom watching a single hole, never mind eighteen.

He had been so angry at her coming to America. Then again, he'd left her little choice.

Of course, he'd been so angry at so much of what she'd done growing up. She hadn't been like Mary and Emma, the good girls who'd stayed on the straight road, dressed modestly, and waited for their husbands to show up. Vivian

102

had found trouble early and often, and discovered that instead of it scaring her, it only made her feel more alive. She had no acuity for cooking, baking, or cleaning and had no intention of acquiring it, either. What she did have, from the time she was a seven-year-old girl standing in a pew in St. Mary's in Fetcham, was the ability to sing.

God held no fascination for her; the Bible was a book of fairy tales that might as well have been written by the Brothers Grimm. But the music of the church, that was something else. There was something aching in the dour verses, accompanied by organ and harp and violin, a sad beauty that touched her in a way little else ever had. Music was transcendent. She loved the way she sounded when she sang. And that when other people heard her sing, they saw not the redhead with the dangerous curves, but something far more real. Something pure.

Nicky's elbow nudged her back into the conversation. 'Tell 'em, Ruby,' he was saying, 'am I right, or what?'

'Ruby' had become his selected nickname for her, though in more intimate moments he had the good sense to swap in 'Honey' or 'My lovely,' which, it pained her to admit, she rather liked. He had tried 'Red' at first, but she had protested, pushing back that it made her sound like a saloon owner. At least Ruby had some style, something Bogart might call Bacall.

'I'm afraid I'm a bit out of my depth,' she said, sipping again.

'I'm telling these mooks that Johnny Podres is

going to mow down that Yankees lineup.'

'Dodgers ain't gonna *make* the Series, so that's gonna be kinda tough there, Nick,' one of the mooks retorted. His date opened her compact, pursing her very red lips, coated in lipstick so thick it looked like cake frosting.

'Never fear,' Vivian said, raising her glass with brio. 'To the Dodgers.'

Nicky quickly grabbed his whiskey glass and clinked. He leaned over, planted a soft kiss on her neck. 'What do you say we get out of here?' he whispered.

Finally.

She had told herself she wasn't seeing him again. She often made that sort of pledge with the men she dated. But then a necklace or a bracelet would arrive in a satin-lined velvet box, Metzger arching an eyebrow in disapproval as she slid it across the desk, and Vivian would think, *Oh, what the hell,* and agree to one more outing with the bookkeeper from Astoria or the car salesman from Westchester.

Nicky, though, had proved a bit more territorial than most. She had one night a week off from the Stork, and she wasn't going to waste it on him. But then he'd showed up at the club twice this week, bearing corsages and sonnets (actually, more like limericks), and she'd weakened. There were worse ways to spend your free night than in the company of a handsome man, eating and drinking at a nice restaurant. It sure beat *I've Got a Secret.*

He'd won her over tonight by reserving a room at the Plaza, complete with room service

— anything she wanted. As he stood to pull out her chair, his eyes looked at her with a combination of benign amusement and raw lust. And she thought, *Right now, I know exactly what I want.*

★ ★ ★

Vivian sat on the edge of the tub, wiggling her fingers under the spigot as she fiddled with the faucets, trying to ascertain the perfect temperature, not too hot, not too tepid. Through the open door, she could hear Nicky on the phone, yelling — actually, it was more like barking — at whatever poor soul was on the other end.

She put the stopper in, watched the tub slowly begin to fill. She grabbed the bottle of bubble bath and upended it over the water, inhaling the sweet smell of jasmine. Their lovemaking had been ferocious — damn, he knew what he was doing — and she relished the thought of a warm, relaxing, afterglow soak in the tub.

She cinched the belt around her silk robe and padded to the doorway, taking a casual look into the room. A naked Nicky was standing by the nightstand with his back to her, the phone still in his ear. She took in the fine lines of his musculature, felt herself stirring again.

' . . . and I am telling you, if that shipment ain't in Hoboken by tomorrow morning, you can tell Mikey Feet that they can start sending his mail in care of Mount St. Mary's Cemetery, 'cause that's where he's gonna be livin'. Or rather *not* livin'.' A pause. 'I don't give a shit,

Lon! That's not my problem! I paid for freight, I expect freight to be delivered. This is business! Stop with this fucking bullshit! I am — ' Another pause, punctuated by the occasional grunt. Vivian could imagine the plaintive case being made on the other end of the line. It wouldn't do any good. Nicky was immune to begging. Except when it came to sex, when he was very good at begging himself.

The call went on for another five minutes, Nicky apparently trying to set some sort of record for how many expletives one could sandwich into a telephone conversation. He slammed the receiver down so violently that Vivian wondered if he'd broken it altogether. He ran his right hand through his hair. It's what he always did when he was upset, as if pulling back his hair could actually clear his head.

'Can I get you something?' she asked serenely from the bathroom doorway.

He turned around, as if he'd completely forgotten she'd come in with him. 'These fucking Jersey morons. Impossible to do business with. I — '

She unfastened the belt around the robe, let it drop to the floor. 'No use getting upset, darling. There must be something I can do for you.'

His eyes never left hers as he walked across the room. He grabbed her roughly, biting her neck, her ear, her hair. She flung her legs around his midsection. 'Tub is almost full,' she whispered. He cupped her ass as he continued feverishly exploring her with his mouth, slowly backing her into the bath.

8

Laura put down her book. She couldn't concentrate. Too many distractions.

Her date with Box to the El Morocco was tonight, but any daydreams had taken a back seat to worry. She looked over again at the clock on her bedside table. Almost 11 a.m. *That's it. If she doesn't show up by noon, I'm going down to Metzger.*

She hadn't seen Dolly since Wednesday. She and Vivian had watched as Dolly had approached Agnes Ford across the Barbizon lobby as if in a zombie trance, then witnessed the peculiar exchange where it appeared that Dolly was helping Agnes with the clasp of her bracelet. And then, suddenly, Dolly had turned and bolted straight out the door of the hotel, vanishing up Sixty-Third Street. Laura had started to go after her and now regretted heeding Vivian's advice. 'Let her go,' Vivian had said. 'Sometimes a girl just needs to tell everyone to sod off and sort out her own melodrama.'

She and Vivian had gone to dinner in the coffee shop before Vivian's shift at the Stork, which must have been when Dolly had slipped back in, hastily packed a bag, and left again. No note, nothing. Laura would have reported her missing right away if she hadn't noticed her suitcase and toiletries gone. The fact that Dolly hadn't packed everything steadied her — it

107

meant she'd have to return at some point.

Doesn't it?

As if on cue, the door to the room opened and Dolly walked in, dropping her suitcase on her bed. 'Hi,' she said, as if she'd been gone for breakfast rather than three days. 'Have you been out yet? The humidity is wicked. The F train was stifling.'

Laura bolted out of her chair, flinging her arms around her roommate. 'Oh my God! I've been so worried about you. Where have you *been*?'

'I went to see my aunt in Park Slope.'

'What?'

'Sorry. I probably should have left a note.'

Laura separated, slid a hand into hers. 'Dolly, what's going on?'

'What do you mean?'

She searched the girl's face. Blank. 'I mean, one minute you're talking to Agnes Ford at the front desk, the next you take off, just vanish on some trip to see an aunt with no warning? It's not like you.'

'We've known each other, what, *a week*, Laura?' Dolly said. 'You have no idea what's like me.'

The iciness in her voice left Laura blindsided. She dropped her hand. 'Of course. You're right.'

Dolly sank down on the bed, kicked off her shoes. She stared at the floor as she spoke. 'Sorry. That was mean. I just . . . I don't want to talk about it, okay?'

Laura's instinct was to push, but she thought better of it. *She'll tell me when she's ready.* 'Okay.'

Dolly returned a wan smile. And then, there they were — sitting right on the desk. Agnes Ford's white gardenias, a bit droopy from three days of heat but holding their own in a full vase of water. 'Oh, yes,' Laura said. 'I'm sorry about those. I tried my best to keep them going, but gardening has never been my strong suit. You can ask my mother. I was absolutely hopeless at the Greenwich garden club. But Metzger told me Agnes had given these to you, and they seemed too pretty to throw away, so I kept them for you.'

Dolly nodded slowly, unblinking. 'Yes. That was very thoughtful.'

'Hey . . . you want to come with me? I'm going back to your favorite place, the bookstore in the Village, to see Connie. Please come. Afterward I'll take you to the San Remo and we can people-watch. It's like the Stork with angry intellectuals.'

'No, no, you go. I'm tired. I think I'm actually going to take a little nap.' She pushed back two more of Laura's halfhearted but well-meaning entreaties. Ten minutes later, Laura walked out the door, headed for the Village.

Dolly lay back on the bed and closed her eyes, waiting for sleep to overtake her. When she got up, she would get a paper sack and put the gardenias in it, walk down the hall, and send them plummeting down the trash chute.

★   ★   ★

'Well, well, look who's back!'

Connie lowered his glasses from behind the

109

small counter. He looked genuinely happy to see her, which pleased her. She loved the idea of being a regular at a little bookshop in the Village.

'I've brought another recruit,' Laura said, holding the door open. 'Hopefully this one won't abandon us for the siren's call of shopping.'

In the lobby she'd bumped into Vivian, who, professing both boredom and hunger, had volunteered to accompany her to the bookstore if there was a promise of lunch at an outdoor café afterward. After brief introductions Vivian went off to explore the books, though Laura strongly suspected it had been years since Vivian had actually read one. Connie kept peering over at her like a smitten schoolboy. 'Your friend,' he said, 'she's rather . . . different. Showgirl?'

'Even when there's no audience,' Laura said.

Connie smiled. 'How was your first week at *Mademoiselle*?'

'Good. At least I think good. Not quite as literary as I had hoped. Too many handbags, not enough E. B. White. But there's three weeks left. I still have time to plan a takeover of the editorial department.'

Connie excused himself to help two older women who'd come in. Laura wound her way through the narrow aisles and found Vivian in Popular Fiction, flipping through a used copy of *Rebecca*. 'Ohhh,' Laura said, looking over her shoulder. 'I adored that book.'

'You American girls and your romance novels. It singularly explains the existence of Johnnie Ray. How to find pleasure in a book where the heroine is mistreated by her husband, pushed to the brink of suicide by the maid, and doesn't even warrant enough respect to be given a proper name? Ask an American.'

Laura swiped the book out of her hands. 'I'll remind you this book was written by an Englishwoman.'

'Barmy.'

'I don't know what that means, and I don't care. You're missing the point, as usual. She's nameless because she's every woman who's ever dreamed of a better life and been scared to imagine it. And Maxim . . . Maxim is scared, too, in his own way. He's haunted by the fact that he killed his first wife. And he knows that his new Mrs. de Winter may be his only real chance at happiness.'

Vivian let out a gaping yawn.

'Another late night with the Italian?'

'You have no idea.'

'Did his mother make you breakfast on this go-round? Or did you just stay locked in his room again and let your hair down out the window?'

Vivian grabbed the book back and hit her in the arm with it.

'Ow! That hurt!'

'Good. I'll have you know that we stayed in a lovely suite at the Plaza. Very expensive, very romantic.' Vivian had a brief flashback of watching Nicky on the phone, threatening to put someone in a cemetery. She was growing increasingly wary of his temper. And, if she was being honest, becoming somewhat addicted to what came after it. The lovemaking in the bath had also been epic.

Laura snatched the book back. 'I'm buying this.'

'Oh, goody. Perhaps you can start a book club with the Women.'

Laura attempted to take a turn swatting with the book, but Vivian artfully dodged it as they wound their way back to the counter. Connie was nowhere in sight, but the bell tinkled again as the front door swung open.

Pete the San Remo bartender grinned as he walked in. 'I should have known,' he said, laughing. He was carrying a stack of books under his arm. 'The Barbizon girl returns.'

Laura felt her face flushing again — she was going to have to work on this — an embarrassment only compounded by regret. Why couldn't she have been wearing a dress? Instead here she stood, inside a dusty bookshop, in a sleeveless blouse, rolled-up blue jeans, and penny loafers. If Marmy saw her, she'd disown her. Or possibly shoot her.

Laura made polite introductions between Pete and Vivian but found herself distracted. She hadn't recalled him looking quite this dashing behind the bar. Or perhaps environment was everything. Standing here, one elbow casually resting on the counter, eyes dancing as Vivian fired off pithy comments about everything from the weather to the end of the Third Avenue elevated, he appeared handsomer somehow, the big nose and the cowlick and the prominent Adam's apple coming together, dovetailing into a more cohesive package. There was something about him, she had to admit. Something she

112

didn't *want* to admit. Didn't she have a date with Manhattan's most eligible bachelor this very night, at the city's most sparkly nightspot?

Focus!

'And what brings you two here today?' he was asking her.

'Oh, you know, um, reading material.' *Pathetic, Laura.*

He looked down at her hand, cocked his head. 'Du Maurier. Hmm. I have to admit, I found it hard to find a sympathetic character in that book.'

'Vindicated!' Vivian exclaimed.

Laura ignored her. 'And you?'

He plopped his stack of books on the counter. 'Connie's lending library. Perfect for the underemployed bartender. He lets me borrow books; I treat to the occasional beer on the house. Everybody wins.'

Laura cocked an eyebrow. 'Weren't you the guy who told me he had no time to read?'

Pete laughed. 'Busted. In my experience, girls like guys who sound busy.'

'Your day off?' Vivian interjected.

'No, I go in later. I'm off next Saturday, though, which is rare. So I want to make sure I do something with it. Thinking about going to the beach.'

Vivian slid an arm around Laura. 'What providence! Laura was just saying on the ride down here that she hasn't been to the beach yet this year and has been dying to go.'

Laura could have murdered her. Taken a pair of hose and wrapped them around her English

113

neck. 'Wait, I didn't really say — '

'Well, hey, I'd love the company, if you're free. And I pack a heck of a lunch. In expertly constructed brown paper bags.' He stared into her eyes more directly than she was prepared for. 'So, whaddya say? You girls want to join me next Saturday?'

It was all over before Laura knew what had even happened. Vivian dove in like an aerial bomber, inventing an excuse for herself and brazenly accepting for Laura, as if she had been given her proxy. Pete would pick her up in front of the Barbizon at ten that morning. He'd try to get his buddy's car, but they might have to take the bus. Was that okay? Laura had found herself so flummoxed that she and Vivian were out the door and halfway down the block before she realized she hadn't even bothered to ask which beach they were going to. She'd left Connie the money for the book on the counter.

Laura stopped mid-stride, grabbed Vivian by the arm. 'What was that?'

'That,' Vivian said, 'was me being a good friend.'

'I have a date tonight with Box!'

'And now you have a date next week with Pete. Oh, really, Laura. What the devil is the matter with you? Don't be all Ethel about it.'

'What does that even mean?'

'It means you could be like those sad girls at the Barbizon who spend their nights dreaming about your choices. Or you could be the girl, as you now are, who has two dates with two very attractive men on two different days, the second

114

thanks to *moi*. I would count this as an unqualified success for someone who has been here for a little over a week. You're working at a fancy magazine in New York City. Perhaps you should start acting the part.'

'I don't want to start 'acting' anything.'

Vivian flung an arm around her, started propelling them down the sidewalk. 'All right, then. Sorry if I acted a bit dodgy in there. I just felt you needed a little push, that's all. I saw the way you looked at him. I thought I was doing you a favor.'

Laura sighed wearily. 'I . . . I've never been good at juggling boys.'

'Who said anything about juggling? Look, go with Box tonight, and if it turns out it's the night of your life and you're ready to start ordering note cards with 'Mrs. Box Barnes' stenciled on them, you simply call Pete and make an excuse and get out of the beach. And if things with Box go just all right or worse, then you've got a little extra deposit in the bank and you can keep the date. No one's proposing marriage here, my pet. A bit early to put all the chips in the fryer just yet. Why don't you just wait and see. Remember: There's a reason the fairy godmother gave Cinderella two glass slippers.'

Laura chuckled. She'd never get tired of hearing Vivian talk. 'There were, I don't know, ten metaphors in that last statement. I don't know whether you're brilliant or insane.'

'A little bit of both, darling. A little of both.'

9

Pacing the rear of the Barbizon mezzanine, Laura felt sick. She clutched once again at her pearls, which had belonged to Vivian's grandmother. 'A woman going out to El Morocco must wear either diamonds or pearls,' Vivian had insisted, and personally hooked the strand around Laura's throat. Laura had worried that pearls were a bit much in warm weather; Marmy would have been aghast. How much time this week had she wasted thinking how aghast Marmy would be at something she was doing or not doing? But the gesture was too sweet, too un-Vivian, to refuse. Besides, she had already ditched the opera gloves. Too much costume for a date that already had more than enough theatricality.

Vivian had already left for her shift at the Stork, delivering some ridiculous goodbye ('Cracking, darling! Best of British!') before scurrying out, but Dolly was now a floor below her in the lobby, awaiting Box Barnes. Laura had begged off the whole Shakespearean 'waiting on the balcony' scene, but Dolly had insisted, convincing her that if she waited in the actual lobby in her ball gown, she'd only attract *more* attention from the girls drifting in and out, and if she waited in their stuffy room, she'd wilt like a week-old violet. Laura suspected this was really all about Dolly wanting an excuse to talk with

Box in front of the others. If it took that to get her out of her recent funk, so be it.

Laura looked at the clock. Nine. She sank onto a settee, willed herself to stop fidgeting. *I need to think about something else.*

Pete.

She hadn't wanted to acknowledge that her mind had drifted to Pete more than once since she and Vivian had returned from the Village. Even as she'd brushed and pinned her hair into soft waves and shimmied into the most beautiful dress she'd possibly ever wear, he had crisscrossed her thoughts. Was it wrong to be preparing to go out on a fancy date with one guy while you were pondering a date with another?

Such was life inside the Barbizon, she'd learned. In short order she'd discovered the hotel was more of a play than a residence, populated by three distinct casts of characters. There were the glamour girls like Agnes Ford who dashed out every night, the echo of their heels reverberating on marble as they disappeared with square-jawed men into idling pastel sedans. Then there were the supporting players, the girls from Iowa and Maine and Louisiana who had won their local chamber of commerce's modeling search or beauty contest and, brimming with bravado and squaring their shoulders, had arrived on the doorstep of the hotel to find fame, fortune, and a rich husband, not necessarily in that order. The Katie Gibbs girls like Dolly were also part of this group, the ones whose nights out meant movies with their girlfriends and eyelash-fluttering at strangers in

117

the coffee shop afterward, or not-so-cozy nights in the television room, their faces blank in the ashy reflection of the tube. And finally there were the Women, skulking about the halls, their faces hardened a little more each day, like individual pictures of Dorian Gray. During the day they ventured out to their jobs as bookkeepers and librarians and English literature teachers; at night they returned to rooms that had become cells.

And then there was her, Laura Dixon of Greenwich, Connecticut, former debutante, Smith junior, *Mademoiselle* college editor, about to go to El Morocco with arguably the city's biggest catch. These were, without question, the bona fides of a glamour girl. And yet inside she felt empty, inauthentic. She loved the dress, loved feeling pretty and feminine and envied, and her heart danced with adrenaline from anticipation of the night ahead. But deep down, didn't she feel more at home in the cluttered, dusty confines of Connie Offing's bookstore, thumbing through an old copy of *Rebecca*? Was she really not the second Mrs. de Winter, shapeless and nameless, swept up in Maxim's world of romance and intrigue but never quite at home?

She hadn't told Marmy about Box. Her mother was difficult to impress, but Laura knew that would have done it, and in some ways that prospect was worse than not impressing her. Laura had managed to put off Marmy's New York visit, decrying *Mademoiselle* obligations that didn't exist. But that wouldn't work much longer. It was bad enough being unsure of who she was in a moment like this; she knew exactly who she was when she was in a room with her mother. And that girl she despised.

Only a few others remained on the mezzanine. It was a peculiarity of the Barbizon that girls took pains not to notice one another on occasions such as this — no one wanted confirmation that the girl next to her had a more inviting evening approaching than she did. Any comparison was done with a faux smile, darting eyes. Laura felt like she was suffocating. She started pacing again. It was like waiting for your name to be called as a finalist at the Miss America Pageant.

'He's here!' Dolly stage-whispered, bounding onto the mezzanine. 'I gotta tell you, he looks really good.' She pulled Laura to the edge of the shadows of the balcony. 'Look.'

There he stood, not far from the elevator bank. Girls buzzed about him like caffeinated bees. More than one dropped pretense and outright stared. His blond hair was once again perfectly cresting. He wore a fitted white dinner jacket and black trousers.

'Please tell me you didn't say anything embarrassing to him,' Laura said.

'Oh, hush up and go.'

Laura picked up her bag and wrap, shot Dolly a questioning look. 'Well, here goes nothing.'

Descending the staircase, she felt like she was in the opening credits of *The Loretta Young Show*, minus the applause. But really, weren't these girls silently applauding? She was tonight's

119

winner, and tomorrow they would all be talking, trying to guess what had happened. And secretly hoping it had all gone very, very badly.

But that was tomorrow.

Box Barnes approached her at the bottom of the staircase, leaned in for a light kiss on the cheek. 'You look incredibly beautiful,' he whispered.

She did the most un-Laura Dixon thing she could think of: Standing there, a hundred eyes on her in the middle of the Barbizon, she extended her arms and twirled, laughing. 'Do you like my dress?' she asked. 'It's new.'

* * *

Laura could not recall having ever witnessed a woman smoking through a cigarette holder, other than in movies. Her arm in Box's, winding her way through the bejeweled and bedecked throng in front of El Morocco, all she could do was stare at the woman with the shocking white hair spun around her head like cotton candy, elegantly puffing through the long silver holder.

Angelo, the club's formidable maître d', gave a barely discernible nod as they approached, sweeping them past the red velvet rope into the club. Flashbulbs popped. 'Box! Over here!' yelled one photographer. Laura smiled. 'Hey, Boxy, who's the girl tonight?' yelled another. Her smile vanished.

He guided her through the crowd, his hand never leaving the small of her back. 'I just noticed,' he said, 'you're not wearing the gloves.'

'They were lovely. But it was too warm out.'

He slipped his hand into hers. 'Good.'

They stepped down the few stairs leading to the main room. It was actually a tad on the gaudy side — the lavender walls, too much crystal, too many centerpieces, too many candles — but watching the coterie of couples waltzing around the dance floor, all of its slightly vulgar qualities faded away, until all that was left was supple light, perfume, the gentle rustle of skirts, and the soft click of shoes. A clarinet tumbled out the notes of Cole Porter.

Her eye caught a stunning couple circling to their left. 'He looks like Errol Flynn,' she said.

Box leaned in. 'That *is* Errol Flynn.'

The host told them he'd seat them in a moment.

'I don't understand,' Laura said. 'Why is everyone crowded onto the right side of the room, when there's all of these empty tables on the left?'

'Because that is Siberia. No one with any self-respect would be caught dead sitting on the left side of Elmo's. Only the tourists, and they only get in on slow nights, which aren't many. Angelo hates them, thinks they diminish the place.' The host waved them over. 'Great. We're ready,' Box said, moving her to the right. 'Let's go.'

It took a good hour before Laura found herself truly relaxing, despite the fact that she never left the security of their blue-and-white zebra-striped booth. They nibbled on small plates and drank champagne, and she fought to concentrate on the conversation, a near impossibility with so much stimulus arriving from all corners. Gowns gathered as they were threaded through openings between tiny tables. The throaty laughter of men drifting by on clouds of smoke from expensive Cuban cigars. Flickering candlelight hidden under tiny lampshades, dotting tables around the room like constellations. The husky urgency in the chanteuse's voice. The quick glint of light on a silver cigarette case being opened and proffered for a lady. The clink of ice cubes swirling in an emptying cocktail glass. The danger of a surreptitious wink.

Laura felt Box's breath on her neck, turned to see him again leaning into her, his hand sliding behind her along the shelf of the banquette. 'You're writing this,' he said.

Oh, that smile. 'What?'

'You're writing this. I can almost hear the Olympia typewriter pinging every few seconds as the carriage slides back and forth inside your head. You're here, but you're not really here. You're still acting like an observer instead of a participant.'

Her avocation had come up in the cab ride over; she'd playfully threatened that she had only agreed to the date because she was going to write a tell-all for *Mademoiselle*. Now she felt embarrassed about it. She took a casual taste of her champagne. 'Not everyone is to the manor born, sir. This is new for some of us. You have to spot me a period of adjustment.'

'It isn't like you're exactly from the wrong side

of the tracks. You grew up where?'

'Greenwich.'

'And you go to school where?'

'Smith.'

'Neither exactly Flatbush. This can hardly be all that new.'

'Knowing how to dance a waltz is not the same thing as having a full dance card. I am not going to inherit a department store in the middle of Manhattan.'

'No. You are going to marry well and raise lovely children in an immaculate center-hall Colonial somewhere in Rye.'

She felt her hackles flare. 'What do you — '

'Wait, wait! That came out wrong.'

'That happens a lot with you, doesn't it?' It carried more bite than she'd intended.

The frankness of his reply caught her by surprise. 'It's what people expect. And I'm stupid enough sometimes to fall into the trap of playing the role.' He shrugged, gulped some champagne.

'You can't just leave it like that. Explain.'

'I have, shall we say, a reputation, of which you are no doubt aware. It gets me into trouble, and it gets me blamed for things I didn't do or say, but if I'm being honest, it also gets me great tables at restaurants and brings in a lot of publicity for the store. But it's a character, a version of me I put out for public consumption. It's not really me.'

Or is this — the candid, sensitive guy — not really you? she wondered. *Is this the act?*

He laughed. 'You're sitting there thinking,

'This guy is full of shit.' Sorry. I shouldn't have said that, either. God! I'm making a mess of this.'

It was her turn for candor. 'Why did you want me to come here with you? We talked for five minutes, and it didn't exactly go well. And by your own admission, you are not at a loss for company.'

He smiled. 'Because you're different.'

'How do you know I'm different? According to you, I'm just some girl who's going to end up in a center-hall Colonial.'

'Ah! Okay. See, let me explain what I meant. That's one possible outcome, and certainly the most likely for a girl with your background. But I don't think that's really the life you're looking for. In fact, I imagine you're looking for something radically different. The only question is whether you're brave enough to actually step off the path you're on, the safe route, and go for uncharted waters.' He grinned, grabbed his glass.

How much time had she spent with this man — a few hours over three very different interludes? And yet already she'd identified his pattern: Charm, disarm, attack. But behind the twinkling teasing in his eyes, she saw something else, something she found genuine, which indicated that he found her worth more than just fleeting interest. But wasn't this the trap every girl fell into with men like Box Barnes: believing *they* were different, they were special, they were the one to turn the frog — or more accurately, the rogue — into the prince?

'I'm getting worried,' he said, turning his gaze

to watch Kitty Carlisle and Moss Hart do the cha-cha.

'What do you have to be worried about?'

'These contemplative silences.'

'Are you afraid of a thinking girl?'

'I'm afraid of a girl who thinks too much.'

She placed her elbows onto the table, crossing her arms. 'Can I ask you something?'

'Fire away.'

'This place. This whole life. The constant parties, the tuxedos, the travel. Do you ever tire of it?'

'Honestly? No.' He looked into her eyes with an intensity she found slightly unnerving. 'And just to be clear: It's not all parties and airplanes. I work hard. Harder than I get credit for. But to your point, I do enjoy a nice life. And no, I don't tire of it. I think it would be disingenuous to say otherwise. *Will* I tire of it? Perhaps. But what is there to tire of? Beauty? Fine wine and fine food? Interesting people saying interesting things? I live a life that I am very fortunate to live, I've never denied that or taken it for granted.' He laughed. 'Well, I may have taken it for granted. But I no longer do. And I see no reason to apologize for it, or to not enjoy it.'

'Hmmm.'

''Hmmm'? What does that mean?'

She shrugged, leaned back into the banquette. 'I don't know. I wish I could be as self-assured in my convictions. I love this, being here, but it doesn't feel real to me somehow. This isn't how the real world lives.' If she was going to consider dating this man, she needed to be able to be

125

honest. He needed to understand she was a girl who spoke her mind, even if her mind was occasionally muddled. These days, often.

He glanced away. 'Who gets to decide what the 'real world' is, Laura? Answer me that.'

They were interrupted by a hand on Box's shoulder. An oily banker associate of his father, named Cathcart or something similarly Old Money sounding, here with his wife to do a smile-and-greet. They demurred Box's offer to join them for a drink but lingered by the booth for several minutes, talking about the music, the weather, the performance of that new musical *Damn Yankees* they'd caught earlier in the week at the 46th Street Theatre. Laura smiled, nodded, tried not to fidget with her pearls. She laughed delicately in all the right places. If Marmy had managed to teach her one thing, it was how to take a social cue.

The waiter brought fresh coupes of champagne. 'Tell me something embarrassing about yourself,' Laura said after the man and his wife had gone. She wasn't completely sure why she was asking. Actually, yes, she was. She needed affirmation, some evidence, that his life had not been as perfect and as flawless as his appearance belied.

He chuckled. 'Wow, you really *are* going to be a journalist, aren't you?'

'Come on,' she pressed. 'Just one thing.'

He pushed his fingers through his hair, searching for an answer. 'Okay . . . Well, reports to the contrary, for the most part I have always been a very obedient child. I was raised with

126

order, you have to understand. When I was seven, I was attending a very fancy private school here in Manhattan. I was originally supposed to go to school in London, but the Nazis had just come to power in Germany, and my parents were nervous about sending me to Europe amid that kind of political unrest.

'My mother has always loved music, so I decided that I would try out for the Christmas musical at school. Mind you, I had very little actual musical talent, but I was determined. Well, it turned out I couldn't sing, and I had no aptitude for playing a musical instrument, either. But I *was* a decent dancer.'

'I look forward to seeing you prove that.'

He nodded. 'So they put me in the big closing number of the Christmas pageant,' he continued, 'which I think had far more to do with my parents' philanthropy than my budding talent. Anyway, the director, Mrs. Powell — it's always amazing that I can't remember where I put my keys this morning, but I will never in my life ever forget Mrs. Powell — she had this station below the stage, almost in the orchestra pit, where she would give us our cues and yell out instructions over the music. Things like, 'Sharper kicks!' and 'To the right!' If you messed up, she was merciless. I'm not kidding. She could have worked for the Gestapo.'

He delivered a casual wave to a couple entering across the room. 'Anyway, the night of the pageant she's stationed in her usual space below the stage, and everyone's parents are there, including mine, which only made it worse,

127

because there is no place in the world that is busier during Christmastime than a department store in New York City, and even then I was savvy enough to realize the kind of pressure my mother must have exerted to get my father there.

'So I'm in the wings, and I am in full panic. I mean, *panic*. I can't remember a single step, and I am sure I am going to go out there in front of all these people — the wealthiest, most important families in New York — and freeze. But then I think to myself, 'I just have to look at Mrs. Powell. She'll be shouting to us along with the music, and if I just do what Mrs. Powell says, I'll be fine.'

'I can't even remember what the song was. It may have been 'Sleigh Ride.' In any case, for the big finale we were all supposed to form this sort of kick line, with girls in the middle and boys on the ends, and I can't remember the steps at all. So I look down and I see Mrs. Powell looking at me and she's yelling, 'Show me those high knees! Let's see those high knees!'

'But what I kept *hearing* was, 'Show me your heinies! Let's see those heinies!' So right there, on cue, I turned my back to the audience, pulled down my pants, and showed everyone my heinie.'

Laura's hands flew to her face. 'You're making that up!'

'Hand to God,' he said, laughing with her. 'I never make up stories that make me look bad.' He reached over, pulling her left hand away from her face and kissing it gently. For a few breathless seconds, their eyes met wordlessly.

128

They were still locked as he pointed to the orchestra. 'Ha! Do you hear that? My favorite Cugat number. 'Miami Beach Rhumba.'' He slid out of the booth, pulling her toward him. 'C'mon. They're playing our song.'

They whirled around the floor to Cugat's catchy mix of horn and staccato percussion, and Laura let herself surrender to the magic of El Morocco and the man dancing her through it. And she thought it impossible to imagine another night when she might again feel this alive.

10

'So,' Dolly said, stabbing at her eggs, 'I think I have been very patient and waited long enough. We're here, we're all awake, we have our food, so it is time to start *talking*, Laura Dixon. From the *beginning*, please.'

That they were even here, eating brunch, was incredible enough, Laura thought. Hadn't she just tumbled into bed six hours earlier? Box had insisted they go to P.J. Clarke's for hamburgers after El Morocco closed at four, and Laura had been astonished to see it crowded with the tuxedos, gowns, and wraps she'd left around the corner, the Manhattan gentry packed into tables gobbling greasy-spoon fare in all of their frippery and finery. Fitzgerald was right: The rich were different.

Dolly had bounded onto her bed at nine like a five-year-old on Christmas morning, pulling at the covers and asking for every 'delectable detail' of her evening. Laura rolled over, covering her head with her pillow, but Dolly had upped the ante, leaving the room only to return in fifteen minutes to relay that Vivian was joining them for brunch to get the whole story.

Vivian had come in a bit later, wearing a man's white oxford shirt, blue jeans, and sandals, and told the pair she was (a) famished and (b) would not consider going to brunch if they were going to be surrounded by 'those old hens' at

Hicks or Elizabeth Norman, and that the Barbizon coffee shop was a non-starter. In a moment of lunacy she'd actually suggested Monte's on the Park, with its spectacular view of Central Park and its equally spectacularly priced brunch ($2.25 a person); Dolly looked sick. She wanted the Automat. ('Of course you do, dear,' Vivian had replied drolly.) The entire thing was giving Laura a splitting headache. Either that, or she'd drunk far too much champagne at Elmo's.

They'd settled for Café Renaissance on East Forty-Ninth ($1.75 — still pricey, but Dolly was willing, in order to hear the dirt). Vivian sat with a fruit cup, two poached eggs, and a Bloody Mary, sucking the straw so hard, her cheeks caved in. She was sporting her oversize sunglasses once again, and Laura was certain it wouldn't be long before Dolly started yelling at her to take them off. She suspected Vivian now wore them just to provoke. Silverware clanged all around them, worsening her headache.

Vivian put down her drink. 'That's the ticket,' she said lustily, smacking her lips. 'Positively delicious.' She turned to Laura. 'Afraid time's up, ducky. We're going to end up at hospital with this poor girl if you don't start telling. Let's hear it.'

The more detail Laura gave, the more insatiable Dolly became, interrupting to ask for additional details as Vivian slurped her way through another bloody. Though Vivian had some queries of her own, as it turned out. Questions ranged from the celebrities present, the dresses, and the handsome men (Dolly) to the musical selections, the jewelry, and the dangerous men (Vivian). And then there were all the questions about Box. By the time Laura had wrapped up with the cab ride back to the Barbizon and Box's tender kiss at the hotel door ('Divine!' Dolly exclaimed), Laura felt as if she'd just read *War and Peace* aloud.

'A chaste peck at the door, after all of that?' Vivian mused. 'Doesn't sound like a swell date to me.'

'It sounds unbelievably *perfect* and *romantic* to me,' Dolly said. She cast a glance at Vivian. 'You know, not everyone's date ends horizontally.'

'Pity,' Vivian said, taking another draw on her straw.

'So, when's your next date?' Dolly asked.

'Her next date,' Vivian interjected, 'isn't with Box Barnes.' She lit a cigarette as she smiled at Laura. 'Remember . . . *two* glass slippers.'

Pete. It was amazing how quickly he'd flown out of Laura's head after she'd heard the orchestra's first notes. Maybe —

'No,' Vivian said, reading her mind.

'No what?'

'No, you are not going to cancel your date next Saturday with Pete. Insurance isn't just for dads and motorcars, Laura. Risk must be spread out in order to be reasonable and smart. You'll have plenty of time to commit to one of your Prince Charmings. One lovely night doesn't mean you should go arse over tit for the first man who takes you dancing.'

'Vivian!' Laura whispered. 'Keep your voice

down!' She looked around to make sure no one had heard. 'You were the one who told me yesterday that if I had an amazing time with Box I could cancel with Pete.'

Vivian shrugged. 'Reconsidered.'

Dolly sighed. 'I should have such dilemmas.'

'Well, ladies, it's time to settle the bill and move on,' Vivian said, reaching for her purse. 'I'm sure there's some other tragic soprano singing Gershwin in the conservatory that Ethel must rush back to.'

'First off, it was Rodgers and Hammerstein, and it wasn't tragic. You're just afraid to admit you actually enjoyed it.' Dolly reached over, plucked Vivian's passport peeking from the side pocket of her purse, and flipped it open. 'Oh, look at this glamorous photo. Vivian . . . *Dwerryhouse?*' She looked up. 'I thought your name was Vivian Windsor.'

Vivian reached over, snapped it back. 'Really! You'd think *you* were the reporter rather than Miss El Morocco over there. Don't be daft. If your last name were 'Dwerryhouse,' wouldn't *you* change it? It literally translates into something like 'dweller at the dwarf house.' I couldn't think of a better, or more fitting, new one than that of the royal family.'

Dolly was hysterical. 'I swear,' Laura said, 'sometimes I can't believe you're a real person. Being with you is like living in a drawing-room comedy.'

Vivian began to defend herself in earnest — it was hard being an original, she argued — as Laura looked to Dolly, but Dolly's attention had

133

drifted elsewhere. Two tables behind, to be exact. Laura turned to see a man eating alone. Even seated, he exuded the burly presence of a linebacker. He was sopping up the remnants of his eggs with his rye toast, every once in a while taking a casual sip of coffee and stealing a glance over at their table.

At Dolly.

'Oh my,' Vivian said, taking in the scene. 'Ethel's baited the hook.'

'Do you know him?' Laura asked.

'No,' Dolly said, her mouth turning into a bright smile as she caught the mystery man's next stolen stare. 'But I'm going to.' She scooped up the cash they'd left on the table. 'You girls head on back. I'll settle the check.' She snuck another glance. 'I'm going to treat myself to one more cup.'

★ ★ ★

'You know, you're sort of like Marilyn Monroe.'

'Really,' Vivian replied. She and Nicky were strolling through Times Square. They'd just left the theater. The thick night humidity was a tonic after the frightful air conditioning inside the movie house. She'd thought her toes were going to have to be amputated. 'How do you figure that?'

'Easy. For one thing, you're sexy as hell,' he said, taking her hand in his. 'Second, you got great boobs, like she does.'

'That's the same thing, isn't it?'

'Not all women with good boobs are sexy. You

134

gotta know how to show 'em off, but still be classy about it.'

'Let me remind you that I am neither blond, speak like I have just run five blocks, nor bat my eyelashes as though it were a sport.'

'You're right,' he said, stopping to graze at her neck. 'You're way better than Marilyn.'

This, she knew, was highly doubtful. She had always been torn about Monroe — she loved her brash ownership of her sex appeal, while at the same time wishing she was just a bit, well, smarter. Like Jane Russell, who had those killer knockers and still looked like she could beat any man at poker, or a duel, or math, for that matter. But she was a brunette, and men, at least American men, were all about blondes. And, to her good fortune, the occasional redhead.

They'd just left the seven o'clock showing of *The Seven-Year Itch*. Vivian thought the plot a bit contrived — too many fantasy sequences involving some middle-aged dullard's erotic daydreams — but it hadn't been a total loss. In one scene Marilyn had airily announced she kept her underwear in the icebox to keep it cool during the summer. That seemed a capital idea if Vivian had ever heard one.

They started strolling east again. He'd promised her food, and for once not Italian. 'What's going on with your friend?' she asked as they crossed Forty-Third Street.

'What friend's that?'

'You know, the friend you told me about who knows the talent agent. You said you could get him to give me an audition.'

'I will, baby, I will. I've just been busy. These longshoremen in Brooklyn are killing me right now. I gotta focus on business. But I'll do it. Don't I always do what I say I'm gonna do?' He smiled at her.

'No. I seem to also recall you told me you were going to look for your own apartment.'

'I said I'd *think* about it. And I thought about it. It don't make any sense. I got a perfectly good setup with Mom and Pop. Why am I gonna go rent some shitty place in Chelsea and throw my money all into some Jew's pocket? I'm saving up to buy a place for after I get married someday.' He turned to her, smiled again, more broadly this time. 'Wouldn't that be nice, a nice house in Brooklyn? Huh?'

I cannot think of anything more dreadful.

They ended up eating at Karachi on West Forty-Sixth, Indian food, which Nicky hated, but she convinced him that chicken tikka masala was simply his mother's stew with different spices, and this seemed to mollify him. There was no liquor served, which he also bitched about, but she told him she'd go with him afterward to whatever bar he fancied for a nightcap.

She should break up with him — what was the point of all of this? She was beginning to really resent that he had just assumed her nights off were his. What was it with Italian men? They all seemed to have such strong-willed mothers, formidable matrons who pulled their sons by the ears into the first church pew when they got out of line, yet when it came to their own relationships with women, they wanted to call all

136

the shots. The American Italians were the worst — constantly blessing themselves with rosary beads and lauding Mama's meatballs while leering at everything in a skirt.

Still, Vivian couldn't bring herself to cut the line. Not yet. There was the matter of his friend's friend the agent; she'd grown desperate for an introduction to someone, anyone, with a connection in show business. If she ever hoped to drop the cigarette tray, she had to get somebody — preferably a paying somebody — to hear her sing.

And then there was the matter of Nicola Accardi himself.

Yes, he lived with his parents. Yes, he had a flaring temper that was on the border of scary. But she wasn't going to marry him, so what did it matter? He was fun, he took her out to nice dinners and the occasional play — they'd just seen *The Pajama Game* last week — and most important, he worshiped her. He told her how beautiful she was all the time. He always smelled nice. He knew what went into a good martini. He had plenty of money to keep things interesting, his brass money clip always fully occupied. He had an even more sizable endowment inside his trousers and knew how to make the most of that, too. He was also the only man she'd ever met who could wear a straw fedora in summer and not look utterly ridiculous.

Most of all, he wasn't one of the rotund 'How you doin', baby?' guys, with their perspiring foreheads and acrid breath, who seemed to

137

populate the Stork in ever-increasing numbers, casually caressing her bottom like a showroom Chevy.

No, she'd hang in a bit longer, see if she could get him to cough up the introduction. *Autumn*, she thought. *If he doesn't come through by autumn, I'll move on. Tell him I'm too busy, picking up extra shifts at the Stork. Or perhaps that there's someone from England who's come back into the picture.* She'd figure it out.

They'd only taken a few steps back on the sidewalk after dinner when Vivian felt a hand on her shoulder. 'Hey, pretty lady.'

She whirled around to see the speaker's face, then instantly flung herself into his arms. 'Oh, Act!!' she screamed. 'Darling Act! Oh, cheers! How are you?!'

They pulled apart and he appraised her lovingly. 'Still beautiful, still breaking hearts, I can see that,' he said, smiling excitedly at her. 'You look great, kid!'

Vivian turned to Nicky, now standing a few feet away. He'd just lit a cigarette. 'Oh, Nicky, come over here. This is — '

The man stuck out his hand. 'Jimmy. Jimmy Stewart. But everybody calls me Act. Because I got the same name as the actor, you see? Vivian and I, we used to work together at the Stork. Nice to meet you.'

Nicky looked warily, shook his hand briefly. Vivian explained that Act had left the Stork a few months ago to take a job with Toots Shor, and that they were old friends and he was a great guy and, oh, the fun they'd had. For the next few minutes, they caught up on each other's news, Vivian chuckling throatily upon hearing the rumor about the former Stork hat-check girl who'd evidently been invited onto Ari Onassis's yacht. 'He has no idea what he's in for,' she said. 'He'll throw her overboard before the second drink.'

'And she'll *still* be talking!' Act roared.

Vivian found herself devolving into girlish giggling, something she generally abhorred. She couldn't even blame the wine — hadn't they just come from a no-alcohol-serving Indian restaurant? She turned to Nicky to share in her giddiness when his cold stare stopped her in her tracks. She turned back to Act, leaned in for the briefest peck on the cheek. 'So lovely seeing you, darling,' she said. 'Must run.'

Act was still saying something — actually, semi-shouting as they walked away — but Vivian kept her head high and eyes forward. She slid her arm into Nicky's, picked up the pace. This had happened once before, with another man she knew whom they'd run into at a fish restaurant. Nicky had darkened almost instantly, pouted for a good hour afterward, until she'd figured out he'd been jealous, the subsequent ridiculous allegation of flirting dripping from his lips like drops from a leaky faucet. She chalked it up to the fact that he'd been embarrassed by his own emotions, which made her happy. He should have been embarrassed. That was yet another thing about Italian men. They all wanted to leer at any décolletage or shapely set of legs within twenty yards, but *you* were supposed to be like a thoroughbred at the races, locked into your blinders and greeting any of the male species with strictly perfunctory *hellos* and *how-are-yous*. Except your dad, perhaps. Dads were probably permitted a bit of affection. Not that he had to worry about that with her.

What had she done in that case to break the spell? She racked her brain to remember. A bawdy joke? No. Didn't matter. What she wanted to do was to tell him to bugger off, walk back to the Barbizon, pick up Laura and Ethel, and go to a lounge and flirt with men as they all got good and pissed.

Odd, she thought, that she would strike up a friendship with those two. So different from her they were, and yet she had to admit she was enjoying them. She'd never had close girlfriends growing up — she wasn't the kind of girl other girls warmed to. She was the girl their boyfriends did.

Perhaps it was an opportunity for her, for the first time, to impart some wisdom, to be a teacher, or the big sister that Mary and Emma couldn't be to her. It was rather thrilling, if she was being completely honest with herself. Laura was a diamond who had no idea she was a diamond, a pretty girl who had been kept in a very lovely cage for her entire life, and who now, fluttering around Manhattan like a nascent dove, spent half her time darting her eyes all around her, fearing she was going to do something wrong or inappropriate and earn the family name a red slash in *Burke's Peerage*. Or whatever the American version of *Burke's*

Peerage was. The other half of the time Laura spent loathing herself for how she was spending the first half. All she needed was a little push. Permission to be unguarded. To not know every answer.

Ethel, she was another story. Cackling like a hen with the other Barbizon wallflowers, cold-creaming their faces nightly to the texture of mayonnaise in the hopes of attracting dreamboat dates who never materialized. They watched too much telly, ate too much sugar, and read too many glossy magazines, all the while laughing at the Women they were inevitably becoming. But Ethel was a good egg. Vivian had her work cut out for her there; it was like trying to tame a puppy who always leapt on you every time you entered a room. Not that Ethel ever greeted Vivian any way but coolly. But Vivian wasn't fooled. Ethel's offhanded greetings belied a naked, desperate yearning to be liked that Vivian recognized all too well in the girls who watched the Barbizon comings and goings like a pack of convent nuns. But perhaps things were turning for Ethel — *Actually, I must start calling her Dolly*, she thought, *I'm being rather unkind* — with her potential bulky beau at the coffee shop last Sunday. She hadn't seen either of the girls since. *Must get a report.*

She heard the rumble of the Seventh Avenue subway beneath them.

Rescue.

Vivian galloped ahead down the sidewalk, perching on a grate just as the whoosh of the train sent a gust of air bursting up from underground. For a few seconds her pleated skirt went swirling around her, as she pouted her lips and attempted to halfheartedly push the dress downward. 'Well?' she shouted in her best kittenish voice. 'Am I like Marilyn now, sweetie?'

Even as he walked closer, his face becoming more and more prominent, she couldn't read his expression. Was that a mischievous smirk creeping up, just barely, from his lips? *Oh Christ, do I even care?* Gorgeous or no, theatrical agent contact or no, this was all getting to be too much bloody work. Living with his mum was one thing. Mollifying his jealous mood swings were another.

To her surprise, he put his hands firmly around her waist and lifted her straight off the ground, his face breaking out into an odd expression she couldn't quite identify. He did a full turn, swinging her around the sidewalk like a little girl. 'You like that, honey? You like being Marilyn for me?'

Before she could answer, he carried her into an adjacent alley, forcefully throwing her against a cool brick wall and pinning her. With the shadows cast from the streetlights, he was almost completely silhouetted, though his black eyes glittered in the darkness. His breath was hot, labored; his chest seemed to almost be heaving. There was an air about him — something primal.

He pressed his body against hers, shoved his hand up her skirt. His fingers, rough and urgent, threaded underneath her corselet, and she gasped, her head crashing back into the bricks, as she felt two of them plunge inside her.

'You like being bad for me. C'mon, baby, tell Nicky,' he whispered, his lips now on her neck, his fingers probing coarsely. Pain zinged through her body. 'Tell me how you like to be bad.'

He said it with fire, with lust. With hatred. Her heart beat uncontrollably, both revulsed and enticed by his emotional violence. She wanted him to stop. She didn't want him to stop. This was frightening. This was thrilling.

All she had to do was scream, kick him in the nuts, and it would all be over. And in that thought — the thought that she was not a prisoner, that she had a choice to make — she lost the battle with herself.

'Yes, darling, oh yes,' she whispered back, her free hand crawling up underneath the back of his shirt, scratching him, clawing at him, branding him. 'I want to be bad for you.'

11

Pretty, glittery, and odd. This was *Mademoiselle* to Laura, or at least the *Mademoiselle* she had been exposed to in the brief period she'd been working inside it. Pretty because it was so very much so: delicate glass vases of bright yellow tulips and daisies dotting the desks, women in pencil skirts and tailored shirts and shiny patent-leather shoes briskly walking up and down halls, their hair pinned in clever updos or worn down in short bangs, all copied from Alexandre of Paris with meticulous care. The thrumming *click-clack* of typewriters and heels on linoleum produced a peculiar lilting concert of femininity that served as the magazine's soundtrack.

Had she truly only been here two weeks? It was hard to believe her apprenticeship was hurtling toward its close — she felt as if it only had just begun. The thought depressed her. How would she ever be able to leave the verve of the city, leave Dolly and Vivian and the Barbizon, to return to the staid world of college in New England?

How can I leave Box?

He'd asked her to dinner during the week but she'd begged off; he'd settled for a cute, if brief, after-work date in the coffee shop. She hadn't mentioned her impending departure, and he'd never asked — boys never thought of or worried

144

about things such as the actual logistics of a fledgling romance. She'd replayed the night at El Morocco more often than was no doubt healthy, but there was so much she wanted to preserve in her mind, details and smells and snippets of conversation she wanted to box up — ha! — and unpack on a cloudy day in the future. Intellectually she realized she had already been given so much on this brief sojourn in Manhattan, more than some girls ever experienced in a lifetime. Yet it didn't feel temporary or like a lark. It felt like a start.

Two weeks in, the college apprenticeship at *Mademoiselle* had been a dervish of parties and events, she and the other editors a makeshift sorority winding their way through New York. She'd been amazed and disappointed at how much of their collective 'work' had revolved around dressing up and simply appearing, graceful mannequins being glided into a luncheon here, a book party there, a gallery opening over here. *Picture, please. Over here, please.* Just last week they'd spent an entire afternoon in the Central Park West salon of some forbidding dowager, sipping tea from Wedgwood cups and looking over the hostess's impressive collection of Colonial-era letters. (Who knew Martha Washington had such lovely penmanship?) One of the girls whispered that the itinerary was originally supposed to have been a visit to the Fifth Avenue apartment of the Baroness Rothschild de Koenigswarter, but that had been scrapped; the baroness was evidently still too broken up over the death of the saxophonist Charlie Parker, who had succumbed in her residence. For her part, Laura wished they could have gone to the Fifth Avenue mansion of the mysterious Russian financier Serge Rubinstein, inside which he had been found strangled in January.

That night it had been a performance of *Inherit the Wind* at the National Theatre. She'd confessed to Box that she had been hoping for *Cat on a Hot Tin Roof* at the Morosco. 'Oh, so *that's* the kind of girl I'm dealing with,' he'd joked. He'd promised to take her next week.

During the days it was busywork, messengering, and inventory taking, reams of papers that needed to be filled out cataloging the never-ending parade of dresses, gloves, shoes, hats, slacks, and scarves that cluttered the office's halls and closets, each hoping to be selected for one of the magazine's fashion pictorials or the holiest of grails, the cover. Yesterday they'd all been herded into the conference room to 'vote' from a series of finalists for the image that would appear on the cover of their vaunted college issue in August, though it was an open secret that the vote, like their input into anything else to do with the magazine, actually meant nothing. Mrs. Blackwell would decide what the cover would be, just as Mrs. Blackwell decided everything at *Mademoiselle*, down to what brand of lotion was stocked in the powder room.

'Oh, I do hope I'm not intruding on your lovely daydream,' Cat Eyes snapped, tossing a pile of folders onto Laura's desk. For the life of her, Laura couldn't understand this steadfast, virulent animosity, which had first reared its head at the initiation that first day, continued right past the luncheon at Barnes & Foster, and only intensified since. There were more than a dozen college editors here for the four-week apprenticeship; why had Laura been the one elected to receive all of the sarcasm and derision?

'Not at all,' Laura replied evenly. Cat Eyes would be the one thing she would definitely *not* miss. 'Do these need to be filed?'

'They *need* to be taken to Mrs. Blackwell's office. If her secretary isn't there, just leave them in her in-box. Then you can go.' She clomped away.

Well, at least it's Friday, Laura thought. Tomorrow she would —

Tomorrow. Saturday.

She'd completely forgotten.

She'd made the date with Pete the bartender to go to the beach. To be precise, Vivian had made the date for her to go with Pete the bartender to the beach. After brunch on Sunday, Laura had decided she didn't care what Vivian thought, that she needed to cancel. Better to concentrate on just one guy, she'd reasoned, especially when she was only going to be in New York for two more weeks. But then she'd forgotten to actually call Pete. And now it was here, tomorrow, and no doubt he'd secured transportation and a picnic basket and God knows what else, and she couldn't in good conscience ditch now.

I should make Vivian go, she thought as she walked down the hall with the files, toward the posh corner office of Betsy Blackwell.

Laura had never been to even the exterior office of Mrs. Blackwell's lair; she suspected this was true of most of the college editors. Only the crème de la crème of the masthead was ushered in — the managing editor, the art director, the fiction editor — along with important guests from the worlds of publishing, entertainment, fashion, politics, and commerce. Laura had always imagined what such an office would look like but held slim hopes of ever finding out. College editors never went *in* the office.

No sign of the secretary; desk light out, typewriter sheathed. Laura saw the in-box on the credenza and started to place the files on top.

Unless.

She looked around. Not a soul. Mrs. Blackwell's door was open, but Laura heard nothing. Could it hurt? Just a peek? After all, when would she get this opportunity again?

Laura slowly stepped toward the office door, passing by completely and quickly glancing in. Empty. She looked around again.

Thirty seconds. Just a quick thirty seconds.

Other than one of Mrs. Blackwell's trademark Sally Victor hats — thrown carelessly on the sofa — the entire office looked more like a salon. Laura's heels sank into the deep pile of the rug.

Internally the office was known as 'the bower,' and Laura now understood why: Its delicate pale green eighteenth- and nineteenth-century furniture, accented by dark green walls, conjured a feeling of being in the reception room of some English country estate. The editor's desk, all romantic curves and Victorian flourish, contained a slender silver vase holding a lone red rose, along with a gleaming silver inkstand. A lacquered gaming table sat nearby, two telephones resting on top.

Laura had been to her father's law office in Greenwich many times, and it was, objectively speaking, impressive: a meticulously curated homage to mahogany and leather and brass, all selected by Marmy, naturally, and all meant to convey an air of power and authority. But this — this was the office of a woman. Of a powerful woman who didn't mind showing she was a woman. A Chinese red lacquer vitrine in the corner held what appeared to be dozens of miniature shoes and antique dolls. A mural by John Burton Brimer dominated the opposite wall, the painting its own testament to the intersection of power and femininity: a collage of dresses and shoes and hats, along with the representation of a typewriter, and a woman who may or may not have been Betsy Blackwell herself. There were awards and plaques and other honoraria given to the philanthropic and influential. Laura walked over to the windows — Lexington Avenue on one side, Fifty-Seventh Street on the other — and clutching the file folders to her chest, watched the light slowly fading in the reflections of the buildings around her. Two disparate but equally important questions flew into her head: *How does someone get an office like this? And, Can I do it?*

'Are you looking for something?'

Laura pivoted, the files tumbling to the floor.

Her eyes zeroed in on those of Betsy Blackwell.

'Oh, no, I . . . oh, Mrs. Blackwell, I'm so sorry, I was just walking these over . . . ' She dropped to her haunches, frantically pushing fallen papers back into folders, manically trying to scoop them off the floor. She popped back up, attempting to fix the askew papers while appearing calm and professional, which she was not, and not like an impertinent apprentice caught snooping in the boss's office, which she clearly was. Laura could see it now ('I came in to find some *girl* in my office'), Cat Eyes firing her for sure.

'Let's not make it any worse, shall we?' Betsy Blackwell said, casually walking over and retrieving half of the files, shaking in a few papers here and there. 'Put the others on the desk.'

'Ye — , yes, ma'am.' *I want to die,* Laura thought. *I just want to fall over and die, right here, on this lovely plush green carpet, and then have the cleaning woman come in with her Hoover vacuum and suck me right off the floor into the bag and throw me out.*

Laura was about to excuse herself with another round of sloppy apologia when Betsy Blackwell cocked her head, seemingly studying her. 'You're the girl who was with Box Barnes at El Morocco.'

'I . . . I am.' Laura mentally took off, running through her memory bank. Surely she would have remembered seeing Betsy Blackwell in the club. Then again, there had been two hundred people there. It would have been quite possible to miss her.

'I see. What is your name?'

'Laura Dixon. I'm one of the girls here for the college issue.'

Mrs. Blackwell had a look on her face that Laura placed somewhere between suspicion and polite amusement. The kind of look one might display holding a particularly winning hand at bridge. 'Radcliffe?'

'Smith.'

'Ahh. The dark hair threw me. The Smith girls are always blond.'

Laura suppressed a laugh. Who knew Connie Offing of MacDougal Books & Letters shared the same sensibility as the editor of *Mademoiselle*?

Betsy Blackwell rested against her desk, one of the messy files still in her right hand. There was silence for a good five seconds, which felt like ten minutes, as the editor took stock of Laura standing in the middle of her office, looking at her as Laura imagined she might a model when a decision had to be made on whether a girl was attractive enough to pull off a photograph of a new hat. 'Where have we placed you?'

'I have been assigned to the fashion department. But I came to New York to be a writer.' *Oh my God. Did I just tell the editor of* Mademoiselle *that I was ungrateful and that the job I was given, the job thousands of girls around the country applied for, was beneath me?* Pinpricks stabbed inside her arms and legs; she felt beads of perspiration forming at her hairline. *Don't faint. Whatever you do, don't faint.*

'A writer. I see. Well, ambition is always

151

admirable, as long as it's backed up by talent and hard work. You've been keeping a journal, then, since you've been in New York?'

Lie! No, what if she asks to see it? Don't lie! 'No, I . . . I regret to say I haven't.' She couldn't remember a single time, not in her entire life, when she had ever felt this insipid.

Betsy Blackwell chuckled, the slow, polite chuckle of a woman who knows how to laugh over lunch in a great hotel. 'Well, let me give you a small piece of advice, dear. Start. Immediately. You want to be a writer. Write. You are in the most interesting city on the entire planet. What do you want to write about?'

'Anything. Everything. I suppose that's what drew me to your windows. I look out of windows and all I see are stories, of the lives of the people behind the windows.'

Mrs. Blackwell glanced briefly over to the windows, then back. 'You are standing in the magazine that has published McCullers, Faulkner, Colette. The magazine that discovered Truman Capote. Embrace your situation while you still have it. No one is going to come looking for you. You need to go look for them.' She threw the file on the desk, folded her arms. 'And, after Smith? What then?'

'I want to get a job. In publishing.'

'What job would you like?'

Laura laughed. 'Yours.'

And there it was. Blurted out, unvarnished and raw, and Laura would later tell Vivian and Dolly that even if that had been it — even if she had been axed, right there on the spot — the look of utter surprise she had managed to place

152

on Betsy Blackwell's face with her audacious answer might have been worth it. But Mrs. Blackwell started to laugh, and then Laura laughed again, and soon the two of them were laughing very loudly, almost cackling, like two girls who'd mistakenly wandered into the men's locker room and, upon realizing their folly, had dashed out together into the hall, clutching each other in teenage hysterics.

'I'm so sorry,' Laura said. 'I answered that question impertinently. I just meant — '

Mrs. Blackwell put her hand up, signaling silence, then circled around her desk and perched daintily on her Louis XIV satin-upholstered chair. She reached for the silver pen in the inkwell. 'Don't worry. As I said, ambition backed up by talent and hard work is nothing to be ashamed of.' She retrieved a piece of pink stationery and began scribbling a letter. 'Good night, Miss Dixon.'

★　★　★

Atlantic City was a revelation. Laura had never really loved the seashore. For the Dixons, the beach had meant various idyllic hamlets on the Cape, but for the most part it had meant Nantucket and Aunt Marjorie's shaker-shingled house near Polpis. As a child, Laura had dreaded the trips, forced to sleep on a lumpy cot in a room that hadn't been properly aired out, if it had been at all, a mildewy turret that reeked of pine-scented cleaning solvent. That was the thing people never really understood about old wealth

153

— you could have it, other people might know you had it, but it was considered pedestrian and vulgar to actually *show* it. Not that Marmy cared. Marmy only cared that they were on the Cape, because that put her in proximity to the really old money, and as a woman who could name every family that had sailed on the *Mayflower*, that was good enough. But the water was always too cold, the beaches too rocky, the lobster too difficult to get to — all that messy work of cracking and peeling and the picking off of shells. And even if the Dixons were on vacation, Marmy's rules never were, translating into a parade of summer dresses and Mary Janes that Laura was never allowed to dirty or muss. She had been a china doll, packed into the trunk and taken on holiday.

Laura leaned back on her elbows on her towel, looking out at the crashing waves of the ocean rolling in. She couldn't believe how different beach resorts could be. Atlantic City was everything that would have made Nantucket recoil: loud, tacky, a carnival town populated with thrill rides, taffy shops, splashy painted signs, and girls who mounted horses, led them up planks forty feet above, and then jumped off into huge tubs of water to various *ooohs*, *aaahs*, and thunderous, wondrous applause. 'SHOW-PLACE OF THE NATION,' the signs blared, seemingly on every corner. Punch bowls and lobster this was not.

Pete bounded out of the ocean, his skin sparkling with salt water, and staggered toward his towel next to hers. 'Sure I can't get you in?

154

The water's amazing!'

He stood leaning over, panting, hands on his knees. His hair flopped into his eyes, water at the ends trickling down, creating rivulets down his face. His body was thin and wiry, and standing here, dripping wet, he looked young, actually very young, like a boy of seventeen who just a few years earlier had been a member of Our Gang with a nickname like Stretch or Slim.

'I'm good here. Maybe in a bit.'

He kneeled down next to her, toweled his hair. 'I can't believe you've never been to Atlantic City before,' he said. 'Did your mom keep you locked in the attic?'

Yes. She did.

He lay back, closed his eyes, feeling the sun bake his skin. She was concerned about him burning, but he swore he never did, despite the Irish bloodline. And you couldn't get more Irish than being named Pete Kelly and working as a bartender. 'So, how was the book? You never told me.'

'You mean *Rebecca*?' she asked.

'No, the other one. The one Connie gave you that you had with you that day at the San Remo.'

'Oh. *Will the Girl and Other Stories*. I loved it. Connie was right. Some people just know how to tell tales.'

'What was your favorite?' His eyes were still closed.

'I think the title one. Actually, you'll get a kick out of this. That's the one that was set in Philadelphia.'

'Get out of town. What's it about?'

155

'Two girls who go to an all-girls Catholic high school named John W. Hallahan. Do you know it? I looked it up — it's a real school.'

'I've heard of it. Unfortunately, I wasn't eligible to attend.'

'The title comes from the announcement the Mother Superior makes over the loudspeakers every morning, to try to keep the girls in line, to show that they are being watched, all the time. She gets on and says, 'Will the girl who was seen at the corner of Such-and-Such and Fifth Street, putting on lipstick, please report to the office immediately. We know who you are.' And it's just this little story about these two girls from opposite ends of the social strata who end up striking up this unusual friendship in this repressive environment. I mean, it was so simple, just a character study, really, but at the same time it was also brilliant, Orwell boiled down to a high school in the middle of Philadelphia. And the writing was symphonic. I think I also liked it because it reminded me in a weird way of my own situation, of how I've come to know Dolly and Vivian.'

'Sounds like you were impressed.'

'Yes. And discouraged.'

He opened one eye, squinting against the sun. 'Why?'

'You read the great authors — Dickens or Dostoyevsky or the Brontës — and you don't compare yourself to them. I mean, how can you? They were the pillars of their day. And that's what is so reassuring. They were of another day. Not your day. But then I read something like

156

this, just quick, little postcardlike stories from a writer who is not a pillar but who is here, right here and right now, sitting somewhere at a desk with his typewriter and creating this stuff, and then it hits me just how difficult it is to actually do it.' She relayed the story about meeting Betsy Blackwell last night, how one of the editor's first questions had been whether she was keeping a journal, and how moronic she had felt to have to answer that she had not.

'So, why haven't you?'

Laura looked at him — at his wide, open, honest face with its quirky features; his hair had dried and was now sticking almost straight up in the back, like a German shepherd's tail alerted to a backyard squirrel.

'You know what?' she said. 'I think I am ready for a dip. You coming?' She bolted up and dashed toward the surf.

★   ★   ★

Hours later, after they had washed up and changed at the bathhouse, they strolled up the Boardwalk. The famous wicker rolling chairs, pushed by strapping men on both sides, rumbled gently past, the younger couples inside them gazing and laughing romantically, the older couples inside them stoic or, in one case, fast asleep. Lights were just starting to twinkle from the honky-tonk amusement piers jutting out onto the ocean, and to their left the windows of the imposing grand hotels lit up in random patterns, as guests dressed for an evening out.

157

They came up to the entrance of the Steel Pier, with its curving arches and whitewashed siding and elegant cupola, the words STEEL PIER spelled out in blazing, white-hot electric bulbs. Pete looked up, pointed.

'Right there. Back in 1930, Shipwreck Kelly sat there for forty-nine days on a thirteen-inch steel disk on top of a flagpole overlooking the Steel Pier.'

'Any relation?'

'Alas, no.'

Laura glanced up, incredulous. 'At the risk of sounding like either a snob or a rube: Why would anyone do that?'

He shrugged. 'That's Atlantic City.'

For the first time he took her hand in his, led her through the archway onto the pier. She didn't know what was more alarming: that she had thought of Box once today, or that she had thought of Box *only* once today. Two Saturday nights — well, technically, this was Saturday day *into* Saturday night — two completely different dates with two completely different guys. Box was movie-star looks, breeding, sly wit, high taste, and excitement; Pete was a slightly gawky, everyday Joe, but fiercely intellectual, funny, genuine, and without guile. On the beach today, he'd casually remarked, 'Teddy Roosevelt once said, 'A man would not be a good citizen if he did not know Atlantic City.'' *Who quotes Teddy Roosevelt? And who quotes Teddy Roosevelt talking about Atlantic City?*

He bought them hot dogs (and was suitably aghast when she confessed she'd never before

158

had sauerkraut). He attempted — several times — to win her a teddy bear throwing baseballs through a hole in a bed sheet and missed every time. 'I was distracted by a girl,' he said, trying to be flirtatious and not quite pulling it off.

'I've been thinking about you,' she said as they sat on a bench afterward and watched the carousel spin by.

'I'm not quite sure how to take that, given that I am, in fact, currently here.' He grinned at her. 'Inside your head are you on a date with a better version of me?'

She inhaled on the straw of her soda, the iciness an assault on her teeth. 'Most guys I know talk all about themselves when they're with a girl, and you don't seem to want to at all. You keep asking me all the questions.'

'Which you keep not answering.'

'That's not true. I've answered everything.'

'Except why you haven't been writing since you've been in New York.'

She glanced at him, unprepared for the look of genuine affection emanating from his hazel eyes. She watched the snapping, popping reflection of the carousel dance in them, but it didn't impinge on their seriousness, a steady warmth that sliced right through all of the light. The hairs pricked up on her arms. She looked away.

'You're right,' she said. 'I didn't. I'm sorry. The truth is I'm embarrassed. It's easy to say you're a writer, to dream it. Doing it is something else. Because what if I do it and it's terrible? What if I'm just deluding myself?'

'You're not deluding yourself.'

'You don't know that.'

'I'm a bartender for the Beat Generation. I'm surrounded by writers every day. I know one when I see one.'

She shook her head. 'I wish I could share your confidence. I've spent two weeks in New York hanging up dresses and putting shoes in boxes.'

He slipped his hand into hers on her lap. 'Do you trust me?'

What's the right answer to that? she wondered. Because she did trust him. The person she didn't trust was herself. Or her thoughts, banging against her brain like a pinball, dreaming of Box one minute, worrying about her future the next, Marmy the next, then wondering how a girl even came to live a life riding on a diving horse, then back to Dolly and whether she'd ever get married to her dream guy or end up like Ethel Mertz as Vivian was convinced, and what would have happened if it had been she, not Mariclaire, who had jumped into the lake in her billowing white gown at her coming-out party . . .

Stop.

Be here.

She forced herself to look back into Pete's eyes, probing, incessant, pure. 'I'm starting to,' she said.

'Okay, then. I want you to close your eyes.'

Her heart sank. It sounded like a cheesy line, something one of the boys in the barn would say to Laurie in *Oklahoma!* as they were sitting in the hayloft, dreaming of life beyond the farm.

'C'mon, please, it's not corny, I promise,' he pleaded.

Now he read minds? She complied, but not without a sigh.

He gently placed his other hand on top of hers, his two palms now cocooning her left hand, his lips almost brushing her earlobe as he whispered, 'Now I want you to picture everything you've seen here, on this pier. The lights, the people, everything. Picture it. As vividly as you can. You have it?'

She took a moment. 'Yes.'

'Good. Now write it.'

'Excuse me?' she said, eyes fluttering.

'Keep your eyes closed! You have to try. And you have to trust me. Again, now picture everything you've seen here, right here, on this pier. Now imagine you're sitting down in front of a typewriter, and there's a clean, fresh, white piece of blank paper, and you're turning the wheel to scroll it in, and now you're putting the bar down to hold the paper. Now you're going to write about what you see here. I want you to read it aloud to me as you type.'

She almost opened her eyes — wide — and told him this was hokey, that it was, in fact, Laurie from *Oklahoma!*, and she wasn't going to do it. Then she pictured his skinny face, crestfallen, wildly embarrassed that this gesture to spark her creativity had been aborted so carelessly, and how it would ruin the rest of the evening, and, really, they'd had such a lovely day . . .

Stop!

She took a deep breath, exhaled, and began. 'Comings and goings. People come, people go.

161

There is the old fat man with the ice cream cone, sitting on the bench by the arcade because he likes to hear the bells and *hoops* and *whooooops* of the games. A teenage boy with his hair perfectly raked wins an overstuffed panda for his girl, who is giggly and failing miserably at hiding the fact she's memorizing every crease of his smile so she'll have something to picture when she is drifting off to sleep later tonight in her bedroom that is too pink. A diving-horse girl, done for the day, ventures out onto the Boardwalk in search of eggs and a bath, in that order, both preferably hot and delivering the comfort she desperately needs after a day spent atop a quarter horse, plummeting into a freezing tub of water. Her hair is still damp as she gathers her jacket around her, chilled by the night breeze coming off the ocean. The little boy by the Giant Slide continues his argument with the man with the long nose and cigar who takes the tickets, arguing he is, in fact, tall enough to measure up to the 'You must be this tall to ride' sign, even though he is two years away from indeed being that tall, but his sister and her friend are already past, and he will not allow his sister to better him in anything if he can help it. A logjam of rolling chairs are stopped, because the couple in the front are kissing, and their pusher could have sworn they said the Steel Pier, but now they are at the Steel Pier and he is clearing his throat and then clearing his throat again so he can get them out of his chair and collect his five cents and get another couple in. Sea mist drifts in from the jetties onto the Boardwalk, and the air is pungent with the aromas of wet wood, hot waffles dripping with ice cream, and roasted peanuts. White lights flash out offers from every side, of dancing to the music of Louis Prima and two motion pictures playing and the General Motors exhibit, making the pier look like a department store at Christmastime. In the distance you can hear the faint, eternal tumbling of the ocean waves, the water dribbling up onto the sand, then retreating in haste, over and over, a timeless constant amid all of the electricity.'

There was a few seconds of silence, the only sounds the noise of the pier around them, and she waited for him to instruct her to open her eyes again but he didn't. When she did and turned to look at him, his expression could only be described as admiring. 'Congratulations,' he said. 'You're a writer.'

Then he kissed her.

★   ★   ★

Pete drove his cousin's car, a slightly dented 1951 Kaiser, through the Holland Tunnel and back into downtown Manhattan somewhere around eight in the morning, and as if to confirm she had lost her mind completely, she readily agreed when he suggested they duck into a Village diner for bacon and eggs before he took her home. The date was rearing up on twenty-four hours, a fact aided and abetted by the fact that they'd ended up at the Club Harlem on Kentucky Avenue until God-knows-what-time, smoking cigarettes and listening to a

163

chanteuse with skin the color of molasses sing about tortured love and loss.

Oh, if the crowd at the El Morocco could see me now, in a rumpled sundress and reeking of smoke, she thought after she finally parted with Pete on Seventh Avenue, insistently declining his multiple offers to drive her uptown. She'd told him to keep her cloth bag with the change of clothes and musty swimwear and drop it off at Connie's bookshop, where she would retrieve it later. 'Not a chance,' he'd grinned. 'I'm holding on to it. This way I know you have to go out with me at least one more time.'

She didn't feel tired. Not at all. Why didn't she feel tired? She had been up for an entire day. And yet she felt like she could stay up for three more. Maybe it was putting all of that scenery and motion into words, just like that, and sharing them with another person. Or simply knowing she could, that she had it in her, that it wasn't just some girlish daydream but a skill she possessed, perhaps raw and unpolished, but which lived in her soul nonetheless.

And much of it no doubt was Pete — honest, clever, open Pete and his skinny arms and bobbing Adam's apple and unruly hair, who brought out a side of her she hadn't even known existed. Or at least allowed anyone to see.

She took her time meandering up the avenue toward the subway, looking in closed store windows the whole way.

By the time she'd made her way uptown and then walked all the way to the East Side and Sixtieth Street, St. Thomas's was just letting out,

164

the summer faithful turned out in their best linen and pouring onto the sidewalk. Laura was a block away when she spied Vivian standing in her regular spot, still dressed in her Stork-uniform black, those whopping sunglasses planted on her face. But even through the dark ovals, Laura could almost make out Vivian's eyes widening, could see her features slowly crawling into arrogant amusement as she played Nancy Drew and watched prim, proper, French-speaking, flute-playing, A-student Laura Dixon, of the Greenwich, Connecticut, Dixons, leisurely sauntering home from her twenty-four-hour date.

Laura walked right by her. 'Not a word,' she said, as Vivian turned and the two of them fell in step behind the Barbizon's churchgoing girls returning home.

12

'Get me the Hellmann's out of the icebox,' Bridget Elizabeth Hickey commanded from her kitchen table. She sat mashing cold boiled potatoes, staring fiercely into a large ceramic bowl.

'I thought Aunt Moya was going to make the potato salad,' Dolly said, retrieving the mayo and plopping the jar and a big spoon on the table.

'She refuses to use anything but that awful Ann Page mayonnaise, which isn't even real, and I am not serving that at your sister's baby shower. I told her to make the deviled eggs.'

'They have mayo in them, too.'

'Not as much.'

Dolly sat down across the table and lit a cigarette.

'A smoking girl now, are we?' her mother said, wielding the masher a bit more forcefully. 'I guess that's what all the girls do down in New York.'

'Mother, please don't start.' Dolly looked around the kitchen. 'How can I help?'

'You can get me a beer.'

Dolly glanced at the clock above the icebox. 'It's not even noon.'

'Do you know what time my day starts? I've been working in this kitchen since six this morning, while you were upstairs pounding sand. I can have a beer if I want one.'

Dolly retrieved the quart of Rheingold, filled a pilsner glass. She'd gotten into Utica around nine last night, immediately been put to work: putting up streamers, ironing the tablecloth, getting folding chairs up from the basement. Later this afternoon, twenty-three women from the Hickey and O'Rourke families would be in this house for her sister Kathleen's surprise baby shower. Dolly had frantically tried to figure out a way to see her girlfriends, but this weekend was about family obligation, and lots of it. There'd be no time for anything but gossip over delicatessen meats and suitably *oohing* and *aahing* over the presents before she would be on a bus back to Manhattan.

'So,' her mother said, 'what's all the news in the big city?'

Dolly took a drag on her cigarette, shaking her head. 'Nothing much.' Her mother was the last person she'd tell about her interesting morning in the restaurant with Laura and Vivian, and what had happened after they'd left. She knew what she'd hear: *You're getting ahead of yourself. You don't know this boy at all. Who are his family?* The fact he had an Irish surname would help, but without the proper parish and county-in-Ireland-his-people-are-from identifiers to inspect, this would prove but a temporary point of interest.

Her father had been her surprising ally in her war with her mother to get permission to enroll at Katharine Gibbs and live at the Barbizon. As the months had passed, Dolly could tell, from the tone of voice in her calls and infrequent

167

letters, that her mother had assumed Dolly's New York tour would prove a phase — a misguided, starry-eyed venture into metropolitan 'fanciness,' as she was fond of calling it.

Dolly should be angry, sitting watching Bridget Hickey turn over five pounds of goopy potato salad with her big serving spoon, stopping only to take a sip of beer, but she couldn't be. Her mother was, quite simply, impossibly Irish. Dolly had been a child through the Depression; her mother had navigated its treacherous pitfalls and scares as a full-fledged adult. There was a fear among that entire generation of anything that smacked of reaching too far, or too high, or of trying to make something of yourself beyond the safe confines of your own backyard, where family and neighbors could look out for you. In the thirties, family and neighbors were all you had.

Kathleen had followed the playbook, married a guy who had been in the service and gotten a job in a local bottling plant that guaranteed a week's vacation and a pension as long as people kept drinking bottled liquids. The fact that he had a head shaped like an overturned bucket and belched constantly was immaterial. Now Kathleen was entering motherhood. Another box checked off the list. Dolly's brothers would no doubt repeat the pattern. Stay in the neighborhood. Get a job with a local company or, better yet, the government. Outside of the priesthood, there was no occupation Irish-Catholic parents in Utica wanted more for their sons than that of mailman or police officer.

168

Dolly couldn't decide which was worse: wanting a more exciting life in New York, or pursuing a more exciting life in New York because you were afraid no one decent would want you as a wife in Utica.

As if reading her mind, her mother said, 'Aunt Theresa will be here at three to help put the food out. Regina is driving her over.'

Dolly felt her back go up. 'You invited Frank's sister?' Frank, the louse who had been her on-again, mostly off-again boyfriend. 'Why?'

'I was at the store and I saw Regina there, and we were talking. She said she could get her father's car and drive Aunt Theresa. Dolly, you know her hip isn't good. And there aren't a lot of women in this neighborhood who drive.'

'Daddy could have picked up Aunt Theresa.'

Her mother shrugged, stabbed a fork into the potato salad, and scooped up a bite. 'Mmm. Creamy. See? This is what I am always telling Aunt Moya. You have to use the Hellmann's. But who listens?' She downed the last of her beer, then got up from the table. 'I have to go get ready.'

Dolly sat, stewing. Her mother lived under the misguided notion that if Dolly had just stayed in Utica, she and Frank would have worked out. The stood-up dates, the broken promises, she was always so quick to explain away bad behavior in Frank that she would have never tolerated from her own children. Why was clear: It was better to be married to a louse than not married at all. Security, that's what mattered. Take what you can get. Go for the sure bet.

Regina will be on me like a bee, Dolly thought. *It won't be five seconds before she tells me all about the new girl Frank is seeing. The old cow. Oh, why didn't I just stay in Manhattan? But I couldn't have done that to Kathleen.* Dolly hadn't wanted to tell anyone about her breakfast guy yet, not until she felt more sure. But if battle lines were being drawn, that called for action. *Maybe I'll just tell Regina a thing or two myself.*

She stubbed out her cigarette, watching the smoke curl lazily up to the light above the kitchen table.

* * *

For the third time in as many weeks, Vivian had almost missed the bus again. Her only answer was to succumb and buy one of those damn alarm clocks, even though she hated that sudden shrill bell that inevitably made her shoot up in bed as if the place were on fire.

The recent humidity had broken, leaving a perfect summer morning for the short walk from the bus stop to the mansion. Strolling down the winding sidewalk, Vivian took in the sights of children on bicycles, free from the drudgery of school, their biggest worries now the possibility of a flat tire or a sudden thunderstorm. Leafy trees framed the street and swayed in a light breeze, scattering beautiful patterns onto the road. Who knew New Jersey could be so beautiful?

She scrambled up the steps of the mansion

and pushed through the door. 'Good morning, Josie,' she said. 'And how are things among the natives today?'

'Quiet, so far,' Josie replied from behind the reception desk. Tiny and wiry, Josie was one of the five-dayers, one of the volunteers who came almost every day of the week, and sometimes even popped by on the weekend. Vivian, by contrast, came only on Wednesdays, relegating her to what Harry Sofronski, who had once tap-danced with Gene Kelly, called 'the special guest stars' here.

It had only been a few months, but the Actors Fund Home, tucked away in the former mansion of an old miser (a woman miser, no less) in leafy Englewood, New Jersey, had proven an unlikely escape hatch for Vivian since she'd started coming in the spring. Arriving in New York in March and knowing no one, she'd been lucky to land the job at the Stork and even luckier to land housing at the Barbizon; Mrs. Mayhew had a soft spot for authentic Europeans, thought they classed up the place. Vivian had imagined her New York life would be nothing but hustle and bustle, endless cab rides to a steady stream of auditions, but quickly discovered that the auditions were few and far between — two, to be exact — and that most of her days were spent either smoking fags or soaking her aching feet after another night shilling them.

Then one of the Stork girls had casually mentioned she had an aunt out here and was going to come visit, asked Vivian if she felt like a little road trip out to Jersey. From the moment

171

she stepped into the mansion, Vivian knew she would come back. The place itself was rather unremarkable — misers weren't exactly known for their décor — but the architecture was brilliant, reminding her of some of the country houses in Bath.

What had really kept her hauling herself out of bed every Wednesday morning were the people who lived here. Old showgirls, vaudevillians, magicians, singers, dancers. Some had done Shakespeare at the Old Globe; others had been contract players for MGM or RKO. They were the exceptions. Most were Broadway hoofers and swings, the extras and chorines hired show after show to flesh out the scenery and fall in line behind the leads. They'd lived lives on tightropes, never knowing where the next paycheck was coming from or if one was coming at all, their personal lives a mishmash of backstage affairs and dressing-room brawls endured for the brief heady adrenaline rush brought by the orchestra's overture and the glare of white lights.

And now here they were, old and wrinkled and broken, waiting for the final curtain. Some were bitter, but most were not. Which is why, Vivian supposed, she kept coming back week after week. She knew she was doing a good thing, a selfless thing, and she had not done many of those in her life. But then, this was not truly selfless, for the stories she heard were priceless. Some she had heard over and over, especially from Gil Mercer, who never seemed to recall that, yes, he had told you the story about the time Gloria Swanson threw an old-fashioned in

172

his face at the Algonquin. But they were all a form of payment for services rendered. A generous payment.

'Anything urgent need doing?' Vivian asked. She spent most of her time simply visiting. Many of the other volunteers measured their worth in tasks accomplished; just last week one had walked into the kitchen declaring, 'I folded the towels!,' as if it warranted a medal.

'Not right now,' Josie said. 'But Sy Schwartzman asked if you were coming today. He's in the library.'

'He wants a rematch at checkers,' Vivian said. 'I beat him senseless last week.'

'What he wants is to see if you're wearing a short skirt.' Josie laughed.

No luck today, Sy, Vivian thought as she walked down the hall toward the library. She was in a simple white blouse and navy slacks. She'd found out early on it was best not to engage with some of the gentlemen who lived in the mansion. More than a few were still alarmingly randy for their age.

Sy was sitting in the corner thumbing through the *Herald-American*. He smiled as she walked up, then started shaking his head. 'Would it kill you to show a little leg, England?' This was his pet name for her. He'd been in London for the Great War and was convinced it was kismet the two of them had met here.

'No,' Vivian replied, 'but it might kill you.'

'You're too much, England,' he said, chuckling. 'I still can't believe you ain't been in pictures yet.'

Sy had been a stage manager for some of Broadway's biggest productions in the 1920s and '30s, though his dream, unfulfilled, had been to be a successful playwright. Unlike most of his fellow residents, he was reluctant to tell stories about the old days, but when he did, they were worth pulling up a chair for. Just last week Vivian had begged him to fill in gaps on a story he'd told her involving Rudy Vallee, a much older Theda Bara, a mysterious manservant named Hendrik, a few bottles of premium vodka, and a tryst in the Fifth Avenue salon of a banking heiress.

Vivian set up the checkers board. 'I know you've been waiting for the rematch.'

'I let you win last week.'

'If only you lied as well as you flirt.' She tapped the board. 'Carry on, then. First move's yours.'

He slid his red piece diagonally. 'I have some moves I could show you, England.'

'Oh, for God's sake!' she said, shaking her head and moving her own checker. 'How many poor chorus girls surrendered to the Sy Schwartzman onslaught, anyway? I bet there's a gaggle of illegitimate children running around the Lower East Side, wondering why they're always craving knishes.'

Sy chortled again, harder this time, coughing up phlegm. He loved it when she got sassy. 'You make no sense to me, England.'

'How's that?' She jumped him, swiped the red piece off the board.

'You're a beautiful, classy girl, and yet you

174

leave New York City every week to schlep out here to play checkers with an old *farshtinkener* like me.'

'You're not my only boyfriend out here, Sy. I like to play the field.'

'Don't shit with me, England. You know what I mean. You work in the Stork Club, for chrissake. You must meet interesting guys every night of the week.'

She smiled at him. How could she possibly make him understand? Make any of them? Last month she'd spent two hours listening to one of the ladies on the lawn talk about working for Flo Ziegfeld. *Flo Ziegfeld*. Afterward, the woman had apologized profusely 'for boring you with my old tired stories.' Vivian could have listened for two more hours and not noticed the time going by. These people were not old stage vets. They were living history books, dismissed by almost everyone stupid enough to think there weren't any pages worth reading.

Her thoughts were interrupted by a commotion on the other side of the library. A woman screaming, 'Just leave me alone!'

Vivian couldn't place her face immediately. Edith something or other. She was one of the ones who kept to herself mostly, not much for chitchat. Which was fine. Not everyone wanted to relive their glory and not-so-glory days as they waited out their last act. She was thin and bony and wore a loose housedress with a pattern of big blue flowers that was at least two sizes too big. She was swatting wildly at an aide. 'I said, leave me alone!'

'Now, Edith, don't be difficult — '

As Vivian walked over, another resident, a man she'd seen but didn't know, was barking from his adjacent chair. He was jabbing his finger in the air. 'See? Didn't I tell you? She's foul! She shouldn't be in here!'

'What's going on here?' Vivian asked.

'It's all under control,' the harried aide replied curtly. 'We just need to get upstairs — '

'Don't talk about me like I'm a child! I am not a child!'

Vivian stepped in front of Edith, careful to keep her sightline but to not crouch down the way one would to talk to a child. 'Of course you're not, Edith. No one is suggesting you are.'

'She stinks!' the old man was screeching. 'She needs a diaper!'

Edith whipped around and flung the back of her hand right against his cheek, sending his eyeglasses flying across the library. Sy started to rise out of his chair, and two women just walking in stopped to see what all the commotion was about. As the aide scrambled to retrieve the glasses and calm the now-hysterical old man, Vivian tried to piece together what was going on. Edith was clutching the back of her dress tightly, and Vivian could now smell the problem. She looked into the woman's eyes and suddenly saw the face of a child staring back at her.

'I . . . I messed myself,' Edith whispered, her body shaking in frustration and embarrassment. 'I'm sorry. It's just . . . I . . . I need . . . '

Vivian slid an arm around her shoulders and began gently walking her out. 'C'mon, girl,' she

176

said. 'Nothing to be upset over. We all have bad days. Don't let that old wanker upset you. All you need is a nice warm bath and some lunch.'

Will this be me? Vivian wondered fifteen minutes later, after she'd stripped Edith, dispatched her clothes for cleaning and bleaching, and poured the old woman into a steaming tub. As she knelt on the floor behind her, gently circling Edith's pruny back with a soapy sponge, Vivian considered that at one point Edith had been just like her, young and pretty and in New York to make a career for herself in show business, and yet in the end she had ended up here. Did she have a family? Did they know where she was, or even care?

Did Vivian's?

A sense of foreboding filled her body. It was all well and good to be the independent sort, to live life by your own set of rules. Until you needed help and discovered the price you'd paid by telling everyone else to bugger off. *I'm truly alone,* Vivian thought. *I suppose in my own way I've always been alone, even when I was living with Mum and Dad and Mary and Emma. But now I am really alone. I've never really thought about it that way before.*

'That feels nice,' Edith was saying, swaying in the tub as Vivian continued massaging her back.

Vivian dipped the sponge back into the water and put it against Edith's skin again, sending sudsy trickles down her back. 'I'm glad,' she said.

13

September 1955

From the journal of Laura Dixon, Monday, September 5:

Labor Day. Has it really been weeks since I wrote in this thing? I started out strong, journaling almost daily. After that episode in Mrs. Blackwell's office, I went right to the stationer and bought a journal and started writing. But then every day became every other, and then twice a week. Some journalist.

Just back from Greenwich. The trains run on a limited schedule due to the holiday, which gave me an excuse to leave the barbecue early. Though it was nice to be there, especially less than a month after the hurricane, which caused so much misery and damage everywhere. The town held up pretty well, thank God. And it was nice to spend so much time with David. Poor David, I worry about him, eleven and alone in that big house and Daddy working all the time and no buffer between him and Marmy. But he seems happy. He wanted to confirm our plans for the three of them to come for a weekend this term at Smith.

I can't believe I didn't tell them.

I am a coward. There's no other word for it,

so I'll just use it. I am a <u>coward</u>. I would say I tried to tell them, but that would be a lie, because I didn't. I'll have to settle for 'I had every intention of telling them.' But there was never the right moment. I knew if I did at the beginning of the weekend, it would ruin the whole thing, and then there was the barbecue, and at one point I thought that was actually perfect — I mean, there was no way Marmy would have exploded in front of the Chadwicks and the Thornes or the rest of them. But somehow, the moment never presented itself. And now I don't know what to do, because as of tomorrow, I am living a lie.

Because I'm not going to go back to Smith. I'm staying here, in New York.

I think back on the summer and I can't believe how much has happened. Moving into the Barbizon, meeting Box and Pete, working at Mademoiselle, and that funny run-in with Mrs. Blackwell in her office, and . . . Well, everything happens for a reason, right? Or perhaps that's just what people say when they can't explain everything that's happened. You need to take it on faith that it will all work out.

I have officially deferred my senior year at Smith until January. Something that is going to become very evident very soon when the bursar's office returns Daddy's tuition check. It isn't like I'm never going back. I'm just not going back <u>yet</u>.

Marmy is going to kill me.

But what's that saying (why am I quoting all

of these old sayings?): 'When opportunity knocks.' How was I supposed to know that Cat Eyes would come up to my desk one day and, with clear bewilderment, pass on a message that Mrs. Blackwell wanted to extend my apprenticeship a month, after the closing of the college issue? I think she was secretly wondering if I was somehow blackmailing the boss. What other explanation could there be? And so there you have it — I was worried I'd be fired for getting caught in the editor's office, and instead I was given an extension. Life is nuts.

And then I saw the job posting on the bulletin board for the editorial assistant position. I would have never applied for it, but Pete insisted.

Oh, yes, Pete. We're still seeing one another, and I am still seeing Box. So despite my efforts, I am seeing two guys, something I am not good at (though given it's now been almost three months, evidently I am) and which I swore I would not do. I was in the coffee shop with Vivian last week complaining that I had told a very funny story about a missing hatbox to one of them, and for the life of me I couldn't remember which one. She laughed at that. Which was nice to see. I'm worried about Vivian, actually. She doesn't seem herself so much these days. She's not as quick with a quip. But every time I ask her if anything's wrong, she swears everything's 'ducky.' She says the mysterious Italian is finally introducing her to some fancy theatrical agent this week. But I still can't shake the feeling something's a bit off.

Dolly, on the other hand, is blossoming. I've never seen her so happy. She's still temping at the publishing house, and she starts her new term at Katie Gibbs this week. Last week she finally formally introduced us to Jack, her big guy from breakfast. I would describe him as the strong silent type. He couldn't be more unlike Dolly, who has gotten even <u>more</u> chatty. But that's what they say, right? Opposites attract. (More old sayings!)

So I start my new job tomorrow, back at Mademoiselle. I'll be making enough to pay my share of the room here, which is good, because I think there is little doubt Marmy will seek to punish me in any way she can once she finds out what I am doing, and that includes pulling the purse strings shut. But that's okay. Maybe it's time I figured out what I'm really capable of on my own.

Letter from Dolly Hickey to Mary Louise Koznarski, September 6:

Dearest Lulu Belle —
Sorry I haven't been able to call. I know your dad won't allow you to accept the charges, and I never have enough change for even a three-minute call. Forget looking for a husband in law firms or doctors' offices — we should be looking for a guy who works for Bell Tel! Anyway, it gives me an excuse to practice my typing, which is hard to do in the

181

room, since it drives Laura mad. Though she's always out with one of her fellas, so it's really not much of a bother.

Speaking of which, I have news: I met someone. (I know, I know! I can hear you shrieking from here.) His name is Jack and he's just the most. He's kind and funny and just the biggest teddy bear you ever saw. (I'm not even kidding . . . he makes me feel DAINTY!!) I was out for breakfast with the girls and he was staring at me, and so I just 'happened' to stay behind to pay the check, and the next thing I knew, we were at a table together, talking for hours! (Okay, it was really just under an hour, but it FELT like hours.) I talked way too much, of course, because you know me and that's what I do, blabber and blabber, but getting information out of him was like pulling teeth! Oh, but he has such NICE teeth! Big and straight and white, not like those old yellow party mints of Charlie Hackel's. What did I ever see in HIM? Is he still dating that girl from Minoa?

Anyway, it's been almost three months now, and I am so happy. I know you are yelling at this page right now, saying, 'Three months?! How can you not have told me for three whole months?!!' because everyone knows I can't keep a secret for five seconds. But I didn't want to jinx it. So I said to myself, 'Dolores, we are going to keep our mouth shut until we are SURE this one is going to stick around.' (You know it's serious when I call myself Dolores.) And here we are!

Oh, you must, must, MUST come down to the city, Lulu! Maybe Jack has a friend and we can double. Oh, wait, I need to tell you more about him. In addition to being very tall and wide (but not fat), he's a graduate student, though now for the life of me I can't remember where. But in addition to his gorgeous teeth, he tells the corniest jokes, and speaking of which, we both love corn muffins! I finally got up the nerve to introduce him to the girls last week. Even Vivian (I told you about her in my last letter. She's the British girl who barged into our room and we covered for her and then she invited us to the Stork Club, only we weren't really invited) was impressed, and she's never impressed about <u>anything</u>.

Anyway, that's my big news. Things at Katie Gibbs are good (I can't believe I'll be finished in five months!), and I am still temping at the publishing house, although I have carefully avoided You-Know-Who and his gardenias. I want Jack to come take me to lunch one day just so I can walk with him right past his desk, happy as a clam!

Well, got to run, Lulu, I have ten pages of shorthand to transcribe before tomorrow. I miss you ALL . . . THE . . . TIME and want you to get your rear end on a bus and come visit!!! Say hi to Rose and the rest of the gang for me.

Love,
Dolly

Telegram from Vivian Dwerryhouse to Mrs. Beatrice Dwerryhouse, 2 High Street, Leeds, LSI 4DY, United Kingdom, September 8:

DEAREST MUM
GREETINGS AND LOVE FROM NEW YORK
STOP MISSING YOU ALL AND WOULD MUCH
LOVE TO VISIT HOME STOP PLEASE ADVISE
SOONEST IF YOU CAN WIRE PASSAGE STOP
ANXIOUSLY AWAIT YOUR REPLY WITH
GREATEST AFFECTION
    VIVIAN.

14

Laura was just beginning to doze off for a delicious dinnertime catnap when Dolly burst through the door, cheeks flushed and ready for a gab. 'Hi, hi, hi!' she exclaimed, arms full of papers and bags, handbag swinging from her elbow like a trapeze. Dolly was one of those girls who always seemed to arrive and leave laden with an assortment of packages and bags.

She dumped her things all over the small side table. 'I love fall!' she said, slipping off her jacket. 'Don't you? What am I saying, of course you do — you're from New England. Is it really as pretty there when the leaves turn as they say? I imagine it must be just breathtaking. Maybe I can get Jack to take me sometime. That would be just dreamy. We could pack a picnic — '

Laura tuned out somewhere around the apple picking. Sometimes she just didn't know where Dolly got the energy. She adored her roommate, but sometimes she just wished she would take that energy someplace — anyplace — else.

Laura had been out late. Again. *How did Agnes Ford and the other models do it?* Laura wondered. Out with one guy this night, another the next, constantly primping — the hours they must spend on their hair alone! — never mind all of the eating and drinking. She'd gained a good five pounds over the summer and had now sentenced herself to pre-work swims in the

Barbizon pool three mornings a week. Which had only served to leave her artificially invigorated every morning, buzzing around the office like a bumblebee as she threw herself into her new position at *Mademoiselle*, only to crash by four in the afternoon, trudging around like she was walking through a field of molasses and craving red licorice.

But last night had been truly wonderful. Wasn't every night with Box wonderful? But then, her nights with Pete were turning out to be just as splendid, in a completely different way. God, she was beginning to sound like Dolly, all over the place. With Box it was theater and carriage rides and candlelit dinners at the St. Regis; with Pete it was hot dogs (to his boyish delight, she'd learned to love sauerkraut) and long walks through the Village and lively arguments about whether *Absalom, Absalom!* could legitimately contend as Faulkner's most underrated work, though Laura insisted that Pete was only arguing that so he could be contrarian because everyone else always picked *As I Lay Dying*. They enjoyed a breezy camaraderie, and it was during this type of jocular interplay that they had their best moments, when she felt the admiration pooling in those big eyes of his.

Last night Box had taken her to '21,' where they'd run into various people of the variety Dolly always called 'the Swells,' as in, 'So, who among the Swells did you see out this time?' That was the thing about Dolly: Laura knew part of her resented that she got to go to these places and Dolly did not, while at the same time

186

wanting every detail of what it was like to *be* in these places, down to the folding of the napkins. Not that Laura could recount the napkins at '21' with any alacrity. She'd drunk far too much champagne for far too long and stayed out far too late. It had been another long road through *Mademoiselle* today — she'd spent the entire day at the New York Public Library on Fifth Avenue, pulling research on marriage rituals around the world — and had been just drifting off when Hurricane Dolly had touched down, whirling at full force.

'Here,' Dolly said, tossing her a thick sheaf of bound mimeographed sheets. 'I brought you a present.'

'What's this?' Laura yawned, thumbing through them. It appeared to be a book manuscript. The front page was stamped: PROPERTY OF JULIAN MESSNER, INC. PRIVATE AND CONFIDENTIAL.

'The most amazing novel,' Dolly squealed in delight, plopping onto the edge of the bed. 'They just bought it, and everyone says it's going to be a blockbuster. It's called *The Tree and the Blossom*. It's the most scandalous thing you've ever read in your life. I was blushing as I typed in the revision notes! It's all about this small town in New England called Peyton Place. You have to tell me if New England is really like this. Because if it is, I'm moving.'

'Can't you get in a lot of trouble for taking this out? It's an unpublished manuscript.'

'Oh, no one's going to care if a couple of girls read it under the covers. I marked the good parts. And look at it this way: Next year, when

187

everyone is talking about this, you'll have already read it! Your coworkers will be crazy jealous.'

The door opened and Vivian walked in, clutching a steaming paper cup of coffee, a newspaper tucked under her arm. 'I'm surprised they let you upstairs with that,' Dolly remarked, slipping off her shoes. The Barbizon matrons were fanatical about the prohibition of food in the rooms. Mice and insects were bogeymen warned of in apocalyptic terms.

'It was the nice one running the elevator today,' Vivian said. 'The one with the bad skin. I only buy a coffee and a biscuit if I see she's on duty.' She nodded toward the manuscript on the bed. 'What's this?'

'Dolly's scandalous novel,' Laura said.

'What's *that*?' Dolly asked in reply, pointing to Vivian's arm. 'I've never seen you with a newspaper in the entire time I've known you.'

Vivian handed the paper to Laura. 'It appears we have a celebrity in our midst. Page twenty-three.'

Dolly scooched over as Laura thumbed through the paper. Their collective eyes were scanning page 23 when Dolly let out a piercing shriek. 'Wow!'

There it was, in black-and-white, right in Nancy Randolph's column in the *New York Daily News*.

I had the good fortune of a long-overdue visit to the always glamorous '21' last night and was delighted to see Doris Duke, looking luminescent as always. She is just back from a pleasure tour of Iran. Among those listening to details of the journey were department store heir and man about town Box Barnes and his lovely date, *Mademoiselle* magazine editor Laura Dixon, whom Box says has just deferred her forthcoming senior semester at college because, he said with moony eyes, 'she can't stand the thought of being without me.'

Laura felt the remnants of her lunchtime tuna salad curdle into the back of her throat. Mrs. Blackwell would be furious, assuming she had inflated her position to a *Mademoiselle* 'editor' when she was but a lowly, and brand-new, editorial assistant. And Pete! Pete would read this, know she had been seeing Box the whole time. And then —

The thought hit her like a truck. *Oh . . . my . . . God.*

A mushroom cloud of panic ballooned around her, interrupted only by a sharp rap at the door. Vivian answered, unveiling the ever-pale, skeletal face of Mrs. Metzger.

'Miss Dixon,' Metzger said officiously. 'Your mother is here.'

* * *

They sat in a back booth in the Barbizon coffee shop, Marmy declining Laura's feeble suggestion they go somewhere nearby. There would be no delay in the reckoning.

Her mother looked as she always did, whether

189

in joy — though Laura could not really recall a day when her mother had ever been truly joyful, at least in the colloquial sense of the word — or distress. Her hair, a mousy brown despite the hours she logged at the beauty parlor, fell in short, brittle waves, giving her the appearance of a schoolteacher who had managed to marry well. Her nails were plain but buffed — Marmy thought nail polish a vulgarity — and she tapped them, slowly, painstakingly, *click . . . click . . . click* on the table as they waited for the waitress to bring them their iced teas. She wore a lemon-yellow dress with a pronounced Peter Pan collar, but the combination, designed to evoke ladylike warmth, somehow only managed to make her appear even more severe.

Walking into the lobby, gripped with growing paralysis, Laura had expected to encounter her father as well. But it turned out that Marmy had come alone to lower the boom. Laura had pictured her family at that morning's breakfast table, David idly chattering on about his friend's baseball card collection as her father pored over the business pages and her mother wanly glanced through the advertisements for Peck & Peck, until she came upon Nancy Randolph and the tale of the young girl who had managed to charm New York's biggest catch. The girl who at that very moment was supposed to be sitting in a classroom at Smith.

Marmy took a delicate sip of her iced tea, added in two carefully measured spoonfuls of sugar, then slowly stirred, like one of Macbeth's witches brewing toads. Laura stared at the drink, at how the tiny agitated crystals gave the glass the appearance of a dirty snow globe.

Her mother gently laid down her spoon. 'All right, then,' she declared tartly. 'I'm ready whenever you are, Laura.'

The shock of her mother's sudden appearance had begun to subside, prompting Laura to try to access the conversation she'd been mentally rehearsing for weeks. Because she had already had this talk, of course — several times, in fact. She had known that she would be found out sooner rather than later. She had composed a thoughtful, even eloquent explanation and defense, refined and edited over time and repetition. One that now completely escaped her in the moment she so desperately needed it.

And so out it came, awkward and fumbling, until she found her rhythm, random phrases and arguments slowly bubbling back into her consciousness from all the practice. She had carefully weighed the decision to defer, she had every intention of completing her degree, but there was something very important happening not at Smith but here, right here, in New York, at this very moment, and she had a duty to herself to see it through. She added that she had been raised well, by parents who had taught her to think for herself, to weigh decisions and act on them, and that her only folly had been in her deception, and for that she was truly sorry.

It got to the point where Laura realized she was repeating herself, skirting into groveling. In all of her trial runs, she had never, ever groveled. Silence was a weapon with Marmy. She defied you to try it, because it was her natural gift to make people uncomfortable and self-doubting, with her pursed lips of disapproval, her arched, half-moon brows, her gray eyes, as colorless as ice cubes. Laura leaned back into the booth and tried to settle into the silence; live with it; wait it out. She watched as Marmy once again lifted her spoon and lazily circled it through her iced tea, once more agitating the unmelted sugar crystals swirling like so much confetti.

Marmy tapped the spoon deliberately on the side of the glass.

'Well, that is quite the tale, I must say,' she said. A skeptical police detective admiring a guilty suspect's outrageous alibi. She looked Laura in the eye. 'And you're happy, here, in this new life of yours?'

Are you happy? Did her mother just ask her if she was happy? Laura dared to meet Marmy's gaze for several seconds and found an expression that was new, foreign, staring back at her. Something that almost seemed like . . . intrigue.

'I don't pretend to know that every choice I make will be the right one in the end,' Laura managed, 'but I do feel confidence that I have the facility to make the best decisions I can at any given moment. So yes, for now, I am happy.' She'd learned that it was always best to engage in conversations with Marmy that sounded like they could have been written by Jane Austen. In one of her initial letters from the Barbizon this summer, she had casually dropped in the sentence 'I can only hope that my patient industry will yield earnest learning,' and done it without a shred of irony.

'I see. Well, your father and I are certainly disappointed you didn't feel that you could discuss this with us before making such a drastic decision, but as you yourself point out, we have raised you to think independently and to use clear judgment, so I must take you on the strength of your conviction that you have exhibited both of them when considering this course.'

Laura's eyes opened so wide she could almost hear her lids snapping. She had expected an immediate order to start packing. Instead she'd gotten something that almost sounded like praise.

She's up to something.

The waitress asked if they wanted to order food, Marmy delicately waving her off as she took another genteel sip of the iced tea. She pressed her napkin to her lips deliberately, the way one might apply a cold compress on a fever. 'And this relationship with the Barnes boy. Is it serious?'

Of course.

Marmy had not come to admonish. Or to berate. Or to judge.

She had come to *verify*.

Laura fought the smile forming at the edges of her mouth. How could she have not seen this coming? Not conjured the image of her mother, prim and self-satisfied, leaving here and slipping behind the wheel of her navy-blue Packard with the white interior, silently humming Tony Bennett as she wound her way back to the

Merritt Parkway? Marmy would be practicing her own internal monologue, the one she would deliver to her friends over bridge about her daughter and Benjamin Barnes: *Yes, we think it's very serious* and *Oh, he's such a lovely young man* and *Of course, it's up to her to decide her future, but he seems very smitten* and *We just want her to be happy, because as mothers all we want is for our children to be happy*. How many times would Marmy sit before her dressing mirror before bed, looking at her reflection and practicing the introduction: 'Oh, yes, you remember my daughter, Mrs. Benjamin Barnes?'

Laura's smirk hardened into something else, and she felt a slight scoff escape. Who knew that a few random lines in a New York gossip column could completely upend two decades of power, two decades of living under the thumb of the pressed and pleated Mrs. Theodore Dixon of Greenwich, Connecticut?

'He's nice,' she replied casually. 'Of course, he's not the only young man I'm seeing.'

Her mother reached for her purse, extracted some lotion, and applied it to her hands. 'I see,' she said, writhing her hands together like a hand mixer. 'Do you think that wise? I mean, Benjamin Barnes is a rather prominent young man. I'm sure you wouldn't want to put yourself into a situation where your other engagements might embarrass him.'

No, embarrass you, Laura thought. Or, more accurately, *Impede your chances of becoming an in-law to one of the most socially prominent families in New York*.

194

She had fantasized about this moment. This very moment. She had lain awake in her cream-and-white bedroom at home, staring up at the roof of the canopy bed, and imagined what it would be like if the day came when she would no longer have to care a whit about what her mother thought, when she would, for once, be holding all the cards. The one in control. Now that it had arrived she felt . . . nothing. She had expected a thrill, but the only emotion she could access was scorn. For her mother and her louche appetite for social standing, and for herself, for wasting all of those years worrying about the opinion of someone as shallow as a glass of iced tea.

'I'm sorry, Mother, but I must be going,' Laura said, sliding out of the booth and delivering a Judas kiss on the cheek. 'I have a date with a bartender.'

15

'Just come in for a minute. C'mon. Just a minute.'

Dolly stood with Jack at the entrance to the Barbizon, pulling at his arm on the sidewalk, trying to haul his impressive frame through the doors. Oscar looked positively flustered, reaching for the door to let them in, then pulling his hand away as Jack insisted he couldn't, then reaching again as Jack jerked a step closer to the building, then back again when he resolutely stated, for the third or possibly fourth time, that the lateness of the hour didn't permit an extension of their date.

'You're being mean,' Dolly said, intending to sound cute but instead coming off peeved.

'I'm sorry. But I have to get back.'

'Back where? What is so important in Yonkers that you can't spend an extra ten minutes in Manhattan?'

'Dolly, please,' he said, leaning in and kissing her on the forehead. 'I have to go. I'll see you soon.'

I'll see you soon.

It was always *I'll see you soon*. Never *I'll see you tomorrow*, or *I'll meet you after work on Tuesday and we'll go see a movie*, or *I can't wait until the weekend — let's make a plan*. Just always, always, *I'll see you soon*. Invariably, he did. Most of the time, anyway. There were those two weeks of silence in August that had driven her to the brink of madness, but then he'd calmly resurfaced, vague as always about his whereabouts ('Family trip' is all she'd gotten out of him), and just when she'd had it, when she was going to demand a firmer commitment, an understanding of what all of this was, or even if there was a 'this,' she'd look into his eyes, or fixate on his pretty teeth, or casually brush her hand against his flat top, which always looked like he was about to enter basic training, and all of her resolve would fly right out of her body like a streamer cut loose at the Fourth of July parade.

She gave him a royal wave as he dashed down the street, smiling weakly as Oscar finally opened the door and the cool lobby of the Barbizon enveloped her. Late Saturday afternoons were always quiet. Girls were out at matinees or lunching with visiting parents or outfit-shopping for that night's date.

Dolly lollygagged, debating whether to go upstairs and take a bath, go upstairs and retrieve *The Tree and the Blossom* and take it with her to the park, or ditch both ideas and simply go into the coffee shop for an ice cream soda, when a voice across the room halted her train of thought. 'Dolly! Over here! Come join us!'

Ruth — Vivian's favorite, the girl who had sung Rodgers and Hammerstein in the conservatory — was sitting on one of the long sofas surrounded by two friends, one a homely girl with spindly limbs and large feet whose name was either Marion or Miriam — Dolly could never remember — and another girl Dolly couldn't recall seeing before. Dolly walked over, pulling up a chair next to Marion/Miriam across from Ruth and the other girl.

'Dolly, this is my friend Helen,' Ruth said, waving to the full-cheeked girl next to her, who looked like Shirley Temple. Not Shirley Temple grown up from *Since You Went Away*, but Shirley Temple from the Good Ship Lollipop, only filled with helium and dropped into a grown-up dress. 'And of course you already know *this* girl.' Marion/Miriam just laughed.

Dolly smiled back, nodded, exchanged all the expected pleasantries about the three topics every girl here never seemed to tire of: the weather, the cute men who arrived for dates, and Agnes Ford and the other models inside the Barbizon, the latter conversation covering their hair, makeup, jewelry, fashions, suitors, latest magazine spreads, and any other ephemera of note. 'We're all gathering in the TV room tonight to watch the Miss America Pageant,' Marion/Miriam said. 'We're sneaking in s'mores!'

'You should come. It's going to be so much fun,' added Helen.

'Oh, I'm sure she has another date, girls,' Ruth said, girlish admiration in her voice. 'Don't you? We haven't seen as much of you lately. I guess you've been too busy with your fella.'

Oh no. Do I have to do this again? Am I really going to keep doing this?

'Tell, tell,' interjected Marion/Miriam, hopping to the edge of her chair.

I'm going to keep doing this.

'Wellll . . . ' Dolly said, trying to will flushness

198

onto her cheeks, 'I guess I've just been having too marvelous a time to notice the weeks flying by.'

'Hold it, hold it! I'm coming into this from the outside,' Helen said, 'so, who is this mystery man?'

Good question. 'His name is Jack, Jack Lyons,' Dolly answered, trying to shove out the memory of an entire afternoon two weeks ago she had spent doodling 'Mrs. John Lyons' and 'Mrs. Dolores Lyons' on the back page of her steno notebook. 'He's a graduate student here in the city.'

'Oh, that's wonderful. What's he studying?'

I have no idea. 'Philosophy,' Dolly answered.

'What college is he at?' Ruth interjected.

No idea of that, either. 'Fordham.' Fordham had its main campus in the Bronx. Jack lived in Yonkers. Close enough. It wasn't like she had not asked Jack these questions herself. But his deftness at answering without revealing anything had proven almost surreal. When she pressed, he became uncomfortable and fidgety, which made her feel insecure, which made her back off, which only fed her frustration that she hardly knew anything about him.

'How'd you meet?' said Marion/Miriam, who of the three definitely seemed the most invested in the whole thing.

Well, at least this one I can actually answer. Dolly regaled them with the story of the stolen glances inside the restaurant after her breakfast with the girls ('Oh . . . her,' Ruth snorted upon hearing Vivian's name), adding a few theatrical

199

flourishes (somewhere along the road of constantly telling the tale she had added a fallen handkerchief and Jack's gallant rescue of same). Unfortunately, the meet-cute story tended to only feed the interrogation, as she was quickly discovering once again.

She told them the truth when she could and her quickly cementing version of the truth when she couldn't. In a bizarre way she was almost proud of the fact that she had memorized some of these anecdotes so well, to the point where she had occasionally questioned whether they might have actually happened. She invented love notes and flowers, long walks in the rain (actually, one short stroll into a hardware store), romantic dinners with loving gazes over candlelight (actually rice pudding at Stouffer's — Jack was addicted).

And what was the harm, really? Didn't she deserve it? After her humiliation with the Gardenia Incident, wasn't she entitled for once to be the envy of other girls, to be the one dating the tall, handsome guy, instead of constantly being the lady-in-waiting for her roommate? Must she spend all of her time watching as Laura hastily unrolled her curlers to get ready for another night out on the town with Box Barnes or going to a set of jazz with her sensitive poet-bartender? Or walking with the girls on Fifth Avenue, observing every man's salacious glance as he surreptitiously let his eyes wander over the hourglass shape that was Vivian Windsor?

Wasn't it her turn?

'So,' Ruth was now asking, 'is it serious?'

This, Dolly had quickly discovered, was where the land mine lay. Answer 'yes' and then everyone will want gory details for days if Jack stops appearing, and expect your heart broken instead of just your pride. Answer 'no' and you were reduced to the desperate girl on her way to being the town trollop.

She had feelings for Jack, no doubt about it — would she keep going to these lengths to keep him in the picture if she didn't? — but her heart, that was firmly under lock and key. At least that was what she constantly reassured herself. She couldn't allow herself to get invested, to have her heart smashed again. Not until she was able to determine what Jack was hiding. Because he was hiding something. Or someone.

She had developed three theories. One, he had a girlfriend, a fiancée, or, God forbid, a wife stashed somewhere, which would explain why, after two months, she was still getting vague answers about his address, why she had yet to meet any of his friends, why she knew little about his upbringing (born in Ithaca, raised in Buffalo) and almost nothing about his family. Several times she had almost come out and just asked, but had then taken the exit ramp, too fearful of getting an answer she didn't want to hear.

The second theory was just as ghastly. He was queer. No one talked about such things out loud, not even in New York, though Dolly suspected they might at the Greenwich Village saloon where Pete Kelly tended bar; the Village types were like that, they liked things that were taboo and seedy, and could pass off talking about them in polite company as intellectual art. Her cousin had dated a guy who had turned out to be queer. After word spread, he had been beaten to a pulp one night by the local boys, then moved out of state to stay with an aunt. No one had ever mentioned his name again.

She clung to her third theory. He was shy. Inexperienced. A big galoot. Just somebody who wasn't all that comfortable around women, or with romance, and was just trying to find his footing. This was the theory that steadied her at night, when she lay in her bed across the room from a deeply sleeping Laura, covers pulled to her chin, closing her eyes tight and praying feverishly that God would give her this one gift. She'd gotten Jack to come into the Barbizon just once to meet Laura and Vivian. He'd been surprisingly affable, if still emanating a slight sense of paranoia, as if the cops were on his trail and he had only a few minutes before his imminent arrest.

Oh God. She hadn't even considered that. *Could he be a criminal?*

'Oh, look at her,' cooed Helen. 'She doesn't want to kiss and tell.'

Dolly almost laughed. Almost. Because the evidence she could never explain away was the kissing. Or, more accurately, the lack thereof. Almost three months and nothing but chaste pecks on the cheek or forehead.

She went to her safety valve and pulled it. 'I wouldn't say I'm ready to buy the car,' she said, smiling just a bit too brightly, 'but I'm definitely kicking the tires.'

★ ★ ★

Walking up Sixth Avenue, Vivian heard the criticism banging inside her brain over and over, like a tropical drumbeat.

You're smarter than this. You have always been smarter than this. How could you have let this happen if you are smarter than this?

She had a million errands to run and couldn't think of one of them. Instead she kept walking, marching, making random right turns and left turns, vaguely heading back uptown, but staying firmly on the West Side, until she found herself back on Sixth Avenue again at Fifty-Ninth, by the entrance to Central Park. She stopped by a cart vendor, bought a sausage sandwich, and walked into the public garden.

She rarely came to Central Park, which was stupid, she thought, since she had most of her weekdays free, when only truant students and young mommies were here. On the rare occasions she did wander in, she left promising herself to return more often. But then life intervened, and she was rushing here or rushing there or late to this or had forgotten that, and it would be weeks or even months before she returned. The great open space reminded her of Hyde Park in London, another urban oasis blooming in the middle of a city. She hadn't spent enough time there, either.

She found an empty bench and sat down,

taking another bite of her sandwich. The Americans may not know how to dance, make tea, or set a proper table, but by God they knew how to make delicious craven food.

Celebrating. That was what she thought she would be doing today, maybe out to lunch with Nicky, then splurging for a new frock at Bloomingdale's or Barnes & Foster, perhaps a pedicure then an ice cream with the girls in the coffee shop, or even someplace fancier. But instead she was trapped — in a dead-end job she hated and in a relationship that was becoming malevolent if not downright dangerous. When she returned to her room in the middle of the night, after yet another exhausting shift shilling cigarettes and enduring the pawing and poking of insolent men, she sometimes looked across at the window and imagined it slowly closing, just an inch more every time, threatening to seal her in for good and suffocate her.

Nicky had finally come through with the audition with the agent, and Vivian had been nervous to the point of almost triggering a breakdown. What she'd needed was some bloody support. She'd briefly considered telling the girls — Laura would have been a good voice of encouragement, and even sweet Dolly would have no doubt brought out her pompoms for a good show — but the pain of looking into their faces if it all went wrong was somehow worse than the nerves.

'How many songs should I prepare?' she'd asked Nicky.

'I dunno,' he'd said, tearing into another bite

of his too-rare steak. 'Just sing great, he's gonna love you.'

Helpful.

In the end she'd brought sheet music for three selections: Dinah Washington's 'Baby Get Lost,' Nat King Cole's 'Nature Boy' (she needed something sentimental), and, for luck, Judy Garland's 'Meet Me Tonight in Dreamland,' the song she'd sung for Nicky that first night after closing at the Stork. She'd tried on at least a dozen dresses before settling on a black polka-dot number that made her pale skin appear almost translucent, and which had a bodice that jutted her breasts out like Jayne Mansfield's and was so tight she wasn't sure she could breathe, let alone sing. Which was probably moot, since she was certain she wasn't breathing anyway.

They'd gone to a small bistro somewhere in the mid-fifties on the far West Side, and Nicky had glad-handed a few men who looked like all the men Nicky knew: slick, shady, stupid. *But now I'm here, I'm finally here*, Vivian thought. *And this is going to work or it won't, but either way I can get out of this and move on.*

Because she knew, as well as she knew her own name, that her time as the girlfriend of Nicola Accardi had gone well past its expiration date. It was almost as if the rough sex in the alley after *The Seven-Year Itch* had flipped a switch, Mr. Hyde steadily appearing more and more as the memory of Dr. Jekyll, the romantic Italian with the rosary beads on his dresser mirror, had faded. After a night in a Midtown hotel last week, he'd been in the shower and she had gone to hang up his suit jacket, flung over a chair. She felt something bulky in the pocket. A gun. How could she not have known he carried a gun? And why did he need a gun?

'Gus, this is Ruby, the girl I've been tellin' you about,' Nicky said, introducing her to a short, stout man with a rubbery pink face the shape of a canned ham.

'Nice to meet you, Ruby,' Gus said, shaking her hand like he was handling a jackhammer. His voice was thin, nasal, as if he was suffering a nasty sinus infection.

'Actually, it's Vivian — '

'So let's hear what you got, kid,' Gus said, lighting a cigar and nodding to his left. 'You can stand up there.'

The stage wasn't a stage at all, just an alcove in the corner with a produce box, covered in a black tablecloth. A microphone stand stood nearby but was empty. There was a beat-up piano to the left.

Vivian extracted the sheet music from her bag. 'Is the player here?'

Gus took a few more puffs lighting the cigar, its tip now blinking red, like a small-town traffic light in winter. 'Nah, nah, we don't need all of that. Just get up and sing a few bars, sweetie. That's all we need.'

Vivian felt a swell of anxiety rising. A cappella? She hadn't practiced anything a cappella. 'Well, perhaps someone could just — '

'Jesus Christ!' Gus interrupted, glaring over at Nicky. The other guys sneered. 'Nick, you didn't tell me you were bringing fucking Lena Horne. I'm busy here. Is she gonna sing or not?'

Nicky grabbed Vivian by the arm, quickly ushering her over to the corner. 'Babe, what are you doin'?' he whispered, his eyes boring into hers. 'Why you makin' trouble? You're *embarrassing* me here. Just sing the goddamned song!'

Vivian shook off his grip. For a fleeting moment, she considered just walking out. But she was so close; she had waited so long. It would be insane to back out now. She shuffled back over to the alcove, apologized to Gus, stepped up onto the tablecloth-covered box. She sang out the first few lines of 'Nature Boy'; she figured it was better to go with a song they were familiar with, especially with no piano to back her up. She hadn't reached 'a little shy and sad of eye' when Gus began barking.

'That's nice, honey, but people don't want this sad-sack shit anymore. They want peppy, bouncy, happy. The kids are the ones buyin' records, not their folks. Let's hear a few bars of 'Rock Around the Clock.''

It was over.

'I'm afraid I don't know that song,' she said quietly.

Gus almost choked on his stogie. 'Well, I can understand why. It was only the fucking number-one hit of the whole summer. Cutie, take some advice: Go buy it. 'Cause that's the future. Let me know when you've learned the words.'

Nicky quickly put an arm around Gus, began to apologize, thanked him for his time. Gus looked at him appraisingly. 'Heard what happened to Mikey Feet,' he said. 'Doctors say he might not make it.'

Nicky nodded his head gravely. 'Yeah, too bad. But you know what they say: Accidents happen.'

Gus's eyes narrowed. 'Yeah. Accidents. They're a bitch. See you 'round, Nick.'

Mikey Feet. Where had she heard that name before? Vivian furiously worked the levers of her memory, trying to remember. She looked at Nicky standing by the door, smoking, his back to her, waiting for her to collect her things. And then she remembered. His back to her, standing nude in the room at the Plaza, barking into the telephone about Mikey Feet. *If that shipment ain't in Hoboken by tomorrow morning, you can tell Mikey Feet that they can start sending his mail in care of Mount St. Mary's Cemetery.*

Oh, bugger.

She let out a deep breath, squared her shoulders. She slowly crept up behind him. 'Darling — ' she said.

He whirled around. 'Are you fucking kidding me with that shit?! I should — '

'There's a call for you in the back. The man says it's urgent.' She said it plainly, authoritatively. *Stay calm.*

He seemed momentarily thrown. 'Nobody knows I'm here.'

'Well, evidently someone does, because there's a call. I believe the man said it's from Hoboken.'

Nicky looked past her for a second. He dropped the cigarette onto the floor, stubbed it out. 'Jesus Christ,' he muttered in an exhale

208

cloud of smoke. 'Wait here.' He stalked toward the back.

He was two seconds out of view when Vivian bolted through the door and into the street, quickly flagging down a checkered cab. Twenty seconds later, she was zooming up Tenth Avenue. She'd turned to look through the rear window. All clear.

That had been two days ago. She knew how this would play out: One night soon he'd show up at the Stork, holding a bouquet of yellow roses because 'red is expected, and with me you never know what to expect,' and he'd flash his sensual smile and make sure his hair was slicked the way she liked it, and the clock would reset and start all over again. Only this time it wouldn't. It couldn't.

Vivian finished the sandwich, tossed the wrapper in a bin as she wound her way slowly through Central Park toward Fifth Avenue. It was still bright and sunny, but there was just the slightest hint of crispness in the air, a small foreshadowing that soon the leaves would be turning, the riotous reds and oranges and yellows of autumn in full bore.

She'd hung on too long to chase an opportunity that had actually been an illusion and ignored the warning signs about a man with whom she had been playing a very dangerous game. Now she was going to have to be clever — very, very clever — to extricate herself from Nicola Accardi, who was not used to being told 'no' by anyone. She felt something gnawing the pit of her stomach and realized it was . . . fear.

He wouldn't give her up without a fight. Perhaps a very bloody one.

I have to get back to England, she thought. *Just for a little while.*

She walked into the Barbizon lobby twenty-five minutes later and headed straight for the desk. 'Any messages?' she asked, silently screaming for a reply telegram from Mum in the box behind Metzger.

'Sorry,' Metzger replied, briefly looking up before turning to retrieve some papers. 'Nothing today, either.'

16

Laura pushed open the door to MacDougal Books & Letters and prayed that no one else was in the shop. Of course, it was rare to find many people in the shop anytime she visited, which both pleased her — more room to browse, more time to talk with Connie — and concerned her. How did you keep a bookshop open if no one ever bought anything?

Not that she was any better. Connie was constantly lending her books, which she took and gobbled voraciously. She assuaged her guilt at accepting his generosity by telling herself her subsequent visits and discussions with him about the works gave him a psychic payment he seemed to thoroughly enjoy. She knew she certainly did. And she had bought a copy of *Auntie Mame* for Vivian.

Connie was sitting at the counter, spectacles on the bridge of his bulbous nose, poring over the latest issue of *The New Yorker*. Or perhaps a ten-year-old copy of *The New Yorker*. With Connie you never knew. 'Ah,' he said, smiling, 'my favorite literary critic.'

Laura smiled and he toddled away from the counter to the back of the shop, no doubt to retrieve two icy bottles of Coca-Cola from the refrigerator. He wasn't supposed to drink it — the doctor had warned it would aggravate his gout — but he convinced himself that drinking a soda pop in the presence of a young protégée somehow didn't count. Laura wandered through the tiny shop and saw that it was reasonably crowded for a weeknight; there must have been a dozen people flipping pages and thumbing through spines. A young couple, clearly in the throes of early, sugary love, sat on the floor in a corner, lazily leafing through a copy of *The Great Gatsby*.

In total the shop couldn't have been more than six hundred square feet, and yet its worn wooden floors, incandescent schoolhouse lighting, and weathered bookshelves came together to create the coziest, happiest sanctuary Laura had discovered in her three and a half months in New York.

Connie walked back around the counter, slid a Coke over to her. 'So, what did you think? Tell me, tell me.'

Laura extracted the copy of *The Man in the Gray Flannel Suit* from her bag and placed it on the counter. 'I thought it was really well written,' she said, 'though if I'm being truthful, I didn't enjoy it quite as much as I thought I would.'

'Really? Why?'

'The plot is about a very unhappily married couple in suburban Connecticut.' She laughed. 'I think perhaps it hit a little too close to home.'

'Or perhaps you were distracted while you were reading it.'

Connie did this now and then. He had the ability to see right through you, as if you were made of wax paper. Laura shook her head. 'You're uncanny.'

'No. I'm just an old man who's grown to be

212

very observant. What's the trouble?'

Where to start? It appeared her problem with dating two men at the same time had solved itself. Laura had left Marmy sitting in the coffee shop to prepare for her date with Pete, where she had hoped to explain the situation and her confusion in it. But she'd never gotten the chance. He'd left a terse message with the front desk canceling, and her subsequent messages, left at the bar, had gone unreturned. She'd dropped a note in his apartment mailbox. No reply. Clearly Marmy wasn't the only one who read the *New York Daily News*.

'Pete,' she blurted out, because, well, why not? Isn't that what she had really come here for, to talk about Pete? 'Our friendly bartender at the San Remo. Also another member of your lending library, as I recall. I don't know whether you were aware we had been seeing one another.'

'Yes,' he said. She searched his face for a clue, something. Nothing.

'Well, then, I am sure you also know that there was an item in a gossip column about me and another guy I've been seeing. A guy Pete didn't know anything about. I mean, it isn't like we had ever talked about dating exclusively or anything. But . . . ' She trailed off. 'I just know he's hurt. And I can't bear that I hurt him.'

'I'm sure. Well. Yes, that is a difficult situation.'

'He's been in here, hasn't he? He's talked to you about this.'

For the first time, Connie's face showed discomfort. 'I wouldn't betray any friend's confidence, including yours, my dear. I can only

213

tell you this: If you have something to say to the young man, you should do so.'

'I'd like to. But he won't return any of my messages, and he ignored my letter.'

'He works down the street.'

'I don't know his schedule.'

'I do. He's working tonight.' Connie glanced at his pocket watch. 'Right now, in fact.'

Laura took an unladylike swig of the Coke, suddenly wishing it was something stronger. She stepped aside to allow two people buying books to check out.

There was no excuse not to go. He was a block away, for God's sake. But Laura had hoped it wouldn't come to this, that somehow she'd be able to stockpile all of the evidence of her good intentions — the calls, the note, the visit to Connie inquiring about his welfare — and then be able to walk away, say, 'Well, I tried.'

But she wasn't trying.

And was she really sure she wanted to walk away?

'I can see that you're conflicted,' Connie was saying as his customers brushed by her and out the door. A light rain had started falling, whooshing a musty, damp air into the shop as the door opened.

'I don't know what to do,' Laura confessed. 'Tell me what to do.'

'Follow your heart.'

'Oh God, Connie. Is that truly the best you've got? 'Follow your heart'?'

'Perhaps I have more faith in your heart than you do.'

'I think that's apparent.'

'To faith,' he said, raising his bottle of Coke.

★ ★ ★

Laura folded the umbrella she'd borrowed from Connie — he had insisted she take it, in large measure, she guessed, so that she would have one less excuse not to go to the San Remo — and tentatively pushed her way into the bar. Rather than act as a deterrent, the rain had acted as an incentive; the place was crowded with patrons who'd run in to escape the downpour and warm themselves with cheap whiskey and cheaper beer. The rain had also mixed the crowd considerably, the artsy writers and angry polemicists augmented by your standard-issue working Manhattanites and the random bewildered tourist.

Pete was down at the other end, thrusting four glasses of beer at a time, swiping cash off the bar, and punching charges into the old rusted cash register. He had a dishrag flung carelessly over one shoulder, and the fabric under the armpits of his blue-gray oxford was stained with sweat. The muggy rain had turned the interior of the bar soupy.

In short order, another bartender slid behind the long oak to assist, but it took Pete a good ten minutes to make his way down toward her end. When he spotted her, his expression, while not quite as inscrutable as Connie's, was nonetheless cryptic in its own way, a mix of subtle surprise, disdain, excitement (or maybe she was inventing the excitement part), and caution, which all too quickly vanished into a hardened look of utter detachment. His hair was in his eyes, making him look raw and sexy in a way she wouldn't have imagined he could.

He slid a coaster in front, looked at her impassively. 'What'll it be?'

This is going to be worse than I thought.

'How about a hello?'

His short, derisive laugh scolded her for her gall. 'I'm busy here, as you can see. Would you like to order something or not?'

'White wine, please.'

He poured her a glass of something that smelled like dirty socks — wine was not what one ordered at the San Remo — and promptly disappeared, never even bothering to collect her money on the bar. She stayed and sipped and people-watched for half an hour, until she lost track of his whereabouts and it became apparent her visit had been pointless. She picked up the damp umbrella and left.

She walked out to find the rain dissipating. It was now a fine, swirling mist, the kind that came so often in Connecticut but for some reason seemed uncommon in New York.

'Cutting your losses?' came the voice behind her.

She startled. Pete was leaning against the building, foot against the wall, smoking. She'd allowed him his anger. But now she felt defiance coursing through her chest. She'd come to apologize and had been met with only sneering derision. It was her turn to be angry.

'I'm going home,' she said. 'By the way,' she added as she turned and began walking up Bleecker Street, 'your wine stinks.'

'Oh, yes, I'm sure the wine list is much, much better at '21,'' he yelled after her. 'Or the Harwyn. Or the Drake Room. Or anywhere else Box Barnes takes his — ' He stopped himself.

She whirled around. 'His what, Pete? Don't stop now. You have something to say, then say it. His what, his 'harem'? Is that what you were going to say? Or was it something more guttural? His 'sluts'? Maybe that's it. Are you shocked, that a girl like me would use a word like that? But that's what writers do, right, Pete? We use the proper words. And we both know that's exactly what you're thinking.'

He bolted from the shadows onto the sidewalk. 'Thinking? You want to know what I'm thinking, Laura? Well, let me save you the guessing game: I'm thinking I am a complete and total chump. Because all this time, while I have been dating a girl I thought was real and honest and open and funny, she's been playing me. The whole time. She's been slumming it with me while she laughed behind my back with her rich boyfriend uptown. Did you tell him, Laura? Huh? Was it all a big game? 'Oh, Box, my darling Box, you should see this bartender down in the Village with all of his moony poetry and silly jokes. It's hilarious!' And then the two of you drank more champagne in the back of his limo? I'm sure it was a great time.'

Her fury was consuming, bubbling like molten lava, ready to spew. But then, standing there in the orange glow of a streetlight, she got a good look at him. Really *looked* at him. Her fury collapsed in on itself and disappeared. He was right: not about her playing him, or about her laughing at him, but certainly about her carelessness, about her casual disregard for how he would feel if he found out, and about the stunning lack of depth it exposed in her character. In the movies it was always the man who was the cad, the unfeeling, selfish brute who cavorted at will and never looked back on the dreams he'd dashed in his wake. It had been she who had been cavalier, who had allowed feelings on both sides to grow — between her and Pete, between her and Box — with little more than airy thought to the fact that at some point a choice would have to be made and that there would be consequences. This could have happened just as easily in the inverse. What would Box have done if he'd come upon her with Pete in a rolling chair on the Boardwalk in Atlantic City or sitting in the window of a coffeehouse on Thompson Street, playfully arguing over Kafka?

'I'm sorry,' she blurted out. She wanted to say more, but the words wouldn't come. She felt the burning of tears, lowered her eyes toward the sidewalk.

They stood in silence for a while. She was starting to shiver from the mist.

'Does he know? About me?'

She shook her head.

'Were there others?'

Her eyes shot up to meet his. 'Of course not.'

'Why, Laura? I swore I wasn't going to ask, but now I have to know.'

'You might not believe this,' she said, summoning the courage to continue to meet his stare, 'but I do, really, honestly care about you. The truth is I met you both at the same time and it just seemed okay at first — '

'Yeah, you see, that's the key phrase: At first. I didn't expect you weren't seeing other guys when we met, Laura. You're a pretty girl. But my God. After that date in Atlantic City? We spent almost an entire *twenty-four hours* together. And then all the other days and nights over the last few months? And you watched me falling in love with you and never thought it might be worth mentioning that you also happened to be dating the city's most well-known bachelor?'

She heard nothing after *You watched me falling in love with you.* She began crying, big, gulping sobs that choked in her chest and heaved from her lips in jerking bursts, as if she were grieving at a hospital bedside. Her voice cracked like an adolescent boy's. 'I'm . . . I'm sorry.'

It was awful, rote, magnificently inadequate. But it was all she could manage.

He went to say something but stopped, and instead simply turned away, slowly walking back toward the bar.

17

The tea was hot and delicious and served in tiny individual pots of delicate porcelain that matched the teacups and saucers, a decidedly feminine pattern of curlicues and flowers swirling around the edges of each. Laura, Dolly, and Vivian sat in the dining room of the Barbizon — 'imbued with Old Charleston atmosphere,' as the brochures declared, a bit optimistically — each making polite conversation in spectacularly unsuccessful fashion.

This had been Laura's idea, and she knew it had been a mistake even before the tier of tea and sandwiches and the perfectly shaped mounds of clotted cream had been placed on the table. She was still worried about Vivian, who seemed increasingly distant, devoid of any of the jaunty joie de vivre she'd exhibited ever since she'd barreled into their room looking for cover from Metzger. So Laura had convinced Dolly that they should take Vivian to a proper British tea, which was served several afternoons right inside the cavernous dining room. She had hoped that perhaps the gesture would lift her own spirits, too. Now, looking at Dolly's similarly pained expression, it appeared all three of them were in desperate need of a boost. And not likely to get it from the other two.

Dolly leaned back in her chair. 'Well, ain't this the cat's pajamas,' she said, breaking through the falsity. 'Three girls all dressed up for tea, and nothing but Gloomy Guses in the lot.'

'Not everyone,' Vivian said, nodding quietly over to a table in the corner. Two of the Women sat, chatting amiably. They were archetypal: dowdy, eschewing makeup or fashionable hairstyles, in nondescript, shapeless dresses with little adornment. The one with her back to them sat with a single long-stemmed rose by her place setting. But the one whose face they could see seemed decidedly content, even occasionally smiling, which was not common for that demographic. At one point she reached across the table and gently laid her hand over the other woman's, whispering something. The gesture lasted only seconds but spoke volumes.

'Are they . . . I mean, do you think they . . . ' Dolly whispered.

'Yes, I do,' Laura answered.

'Oh my!' Dolly said. 'I mean, I'd heard rumors of that sort of thing among the older ones, but out in public? In the *dining room*? I'm speechless!'

'Well, that would be a first,' Vivian replied, and for the first time today the three of them laughed. Vivian delicately balanced the strainer over her teacup and began pouring, still stealing the occasional glance over at the far table. 'And don't be so hasty to dismiss Sapphic attachment, darling. I'm beginning to appreciate its merits more and more every day.'

Dolly giggled, less from the comment but more from the way Vivian pronounced *appreciate:* appree-see-ate. She loved how the English talked. Everything always sounded better. She'd decided that if she was ever declared terminally ill, she wanted Vivian to be the one to deliver the news.

Laura quickly felt the cloud of melancholy descending over the table once again and opted for a preemptive strike. 'Okay,' she said, grabbing her teaspoon and gently tapping it a few times against her teacup. 'Who's going to go first?'

'Pardon?' Vivian asked.

'Dolly's right. We look like we're at a funeral. We're friends, and friends confide in one another. So let's have it. Dolly? You first.'

'Wh . . . Why do I have to go first? Your problems are probably a lot more interesting than mine. You go first. Or the House of Windsor over here.' Vivian said nothing. She took a sip of her tea, gingerly placed the cup down onto the saucer.

'Fine, then, I'll go,' Laura said. And go she did: with the story of the horrors of the past few weeks, how after standing up to Marmy she'd gone to see Pete, and everything that happened afterward. A week after his blistering indictment of her on the rainy street in the Village, she'd written him a letter and left it at the bookstore with Connie but again had received no reply. When she reached the part about Pete confessing he'd fallen in love with her, Dolly openly gasped. Even Vivian raised an eyebrow. 'Oh dear,' she said, returning to her milky tea.

Laura sank back into her own chair. 'I should have just gone back to Smith.'

'Why on earth would you say that?' Dolly interjected. 'You were dating two good guys. One of them broke it off with you because he didn't know about the other. But keep something in mind, dearie — you've still *got* the other. That's a lot more than most of the girls can say in this place. And not just any other, either: Box Barnes. You make it sound like if you had been forced to choose, you would have picked the bartender. Don't you love Box?'

This is where Vivian would have normally erupted, raising her cup and issuing some pithy accolade like, 'Hickey for the prosecution!' But she remained silent, eyeing Laura cautiously. 'You're being very quiet,' Laura offered.

'I think our Dolores here has posed an interesting question. And I think it would make you feel better to answer.'

'What if I don't know the answer?'

'Then perhaps you really do know the answer.'

Did she? Laura pondered the question, looking over again at the two women at the corner table. It was nice to see at least a few of the Women happy, that was certain. Laura didn't realize how rare it was until now.

Is that what love looks like? she wondered. Love had to be deeper than that, than a glance over tea, which was indicative but not dispositive. She laughed to herself. Wouldn't Mrs. Harris, who had taught her eighth-grade grammar, be proud of her command of the language? Be proud that her pupil was now in New York, working for *Mademoiselle* magazine?

Stop it! she admonished herself. She questioned whether everyone else's mind was as jumbled as hers seemed to always be, a random traffic jam of disparate thoughts: thinking about life's big questions, along with what she wanted for dinner, where she had last worn her silk scarf, trying to remember the name of the restaurant Box had taken her to last week, and the name of Audrey Hepburn's princess character in *Roman Holiday*. She worried that it was some sort of disease she had, this propensity to think in odd puzzles, problems and worries and joys and memories and random song lyrics all crashing into one another inside her head. Did everyone walk around like this, trying to sort it all out every moment of the day? Or was she some wild schizophrenic, headed for a psychic break?

'I'm very fond of Box,' she finally managed, instantly hating how it came out.

'Oh, I'm sure he'll be quite relieved,' Vivian muttered.

'Well, I think you're nuts,' Dolly offered. 'He's absolutely dreamy, he's rich, and he's obviously cuckoo for you.' She shook her head. 'Pretty girls and their problems.'

'You need to stop saying things like that,' Laura said. 'It only demeans you. And me, for that matter. But particularly you. It's unattractive.'

'I have to agree,' Vivian piped in. 'Your self-esteem cannot still be this low, not with that lumberjack you're snogging.'

Laura delivered Vivian a cautionary look

224

— the things that could come out of the girl's mouth — while also being secretly pleased: The old Vivian was making a long-overdue guest appearance.

'Well, truth is,' Dolly said, evidently freed by both Laura's own confession of misery and this sudden vote of confidence, 'things with Jack aren't really . . . progressing.'

'Oh my,' Vivian said, looking around for the serving girl. 'I'm going to need more tea for this.'

Ten minutes later Vivian had a fresh pot and Dolly had finished her own tale, of Jack's secrecy and her theory that he was either married, homosexual, or — God willing — simply inexperienced with women. She was amazed that instead of feeling embarrassed or ashamed, she actually felt . . . lighter. The weight of carrying around her faux romance was slowly lessening, if only within the confines of the room.

'I wouldn't worry about it,' Laura said. 'Men come at these things each in their own way, and in their own time.'

'You're off your trolley,' Vivian retorted. She reached for a biscuit and the clotted cream. 'Am I the only one eating?'

'You don't know — '

Dolly cut Laura off. 'No, no, I want to hear what she has to say. Because no matter how rude she gets, at least I know she's always telling me the truth. Go ahead, Vivian.'

'Personally, he sounds like a bender to me,' Vivian said. 'Not that I mind them, of course. We have a waiter at the Stork of that particular variety who's actually quite lovely, and I've had one or two help me pick out some darling clothes at Tomas. But for your purposes, it's a waste of time. Luckily it's all easily sorted out. The next time you're alone, simply kiss him, good and cracking, then grab him by the knob. If it's all mashed potato down there, then you have your answer.'

Dolly sighed wearily. 'It's as good a plan as any. I certainly can't keep going around like this. The uncertainty is worse than having no boyfriend at all.'

'And you, Lady Windsor?' Laura offered. 'Now that we've both offered true confessions, what's been eating at you lately? You haven't seemed yourself.'

I should tell them, Vivian thought, and for a moment she almost did. They were the closest thing she'd ever had to real girlfriends. And yet something held her back. She was afraid. Not so much of their judgment — she was used to that from people — but of their pity. She couldn't face the prospect of their pity.

'Another time, my loves,' she said, rising from her chair and leaning over to give each girl a peck on the cheek. 'All of this tea has wreaked havoc with my kidneys, so must dash to the loo, then into the lift to get some rest before work. But thank you for the tea and the chat. I'm feeling better already.'

Do it, she willed herself, hurrying down the stairs toward the mezzanine.

Do it now, while you have the courage.

A few minutes later she slipped into a phone booth, lifted the receiver, and swung her finger around the dial. 'Operator,' the nasal voice intoned.

'Overseas operator, please. I'd like to phone England. Reverse the charges.'

★   ★   ★

Wednesday night had somehow turned, unofficially at least, into Laura's weekly date night with Box. They saw one another other days as well, and most weekends, but Wednesdays had somehow turned sacrosanct, even though neither of them had officially claimed it for the other. Laura worked late, typing up notes for a writer about a Broadway actress the writer had interviewed, and felt almost too tired to go out. But she had begun looking forward to these Wednesdays more and more, in part because they tended to be more relaxed than the weekend, often nothing more than she and Box sitting in some red-sauce joint, slurping spaghetti and talking about their day-to-day lives.

Laura was standing in the lobby of the Barbizon when the matron on duty behind the front desk beckoned her over with the crook of her finger. 'Letter came for you,' she said, thrusting an envelope that had her name and the hotel's, but no stamp. Hand-delivered.

She plopped down on one of the sofas and ripped it open, silently praying for Pete's handwriting. Instead she unfolded a flyer and a piece of stationery with the logo for MacDougal Books & Letters across the top. A note from Connie.

Dearest Laura, As soon as I booked this reading, I thought of you. I hope you can make it — I know you're a fan! C.

She picked up the flyer.

PLEASE JOIN US FOR A SPECIAL EVENING WITH CHRISTOPHER WELSH, AUTHOR OF 'WILL THE GIRL AND OTHER STORIES,' AS HE READS A PREVIEW CHAPTER FROM HIS NEW NOVEL, 'WONDERLAND.' SATURDAY, NOVEMBER 5TH, 7 PM. COFFEE AND PUNCH RECEPTION WITH THE AUTHOR FOLLOWS.

That was a month from now. She wondered if Pete had ever bothered to read *Will the Girl* after her review on the beach in Atlantic City. She doubted it. Surely he would avoid any reminders of her at all. Perhaps he had stopped coming into Connie's shop in fear of bumping into her.

'Penny for your thoughts,' came a voice as Box leaned down and kissed her. He was in a henley and blue jeans, accented by a tight black leather jacket. It made him look like a college student dressing up as Marlon Brando in *The Wild One*.

'This is a new look.'

He smiled, stepped back. 'What do you think? I'm trying to branch out of the whole New York-to-Newport axis.'

'I'm reserving judgment. Where're we going? I'm guessing neither the opera nor the Plaza.'

'We,' he said, sliding his arm around her, 'are going to my apartment. I have a surprise for you.'

She felt a sudden unease. 'Who else is going to be there?'

He laughed. 'Is my company not entertaining enough for you?'

'I just . . . I've never been to your apartment.'

'Because I've never made you dinner before. I guess there goes the surprise. But I feel it's time I share my exceptional culinary skills, so you can see there is more to love about me than just my amazing hair and my employee discount at Barnes & Foster.'

They stood by the exit, Oscar the doorman looking at them through the glass expectantly, again trying to gauge whether to swing open the door because they were going to walk out or whether he was about to witness the start of a fight between a girl and her boyfriend, played out in the lobby for all to see. Some of the Barbizon brawls — crying girls, boys standing palms up, baffled — were legendary. Even Agnes Ford had engaged in one.

Laura and Box had kissed, of course, often passionately — in a carriage clip-clopping through the city, in the mezzanine of the Imperial Theatre — and she had allowed things once or twice to progress to 'second base,' Box's fingers and hands dexterous and warm on her breasts, causing sensations she had only read about. But it was precisely this expertise of his that was causing her so much distress in this moment: After four months and a romantic dinner in his apartment, a dinner he had made himself, what would he expect then? And was she prepared to give it to him?

'You know how I know you're a writer?' he asked, devilment sparkling in his eyes as poor

229

Oscar still lingered outside, waiting for a sign.

Something in his eyes put her at ease. He had that ability. 'No. Tell me.'

'Because I can read you like a book,' he said. He leaned over, brushing his lips on her temple. 'You worry too much,' he whispered. 'I wasn't planning on serving the dinner in the bedroom. There'll be time enough for that in the future.'

And with that he put his arm around her waist as the front door of the Barbizon swung open, Oscar smiling broadly as Box Barnes and his lovely girlfriend Laura Dixon stepped out into the crisp autumn evening.

*   *   *

His apartment, in a whitewashed slate building on the Upper East Side, was more masculine than she'd imagined, though intellectually she knew that made little sense. For some reason, she had always pictured him living in Gene Tierney's apartment in *Laura*, replete with crystal chandelier and an imposing self-portrait in oil hung above the fireplace.

Instead she found an attractive, spartan, open space of gleaming oak hardwood floors and beige throw rugs, with long windowpanes framed in black metal and accented with plain white shades with pull cords, each of which covered precisely half the window. Facing the fireplace in the living room was a long sofa with a rounded back covered in forest-green velvet, along with a glass coffee table stacked with art books and a

230

black Ludwig Mies van der Rohe Barcelona chair. Built-in mahogany bookshelves on either side of the windows held an eclectic assortment of novels, war histories, biographies, and essays, along with what looked like several scrapbooks and photo albums. A pewter Hans Arne Jacobsen pendant lamp hung above the rectangular dining room table, which like the bookshelves was mahogany and burnished to a shine.

Laura sauntered into the tiny galley kitchen, sipping her chilled glass of wine as Box stirred creamy white sauce on the stovetop, a large pot of spaghetti bubbling on the opposite burner. 'That does not look like something Agnes Ford would eat,' she said casually.

He turned to look at her, his expression flat. 'Why would you mention *her*?'

She eyed him quizzically. 'Because she's a famous model and very skinny and she happens to live in my building and periodically appear in the magazine I work for,' she answered.

He muttered, 'Oh,' then returned to his stirring. 'Fettuccine carbonara,' he remarked, a bit too eager to return to the subject of the cooking. 'I want you to know I only make this for very special guests.'

'Like Agnes Ford?' she said, and instantly regretted it.

His eyes glazed over. 'What's that supposed to mean?'

'I . . . I don't know. You tell me. It's just when I mentioned her you seemed to jump. Do you know her?'

'Of course I know her. She's a model in New

York. I run a department store.'

'That's not what I meant.'

'Then by all means, Laura, why don't you tell me what you mean? You know how I love your outspokenness.' He turned up the burner on the fettuccine, his eyes never leaving the stove.

Too far down the road to turn back now. 'All right,' she said quietly, placing her wineglass on the kitchen counter. 'Did you date her?'

'I thought you had already done all of your research on me.'

She winced. A few weeks into their relationship, she'd made the mistake of telling him that she'd spent the better part of an afternoon in the Street & Smith's library, scanning through whirring panels of old microfiche to read gossip column accounts of his many, many (many) dates. She thought it would show Hepburn spunk. Instead, he'd been livid, accusing her of succumbing to jealousy and the vacuous thirst for scandal that was a well-known trait of the Barbizon girls. Worse had been how he had *looked:* hurt and betrayed. They hadn't spoken for the following three days; it had taken her that long to realize he'd been right. She'd gift-wrapped a box of matches and dropped it at Barnes & Foster, with a note that said, 'I used these to burn the microfiche. I'm sorry.' They'd never discussed it again.

'I'm not accusing you of anything. I'm simply asking if you dated her.'

He put down the spoon, turned to her. 'Yes, I did. And for the record, she was the one who ended it. Though that doesn't really fit neatly into the 'Box Barnes, noted womanizer' narrative that plays so well in the rags. Of which I too often forget you are a part.' He glanced back over at the simmering noodles. 'Dinner'll be ready in a minute. I'll refill your wine.'

She took hold of his forearm as he tried to pass her to the icebox. 'I'm sorry,' she whispered. 'You have to be patient. This is all very new to me.'

'I've been patient, Laura. I've also made mistakes. The difference between us is yours aren't archived at the public library. Yes, I've dated a lot of girls. Yes, I've treated a fair number of them badly. I was young and stupid, and I couldn't handle all of the attention. That's not an excuse, merely an explanation. But I've tried to . . . change. You've been a big part of that. That night at the Stork, I was just so ashamed of the way I behaved. I knew you deserved better, and I wanted to *be* better, to deserve you. But it'll never work between us if you don't learn to trust me.'

'I'm trying. But you don't understand what it's like on the other side of this, to be the girl who's dating the guy every other girl wants.'

'That's not true. I'm — '

'It *is* true. You may not look at those girls at the Barbizon, or in the theaters, or in the restaurants, and that's to your credit. But I do. I can't help it. They're everywhere.'

'Including the San Remo?'

The blunt force of the sneak attack staggered her, and she felt her heart pounding. She was about to ask what he was talking about, but she knew what he was talking about and, further-more, *he* knew that she knew what he was talking about. They'd crossed over the line of playful hide-and-seek.

'You've been spying on me?' She said it slowly, carefully, half accusation, half incredulousness.

'That's right, Laura, I've been in a trench coat and a fedora and dark glasses, shadowing your every move.' He shook his head, brushed past her to retrieve a quart of beer from the icebox. 'Not all of my haunts require a tux, Laura. I have friends in low places, too.'

'And you never said anything.'

He poured the beer into a Pilsner glass. 'No. Because it wasn't any of my business. We were dating. We didn't have any exclusive understanding. Which is why your jealousy is so irritating.'

'I am not jealous. I asked a simple question, that's all. And I'm not the one who was getting secret reports on *your* dating life.'

He took a hard swig of his beer. 'Are you still seeing him?'

'Don't you know the answer?'

'Laura, please. To borrow your phrase, it's a simple question. Are you?'

She was inclined to sass, to tell him it was none of his business. But the truth was that it was, in fact, his business. Just as it had been Pete's. 'No, I'm not. It ended weeks ago.'

There was silence for a good minute, the only sound the increasingly ferocious bubbling of the boiling water on the stove. Laura stepped over, flicked off the gas. 'The spaghetti's going to be overcooked.'

When she turned back around he was directly in front of her, his arms around her, pulling her close. 'I know I'm coming off as a jerk, and I don't mean to. I have a past, and it's only logical you'd be wary. But I know you feel it, Laura. I know you feel what's in my heart, and what I hope is in yours. So let's commit to it, right here. Right now. From here on out, nobody else. Just us. Because I think . . . ' She could see how desperately he wanted to say the words but couldn't yet. She pressed her index finger to his lips, searched his eyes.

'Just us,' she whispered.

And then she kissed him, his mouth hungry on hers, until dinner was forgotten.

18

'Viv? Viv? Sweetie, you okay in there?' Barbara, one of the coat-check girls, was knocking gently on the door.

'I'm fine, fine. Sorry. Just some bad shrimp from last night, I'm afraid. Out in a jiffy.'

Still kneeling, she weakly pushed down the lever to flush the toilet, then fell back on her haunches, resting the back of her head against the stall door. *Good Christ, Vivian,* she admonished herself, *how did you get here?*

The clock was ticking, ever louder, every day. Her telegram to England, sent before this latest terrible development, had gone unanswered. Her collect phone call last week, unaccepted. ('We don't take no collect calls in this house, especially from the likes of her,' her father had snapped to the overseas operator before abruptly hanging up.)

Oh, how foolish I've been. How utterly, totally, completely foolish.

Because England was where her road had really diverted, she realized now. Back there, at the engagement party, where she'd decided just for devilment to see if Emma's fiancé would go a round with her if she worked him hard enough, just so she'd always have that for herself, the knowledge that she could have had him if she'd wanted him, that Emma — smart, educated, always-our-good-girl, always-better-than-Vivian

236

Emma — had, for once, lost in a battle of the Dwerryhouse sisters. Every year growing up, she had watched her parents dote on Emma, praise Emma, nurture Emma, leaving her the prodigal daughter who just hadn't left home. Until she did.

If only Mary hadn't found them. What harm would have come of it? A knowing smile, a wink to herself in the years hence, a silent satisfaction that for once she had triumphed? But Mary *had* found them, out by the shed in the rose garden, and had of course done what Mary always did, run and tattle, and of course Aunt Maude had been close enough to see the two of them hurrying up the path, Devin's shirt-tail still untucked. They'd only kissed, maybe a bit of fondling, but the damage was done.

Emma had milked it for every ounce, canceling the wedding, shrieking that her life was over, that Vivian had always been jealous, always hateful, always there to trip her up when she had been nothing but kind and giving. Her parents' wrath had been swift, brutal, and, it now appeared, permanent.

And what had she cared? She had always planned on coming to America anyway. So she took the money they shoved at her to disappear and happily obliged. And things had been going good — or at least okay — until Nicky had showed up. Slick, pretty, possessive Nicky and his wad of bills, asking her to sing to him that night, filling so many of her nights afterward. She had been so casual, so sure she could discard him into the bin like a piece of used tissue, as she had done with the men who had come before. She'd stupidly hung on too long, clinging to the chance for the audition and succumbing to the dark pleasure of channeling Monroe.

And that's when the trouble had really started. He had begun popping up unexpectedly, checking on her. They'd have a down-and-out row — they'd just had another two nights ago — and she would think she was free of all of it, only to have him reappear three days later, yellow roses in hand, begging forgiveness and confessing to the sin of simply loving her too much. He'd become addicted to spontaneous, dangerous sex, which had left her no time to plan. Which is how she had ended up sick as a dog on the floor of the loo.

There was no money and no one to send passage. England was out. She knew no one outside of New York. And she had to get out of New York. Especially now. It was going to be extremely difficult to break it off under normal circumstances. If he found this out, he'd never let her go. Ever.

But suppose I do get out. Then what? she wondered. Spend nine months in hiding? Give the little thing up, then saunter back into the Stork, pick up her cigarette tray, and start serving again?

There has to be a way out of this. I have a little time. I just need a bit more thinking to find the answer.

★ ★ ★

And then the answer walked through the door of the Stork Club. Vivian heard him before she saw him.

'Hey, Babs! Looking great, kid! How ya doin'?!'

Act.

It was still a half-hour before opening, and Vivian was stocking her tray. She quickly darted out of the supply closet and found none other than Jimmy Stewart himself, *her* Jimmy Stewart, 'Act,' leaning by the entrance to the coatroom, charming the knickers off of wide-eyed Barbara.

Vivian was not a person of faith, despite how handy the church had turned out to be as a cover for her Sunday-morning entrances back into the Barbizon. But surely this was not merely Act. This was an Act of God.

'Well, if it ain't Rita Hayworth herself!' he said as she walked toward him, arms outstretched. He hugged her tightly. She could not recall a time in her entire life when she had ever been so glad to see another person.

He looked good, as he always did, just as he had that night in June, the night of the infamous post — *Seven-Year-Itch* shag in the alley that had sent her tumbling down the rabbit hole in which she now found herself trapped. He wore a dark gray suit and a navy raincoat and held a black-banded gray fedora in his hand.

'You look terrific, kid, as good as the last time,' Act said, holding her by the arms as he appraised her. 'You still kicking around with the Eye-talian?'

'Something like that,' Vivian managed. 'What

239

brings you here, Mr. Stewart?'

'This,' he answered, waving a long white envelope with the Stork logo emblazoned in the corner. 'Been thinking about moving on from Toots. Me and the bandleader not seeing eye to eye these days. Mr. B. was nice enough to offer a reference if I needed it. So I decided to swing by and pick it up. And you, sweetheart? How you been? Life treatin' you good?'

This was her chance.

Take it.

'Why don't I tell you all about it as I walk you out,' Vivian said, threading her arm through his. 'Barbara, I'll be right back. Just going to do a quick catch-up with our Act here.'

Telling the truth turned out to be far harder than she'd anticipated. Five minutes of inane small talk had passed outside the club, and she hadn't gotten to anything of importance. He looked at his watch.

'Well — '

'Act, darling, I need a favor,' she blurted out.

Her desperation mushroomed through the air. He placed a hand on her arm. 'Honey, what's wrong?'

Vivian looked around, careful that no one was within earshot. She found herself shivering. She looked him squarely in the eye. 'I'm in trouble, Act. The worst kind of trouble a girl can get herself into.'

She forced herself to look at him. There was no recrimination, no harsh verdict. Only grave concern. 'I see. How far along are you?'

'Not much. But enough. I need help. And I

240

have no one to turn to. I'm so sorry to put you in this position, darling. If I — '

He grabbed both of her hands in his. 'Hey, hey, there's no need for that kind of talk. We're friends, Viv. Always. You had my back with Mr. B. more than once, and don't think I forget it, neither.' He looked up, as if searching the sky for options. 'I have a sister in Ohio. I could call her — '

'No, Act, you don't understand. I need to *correct* this situation. To make it . . . *disappear.*' She watched the impact of her request slowly creep across his face. 'I know you know a lot of people. All sorts of people. Maybe the sort of people who help girls out.'

He nodded. 'I got ya,' he said softly. He was quiet for a bit, and she couldn't tell whether he was thinking of how to help her or having some sort of internal moral debate. 'Let me see what I can do. I'll call you here at the club in a few days. A week, tops. Don't do anything or talk to anyone about this until you hear from me, okay? We'll get you all taken care of. Good as new. Don't worry. Act's got your back, sweetie.'

Vivian flung her arms around his neck, kissing him on the temple. 'Oh, darling, *darling* Act. I knew I could count on you,' she said. 'Thank you.'

In her rush of relief, she never noticed Nicola Accardi standing in a doorway across the street, his latest bouquet of yellow apology roses wilting in his hand.

★ ★ ★

241

'So, what did you think?' Dolly asked as they walked out of the movie theater and headed up Forty-Second Street. They were going for pastry and hot chocolate at the Coffee Mill on West Fifty-Sixth.

'I don't know,' said Ruth, with a bit of a whine. Dolly had come to notice that whenever Ruth was in a bad mood or commenting negatively about something, she always sounded like she was in the midst of a terrible stomachache. 'I'm getting tired of all of these movies where the women are either sexpots or absolute drips. For once I'd like to see myself in a movie.'

'Oh, *that* would sell tickets!' howled Miriam. Dolly had finally confirmed it was Miriam, not Marion.

They'd just left a screening of *My Sister Eileen*, which Dolly had originally wanted to see with Laura, given that it was about a girl trying to be a writer in New York, but pinning Laura down had become downright impossible. 'I kinda liked it,' Dolly chimed in. 'But I like this sort of stuff anyway. I thought the songs were catchy. And that Jack Lemmon . . . swoon!'

'Double swoon!' added Miriam, patting her heart.

They were about to make the left to go uptown at Seventh Avenue, still giggling over Lemmon, when Dolly saw him standing in the flashing glow of Times Square, laughing.

His back was to her, but she knew it was him. Frank. Her Frank. Frank from Utica, Frank who had been her fella but who had never quite

242

embraced her as his girl, who had ridiculed her for her weight and always kept her at arm's length, like a shopper mulling over a purchase but really convinced there was a better deal to be had two racks over.

Dolly unconsciously began drifting toward him to get a better look. The girl on his arm was short, shorter than Dolly by at least an inch, but slim and sandy-haired. She kept turning in profile to say something to him, exposing beady eyes that were too close together, giving her the appearance of a slightly softer, younger Miss Gulch, without the bicycle and the agenda to kill Toto.

Dolly couldn't stay away, even as she was engaged in an internal dialogue begging herself not to do this, to not be *that* girl. She ran up behind them, put a gentle hand on Frank's shoulder. 'Hey, stranger!' she said, in a syrupy voice she didn't even recognize.

Miss Gulch whipped around first, followed by him. Dolly took a step backward. A stranger's quizzical face looked back at her. 'I'm sorry, do I — '

'No,' Dolly hastily replied. 'I'm . . . I'm so sorry. I thought you were someone else. I'm sorry. Sorry.' She began backpedaling down Forty-Second Street, bumping into pedestrians as the man shrugged and walked away with his date.

'Honey, what is it? What's the matter?' Ruth was saying, tugging on her jacket sleeve.

Dolly turned, plastered on the biggest fake smile she could muster. 'Nothing! I thought I

243

saw someone I knew. Now,' she said, walking ahead authoritatively, 'I hope they have rice pudding. I'm starving.'

By the time they sat down at a table, the voice inside her head, the one she had paved over with inane jibber-jabber during the walk here, returned in full force. Because no, it had not been Frank in Times Square with another girl. But he was out somewhere with another girl. While she was here, dating a phantom who had once again begged off this week, vanishing into his cave. Wherever that was.

There is just something missing in me. They all have something I don't, and I'm tired of trying to figure out what it is. I can't be Laura. I can't be Vivian. I'll never be them. I am Ruth, and I am Miriam.

I am the Women.

I go to movies and I am going to grow old alone and be an aunt and grow geraniums in pots and volunteer at church bake sales and work in an office until one day they hand me a bouquet of flowers and a silver picture frame and wish me well in retirement. That is my destiny. I need to accept it. I need to stop believing there is a guy out there for me. Because there isn't. There just isn't.

She ordered coffee and a slice of apple pie á la mode, then slowly tuned back into the conversation, Ruth fretting about how she was ever going to save enough money for that alpaca coat at Bonwit's.

19

Like Mrs. Blackwell herself, editorial meetings at *Mademoiselle* were brisk and officious. The senior staff met weekly and sometimes more than that in her soigné office, but once a month the entire staff poured into the conference room for an update on the current issue and logistical planning for the next several. Laura had attended her first meeting in July, and like her fellow 'college editors' at the time had served merely as window dressing, there to look pretty, stay quiet, and observe. Now, as an editorial assistant, she was supposed to take diligent notes on anything to do with features, and to have with her any and all backup material that might be associated with stories that were scheduled for upcoming issues.

She was stationed in her usual spot, in the back with the other entry-level girls, away from the long, shiny conference table. Mrs. Blackwell sat at the head, perfectly accessorized in a gray Mainbocher suit and pearls, peering over her reading glasses as she looked over a contact sheet of fashion photographs. She appeared peeved.

'I asked for hats with the coats,' she announced. 'Half of these photos have no hats.'

There were a few seconds of awkward silence before one of the art directors spoke up. 'Well, yes, I know that's what we'd discussed, but some of the hair was so beautiful we thought it was a shame to hide it all under hats, so we — '

'Must I go on every photo shoot to ensure that my instructions are carried out? Is that where we are, Bill? Because no self-respecting girl goes out in the middle of winter with a lovely coat and no hat. Because, you see, it doesn't matter if her hair looks smashing if it's covered in sleet and snow. Or if she catches the flu as a result.' She flung the contact sheet back on top of the file. 'I want the red Vera Maxwell and the beige Scaasi reshot — with hats.'

'Of course, Mrs. Blackwell,' Bill replied, writing furiously in his copybook.

The rest of the meeting passed by in a similar vein — Mrs. Blackwell complaining about a boring story on the overshirt trend ('If it were any more dull we could prescribe it for insomnia'), wondering why she was being forced into hosting a luncheon for wives of the armed forces ('They're not our readers, and I don't understand who decided my time was so irrelevant that I could do this'), and pointedly dressing down two beauty assistants in the rear of the room who were caught chewing gum ('This is not the girls' room at Chumley's, ladies').

Woo boy, Laura thought as she exited the meeting with the others. *I'd hate to be in her crosshairs today.*

She was halfway down the hall, coming back from the managing editor's office, when she spotted them sitting on top of her desk, a tall crystal vase of what appeared to be two dozen long-stemmed lavender roses.

246

There were a handful of girls congregated around her desk as she approached, their faces conveying the mixture of giddiness, envy, and jealousy she had come to recognize since the day she'd walked back into *Mademoiselle* after the item about her and Box had been published in Nancy Randolph's column. Last week her name had popped up in Ed Sullivan's, as the 'young *Mademoiselle* editor who's charmed Box Barnes.' Still, flower deliveries weren't uncommon at *Mademoiselle*. It was, however, unusual to see this many girls standing at her desk, ogling.

Laura downplayed her own bursting of joy — better not to appear gloating — and plucked the card from the bouquet and opened it. Inside were three simple words.

LOOK BEHIND YOU.

She spun around, and there stood Box a few feet away. The tittering over the flowers suddenly made sense. 'Surprise,' he said, walking over and kissing her. Laura could hear the sighing all around her, felt her cheeks reddening with conspicuousness. 'Have time for a quick cup of coffee?' he asked.

A few minutes later they were in a diner around the corner. 'What are you doing next Saturday night?' he asked.

'Don't know yet. Hopefully whatever it is you're doing next Saturday night,' she said, laughing.

'I was counting on you saying that. My folks have decided to throw an impromptu cocktail party for their thirtieth wedding anniversary, and I wanted to know if you would come with me.

They were actually supposed to have it for their twenty-fifth, but then Dad ended up having his gallbladder out. So they're going for thirty. What do you say? Ready for the whole Barnes experience?'

Meeting the family. Wouldn't Marmy be impressed.

'Of course, I'd love to. Where is it?'

'Their place, Seventy-Third and Park. I'll pick you up around seven.'

Laura nestled into the booth. 'What will I wear? This is pressure.'

'Well, as it happens I — '

'I know, I know, you know a great department store. That was not a hint. I'll buy my own dress.'

'Why don't you just wear the one I bought you for our night at Elmo's?'

'Because the Barbizon has already seen me in that. And what fun would that be?'

He provided a few more details, and the more she heard, the more nervous Laura got. This was not going to be some idle cocktail party for two dozen people. This was a full-blown extravaganza, with a band and butlers and Veuve Clicquot inside the Barneses' Park Avenue penthouse. She was half listening, trying to figure out how she was going to afford a decent dress for a soirée this fancy, when she caught a snippet of his lament about a singer. Evidently the band's female singer had been called back home on an emergency of some kind, and Mrs. Barnes had reluctantly decided that a strictly instrumental affair was her only option.

Laura leaned forward. 'Vivian could sing!'

'Vivian the British redhead?' He'd met her one night after the theater, when Laura had arranged for them to see Vivian and Nicky for a drink. Any hopes for fraternal bonding among the boys had quickly dissipated. It became very clear, immediately, that Nicky thought Box a spoiled prig, and Box thought Nicky an uncouth thug. Reading his thoughts, she said, 'She wouldn't bring the Italian. It would be work. But I know it would mean so much to her to sing in front of a crowd like that. Please, please . . . can you just consider it?'

He put his hand on hers. 'I will consider anything for you. Tell you what: Why don't I come to the Barbizon this week and hear her sing something? Although I don't know if those prison-guard matrons will let me outside the lobby.'

'No, no, they will. You can bring male guests to some of the lounges if you get a pass. I'm sure we could get you into the one with the piano. Oh, this is going to be great!'

Back at the office, Laura spent the afternoon peppily typing correspondence. For the first time since she'd come to New York, she was feeling the true magic of the city. She had a job at one of the nation's most prestigious magazines. She was dating a handsome man who adored her. She'd made wonderful friends — and gotten out from underneath the oppressive watch of her mother. Everything was falling into place . . .

'Mrs. Blackwell wants to see you,' Cat Eyes harrumphed, passing by her desk. 'Now.'

249

This day just keeps getting better! Laura thought. She grabbed her leather-bound notebook — Mrs. Blackwell had a well-known aversion to steno pads, which she thought made a girl look working class — and headed down the hall. She wished she'd had time to pop into the ladies' room to reapply her lipstick.

Laura tapped lightly on the open door. 'You wanted to see me, Mrs. Blackwell?'

The editor sat at her French provincial writing desk penning a note in her elegant script but never looked up. 'Come in, please, Miss Dixon.'

Laura didn't know what it was — her lack of eye contact, the flecks of ice in her tone, her rigid posture behind the desk — but instantly she knew that this was not going to be the convivial encounter she'd imagined. Betsy Blackwell was angry. From the forceful strokes of her pen, quite so.

Laura stood in front of the desk, the adrenaline flowing like a dam break, the drop of anxiety into the pit of her stomach hard and fast. For what felt like an hour, the only sound in the office was the editor's strident scribbling. Finally, Mrs. Blackwell put down the silver pen and looked up. Her stare was pure poison.

'How long have you been with us now, Miss Dixon?'

Laura cleared her throat. 'Um, about four months, ma'am. Two as a college editor, and now almost two as an editorial assistant.'

'I see. And you're enjoying your work here, are you?'

'Very much so, ma'am.'

250

'And you'd like to continue in this position, I assume?'

Oh my God! What's going on? 'Yes, ma'am.' It was almost a whisper.

'I see. Well, that's most reassuring. You might understand my confusion, given your rising public profile as a celebrity both in and outside of this office. One might gather from the press that it was you, rather than I, who was editing this magazine.'

The *Daily News* item. Ed Sullivan. Box's visit. Too many roses. 'I'm sorry . . . if you feel I have shown any impertinence,' Laura said, slowly and carefully. 'I am, of course, extremely grateful for this opportunity. I'm afraid I am a bit out of my depth with some of these columnists.'

'That is apparent. Perhaps it might be wise to step out of the glaring spotlight of your apparently very active social life and concentrate a bit more on your professional duties. There is so much competition in publishing today. I would hate to see you take a step backward in your career.' She put her reading glasses back on, picked up her pen. 'Of course; that's only my opinion. Your life is your own. Good afternoon, Miss Dixon.'

'Thank you, Mrs. Blackwell.'

As she walked to the door, Laura heard a final warning emanating from behind the desk. 'There's an old Chinese proverb that might be worth remembering,' Mrs. Blackwell said. ''The light that burns brightest burns briefest.''

★ ★ ★

Can I do this? I mean, can I really, truly do this?

Dolly estimated that she had asked herself this at least a hundred times in the last hour alone. Maybe more.

I can't do this.

You have to do this!

She flopped back onto her bed, rubbing her eyes. She felt a headache coming on.

The door opened and Laura walked in, tossing her bag on the dresser, then slowly pulling off her gloves, one finger at a time. Dolly propped up on her elbows. 'You look terrible,' she said.

'It's lovely to see you too, Dolly.'

'Bad day?'

'The baddest. I just want to get out of these clothes, get into a hot tub, and then go to bed.'

Dolly looked over at the clock. 'It's not even seven.'

'Precisely,' Laura said, kicking off her heels. 'I swear if that girl down the hall with the frizzy hair has tied up the tub again, I am going to take an ax and chop down the bathroom door.'

'I wouldn't worry about it. I saw her in the coffee shop a half-hour ago. It looked like she was waiting for a date.' She eyed Laura warily. 'Wanna talk about it?'

'No.' Laura began peeling off her stockings. 'You look nice. Going out?'

'A date. With Jack.'

'Ah! The elusive one returns. See? I told you. Where are you going?'

'Just to the diner. I have a — ' She stopped herself.

Laura stopped. 'You have a what?'

For once in your life, Dolores Mary Hickey, do not go blabbing all of your business all over town. For once! 'Nothing,' she said, scooping up her sweater and handbag. 'I better get downstairs.'

She was in the elevator, staring at the back of the zaftig elevator operator and lumbering toward the lobby, before she dared to even allow herself to complete the aborted sentence inside her own head.

I have a plan.

20

The girl was young — she couldn't have been more than eighteen, nineteen at best — and had long, blond hair that Vivian knew would, when the time came, be swept up into a glamorous updo, smooth and silken, like a just-fired piece of pottery. But for now she stood in the middle of the tiny stage at the Stork looking slightly disheveled, and more than a little panicked, as all singers did before their big shots, before their debuts at notable nightclubs. Vivian had seen the look before. She'd just never had the opportunity to see it on her own face. Perhaps she never would.

Mr. Billingsley sat at a nearby table, nervously thrumming his fingers. He was always nervously thrumming his fingers, as if he were the owner not of a successful nightclub but rather of a grand theater packed with patrons, and his mezzo-soprano was locked in her dressing room, refusing to come out. The only time he seemed truly relaxed was during his weekly Friday luncheon that he hosted for the models living inside the Barbizon, a courtesy he extended to ensure their regular attendance inside his nightspot and, it was presumed, to satisfy his own desire to be alone in a room once a week surrounded by beautiful women.

'Fresh meat tonight,' Bennie the busboy whispered.

'What do you know about her?' Vivian asked.

'Nuttin', really. Same old stuff. She's sleeping with the right guy who knows the right guy who knows Sherm.' He stopped for a minute, appraising the new singer more closely. 'Bet she cleans up nice, though.' He vanished through the kitchen doors.

'Okay, let's try it from the top,' the bandleader was saying. Vivian kept standing, absently futzing with her tray, her eyes never leaving the stage as the ingénue delivered a serviceable if shaky rendition of 'Come on-a My House.' Mr. Billingsley hated ballads. He felt they brought down a room, got people out of a party mood — death in the nightclub business, which counted almost exclusively on not only getting people into a party mood, but keeping them in it a good, long, lubricated while. This was often a problem when auditioning singers, most of whom came from a place of torchy yearning; ballads were their stock and trade. They often came to the Stork for their 'big break,' only to have the torch quickly extinguished, a steady stream of peppy standards fit for the Andrews Sisters in their wake.

No stage presence, Vivian emitted in silent verdict. *I hate that song. But I would have sold it. And the patrons would have bought it.*

But what did it matter, anyway? Her 'one shot' had turned out to be a sham. She'd gotten herself into what polite society delicately called 'trouble.' She had no money. No family to turn to. And a beau — she was being kind; it simply sounded better than 'brute' — who had gone

255

from pursuant to attentive to tenacious to controlling. What came after controlling? And did it require a gun?

Bennie rolled a cart of dishes by. 'Babs says you got a visitor out front.'

Vivian closed her eyes. This had been the most recent development: the surprise pop-in at the club. Stunningly, most of the other girls never scratched beneath its surface, saw it for what it really was, instead devolving into misplaced, dewy-eyed envy at Vivian's good fortune in landing a romantic rake. Nicky brought flowers, chocolates, and once, curiously, a record album by Al Martino.

She took in a deep breath, whooshed it out, and walked into the lobby. She had a part to play.

He turned around as she approached, and her heart leapt. 'Act,' she said, stepping into his embrace. 'Darling Act.'

He smiled at her, took her hand in his. 'Come, walk out with me.'

They went outside, under the red awning above the entrance that proudly displayed in stenciled letters STORK CLUB. 'Viv, are you really sure you want to go through with this? There are other ways to deal with this, you know. I can arrange to get you of town, taken care of, until the — '

She cut him off. 'Yes, I'm sure. Really.' She couldn't allow him to complete the sentence, to hear the phrase 'the baby's born' out loud. As long as no one said it out loud, she could pretend it wasn't a possibility, that all of this wasn't really happening at all. She looked at him seriously. 'I do appreciate everything you're doing. I know I've left you at sixes and sevens.'

'I'm glad to help. Any way you need.' He dove into his pocket, fished out a scrap of paper. 'Here's the address where they can . . . take care of you. It's in the Bronx. I got you an appointment two days from now, at noon. You have to go around to the side entrance. The building's not well marked, so it doesn't look like anything, but it's the right place. There's a sign on the side door that says 'Private Office.' Just ring the buzzer, and when the intercom comes on, tell 'em you're there to see a Mrs. Hutchins.'

'Mrs. Hutchins? She's a doctor?'

'Not exactly. She used to be a midwife. Now she just sort of . . . fixes things. It's all on the up-and-up. I wouldn't send you anyplace that wasn't safe. It's quiet and out of the way, and they'll have you all taken care of in few hours. But you're probably going to have to call in sick to work that night.'

'Who do I pay?'

'Don't worry. I took care of it.'

'Act, I can't — '

He cut her off. 'Vivvy, listen to me: I got it. You asked for my help, and my help is what you're gonna get. I know you hate asking anybody for anything, but this is one time when you're just going to have to swallow it. I'd go with you myself, but they don't like men coming in. Makes people suspicious.'

She felt tears coming on. Maybe it was her

hormones, or just the shell she'd built around herself, buried herself inside for so long, finally cracking. She hugged him tightly, clutching the piece of paper. 'I can't thank you enough, darling. Truly.'

'You're going to be okay, kid, don't worry. My number's on the bottom of the paper. Call me after, let me know how you're making out, if you need anything, okay?'

She nodded. 'Okay.'

Vivian walked back into the Stork, exhaling again, for the first time feeling some of the weight lifting off of her shoulders.

Act replaced his fedora and turned onto Fifty-Third. He didn't see the figure crossing diagonally from the other side, casually following him up the street.

★ ★ ★

'I couldn't eat another bite,' Dolly said as she and Jack crossed Houston Street onto First Avenue. This, of course, was a lie: he'd decided they needed a change of scenery and dragged her down to the Lower East Side to Katz's Delicatessen, and she'd been dying, *dying*, for one of Katz's famous hot pastrami sandwiches. But if months living inside the Barbizon had taught her anything, it was that girls were supposed to eat daintily with their dates. It was fine for him to wolf down a big, juicy Reuben, but you were supposed to settle for the scoop of chicken salad on lettuce or, if you were feeling wild, perhaps a BLT.

'I'm stuffed, too,' he said, laughing. 'Wanna walk a bit?'

'Sure.'

They talked about the things couples talk about when they walk through the streets: movies, television, their families — Jack's brother and sister-in-law were expecting a child any minute. She was making progress, unearthing his family tree (two brothers, both married, no sisters), his favorite passion (the Dodgers), and what scared him the most (dancing, which he confessed he had 'no aptitude' for).

He seemed chattier tonight, more relaxed. All the better to implement the Plan, which she'd divided into two parts: Warm-Up and Brazen.

'It gets so chilly in October,' she said, rubbing her arms. She had deliberately worn a sweater far too delicate for the weather. 'You forget how cold it can get at night in the fall here.'

'You're cold,' he said. 'Here, take my jacket.'

'Oh, no. I don't want to do that. Let's try this.' She nuzzled close to him, leaning her body into his, simultaneously placing his right arm over her shoulder as she slipped her left around his waist. 'Oh, that's better. Good and toasty.'

They'd walked a good block when he turned to her and said, 'This is nice, walking with you like this.'

Dolly smiled, careful not to smile too much, saying nothing, as inside her brain exploded: *Yes! Yes, yes, yes, yes, yes, yes!!*

It was absurd to be this happy, over a guy whom she had technically been dating for months, for the simple act of him finally showing some affection. Affection she'd had to manipulate into existence. She was just as thrilled to push that thought right out of her head, to simply luxuriate in what was happening between them right now. No matter what else, no one could take this away from her, this moment on First Avenue, strolling uptown with the guy she was crazy about, the guy who was dating her, not any other girl at the Barbizon, the guy who had his arm draped around her for all the world to see, declaring, *This is my girl.*

When they reached Union Square, he said, 'We should probably catch the subway from here,' because, after all, they weren't going to walk all the way up to East Sixty-Third Street, no matter how lovely an evening it was, even though she would have walked up all the way to East Sixty-Third Street, and probably 163rd Street, if it meant pouring even more into this memory that wasn't yet a memory.

She looked around, searching for a place for the next move. Did she really want to risk completely ruining Part Warm-Up to instigate Part Brazen? Maybe she should take what she'd gotten, save the rest for another day.

No, that's not what we agreed to, Dolly told herself, wondering if other people talked to themselves in the plural. *We said we were going to implement the Plan, and we are going to implement the Plan. Don't chicken out now.*

She looked around as they descended the subway steps. She could hear people on the platform below, but took a quick glance behind her and saw no one else following them down.

Now.

In a lightning-quick motion, she took hold of his arm, turning him around on the step below her midway down the stairs. He looked at her with both expectancy and slight bemusement, as if he thought she was going to say something very important and he needed to pay attention carefully. 'What is it? What's wrong?'

'I . . . nothing. I — '

She grabbed his face with both hands, pulled it forcefully to her own, and kissed him, boldly, passionately, hungrily, like Jane Wyman after she discovered Rock Hudson's true identity in *Magnificent Obsession*. She darted her tongue into his mouth, kept her hands around his head like a vise. And as he responded, returning the ferocity of the kiss and pulling her into an embrace so snug her left foot lifted off the step, she thought she might just pass out, right there on the subway staircase, and realized if she did and cracked her head and bled out all over the platform, she wouldn't care, because it would have been worth it.

The sound of footsteps behind them broke them apart. A pair of smirking teenage boys threaded their way past. Jack looked into her eyes and broke out into a grin that came and then went, his eyes admiring but slightly scared. What did it matter? She'd spent enough time trying to read the tea leaves of his heart. She wouldn't anymore. The moment may have been over, but it was hers and only hers. She would preserve it no matter what.

She grabbed his hand. 'Let's go. I hear the subway coming!'

They scrambled onto the uptown number 6 train just as the doors closed, Dolly already reconstructing how she would relay the entire story to Laura, detail by delicious detail.

21

'Well, don't you look posh?' Vivian said as she entered Laura's room. Laura stood in front of the dresser, screwing on her earrings.

'Thanks,' she said. 'Though I would give my eye teeth for a full-length mirror. It amazes me that in an entire hotel full of women there is not one full-length mirror for public consumption.' She turned to Vivian. 'You look 'posh' yourself.'

'Just an old frock I keep on hand in case someone calls to ask me to sing for the upper crust.' She wore a plain but beautiful form-fitting dress of deep garnet that hugged her every curve, ending tightly midway between knee and ankle. Her lustrous red hair was swept back dramatically on one side, held in place by a stunning clip of twinkling jewels in the shape of two angel's wings.

'Good Lord,' Laura said, coming over to inspect the barrette. 'Are those real?'

'I imagine so. A gift from Nicky.'

'He's very generous.'

'Among other things.' She didn't say it as a compliment. 'Where's Dolores?'

Laura had never asked Vivian why she had suddenly stopped calling Dolly 'Ethel.' She didn't want to jinx it. But every time she heard her use Dolly's actual name, it still threw her, just a bit.

'She's getting dressed in Ruth's room. I think

she sees this more as a great unveiling.'

'Do I even want to ask what she's wearing?'

'Something borrowed, something blue, even if she's not getting married. Box arranged for her to take something from the racks. But I have reminded her three times now that she cannot keep it and absolutely cannot spill anything on it.'

'A gauntlet thrown down if ever there was. I'm amazed you managed to get her invited to a party thrown by Box Barnes's parents.'

It hadn't been easy. It was one thing to get Box to advocate for Vivian singing — Vivian was a singer by trade, or at least by aspiration, and the Barbizon had enough of a reputation for housing starlets that after she'd sung for Box earlier in the week, it hadn't taken all that much to get his parents to accept his recommendation and agree. Dolly was another story. But as soon as Laura had confirmed Vivian had the singing job, she'd known she *had* to find some way to get Dolly into the party. It would have killed Dolly not to come. And like most of the girls in the hotel, she was still mourning James Dean, killed in that awful car crash.

Though she had seemed noticeably brighter since things with the mysterious Jack were finally progressing. Dolly had relayed the story of their subway kiss as if it were the greatest love story ever told.

Vivian, too, seemed a bit lighter. Laura had been meaning to talk to her, find out what had been bothering her. Now here they were, alone. 'We had to come up with a tiny white lie,' Laura said. 'Box told his parents that Dolly is my roommate — from Smith. And that we had this visit planned ages ago, so would it be okay if I brought her. So as long as no one else from Smith shows up and starts quizzing Dolly about Mountain Day or Paradise Pond, we should be all right.' She drifted back over to the bureau, dropping lipstick and mints into her clutch. 'And you?' she asked, a bit too airily. 'How are you?'

'I'm well, thank you.' Even with her back to her, Laura could feel Vivian's eyes on her, wary, alert. Vivian was not the kind of girl you could glean information from through polite chitchat. It was direct or nothing.

Laura sat down on the bed next to her. 'Vivian, we're friends, aren't we?'

'Of course. Someone has to guide you through these delicate years of your burgeoning woman-hood.'

'Come on, I'm serious. I consider you a friend, a good friend. I hope you consider me one, too. We haven't known one another long, but I care about you. If there's ever anything you need to talk about or are worried about, I hope you feel you could tell me.'

She looked into Vivian's face, pleading for an opening. These past weeks had been confusing — at times Vivian would pipe up with her snappy British comebacks; during others, she would appear completely shut down, either walking by distractedly in the lobby or vanishing from view for days, not answering knocks to her door. Looking at her now Laura could see a glimmer of something, a small chip in Vivian's always-stunning façade, and yearned for a gap that would become wider, so she might discover what was really going on underneath. She could almost hear Vivian internally arguing: *How much do I trust this girl?*

'Well, truth be told — '

'Ta-da!!!' Dolly yelled as she burst through the apartment door. 'Dolores, the Countess de Barbizon, will now receive her subjects!'

It was the happiest Laura had ever seen her. Dolly practically shimmered in her loaned Charles James gown, which featured a relaxed bodice draped with gray chiffon, overlaid with delicate lace that wrapped at the hips and was secured with a pearl fastener before blossoming out into a full ball skirt that tickled the ankle. Vivian walked over to her, delivering a tender side hug. 'Breathtaking, my dear. I knew you had it in you.'

Vivian flung her wrap over her shoulder and headed for the door. She was going to catch a quick smoke and would meet them outside.

* * *

Franklin and Topsy Barnes — her real name was Millicent, though everyone in New York, including its best society columnists, called her Topsy, because that was what rich old moneyed people did, they came up with ludicrous nicknames — stood in the foyer of their grand Park Avenue penthouse as if they were an ambassador and his wife, welcoming guests to

266

their first state dinner. Box's father was stocky, with a bright, flushed complexion the color of Pepto-Bismol, appearing the way that English lords did in Revolutionary War paintings. Topsy was more serene, her face all sharp angles and taut lines. She was the kind of woman people called handsome.

'Mother, Dad, I'd like you to meet Laura Dixon,' Box said in introduction, as Laura extended her hand. 'And this is her visiting friend, Dolores Hickey.'

'I'm just so honored to be here,' Dolly gushed, instantly feeling like she already sounded like an imbecile and thinking, *How am I going to get through this whole party without sounding like someone who doesn't belong here?*

Laura had wanted to bring a gift, but Box had steadfastly forbidden it — evidently bringing gifts to the affluent was a social error of the highest order, a notice that Marmy had evidently never received. Just last year her mother had thrown herself a birthday brunch and not only expected but fully encouraged beautifully wrapped presents.

'So this is the young lady we've been hearing about,' Franklin said.

'And reading about,' added Topsy, with a petrified smile that threatened to snap her face in half. Thus began a series of quick peppery questions, ranging from Laura's collegiate status ('Oh, I see,' was all Topsy managed upon hearing of Laura's semester deferment) to her debutante ball to her parents' biographies. When the quiz progressed to the location of Aunt Marjorie's house on Nantucket, Box said, 'Lots of people left to greet, Mother, don't want to monopolize you,' and swept Laura and Dolly into the grandeur of the Barneses' apartment.

The room glittered with the flickering of a hundred tapered candles. The buffet featured duck à l'orange, rare roast beef with a creamy horseradish sauce, goose with chestnut stuffing, and shrimp and crab étouffée, a banquet fit for the Ghost of Christmas Present. Laura sipped a gin fizz as two men next to her argued about whether Ike had really suffered a heart attack in Denver last month, and whether his administration was covering it up. 'Nobody wants Dick Nixon in the White House, that's for sure,' one of them was saying.

A little while later Topsy Barnes reappeared, putting a gentle arm around Box. 'My dear,' she said to Laura, 'would you mind if his mother stole Benjamin away for just a moment?'

'No, of course,' Laura said, and wandered off to find Dolly.

Box's eyes remained straight ahead. 'Don't start, Mother. Please.'

'On the contrary,' Topsy said, deftly plucking a flute of champagne off the tray of a passing waiter, 'I wanted to congratulate you. She's exquisite.'

Box took a swig of bourbon. 'You've left off the last half of that sentence: ' . . . as opposed to that last tart you were seeing.''

'Now, now, dear, it's our anniversary party. Let's be cordial, shall we? But I will say, this one is a vast improvement. A Greenwich debutante who attends Smith.'

Box spied Laura across the room. 'She makes me want to be a better person.'

'Do you love her?'

Box eyed her evenly. 'Since when do you care about whom I love?'

'Your father and I only want your happiness, Bennie.'

'My father and you want to make sure that your money stays where you can control it.'

Topsy delivered a short, brittle laugh, the kind perfected through years of charity golf outings and opera galas. She leaned over and kissed Box on the cheek before drifting back into the midst of her fine party.

* * *

It was an hour and many introductions later — to a Broadway actress, to the vice president of Macy's, to a congressman — when Laura found Dolly, now standing in a corner, delicately navigating a stuffed olive into her mouth. 'How do fancy people eat?' Dolly asked. 'Seriously! This is like trial by fire, to see who can eat the sloppiest food and stay the neatest. And another thing: All of this food is nothing but cream and butter! How do these women all stay so thin?'

'Cigarettes, scotch, and diuretics,' Laura answered.

'Wait. Box is making an announcement.'

Box was standing in front of the twelve-piece orchestra, welcoming guests. With his sister by

269

his side, he gave a brief but loving toast to his parents, culminating in the assemblage raising glasses to assorted *Here-heres*! 'As a special treat,' he continued, 'I'd like you all to welcome a very special guest we have with us tonight, one of the fastest-rising stars in New York's musical scene. Ladies and gentleman, I give you the stylings of the lovely Vivian Windsor.'

Dolly slipped her hand into Laura's, and like proud parents they watched from the back as Vivian walked behind the silver microphone amid polite applause. *I love him for doing this*, Laura thought.

Or maybe I just love him.

As Vivian sang her voice became more tremulous, clear and beautiful in its convincing desperation and longing.

> '*There's a somebody I'm longing to see*
> *I hope that he turns out to be . . .* '

'Someone to watch over me. How about it?' a voice whispered in Laura's ear; Box, reaching an arm around her waist. Delicately drinking her punch, Dolly tried not to sneak peeks and was thoroughly unsuccessful.

'How about what?' Laura asked.

'Someone to watch over you.'

'Are you volunteering for the job?'

'Are you accepting applications?'

They laughed, and he took her hand. 'C'mon. Let's get some air.'

'The orchestra is right by the terrace door.'

'I am a man of many methods. C'mon.'

270

Laura was about to protest — she didn't want Vivian to watch her dashing out in the middle of her set — but Dolly's wild shooing motions and urgent mouthing of *Go, go!* finally made her relent.

They slipped out of the front door and hustled down the hall, walking past the elevators to the stairwell. A minute later they were on the roof, which to Laura's surprise had been landscaped with huge stone urns and patio chairs and tables, and had clearly been used for summer entertaining. Laura turned to see New York laid out before her like a magic carpet, Central Park on the right, the twinkling lights of the Plaza to the left. She gathered her wrap around her. 'It's beautiful up here.'

'So are you,' he said, folding her into his arms and kissing her.

'You're always surprising me,' she said.

'The roof can be an oasis. It can take you away. Out of yourself.'

'It's like *To Catch a Thief*. Only we're in New York instead of Monte Carlo.' They'd seen it last month. She nuzzled her head into his chest.

'You're still chasing Grace Kelly.'

'I'm lucky this isn't seven years ago. Or you'd be standing up here with her and not me.'

'I could stand here with you forever, Laura.'

She looked at him, her eyes shining. The pale moonlight washed over the roof, gave it the feeling of standing inside a painting. 'I can't imagine anyone ever saying anything lovelier to me.'

'I'd like to try,' he whispered. He stepped back

271

and in one swift motion dropped to his knee, gazing up at her. 'I love you, Laura Dixon. And I don't want to ever have to imagine my life without you. Will you marry me?'

22

Vivian stepped off the number 5 train, avoiding eye contact with anyone, hidden beneath her head scarf and sunglasses. The calendar said late October but the weather said deep winter, and there was a kind of camaraderie wrought by the unseasonable cold that seemed to spread among the passengers as they scrambled up the steps onto the street, bundling against the headwinds as they dispersed.

Vivian didn't feel it. Not the cold, not the wind, not anything. What she needed was focus. Fretting about the weather was a distraction she could ill afford. At least the day was finally here. She would take care of this, bolt-cut this final shackle to Nicky, and move on. She had enough money to get out of New York — maybe not that far, but at least far enough where he wouldn't find her. She would book bus fare to somewhere in the Midwest — somewhere nondescript, anonymous — and would get a room, get a job, hide. She'd start over. Wasn't that her expertise by now, reinvention? Kansas City — that sounded suitably awful. Or perhaps Wichita. At least that had a certain scratchiness to it, like an old saloon town. She would spend a year keeping her head down and her savings up, until she had enough to get all the way to L.A. Anything could happen to you, or for you, in Hollywood.

Vivian separated from the other riders, looking

at the directions she'd managed to scribble from the street map. A few more blocks straight ahead, then a left, then a quick right. She picked up the pace. She was early, but in a situation like this it never hurt to be too early.

I need a cigarette.

She leaned against the pole of a traffic light, her hands shaky as she flicked the lighter to life and inhaled a long, slow drag. A woman pushing a stroller was approaching. She looked tired. Her hair was an ashy blond, and she wore an open heavy wool coat thrown over a summer blouse and cigarette pants. She was pushing the stroller with her left hand and holding the hand of a little girl of about four in her right, yanking the child like a rag doll every time she dared to dawdle.

The girl suddenly ripped free of her mother and dashed to retrieve a perfect crisp leaf under a nearby oak tree. 'Look, Mommy! Can we put this in my book?'

'Deborah Elaine Marks! You come back over here right now!'

Undaunted, the girl skipped over and held up the leaf to show her mother, as if she were presenting a priceless piece of art.

The mother slapped the leaf out of her hand and grabbed her wrist. The girl dissolved into tears of protest.

'Oh, I'll give you something to cry about, missy,' the mother barked. Vivian stood, her mind going back to a moment at Franklin and Topsy Barnes's party. Later in the evening a gentleman had approached her, introduced himself. He was chairing a gala at his country club out in Westchester, he said. Might she be available to sing? In May.

Vivian stamped out the cigarette butt and pulled her coat around her, began walking again.

At first she thought she had the wrong place. Then she saw the sign, barely discernible from the sidewalk, with its tiny letters: PRIVATE OFFICE. For the first time today, she wished she hadn't come alone. She'd almost told Laura the truth, asked her to come — what if something went wrong? But it was better this way. Better not to involve anyone else. This was her mess.

She took a deep breath and buzzed the intercom. It crackled to life. 'Hallo. I have an appointment to see Mrs. Hutchins.'

The door opened, and she gasped.

'Hello, Ruby,' Nicola Accardi said, his dark eyes slicing into her. 'Come in. I've been expecting you.'

* * *

The question popped out at Laura on every corner, in every stoplight, in the face of every passerby she saw as she stared out of the window of the taxicab:

What are you going to do?

Dolly sat on the other side, chattering on about one of the many dramas playing inside the Barbizon. Laura didn't hear a word. She kept staring out the window, through the blur of folks hurrying along Fifth Avenue, for an answer.

275

Box's proposal had been romantic and impulsive, but also sudden. As a young girl, she had often daydreamed of her marriage proposal, of sitting in a tree swing somewhere in a park after a lovely picnic lunch and having her great love fall to his knee, ring box in hand, and pledge his undying troth. As the years passed, the proposal changed — sometimes it was on the beach, sometimes in the corner booth of a swanky restaurant — but there was always one constant: She knew it was coming.

Even now, she couldn't remember specifically how she had responded after he'd asked. He'd been hurt, she could tell, that she hadn't instantly fallen into his arms, ready to go back to the party and make the grand announcement. Eventually she'd managed to explain that she was simply out of breath; that she needed time to really think about it; that, yes, she cared deeply for him; yes, of course she had thought about marrying him; and yes, she thought he was the moon and a thousand stars. But she was practical. He hadn't even met her parents, and they had a lot to discuss before they could be sure it was the right thing to do: How soon would he want to start a family? Would she go back to Smith? Would she have to quit *Mademoiselle?* And this way he, too, could have the time to be absolutely sure. And, she'd said with a smile, at least go shopping for a ring.

Two weeks later, she was as confused as ever.

You do love him, she thought. *You know you do.*

What was holding her back? He was the prince of the city. So why couldn't she silence this little voice, deep inside, asking, 'Are you sure?'

'You're not listening to a word I've said!' Dolly said in exasperation, smacking her arm. 'Where are you, anyway? It's like you're in outer space these days!'

'Sorry. I'm a bit preoccupied.' She'd told no one. She most certainly was not going to tell Marmy until she absolutely had to. She didn't need any more clutter inside her head. But what was this constant ruminating getting her? She had to tell someone.

'Actually,' she confided, 'I've been keeping a secret.'

If there was anything that got Dolly more excited than having a secret, it was hearing one. Her eyes lit up like firecrackers. 'What?'

Laura said it casually, the way you might tell someone you were going shopping tomorrow. 'Box asked me to marry him.'

It went the way Laura expected: Dolly's jaw dropping, eyes ballooning, mouth inhaling, hands flying to her face, then grabbing onto Laura's forearm like a wrench with a lug nut. 'Far-out! I am so *thrilled* for you!!' She almost leapt across the back of the cab, crushing Laura in a bear hug. The cabbie gave a glance in the rearview.

Then: How did he propose? When? When were they getting married? In New York or out on the Cape? Was her mother ecstatic? Where would they live? Had they talked about children? When was the *Times* announcement going to be

277

published? Did Vivian know? Would it be in *Town & Country*?

Laura knew she'd just made a huge mistake.

'Honey, honey,' she said quietly, interrupting Dolly's game of *Twenty Questions*. 'I haven't given Box an answer yet.'

Dolly didn't seem to know what to do with this information. Evidently it had never occurred to her that someone — at least anyone with her mental faculties intact — might actually debate a marriage proposal from Box Barnes.

'It's just a lot to think about,' Laura said, relaying how Box had caught her off-guard on the roof the night of the party, and how she had concerns about their future, her work, all of it. 'When I get married I want to make sure I do it once, and that I do it with the man I know will make me happy, and I will make happy, for the rest of my life. Is that so unreasonable? It's the biggest decision I am ever going to make. I want to feel completely sure about it.'

Dolly seemed to be trying to actually consider this, though it still appeared to completely baffle her. 'How did he take your . . . delay?'

'He understands. I'm doing this as much for him as I am for me.'

'Do you love him?'

'Yes.'

'Then that's all that matters, you silly goose!'

There was something to be envied in that sort of simplicity of conviction. Laura wanted to believe that love was all that mattered. But her own parents' marriage — a slow, steady descent into a chilly garden-party partnership — told her

278

otherwise. She leaned forward in the back seat. 'It's here on the right, driver,' she said, as the cab slowly pulled to a stop.

★ ★ ★

Dolly had asked to come to Christopher Welsh's reading for one reason, Laura knew — she was as curious as Laura was to meet an actual author. Dolly admitted she would have much preferred meeting Grace Metalious, the housewife who had written the spicy novel about Peyton Place, but circumstances being what they were, she'd settle for the writer who had captured Laura's attention.

Laura had come for a slightly different reason. She admired Welsh's stories, yes, but more than that she loved how he threaded them together, into one interconnecting narrative that leapt off the page. Deep down she knew there was another reason she'd come. She'd wondered if Pete would be here.

The back of MacDougal Books & Letters had been arranged with a small podium and three small rows of folding chairs. There were about half a dozen people already here; Laura recognized two of them as beats from the San Remo. Connie was at the front, hurrying back and forth between the podium and a side table, where he'd set up a coffeepot and pitchers of cider, soda, and iced tea, along with a tray of sad-looking cookies. His rear left shirttail had come undone from his trousers, and his brow line showed nervous beads of perspiration.

'Why, hello!' he said warmly as Laura approached. He gave her a warm hug as Laura reintroduced Dolly.

Connie filled Laura in on the Village gossip and his own recent adventures, including his recent auction bid on a letter from Jane Appleton Pierce, wife of President Franklin. 'Did you know that her eleven-year-old son was killed in a train accident *two months* before the inauguration? Horrible. She spent the entire four years of the administration in mourning. Draped the entire White House in black.'

'And people think Mamie has it tough,' Dolly said.

Laura chuckled. 'Who thinks Mamie has it tough?'

Connie was about to issue a comment when he spied someone over her shoulder walking in. 'Ah! Our guest of honor has arrived.'

Laura turned.

Pete.

It took only a few seconds for all of the pieces to tumble into perfect, interlocking place. The banter at the San Remo the day she'd first walked in during the summer, her putting his own book on the bar. The probing of her opinion of it that day in Atlantic City. His insistence that she was a writer if she believed she was a writer, his experiment of making her close her eyes and describe the scene on the Steel Pier . . . It all made perfect sense now — why she had been so torn, why she had started to fall for him. He'd understood her from a perspective no one else could.

'Hmmm,' Dolly was saying in her ear. 'He's cute, in a sort of lunch-pail kind of way.'

Laura couldn't speak. Her gaze was fixed on Pete, who was shrugging off his pea coat and laughing with Connie. For the briefest of seconds their eyes met, his stare empty, impenetrable. She wanted to walk out but knew she couldn't. He'd already scored the element of surprise. 'C'mon, let's sit down,' she said.

Following Connie's introduction, Pete gave some brief background on his new novel-in-progress, *Wonderland*, an allegory of Alice in Wonderland about 'a young girl trying to find herself in the big city,' and before he shared a word of it, Laura knew instinctively that it was about her. Or at minimum a version of her. For fifteen minutes the cozy audience sat rapt in the back of the bookstore listening to his lively storytelling, relaying a passage about the heroine as she found herself torn between two very different men who were in some ways nothing like Pete and Box, but who were also very clearly Pete and Box. His eyes occasionally grazed her sightline in the back row but never lingered. Connie stood to the side, beaming like a proud papa.

After the reading and a few questions from the audience, Connie stepped to the front. 'We invite you all to stay and enjoy some refreshments with us and to meet Christopher. Copies of Chris's first collection of short stories are available for purchase and signing.'

'I'm actually glad I came,' Dolly was saying, sliding an arm into her coat. 'Can I borrow his book from you?'

'No,' Laura blurted out. 'Sorry. I mean, the whole point of coming to a reading is to support the author. You should buy a copy, get him to sign it.'

Dolly did, seemingly thrilled to be chatting with a real live author as he scrawled a dedication. Laura remained glued in her chair, unable or perhaps simply unwilling to move, hoping to make him feel as uncomfortable as she did. The more she rolled around his deception the angrier she became, both at him and also Connie, who had clearly known that she had been dating Christopher Welsh the entire time and never bothered to say a word.

To her surprise, Pete broke free from a conversation with three young men, walked over, and wordlessly sank down onto the chair next to her. They sat in silence for a full thirty seconds, both looking ahead at the leftover crowd still mingling by the refreshments. To the right, Connie erupted into laughter with a middle-aged couple. Evidently he'd moved on from discussing Jane Pierce's mourning.

'I know you're angry,' he said quietly, still staring ahead. 'But it's not what you think.'

'How could you possibly know what I think?' The words came out in a hiss, and she scolded herself for it.

He exhaled wearily. 'I wanted you to get to know me, the real me, not some guy on a printed page. I was going to tell you. Actually, I had planned on telling you the night I read about you and Box Barnes in the paper. It just didn't seem to matter after that.'

Laura shook her head. 'It would have mattered. It does matter.'

'Why? Because I would have been a more worthy competitor for your affections if you'd known I was a published writer?'

'Don't you dare try to play the victim here. The secret you've kept is far bigger and far more meaningful than the one I did.'

'That's open to question.'

She laughed derisively. 'I love the new stuff. Very creative. Wherever did you get the idea?'

'She's not you.'

'You could have fooled me. Oh, wait. You did.'

'Believe it or not, you're not the only girl to ever come to New York to try and find out who she is. Yes, there are elements of you. I would never deny that. But there are elements of a lot of other people, too. That's what novels are: They're amalgams of archetypes, collections of random traits one observes in other people through life, blended into fresh characters.'

'Please don't lecture me like I am some freshman sitting in your writing seminar.'

'I'm sorry. You may be angry with me for not telling you who I was. But you seem to be conveniently forgetting that you left out a rather important detail of who you were. I risked my heart on you and lost. Can you honestly say you did the same?'

She remained silent. She wanted to hold her anger but instead found her fury slowly dissipating, like the air out of a flattening tire. Why couldn't she stay mad at him? ''Christopher Welsh'?'

'Christopher is my middle name. Welsh is my grandmother's maiden name. I didn't think anyone would take 'Pete Kelly' seriously as a literary figure.'

Her laugh was laced with something bitter. 'That's funny. I did.' She stood up, grabbed her coat. 'Well, at least you got what you wanted from me, right?' she said. 'An unvarnished review of your work. And lucky for you, it was a rave. Delivered without agenda.'

'That isn't what I wanted from you,' he said, rising. 'And you know it.'

She looked away, digging into her handbag to retrieve her copy of *Will the Girl and Other Stories*. 'Here,' she said, handing him a pen. 'Sign it.'

He hesitated but then took the pen and, leaning the book against the back of a folding chair, jotted down the inscription and handed it back to her with the pen. She took both, casually dropped them into her bag, and, coat over her arm, walked silently out of the shop, Dolly scurrying from across the room to catch up.

Later that night, alone and locked in the security of the hall bathroom, she extracted the book and opened it to the dedication page. *To Laura*, it read. *One of the city's finest new writers*. He'd signed it simply, *CW*.

She didn't know why she was crying.

23

No matter how many times she entered it, Dolly never lost her sense of awe at the sheer majesty of Central Park. To her it was like its own city within a city, or perhaps more of a kingdom, the kind of place where there should be a castle in the middle, complete with a moat and a drawbridge and a turret soaring to the clouds with a pretty lady fair peeking from the window.

Jack had called and asked to meet, told her he needed to talk to her about something, and had suggested the park. Her initial reaction had been panic — *He's going to tell me something awful* — but the more she thought about it, the more she'd been able to convince herself otherwise.

The last few weeks had been, in a word, heaven. Since her brazen overture to him in the subway, it seemed like he had come alive, at least in the romantic sense, affectionate and flirtatious and even occasionally earthy. It was as if someone had cut him free of a self-imposed restraint, and he seemed to relish her in a way he hadn't before, in her kisses and her touch and her fingers through his bristly hair. She'd switched on a light somewhere inside him, and she couldn't fathom that he'd ever want to return to darkness. Thank God, she'd ignored all of that advice in *Cosmopolitan* about the virtues of patience and coy, ladylike aloofness.

A police car sat idling up ahead, and she

quickly dashed toward it, stooping down in front of the passenger side-view mirror to check her hair, hat, and lipstick. She gave the cop behind the wheel a casual wave of thanks. He smiled, tipping his finger to his hat.

They'd agreed to meet on a bench near the Great Lawn, and as Dolly took a seat, smoothing her beige wool coat underneath her and daintily crossing her ankles behind her, she hoped she hadn't gotten the location wrong. Central Park was lovely, but it was also enormous — 843 acres enormous. You could spend days inside it and not find one another.

A few minutes later, he walked up. And she knew.

His face was slack, pallid, his jawline too rigid. His hands were shoved deeply into the pockets of his trench, and even as he issued a gentle 'Hi' as he approached, it wasn't enough to diffuse what his body language was not simply telling but screaming. She felt the pit of her stomach twist into a knot so painful she almost cried out, as her mind pleaded that what she was about to hear would not be what she was about to hear.

He sat down on the bench next to her, looking out at a group of children playing.

She searched his profile for something, anything to allay her exploding fear. A few months. A few wonderful, intoxicating months when she'd been smart enough to hold back, to stay guarded, to perhaps keep an illusion going for her girlfriends but always telling herself the truth inside, to protect, to make sure she didn't believe her own publicity, to make sure that she never took her focus off of her duty, which was to protect the heart she had already subjected to too much disappointment through poor judgment and bad luck and needy craving. Then the night in the subway had happened, and she'd let go because she was so very tired of *not* letting go. The jury verdict had come in and she'd been declared loved, and she'd basked in it, submerged herself in it, drowned in it. It was finally her turn. And now it was over before it had ever really started. Laura got a proposal, and she got what she always got: The excuses varied, but the delivery was always startlingly constant. He would tell her what a great girl she was, how she was going to find the right guy to appreciate her, how he was messed up or unfocused or whatever excuse guys accessed to open the escape hatch and parachute out, and then he would kiss her chastely and walk away, exhaling a mental *Well, that's done* as he wound his way through Central Park to the rest of his life, never once looking back at the scorched earth he'd left behind.

He glanced over. 'You look nice.'

Dolly closed her eyes, forced herself to breathe.

'Thanks for meeting me,' he began, more of a stammer than statement, and for a second she wondered if she should just stand up and walk away first — some shred of dignity in the closing act. But the little voice inside her head said, *Don't jump to conclusions* and *Maybe he's just tired* and *Hear him out* and all of the other trite things the mind conjures in its fey efforts to

287

overtake the raw truth of the heart, and in her hesitation she sentenced herself to the entire awful scene. She would spend the foreseeable future going over every second of every date they'd ever had, going all the way back to that first eye contact across the restaurant, looking for the clues she'd missed that would have told her that she hadn't had any true happiness at all, and beating herself to a pulp for the wrong comment she'd made this night or the wrong dress she'd worn that day, and asking herself, over and over and over, how he could have seen emptiness where she saw blossoming love.

The November chill seeped into her bones, and she began to shiver. Jack reached out for her gloved hand. 'Dolly, you know, you are one of the most special girls I've ever — '

'Stop.' She looked directly into his eyes, hunting for reprieve and failing. 'I don't think I can take the whole speech, Jack. Correct me if I am wrong — please, *please*, correct me if I'm wrong, because I have never, ever in my life wanted to be wrong as much as I do right now — but you're ending things, am I right?'

He looked back at her but couldn't hold her stare. 'It's more complicated than that.'

'No, it's not. It's a yes-or-no question, Jack. Are you or aren't you?'

He shook his head. 'I can't . . . It's . . . It's my fault. All my fault. Believe me, I know that, and I feel more horrible about it than you could ever know. I really liked you. Like you. I just . . . I had no right to let things get this far when I knew I wasn't . . . '

'What? Wasn't what?'

He sighed, threw his head into his hands. 'Available.'

She sat paralyzed. She wondered if she would ever be able to move again. Years from now they would find her, a skeleton in a plain cloth coat and hat, tethered to this park bench like a haunted house attraction. 'You're married,' she whispered, through the catch in her voice.

He shook his head. 'No.'

'Engaged, then?'

'No.'

'Well, then, how serious is it? I don't understand. You said you're not available. Who is this girl —'

'Dolly, there is no other girl, I swear.' He squared up and tried to regain his composure, as if he were delivering a presentation in front of a boardroom of clients and had forgotten his storyboards. Her eyes traveled wildly around his face, trying to unearth clues in every tic and movement. 'It's just so complicated. I should have never let it get this far —'

'Stop saying that! Don't treat me like I'm some sort of bad mistake you're going to regret for the rest of your life.' Tears began streaming down her cheeks. 'I don't understand any of this. Are you . . . are you' — she fought to spit the word out — 'queer?'

He spun around, horrified. 'Of course not!' A couple walking by glanced over, embarrassed to witness the dramatics. Jack popped up off the bench, once again shoved his hands into his coat pockets. 'I know I owe you a better explanation,' he said. 'I do. I consider myself an honorable man, and yet I am standing here acting dishonorably. I regret it, bitterly. And I accept that this is all of my own doing. You're blameless. I apologize, deeply, for hurting you, for leading you on. You were just such a . . . ' He trailed off.

She reached out to grab his sleeve. 'Jack, please. Let's go somewhere, get a cup of coffee, talk about this. You're not making any sense. I know you care for me. I know it. A girl can tell when a guy is real. You're real.'

He leaned down and delivered the kiss she'd known was coming all along. 'I am so sorry, Dolly. Truly sorry. I hope one day you can find it in your heart to forgive me. But I can't do this. I'm sorry.'

She sat, still as a statue, until she could be certain that he had rounded the park path out of view and earshot. And then she collapsed, suddenly and violently, into tears for the next hour and a half, darkness engulfing Central Park and the lonely form of the sobbing girl within it.

★　★　★

He was going to kill her.

Opening her compact in the ladies' room, it crossed Vivian's mind that not only had she almost been murdered, but that once again she was right back where she'd started, in the very same ladies' room she had retched in the day Act had shown up for his reference. She pressed the powder puff into the beige makeup and slowly began applying it to her swollen cheek. The welt,

290

red and purple speckled with yellow, sent pain scorching through her face as the pad made contact, and she winced. She'd have to endure it. She couldn't sell cigarettes with a huge bruise on her face. Luckily she had the long-sleeved dress on tonight. No one would see her arm.

She'd tried to run. She knew that nothing good would come by going through that door in the Bronx, Nicky on the other side of it, but in her shock at seeing his face she'd hesitated, and before she knew what was happening, he'd pulled her in and slammed the door. The words — evil, masochistic, foul — had come first, a low growl that quickly accelerated into violent screams. Vivian had no idea if there were other people left inside the office, whether there was another young woman now cowering somewhere down the hall, shivering in fear in a dressing gown and wondering if she was going to be next.

Nicky hauled back and punched her right in the face, sending her careening across an examination table and tumbling into a corner. Vivian had seen raw anger up close, witnessed it more than once in her own house growing up, but never in her life had she seen such ferocious hate in a man's eyes. As she put her hands to the floor, trying to get to her feet, he'd yanked her up by the arm and pinned her to the wall.

'You think you were going to get away with it, you dumb British bitch? Huh?! You were going to kill my bambino, my son? Fuck you! You think you can do this and not answer to me? To God?!' He shook her violently, his breath hot and acrid on her face. 'You're lucky you're carrying my precious child. Because if not, I would *kill* you right here, right this minute!'

He'd raised his hand to strike her again, and she'd yelled out the only thing she could think to yell out. 'No, Nicky! The baby! You'll hurt the baby!'

His fist was still in midair, his body shaking with rage, when he shoved her away, then turned and upended the exam table, sending it crashing into a wall full of supplies that clanged and clattered onto the floor. Vivian had stayed still with her back against the wall, watching a pair of forceps spinning on the floor, like a child's top. Exhaustion, fear, defeat, hopelessness, and regret heaped, one on top of the other on top of the other, inside her, and she slowly felt herself sliding back down onto the floor. She couldn't remember the last time she'd felt so lost.

Minutes passed — it could have been one, it could have been ten, she couldn't recall now — and he had finally bent down in front of her, reached out to stroke her arm, moved her hair out of her face, gently. He'd slowly pushed past her weak resistance and taken her in his arms. 'Shhhh, shhhh, honey,' he said, stroking her head. 'Ruby, why do you do this? Why must you make me so angry? We are going to have a baby. A little boy. We'll call him Nicola. I know it's a boy. A father knows these things. It's going to be great. You'll see. We are going to have a wonderful life together. We're going to be a wonderful family.'

Vivian fantasized about killing him, right there on the spot. Of breaking free and finding a knife and stabbing him right through the heart. But she was too weak, and too damaged, and too afraid, and so she'd simply remained limp in his arms, like a sack of flour, until she could compose herself enough to whisper the words she knew she must. 'Of course, Nicky. I was just frightened. I'm sorry. I love you.'

As she now took a hard look at herself in the bathroom mirror, Vivian surveyed her face like a detective. You could still see the faint outline of the bruise, but in the club lighting of the Stork it would be okay. She had considered calling out sick or asking one of the other girls to switch days. But that would have been worse, made Nicky even more paranoid. He'd be in tonight to check on her. She was safer inside the club, around other people, acting as if all was well.

She studied herself again, harder this time.

What are you going to do?

She would call Act. Yes, call Act. She would take his money and get out. *Nicky is going to follow me everywhere.* But he couldn't follow her inside the Barbizon. She'd get Act to give the cash to Laura at the magazine, and then Laura would give it to her inside the Barbizon. *Okay, okay, this is good. This is good. This could work.* She'd dye her hair, change her appearance just enough in case Nicky had the hotel staked out. And then one night she would calmly walk out with some other girls and get into a cab to Port Authority, then on a bus going to anywhere. Because now there was only one way out.

Run.

She applied lipstick, put a brush through her

293

hair, then threw everything into her bag and walked out of the ladies' room.

She heard crying.

A half dozen people were sitting around a table by the dance floor. Barbara was sobbing into a handkerchief, as were several other girls. Vivian caught Bennie the busboy's somber eyes.

'What is it? What's happened?' she asked.

'It's Act,' Bennie said. 'He's been murdered.'

24

Laura had known things were bad when Dolly begged her to have lunch at Cortile on West Forty-Third Street. In the five months they'd lived together, she'd recognized the pattern: When she was happy, Dolly liked to eat. When she was sad or upset, Dolly liked to eat more. A *lot* more. When the feasting didn't work anymore, her dark moods got even darker, with curses and tears of frustration when a dress zipper wouldn't close or hose developed a run before she'd slid them up her leg. Laura had suggested — gently — that Dolly join her for the pre-work swims in the Barbizon pool and had been met with a reaction that registered somewhere between incredulity and horror. Cortile's specialty was fried chicken and waffles, and its location only a few blocks from the Katie Gibbs school made it a particularly friendly port for Dolly when she was literally feeding her demons.

Dolly had looked so awful — drawn, disheveled — when she'd walked back into their room after her meeting with Jack in Central Park that Laura worried that she'd been mugged. She'd been able to drag out that Jack had ended things and done so seemingly without any warning or explanation. Laura knew Dolly needed answers, answers she could only get from Jack, and had given up any hope of doing so.

Instead, she had submerged herself in a sea of bread and chocolate.

I hope I'm doing the right thing, Laura thought as the waiter slid her chef's salad onto the table.

'So, what's going on at *Millie* today?' Dolly asked. Laura had once casually mentioned that girls inside the magazine called *Mademoiselle* 'Millie,' and Dolly, thrilled to know such a frilly state secret, took constant joy in now referring to it by its nickname. 'You working on any big stories?' She picked up the syrup, slathering her plate of waffles.

'I don't get to work on 'big stories,' you know that,' Laura said. 'I get to transcribe notes and run errands and make carbon copies and deliver film, and occasionally write a very brilliant caption about a hat.'

'Yes,' Dolly said, stabbing at her plate. 'Well, I certainly understand what it's like to be stuck.'

Laura brushed by it. 'But it's been good today. Mrs. Blackwell is in Paris touring some of the fashion houses, so the office is pretty quiet.'

Too quiet, in fact. She had too much time to think, too much time to wonder. Box's proposal popped up everywhere she turned: in the bathroom mirror in the morning when she was brushing her teeth, in store windows, at the bottom of her coffee cup. There was no escape.

Why are you trying to escape?

Earlier in the week, he'd casually mentioned that he'd been to Cartier, a sure sign that her engagement ring was forthcoming, and with it the need for a definitive answer. But the more she'd thought about it, the more certain she was becoming in what that answer would be. There was a difference between what you want out of the world and what the world is prepared to offer, she now understood. It was folly to look past the wonderful in search of the exceptional. Life was exceptional if you decided to make it so, not because someone handed it to you. Whenever she was with Box, the world was a beautiful and interesting place, one where he was thrilled to play tour guide. She had yet to tell him she loved him. Not because she didn't, but because of her fear of what would happen if she did. That by risking her heart with Box in the way she had been unwilling to with Pete, she, too, could end up sitting like this, burying her sorrows, perhaps not in sugar but in something far worse. She was, after all, the daughter of a woman who never refused a fourth Sazerac sling. Or a fifth.

This was neither the time nor the place to discuss all of that. She wouldn't pour salt into Dolly's wound. Instead, she hoped to apply some salve. Because what Dolly needed was a proper closing act, one she was never going to find in a plate of self-pity and waffles.

Laura clicked open her purse, took out a folded piece of paper, slid it across the table. 'Here.'

Dolly was still chewing on a piece of chicken. She took a long drag of her Coke. 'What's this?'

Laura exhaled. 'It's Jack's address in Yonkers.'

Dolly stared at the piece of paper like it was radioactive. 'Where did you get this?'

'Everyone has to file a tax return. Even Jack.'

'Tax returns aren't public record.'

'Box has a friend who works for the IRS. He called in a favor.'

Dolly threw her arms up. 'You told *Box* about this? Oh God, why not give an exclusive to *Confidential*? I'm so humiliated.'

'I told Box I needed a favor for a friend. That's all. He doesn't know that 'John Lyons' and your Jack are the same person. Remember, they've never even met. The point is, you need to get to the bottom of this or you'll just keep torturing yourself. Not to mention eat yourself into an early grave.' Laura reached across the table, took Dolly's hand in hers. 'Go see him. Make him tell you what happened. Tell him you're not leaving without an explanation. You're owed that.' Her mind flashed to Pete, to the explanation she had owed *him*. 'You're owed knowing that this was not your fault.'

'How do you know this wasn't my fault?'

'Because I know you. You are the sweetest, loveliest — '

'Please stop. I can't take the 'you're great' speech right now.' A tear splashed down her cheek.

'Don't let him do this to you. Find out what happened, and then walk away.'

Dolly gripped Laura's hand tightly and with the other swept aside her plate and slid the piece of paper closer. 'Okay, Nancy Drew,' she said, nodding. 'I'll go get me some answers.'

★ ★ ★

The bus rocked, almost like a baby in a cradle, as it headed toward Yonkers. Dolly sat in the next-to-last row, thankful that it was only half full. Not too many people had occasion to leave New York City for Yonkers on a Saturday morning, and for this she was thankful.

She'd thought of putting on a nice dress ('You're all 'Doll-ed' up,' he used to chide her when she turned up particularly coiffed for one of their dates) but had ultimately settled for a blouse and simple blue jeans under her coat. They'd had a bit of an Indian summer spell of late, a welcome change from the last few chilly weeks, and she hoped the weather might stay temperate through Thanksgiving, when she'd be back in Utica with the entire teeming Hickey clan.

I had actually thought maybe Jack would be coming home with me, she mused with a twang of bitterness. Once — just once — she wanted to be the one bringing home the boyfriend.

But it never happens. Laura doesn't want me to talk badly about myself, think badly about myself, but how could she possibly understand? She's about to marry a handsome millionaire. Oh, she says she hasn't given him an answer yet, but she's going to, and we all know what it's going to be, what it always is for girls like her. And she'll have her beautiful mansion and gorgeous kids and a maid and throw elegant dinner parties, and I'll be sitting in an office somewhere, taking dictation, watching another guy send gardenias to some other girl.

I don't want to be like this. I am so tired of being like this.

Why am I like this?

The rocking was making her drowsy. She felt her lids growing heavier. *If only I could fall asleep*, she thought. *If only I could fall asleep and have a wonderful dream, and have the dream be my life, and I could never wake up and then live in the dream and I would never have to be tired again.*

Because she *was* tired. Tired of always smiling, tired of being the one who was always gossiped to and never gossiped about. She would never look like Laura or Vivian or Agnes Ford, and that was okay. Most girls didn't look like them. Ruth didn't. Miriam didn't. But the Ruths and Miriams didn't seem to mind like she did, didn't seem to have that burning jealousy flaring up all the time inside. The one she paved over with a smile made for S.R. toothpaste.

And it wasn't as if she had chased Box Barnes. She had gone after Jack, big, lumbering Jack, who had nice teeth but also a flat head and bad arches, and who always wore his pants too high at the waist. Over and over and over, she had searched every moment between them since their first meeting, trying to find out what had gone wrong, what she had done or what she hadn't done, tried to pinpoint the exact second when they'd gotten knocked off course. Laura had been right: She needed answers. She wouldn't depart Yonkers without them.

'Miss?' the bus driver yelled from the front,

300

staring at her through his rearview mirror. 'This is your stop.'

Dolly was standing on a street corner, fumbling with her map, when she looked over to see an elegant gray-haired woman in a cobalt blue coat and matching pin standing nearby. The woman had a small Scottish terrier on a leash who pulled away and ran to Dolly.

'Oh, I am sorry,' the woman said. 'He loves pretty girls. Do you need some help, dear?'

'I'm afraid I'm a little lost,' she said.

'Where are you trying to get to?'

'James Street,' Dolly said.

'Oh, well, you're not too far. What's the address?'

Dolly crumpled the map under one arm, dug into her coat pocket for Laura's piece of paper. '265 James Street.'

'Of course!' the woman said. 'The most beautiful address in the area. It's three blocks that way, turn right, then your first left. You can't miss it.'

Dolly was intrigued. *The most beautiful address around?* What did that mean? 'You know the place?' she asked.

'Well, of course, dear,' the woman repeated. Then she told her why.

* * *

The look on Box's face was just what she had been hoping for, a mix of shock and amusement. 'Surprise,' Laura said, sweeping past him into his apartment and toward the kitchen.

301

'Did we have a date tonight that I forgot?' he asked, one eyebrow devilishly arched, which he knew made him look even more handsome, resulting in him doing it more often than was called for. He leaned against the kitchen doorway, watching as she started to extract groceries from two bulging sacks.

'No, but as Grace Kelly remarked to Jimmy Stewart in *Rear Window*, the element of surprise is always the key to a good sneak attack.'

'Again with Grace Kelly. Can we switch over to Ava Gardner? She's more apt. She's a brunette.'

'There's nothing wrong with having a role model. And let's not forget, Grace and I were practically roommates.'

'Do I even want to know how you got past my doorman?'

'A woman has her ways.'

He laughed as he embraced her from behind. 'And what are we making?'

' 'We' are not making anything. 'I' am making you dinner to make up for the lovely fettuccine carbonara we never got around to having the last time. So it's steak Diane, along with some lovely roasted potatoes and a nice tossed salad. And, of course, this.' She extracted a bottle of red wine from a paper bag.

'Wow. This dinner just got a whole lot better. Are you seriously going to flambé a steak in my apartment? Should I have the fire department on alert?'

She threw a dish towel at him. 'Get out of my kitchen!' she said.

'I'm going to go wash up,' he said, stealing a kiss on his way out, 'and then I will come back and set the table. I'm already starving!'

Laura slid the frying pan onto the stove, salted it, and turned on the burner, then the oven to preheat for the potatoes. A sense of calm and contentment settled over her. Perhaps for the first time since she'd arrived in New York months ago, she felt . . . grounded. She'd had excitement and drama and glamour, but this felt more real, more . . . solid. She was in the apartment of the man she loved, making dinner —

No. Not just the man she loved.

The man she was going to marry.

As she stood at the sink, the cold water now turning her hands a rosy pink, Laura could see her life unfolding, really unfolding, for the first time. She and Box would live here, or perhaps a bigger place, and then would come a house, and babies, and Thanksgivings and Christmases and summers on the Cape. Her adventure may have begun in June, but her life was really starting this very minute. Because it was time to give him an answer to his proposal.

She was getting engaged.

She hummed as she began excitedly unpacking the ingredients from the sack, pulling out the two filet steaks wrapped in brown paper, along with the shallots, cream, and butter. *Hold on* —

She went rifling through the empty sack. Neither the mustard nor the Worcestershire sauce was here. The clerk at Ottomanelli Brothers must have forgotten to put them in the bag.

Her heart sank. How was she going to make a dream dinner for the night she was getting engaged without the proper ingredients?

She'd get them to deliver them. She grabbed the market's card from her purse, then dashed into the living room and picked up the phone.

She heard Box's voice, in midsentence on the bedroom extension. ' . . . explained to you, babe, this isn't my fault. Like I said, it's a surprise, I had no idea she was coming.'

'How come it's always me who's getting the surprises, and they're always the unpleasant kind?' a voice snapped back from the other end of the line. Female. Cold. It sounded vaguely familiar, but Laura couldn't place it.

'Look, I'll make it up to you. Don't I always make it up to you?'

'For once I would like to come first. Why is that so much to ask? I've been very patient with this whole situation. Very few girls would be.'

Laura felt her heart beginning to constrict. She was having trouble breathing.

No. No, no, no.

'You're being unfair,' Box whispered. 'I'm in a tough spot here. You know the situation with my trust. I've got to get married to get it. There's no other way. And I've got to marry someone — '

'Your parents approve of. I know, we've had this discussion before, remember? You don't have to remind me that your parents think I'm trash.'

'That's not true. They just never got to know you.'

'Right! Because they think I'm trash. Well, I'm not. And I am tired of you and them treating me like I am. Do you know I was on a commercial shoot today? Well, I was. For Old Gold cigarettes. With Ted Williams, no less. Did you know he was the comeback player of the year in baseball this year? Well, he was. And he's just gotten a divorce. And he was paying *a lot* of attention to me.'

Of course, Laura realized. *Agnes Ford*.

Box was still talking, all hushed urgency and promises, but Laura had stopped listening. There was no point in hearing another word.

She dropped the receiver onto the sofa, grabbed her hat and coat, and fled the apartment.

25

The seconds bled into eternity, and Laura realized she had no idea how long she had been wandering around the Upper East Side of Manhattan. An hour? Two? Ten? She found herself meandering through the streets as if she were dreaming, and any minute the alarm would go off and she would see Dolly sitting in front of their mirror, removing the nightly bobby pins from her hair.

She passed small café windows, their cozy glows illuminating patrons laughing over coffee or dithering over whether to order dessert. Shop windows showed paper pilgrims and ceramic turkeys, a nod to Thanksgiving, only a week away. She'd invited Box to Greenwich for Thanksgiving, to meet her parents and — ha-ha — to show them the ring. Now she would go home and face General Marmy alone, report that she'd gotten attacked on the flank, lost the war. Or maybe she'd just stay here and sit in the Barbizon coffee shop and eat dry turkey over white bread and mashed potatoes in lumpy beige gravy.

She crossed streets and rounded corners, bumping into happy couples, weaving through briskly walking loners, observing two overweight policemen flirting with two young women who themselves might have been Barbizon girls. They had the look.

The streets were dry and fast, a mad confluence of Checker cabs and Dodges and Chevys and the occasional foreign sports car, honking and turning and looking for parking and fighting for parking. The blood of the city continues to pulse, no matter whose heart is full or whose is breaking or whose is giving out. She remembered standing in Grand Central the day she arrived, determined she would write the stories of the people inside it. Instead, she'd written captions about shoes and scarves. A writer? She'd been too busy dancing.

She hadn't cried yet, which surprised her. Maybe New York had toughened her. Or maybe, deep down, she just wasn't so surprised to find out Box had been a fraud.

After all, aren't I?

She was half a block from the Barbizon when the thought hit her: *What if he's here?* Had he seen the telephone receiver dropped on the couch, then jumped into a cab to come find her? Was he now parked in the lobby, sitting with a bouquet of roses and a thousand apologies, waiting to pounce, to tell her what a colossal misunderstanding this all had been?

Laura practically tiptoed into the hotel, eyes quickly darting around to every nook and cranny, but a preliminary sweep turned up nothing. The space was eerily quiet, the gleaming floors undisturbed by the *click-clack-click-clack* of heels. Even the huge potted ferns looked fatigued, arching toward the middle of the room as if they'd decided to indulge in the luxury of a nap. Laura hurried over to the reception desk, where Metzger sat, reading Anne Morrow Lindbergh's *Gifts from the Sea*. 'And how may I help *you*, Miss Dixon?' she said, never looking up from her pages.

'Has anyone been in asking for me?'

Metzger kept reading. 'No. You were expecting someone?'

Laura didn't know what it was — Metzger's barely concealed contempt, the nervous energy pulsing through her own body, the sudden realization that she'd invested almost her entire New York experience in living someone else's lie — but the weight of Box's betrayal tumbled down on her with sudden, shocking force, almost knocking her to the ground. She placed her palms on the reception counter to steady herself. But she couldn't stop the tears.

Metzger's eyes darted up from her novel. 'I see,' she said. She placed her bookmark, stood, and beckoned one of the other managers from across the lobby. 'Mona, can you take the desk for a few minutes?' she asked. 'Miss Dixon and I are going in the back to have some tea.'

* * *

Perhaps it was the haze of tears still pooling in Laura's eyes, but in the warm light of the room, Metzger looked kinder, softer than she did when she was remonstrating her charges throughout the Barbizon, the forbidding Catholic school nun minus the wimple. Laura hadn't even known this space existed. Tucked in back of the reception area, it was a small sitting room with a wallpaper

308

pattern of yellow roses with green stems, and a plush love seat and coffee table. There was a club chair and a small television in the corner, and another doorway that led into a galley kitchen, where Metzger now emerged, carrying a tea tray with a pink floral-patterned teapot, two cups and saucers, and a small plate of butter cookies. Laura stood by the petite bookcase on the other side of the room, trying to calm herself by scanning the spines. Her eye caught two black-and-white photographs in pewter frames sitting on top.

They were each pictures of young handsome men. The one on the left was wearing a sailor's uniform.

'That's John,' Metzger said as she busied herself setting the tea out on the table. 'He was Olive's husband.'

Olive ran the elevators most weeknights and the occasional Sunday. 'What happened to him?'

'Wrong place, wrong time. They got married when he was on leave. Then he got new orders. He was so excited: 'They're sending me to the Pacific!' Which they did. To Pearl Harbor. Six months before the Japanese decided to drop by for an unannounced visit.'

Laura pictured tiny, frail Olive, excitedly making plans for a home and family, only to turn on the radio to find out her new husband was dead. Laura pointed to the other photo, to a man who was equally striking, though in a different way. This man was in a suit and carried himself with a certain kind of élan, encased in an aura of good breeding. 'And him?'

'He belongs to me,' Metzger said, now perching on the end of the sofa, pouring the piping tea. 'Or he did. That's my Rudy.'

Laura studied the portrait, conjured an image of Nick Charles waiting in a café for Nora and Asta. She tried to picture this man romancing icy, detached Metzger. 'He was killed in the war also?' she asked.

'In a manner of speaking. He was a college professor from Poland, who had come to New York as a visiting instructor. We met at NYU. He was so very charming. You can discern that just from the photograph. We were to be married. But then in the late thirties, he was called back to Poland for a family emergency and never returned.'

'What happened?'

'Hitler happened. Rudy was an intellectual and a Jew. He was gassed at Treblinka in 1942.'

In 1942 Laura had been seven years old, worried about angering Marmy if she dirtied her party dress, as Metzger waited in New York for her lover's return, only to have her dream end before it began.

Laura took a seat on the sofa. 'I'm so sorry. You said you were to be married. So you married later, then?'

'Oh, no. I have never been married.' She smiled at Laura's perplexed face. ''Mrs. Metzger' comes from a very old tradition of English estates. You see, a woman who worked 'in service' would be called 'Mary,' for example, until she was old enough to be called 'Miss Smith.' If she reached a certain age and was still

310

unmarried, one day she was suddenly called 'Mrs. Smith.' It was considered more stately and dignified. It projects more authority.'

'But certainly you had opportunity,' Laura interjected, then immediately admonished herself for her impetuousness. But she felt a window opening onto a universe within the Barbizon she had never known existed and couldn't curb her curiosity. And she was desperate for distraction from her own life. 'I mean, you could have married if you had chosen to.'

Metzger smiled ruefully. 'Not all of us get multiple rides on the carousel, Miss Dixon. Some of us only go around once.' She picked up a butter cookie, dunked it into her tea. 'Now, I invited you to tea so we could discuss you. I am fairly familiar with the sight of a girl dissolving into tears in the lobby of this building, but I must say I am a bit surprised to see you among the number. Trouble with your Mr. Barnes?'

Laura felt her face flush. She felt embarrassed. 'I . . . It feels silly to talk about it.'

'That's the problem with all of you girls,' Metzger said. 'You all think you're the first ones to ever have your hearts broken. You look at us like we're ghosts who've never been in love or dreamed a dream. You look down on us. And on 'the Women' — don't look so surprised, of course we know you call them that — and you think you're so much smarter than we are. When the only thing you really are is younger and luckier.'

Laura stayed silent. How were you supposed to answer that type of withering charge? She had

311

come here under the pretense of getting comfort from an unexpected corner and now felt under siege. Perhaps sensing this, Metzger did something unexpected: She reached over and placed her hand on Laura's arm. 'Tell me what happened,' she said. 'You'll feel better.'

And just like that, out it came, like a wave crashing across a jetty. And not just the story of Box and Agnes Ford and the clandestine phone call, but all of it: Marmy, Pete, Mrs. Blackwell and *Mademoiselle*, her delusions of a grand marriage, her desire to be a writer, her fear that she would never be that writer at all.

Thirty-five minutes and two humiliating outbursts of tears later, Laura sat, swirling the tea leaves at the bottom of her cup, waiting for Metzger to issue some sort of verdict. Was this the part where she told girls to pack up and go home, where she warned that not every young woman was ready for the big city, and sometimes it was better to return from whence you came?

Instead, Metzger started clearing the coffee table, slowly stacking the cups, napkins, and spoons back onto the tray. 'Do you have any advice to offer?' Laura said. 'I could sure use some.'

Metzger shook her head, the veil of inscrutability dropping once again. 'Girls don't come to the Barbizon for answers, Laura.' It was the first time since she'd arrived in New York that Laura could recall Metzger addressing her by her first name. 'They come to find out what questions they need to be asking.'

Laura stepped into the phone booth on the mezzanine and picked up the receiver, taking one more glance at her watch. If she timed it right, Marmy would be in the bath following her weekly mahjong game, where she threw out tiles as she casually character-assassinated any woman who'd recently earned her ire — *She didn't buy any tickets to the charity ball* or *She had the nerve to hire that caterer she knew I was going to use for my party* — with the ruthlessness of a military sniper.

Laura gave the operator the number and prayed that he, not she, would pick up.

'Hello.' His voice, deep and resonant, steadied her.

'Hi, Daddy.'

'Well, this is a nice surprise. Is everything all right?'

No, Daddy, it's not. My heart has just been smashed to pieces, and I'm alone and scared and unsure, and I just want you to tell me that it's all going to be okay, because you're my dad and you wouldn't let anything bad happen to me.
'I'm fine,' she said, choking on the second word. Why had she made this call at all? Now that he was on the line, the only thing she could think of was how desperately she wanted him off it.

'Have you been reading your stock tables?' he asked. She heard the rustling of a newspaper, pictured him standing at his desk in the library, flipping through the *Courant* or the *Times*. He did his catch-up reading at night. He'd taught

313

her how to read the stock tables when she was only eight — 'It's important to know how the world works, honey' — and loved to boast to his golfing partners about his daughter's growing knowledge of American commerce. But he loved her in a way that was palpable, in a way Marmy never could. Perhaps not unconditionally, but genuinely. The problem was his love was a moving target; out of nowhere he would say something or make a loving gesture that made your heart bounce, and then wouldn't do or say anything like it again for months. Years.

'Actually, Daddy,' she said, fighting to keep her composure, 'I've . . . I've had a rather tough day. I just wanted to hear a friendly voice, I guess.'

Ask, Daddy, please ask why. Please, let me tell you. Please. I don't know why I need you to do this right now, but I do.

'Well, that's New York for you, kitten,' he replied. 'Up one day, down the next. Now you can see why I decamped for Connecticut. Did you want to talk to your mother?'

Tears again began streaming down Laura's face. She managed to eke out, 'No.'

'Everything else okay, then?' More rustling.

She cleared her throat. 'Yes. I have to go. I'll see you soon. Bye.'

She hung up the receiver but kept clutching it as she sat in the quiet of the phone booth, the only sound that of her heaving tears.

* * *

314

'Pass the gravy, honey.'

Vivian reached over and handed the heavy china gravy boat to one of Nicky's uncles — Luigi? Or was that the one with the ill-fitting suspenders who did all the belching? — then returned to her veal. The food, at least the part she'd managed to eat, was delicious: hearty, homemade fare that was foreign to her existence flitting around New York restaurants.

They sat at a long table in a cluttered square dining room in Jersey City. Ugly, crowded, and smelly, it was the antithesis of Englewood, where she had spent all of those secret Wednesdays going out to play checkers with Sy at the old actors' home. Cranky Sy, always flirting with her. If he could see her now.

'She's not eating,' Nicky's mother was yelling from the other end of the table, jabbing her fork in the air. 'Nicola, why does she not eat? She doesn't like my cooking? She is too skinny!'

'Ma, she's eating, she's eating,' Nicky replied. 'Eat,' he whispered urgently. 'You're insulting my mother!'

Vivian scooped up another forkful, inserted, chewed, smiled. Repeat. This was her life now. She followed orders. Nicky had murdered Act, as casually as he might have picked up his laundry. She had a recurring nightmare of Act, terrified as he was being slowly beaten to death, begging for his life, finally succumbing to the pain and telling Nicky about Vivian's appointment in the Bronx. Act's blood was on her hands. The bars may not have been visible, but she had now been sentenced to prison.

315

A woman in a flowered housedress seated near Uncle Luigi was complaining about the declining quality of tomatoes. A young man with an olive complexion and movie-star features issued a report on his first week working for the pencil factory, which was ultimately decreed a success. Two small children, a boy and a girl, chased one another around the table, ignoring commands to stop, until they got on Uncle Luigi's nerves so badly that he flung his hand out like a whip, walloping the boy in the face. No one said a word.

She and Nicky had come here, to 'Sunday dinner,' to announce their engagement. Or, more specifically, for Nicky to announce their engagement. His family wouldn't be happy he'd knocked up a girl — a Brit, no less — but family was family and his mother, after she spent a suitable amount of time weeping and lamenting and screaming, would accept the situation and live with the shame showered down by the other women in her Brooklyn neighborhood. Nicky thought it might be good to start over someplace else, like here in Jersey City, where they could move into this house, with his grandparents. His grandmother could teach Vivian how to cook and clean. Then, after the baby was born and things were settled, they could look for their own place. Have more babies. Then they would be the ones having the Sunday dinners.

He'd told her all of this almost as an aside, as if it were all just a formality and he was just making sure she had her copy of the schedule. Her wants, her desires, had ceased to matter the day he'd caught her trying to rid her body of his progeny. From now on she would simply be an accessory, a necessary accoutrement to give birth to his children and iron his shirts and dress up. He'd have the bonus of a beautiful, exotic foreign wife who could sing 'Jingle Bells' on key at the family Christmas party.

She had managed only one slight victory, and that was convincing him to hold off on the engagement news. It was, she gently argued, too much to spring her on his family for the first time, the report of their impending marriage and child on the way as well, all in one pasta-laden sitting. Better to get the family used to the idea of her first. He'd considered this much more thoughtfully than she'd imagined he would and had mercifully seen it not as a delay tactic or an affront to his masculine authority, but as a gesture of kindness and sensitivity to his family. After all, it was going to be bad enough that they were going to have to get married by a judge in the city hall, not at Our Lady of Loreto. At least not until Vivian had converted. He'd already made an appointment for her with Father Agnelli just after New Year's to get her started.

'Apologies,' she said, rising from the table. Almost immediately, the men rose with her. The Italians were nothing if not gallant. 'I need to use the loo. Could you tell me where it is?'

'Huh? What's she talkin' about?' Nicky's mother shouted.

'The bathroom, Ma,' Nicky said. 'Top of the stairs.'

Vivian could still hear Mrs. Accardi as she

ascended the steps. ' . . . don't understand half the words that come out of that girl's mouth.'

'She seems a little uppity, if you ask me,' a thin voice said. 'She thinks she's Deborah Kerr.'

'Oh, I *loved* her in *From Here to Eternity*!' squealed the cousin with the bad teeth.

'What does a guy have to do to get more rigatoni?' Uncle Luigi complained.

Vivian entered the tiny bathroom and closed the door. Standing at the sink, she willed herself to be sick. At least that way she might be able to net an opportunity to lie down or, better yet, to leave.

She took a long look at her reflection in the mirror. Her complexion, once smooth and snowy white, was now ashy. Her face was slightly rounder, and would get rounder still as the months wore on. But it was her eyes that gave her away. They were hollow, vacant.

Dead.

You know what you have to do, she told herself. *There's only one way out of this. Be smart. Make a plan.*

Don't be afraid.

26

December 1955

'I hate holiday travel,' Dolly said as she slid her bulky powder-blue suitcase next to her. She began unbuttoning her coat. 'I don't understand how people do it effortlessly.'

'They have help,' Laura replied, placing her own luggage and hat-box to her left as she flung her coat onto the back of the adjoining chair. 'They hire people to carry their bags for them.'

'That'll be you soon enough,' Dolly smirked. 'Mrs. Benjamin Barnes will not be hauling her own luggage all over Europe.'

Laura nodded slightly, looked away. She began pulling off her gloves.

Maybe it's time to tell her, she thought. *If not now, when?*

'You know, now that you mention that,' Laura started, 'there's been — '

'Well, hello there!' Dolly exclaimed, looking over Laura's shoulder. Laura turned to see Ruth and Miriam approaching their table. 'I thought you girls had already skedaddled out of town!'

'That was the plan,' Ruth said wryly, 'but this one couldn't get off work early.' Miriam, whose family was in Nebraska, was going to be spending Christmas with Ruth's clan in South Norwalk. The pair had stopped in here, at the Oyster Bar inside Grand Central, for a quick

319

round of Gibsons. 'I'm just keeping Laura company until her train,' Dolly said, 'then I am going to haul myself over to Penn to catch my own back to Utica. Come join us!'

Mercifully, the two girls demurred, and after half-hugs and a promise to get together for dinner after New Year's, they continued on their travels. 'Sorry,' Dolly said, turning back to Laura. 'Were you about to say something?'

'Nothing important.'

The waiter came with menus, and they ordered drinks. 'I love the fact that we're sitting in the Oyster Bar getting ready to go home for Christmas,' Dolly said as she scanned the offerings. 'It seems so . . . continental.'

Laura measured her across the table. What an odd duck Dolly could be. It had been over a month since she'd handed her Jack's address and told her to get some answers, and yet Dolly — who couldn't keep her mouth shut if you surgically stitched it so — hadn't mentioned it. She'd been growing her hair out and she actually looked a bit more slender, a sign her eating binges had abated if not disappeared altogether. Laura had asked Dolly about all of it, the trip to Yonkers and the subsequent new look, only to be met with an airy response that it was best for everyone to just move on, and that was what she was doing. Discussion over.

And really, what right did she have to pry? She was holding on to her own secret. Both Dolly and Vivian had remarked that they hadn't seen Box at the Barbizon of late, that Laura didn't seem to be going out as much. She, too, had produced her own dismissive, catchall excuse, that the holiday season was madness when you ran a department store. This had been enough to explain Box's absence for the last few weeks. Though it wouldn't hold after Christmas was over.

He'd come to the Barbizon a few days after the disastrous dinner that never was, as she knew he would. She hadn't returned his calls or acknowledged the two bouquets of flowers he'd sent, each with a plaintive note asking for a chance to explain. Finally one afternoon a girl Laura had never seen before knocked at her door, carefully reciting that Box was in the lobby and to tell her that he was going to stay there and wait for her as long as it took, because she had to leave the building sometime. The girl had then broken out in an awkward smile, as if she'd just recited the winning word in a spelling bee.

Laura had made him wait another hour, then walked matter-of-factly into the lobby, silently cursing herself for applying perfume and lipstick before coming down. But she'd had little choice: She didn't want him to see her as she really was — pale and tired, her eyes bleary from all the crying.

They'd exchanged the briefest of terse greetings before they walked into the coffee shop and taken a back booth. A scene witnessed by half of the Barbizon was not at all what Laura wanted, but the thought of having to walk even a block with Box somewhere else was too awful to imagine. Better to just get it all dispatched quickly.

They talked — actually, he rambled was more accurate, about early Christmas season sales at the store, about his parents' upcoming trip to Mexico, some story about his sister she couldn't follow and didn't care to — until the coffee came, and a painful quiet settled over the booth. 'I am so sorry, I can't even put it into strong enough words,' he said finally, looking down as he stirred his cup.

'I know you are.'

'She doesn't even — '

Laura put her hand up. 'No. Not another word about . . . her. It doesn't matter. You've apologized. It's over. There's nothing more to say.'

'That's not true, Laura. I have so much to say. If I can only get you to listen. To understand.'

'Understand what, exactly? That you needed a wife who would pass inspection and Joanne Connelly wasn't available? That you were going to marry me and carry on with another woman right from the start? That you lied to me the entire time we were together? Do you know what I've been spending my days thinking about? Do you? That I came this close to ruining my entire life. My God, how stupid I've been. You two must have been roaring with laughter behind my back.' A small stab hit her heart. It was the exact charge Pete had leveled against her.

'You've got it all wrong. It wasn't like that. I wasn't seeing her the whole time. My parents — '

'Stop! Just stop. I don't want to know. I don't want to know. We're all done.' She began

322

scooting out of the booth. Box grabbed her forearm, pinned it to the table.

'Please, please. I did love you. Do love you. You can ask my mother. The night of the anniversary party, the night I proposed, I told her that you make me want to be a better person.'

She shook her arm free. 'Evidently not enough.'

'My father has had a mistress for years.'

Laura found herself almost speechless. 'So that's it? That's your excuse? 'It's good enough for Dad, so it's good enough for me'? Do you hear yourself?'

'It's all I've known. I'm not saying that to excuse my behavior. I'm not. I am just trying to get you to see where all of this is coming from. You do make me want to be a better man. I don't want anyone but you. It's all over with her. I love *you*.'

Laura sat back in the booth, withdrawing her hands to her lap. She'd never seen such a look of pure anguish on a man's face. Strangely, she actually believed that he did love her. But he no doubt had also told Agnes Ford that he loved her. And who knows who else. It was no longer about love, anyway. It was about trust. And that had been broken. Smashed, actually. Irrevocably, permanently smashed.

'You know what I keep thinking?' she asked. 'How indignant you were that night you were cooking me dinner in your apartment, when I had the gall to ask you about her. How *affronted* you were.'

'You don't understand.'

'At last, a point of agreement.' She slid out of the booth. 'I have to go. Please don't contact me again.'

A rowdy burst of laughter nearby took her out of the memory. Laura glanced around the Oyster Bar, taking in the assorted faces slurping the bar's namesake product, drinking martinis, laughing over cigarettes and platters of cold lobster salad. In an instant another memory returned, of her standing in this very train station, listening to Marmy correct her grammar as she daydreamed of sitting here, inside the Oyster Bar, flirting with a visiting businessman and drinking a Tom Collins. *That was six months ago*, she thought. *Who could imagine that your life could change so much in six months?*

The din inside the restaurant was very loud, a direct result of its stone archways — but above the chatter and clattering silverware and revelry, you could still hear the faint sound of Perry Como crooning 'Home for the Holidays.' Fitting.

A band of men in almost identical gray suits, fedoras pushed back from their brows, stood laughing raucously at the bar, arguing over who had blown the client presentation and finding general agreement and hilarity in blaming someone named Sid. Next to them, a single man, perhaps in his mid-fifties, dressed neatly but not expensively, sat silently sipping a scotch and staring somberly at his own reflection in the glass behind the bar, evidently trying to delay his trip home for as long as possible. Laura wondered how many nights her own father had sat just like that, parked in some out-of-the-way saloon, dreading the ride home to dinner with Marmy and his children. She turned to see two young couples at a table, diving into a messy platter of assorted seafood. One couple chortled almost uncontrollably, feeding each other snippets of lobster; the other sat across from them almost dead still, backs plastered to their chairs, as they pushed lettuce and crabmeat and lemon wedges around on their plates with their forks, trying to muster banal contentment and failing miserably. *The great divide*, Laura thought, *between those who are happy and those who are not.*

Wouldn't Pete be proud of her, sitting here, mentally writing the Oyster Bar?

'What are you having?' Dolly was saying, and Laura turned to see the waiter standing, a bit harried, waiting for her to order.

Laura smiled weakly. 'Tom Collins, please.'

'Okay,' Dolly said after he departed, 'are you ever going to tell me what's going on with you?'

Laura eyed her evenly. 'I don't know. Are you?'

Dolly shrugged. 'There's never anything going on with me.'

'That's not true and you know it. What happened when you went to confront Jack?'

'Jack's ancient history. Why haven't you been seeing Box? And don't give me this crapola about Christmas shopping, either.'

There was silence between them for a minute until the waiter returned with the drinks. Dolly raised her sidecar in toast. 'What shall we drink to?'

Laura thought for a second. 'To Metzger.'

Dolly smiled. 'To Metzger.'

'Actually,' Laura said, putting down her tall lemony cocktail, 'we should probably be making a toast to Vivian. She should be here with us.'

'Yeah, it's too bad. She was being very mysterious about her plans for tonight. I wonder where Nicky's taking her. And what kind of jewelry he's buying her for Christmas. I'm sure he'll miss her when she's in London.'

Laura leaned forward. 'Dolly, did Vivian seem . . . off to you?'

'What do you mean? Vivian always seems off to me. That's what makes her Vivian.'

'No, I'm serious. Something doesn't seem right to me.'

'Oh, you,' Dolly said, taking another long sip of her sidecar. 'Always looking for a tale to be told.'

Not this time, Laura thought. A few days ago Laura had asked Vivian to come with them for a final 'girls' toast' before Christmas break, and Vivian had agreed. Laura had been relieved; Vivian's cool behavior of the last few months had positively metastasized into almost complete withdrawal in the last several weeks. She sometimes disappeared from view within the Barbizon for days. Whenever she did resurface, there was always a reason, always an excuse for her prolonged absence — a nagging sinus headache, an extra shift at the Stork, a trip to the post office to ship Christmas presents back to

England — something just plausible enough. But Vivian was depressed. She looked puffy, tired. Laura recognized the signs. It was like watching someone tumble down into a sinkhole, and you were powerless to pull them out.

Tonight they'd expected Vivian to swan through the door to their room inside the Barbizon at any moment, as she always did when they were going out somewhere. And especially when she knew they were going away for the holidays. And yet Vivian didn't seem to come to their room at all anymore. She had never wanted them to come to her place, reasons unknown, and somewhere along the line a tacit under-standing had come to pass that whenever they'd made plans, Vivian would come to them, never vice versa.

But when she didn't show and with the clock ticking, Laura had gathered Dolly and the two of them had gone down to Vivian's room five floors below. They were surprised when she answered the door. She wore no makeup, only a silk bathrobe. Laura had been even more surprised when Vivian had casually waved them inside.

Laura had always gotten the impression that Vivian lived amid a fair amount of chaos. The lone other time she'd been allowed in this room it had been a circus, a display of boxes and empty cigarette cartons, of hangers on the floor and dresses thrown over the backs of chairs. In her mind, Laura had always imagined Vivian living with a yellow parrot inside a big gold cage hanging from the ceiling, a bird she never fed but whom, like Vivian, always managed to survive nonetheless. But when she and Dolly had walked into Vivian's tiny unit tonight, they'd found only a tidy, orderly, spartan room, one that gave the impression that its occupant had either just arrived or was about to depart for good. It felt sterile, charmless. A suitcase and a hatbox sat by the door.

'I thought you were coming with us to the Oyster Bar,' Laura said.

'Oh, so sorry, my pets, but Nicky simply insisted we have a cozy dinner before I leave, and I couldn't possibly disappoint him. And I am horribly late, as usual.' She put down her hairbrush. 'So I'm afraid we'll have to toodle-oo here.' She reached into her dressing table drawer, extracted two pale pink envelopes. 'Just little holiday greetings to my two favorite Barbizon girls,' she said, handing them each a card. 'But you must, must promise to follow the instruction, or the wishes expressed won't come true.'

Laura read her own name in florid script, with a line underneath that said, 'Vital: Do not open until Boxing Day.'

'When's Boxing Day? And what is it?' Dolly asked.

'December twenty-sixth,' Vivian replied. 'It's a very old English holiday. Back in the day, it was the day when the lords and ladies who ran the grand estates and the factory owners would give their servants and workers their Christmas gifts.'

Laura laughed. 'Are you implying we are your servants?'

Vivian laughed as well, and Laura's heart fluttered; it was the biggest, throatiest, joyous, most Vivian-like laugh she'd heard in ages. 'Oh, well done, darling! Not at all, not at all. I wish I had been that clever. No, no, nothing like that. Just a small something to express love and joy come to you, and to you your wassail too, and all of that.' She looked at both of them. 'You two — '

Something seemed to catch in her throat, and she stopped. It was the first time Laura could ever recall seeing Vivian appear . . . vulnerable. Her eyes were shining.

'What a nice thing to do,' Dolly said, appearing genuinely moved.

Vivian stepped forward, drew Dolly into a hug. 'Always remember you're wonderful, my Ethel,' she whispered to her. 'Don't forget it.'

Vivian had hugged Laura just as close. 'Cheers, darling,' she said. 'To watch how you've blossomed in these few short months has been nothing short of smashing. Happy Christmas.'

'To you, too,' Laura replied. 'I'm sure yours will be a lot more interesting than mine. I picture you at some grand estate. Like Manderley!'

Vivian had smiled resignedly. She looked incredibly fatigued, which Laura attributed to the fact that her face was now plain, unadorned by cosmetics. Vivian hugged her again, tighter this time. 'Alas, no, my dear. I do not get to be the second Mrs. de Winter. I am the first Mrs. Rochester.'

Sitting in the Oyster Bar sipping her drink, Laura felt Vivian's words now swirling through her brain, teasing her. *What had she meant?* Her room had been too neat. But then a lot of people cleaned up before they went on a trip, not wanting to come home to disarray. But still, something wasn't right.

'Where are you now?' Dolly sighed.

'English literature.'

'Pardon?'

' 'The first Mrs. Rochester.' It's from *Jane Eyre*.'

Dolly shrugged. 'So?'

Laura felt her brain shifting into overdrive. Box's words the night of his parents' grand party: 'The roof can be an oasis.' Mariclaire, sopping wet and wrapped in a blanket walking away with her shamefaced parents at her coming-out party, blithely stating, 'Sometimes, you just have to save yourself and jump.' Bertha Rochester, the tortured, insane first wife in *Jane Eyre*, committing suicide as she flung herself from the top of Thornfield Hall.

And just like that, the pieces tumbled frighteningly into place. 'Oh my God, oh my God,' Laura yelled as she jumped up, attracting looks from two nearby couples and the coworkers of Sid. She began frantically rifling through her bag, lipstick and compact and handkerchief and comb tossed onto the table as she dug to the bottom.

'What?!' Dolly looked on, alarmed. 'What's going on?'

Laura found the pink envelope, ripped it open. As she scanned the note inside, she felt herself getting dizzy. She grabbed her coat. 'We have to go. Now!!' She tossed a few dollars onto the table and raced out of the Oyster Bar, not even

330

bothering to take her luggage, as Dolly ran to catch up.

* * *

Good enough, Vivian thought, puckering one more time into a piece of tissue. She leaned away a little from the dressing table, made a final appraisal. Maybe a touchup with some light powder. She snapped the compact shut, stood, and stepped back from the mirror. One last long view: tailored wool suit (fifteen dollars at Oppenheim Collins on West Thirty-Fourth Street), a single strand of pearls, kid gloves, and her hat. Since she was old enough to understand fashion, she has abided by one credo and one credo only, and that is from Edna Woolman Chase, the editor of *Vogue*: 'Fashion can be bought. Style one must possess.'

She slipped her arms into her coat. She would not be outside long, but still, she would be outside. She took a deep breath.

I'm ready.

Should she bring her bag? Yes, it will have her identification inside. Vivian slid it onto her crooked forearm, then downed the final gulp of whiskey from the crystal tumbler on her dressing table, felt it barrel down her throat, warm and bitter. A small smile escaped as Vivian glanced at the suitcase and hatbox beside the door. Both were empty. Thank God, neither Laura nor Dolly had the chance to pick them up before they'd left. She'd have been found out. And then what would she have done?

She stepped out into the hallway. Quiet. It is Friday, the last before Christmas. Most of the girls have left already. The lucky ones are sipping champagne, on dates at the Stork or the Harwyn, others already on trains or buses back home for the holidays, bags packed and brimming with lies about their fizzy days in the big city. The Women are the only ones left behind, each locked on the other side of her door, her only company tepid tea and crossword puzzles.

Vivian passed the elevator bank. If she stepped into the elevator, there would most certainly be questions from the operator, one always desperate for a story. Instead, she exited the door at the end of the hall that leads to the stairwell, and began a slow, steady ascent up the steps.

It was fifteen minutes before she pushed the door out, felt the whoosh of crisp night air rush at her. She was winded from walking up so many flights in heels, but the biting chill felt good seizing her lungs. She stepped onto the veranda, looked out onto New York — on beautiful, wonderful, dizzying New York, teeming with life, each tiny lit window a tale: of someone, of something, of heartbreak and triumph and joy and agony and stupidity and sorrow and sex and laughter and betrayal and loneliness.

She took in another deep breath, placed her hands on the balustrade. *It is*, she thought, *a glorious night to die.*

27

The sound of the door swinging violently open sent Vivian whirling around. She watched as Laura and then Dolly burst through, running to where she stood by the railing.

'Stop!' Vivian thundered, holding out her palm. 'Not one more step! I mean it!'

Dolly was behind Laura and, in exhaustion both physical and mental, plopped onto one of the metal chairs still scattered about the veranda, the cushions that welcomed so many girls for sunbathing long packed away in winter storage. Laura remained perfectly still in the middle of the terrace, her eyes fixed squarely on Vivian.

'Vivian,' she said breathlessly. 'Come away from the edge. Come talk to us.'

Vivian held her ground, pressing her lower back against the top of the balustrade. 'What are you two doing here? You should be on trains going home on holiday.' She eyed Laura coolly. 'You read the card.'

'It all just sort of hit me, what you might be planning. I just put it all together as we were sitting in Grand Central. And so, yes, then I opened the card. And I . . . ' She started to well up. 'Oh, Vivian, please. Please. Come down!' Laura held out her hands, beseeching. 'Just come away from the ledge and talk to me!'

Vivian didn't move. 'There's nothing to talk about. It's all over.'

Dolly bolted up out of her chair. She'd thought Laura had gone mad until she'd read Vivian's own card to her as the cab had gone racing back to the Barbizon. She didn't know what to say; the whole situation felt surreal, as if she were watching a film rather than being there herself. She felt ill-equipped for the task in front of them. But she had to try. *Just stay calm. As long as we're calm, she'll stay calm.* 'Vivian, whatever it is, we're your friends,' Dolly said. 'We can help you. It can't be so bad that you would consider doing something like this. You have a lot of life left to live.'

'My life is over.'

'Vivian, what happened?' Laura asked. 'Talk to me. Please. Tell us what's wrong. Perhaps we can help you find an answer — '

'There's no answer!' Vivian screamed.

For a minute that felt like an hour, the three of them simply stood on the terrace of the Barbizon, twenty-three stories above East Sixty-Third Street, each girl cemented in place. The temperature had started to drop. Finally, Vivian spoke again.

'I'm pregnant.'

Laura ignored Dolly's gasp behind her. *Okay,* she thought. *Okay. It's a bad situation, but it's not the end. We can get her out of this. We just have to get her to see that she has another way out.*

'Okay, then,' Laura said slowly. It was, she knew a delicate balance: too forceful and you could trigger anger; too coddling and you come off as patronizing, treating her like a child. 'I can understand why you would be scared. It's a scary thing. But, Vivian, let me ask you one question: Do you believe we are your friends?'

Vivian didn't hesitate. 'I do.'

'Okay. Good. Because we are. Aren't we, Dolly?'

Dolly took a giant step to stand next to Laura, instinctually grabbing Laura's hand and squeezing it. She found Vivian's detached affect unnerving and began to shiver. 'I'm confused,' she said finally.

Laura could have killed her. *What kind of thing is that to say?!* 'As your friends,' Laura continued, breezing right past Dolly's comment, 'we're here to help you. We can help you. We can help you figure everything — '

'No,' Vivian said. Her face had taken on an odd expression, intrigued and contemplative. 'Please, Dolores, do tell: Why are you confused?'

'I mean, you're pregnant,' Dolly said, almost in a whisper, her face incredulous. 'How could you consider killing yourself if you're pregnant? How could you kill your own baby?'

'Dolly!'

'No, no, Laura, it's a good question. The answer, my dear, is that I am saving this poor, unfortunate child. That's what mothers do, is it not? They protect their children. And I am protecting this one from a life in a prison camp.'

Dolly's face devolved into utter confusion. But Laura understood instantly. 'Nicky,' she said. 'He knows.'

'Oh, far more than that, I'm afraid. He has our entire lives planned out in Brooklyn. Or perhaps

New Jersey. I am to be a good hausfrau and bake pies and learn how to make spaghetti and go to Mass every Sunday. It's all been arranged, you see.' She looked up at the sky, her laugh brittle. 'What a beautiful disaster.'

'It doesn't have to be,' Laura said. 'You don't have to live a life you don't want to live, Vivian. I know it seems impossible, but we can help you. My father is a lawyer — '

'Oh, rubbish!' Vivian yelled, her eyes flashing. 'Don't you see? This isn't one of your petty dramas, trying to decide which boy you're going to pick as Romeo to your tortured Juliet. Really, Laura, sometimes I wonder if you've grown up a day since you've arrived here. Wake up, my darling! Have you spent your entire time in New York learning absolutely nothing? Torn between two men and gleaning nothing from either. Did you really not know Box Barnes was still carrying on with the model?'

Laura felt her throat closing. 'How did you — '

'I work in the Stork Club. It's the city capital for gossip.'

'And yet you said nothing.'

'I . . . I was going to. Honestly. But you seemed so happy. And it wasn't like he was coming into the club with her. I had no proof. Just idle rumor.'

Laura tried to contain her anger. 'It was an idle rumor that I should have heard. From you.'

Dolly turned to her. 'You broke it off with Box? Because you found out he was two-timing you? With who? What model?'

336

'Not now.' Laura was still staring at Vivian. She hadn't really known Box; it turned out perhaps she really hadn't known Vivian, either. Maybe nobody really knew anybody.

It was neither the place nor the time for this. But she couldn't help herself. 'I would have never kept a secret like that from you,' Laura said. 'I was going to marry him. And you would have stood there, silent, and let me do it?'

'Some lessons we must learn for ourselves.'

'This isn't Glinda and Dorothy and tapping your heels three times, dammit!' Laura roared. 'This was my *life*, Vivian. Just like I am here trying to save yours.'

'I didn't ask you to do that.'

'Stop it! Just stop it! Don't you get it? You've just proven my point. I was blindsided by Box's betrayal, Vivian. But you weren't. You suspected it all the time, I bet, probably even before you heard the rumors of him and Agnes Ford. That's because your instincts are good, Vivian. They're valuable. I need you, Vivian. So does Dolly. You're *needed*.'

'Greeting-card sentiment,' Vivian said.

'No, no. So much more than that. You're not the only one who picked the wrong man. The important thing now is that you have options — '

'Are you daft?!' Vivian screamed. 'Do you really think that I would be standing here, exercising this one, if I hadn't considered every other possible alternative? Do you know what Nicky's capable of? Do you?! I had a friend, a very good friend, who I had turned to and who was helping me. Do you know where he is now?

337

In a cemetery, that's where. He was *murdered* because of me. Because that is what Nicky is. That is what he does. You can't help me. No one can help me. Anyone who tries to help me ends up dead.'

'Vivian, you *have* to go to the police. They'll lock Nicky up. You'll be safe.'

'I'll never be safe. Never. They'll never send him to prison. Men like him never go to prison. And he'll find me, no matter where I go, where I try to hide. And he'll drag me back, force me into his form of slavery. Either that, or he'll kill me. And he'll ruin any child unfortunate enough to be born to him.'

Dolly had been quiet, her face nothing but pale quivering and abject terror that at any minute Vivian would turn around and leap. But something in her seemed to crack under the combination of the situation and Vivian's immovable stance.

'The child!' Dolly suddenly interjected, fury in her voice. Her face was flush with anger. 'You're killing your own child!! Anything is better than that! Anything, you hear me?! If you do this, you're no better than he is!! You're a murderer!'

Laura's hand was swift and brutal as she slapped Dolly clean across the face. The force of the smack sent the girl teetering back, until Dolly grabbed the arm of a chair for support.

The three of them once again, suffocating in the chill and the silence.

'Perhaps you're right, Dolores,' Vivian finally said. 'Perhaps I am simply a coward.'

Dolly straightened up, muttering, 'I'm sorry,'

as she walked toward Vivian, arms outstretched.

'No! Stay back.'

Laura pulled her by the sleeve. Dolly shrugged her off.

'I don't think you're a coward,' Dolly said. 'I just don't understand a woman who wouldn't want a *baby*. Who wouldn't want a home with a man who loves her? Yes, maybe he's controlling. Maybe he even killed someone. I don't know. But men mellow over time. Some of us . . . some of us would give anything for the life you're describing. Some of us . . . have nothing.' She dissolved into tears. Soon her body was shaking from the force of them, and she dropped to her knees a few feet in front of Vivian, like a supplicant praying before the Madonna. 'I'm sorry, I'm sorry,' she sobbed. 'I don't even know what I'm saying.'

Laura glanced at Vivian, saw softness and pity creep across her face. She seized the opportunity. Vivian was suddenly invested in someone else's trouble. It would buy some desperately needed time. 'Oh, sweetheart,' Laura said, dropping onto her haunches to slip an arm around Dolly's heaving shoulders, 'what happened when you went to Yonkers? What happened with Jack? Don't hold it all in. Tell us.'

Vivian stood like a sentry as Dolly cried for a few more minutes, Laura rubbing her back. Once she'd calmed down enough, she sat back on her heels, her face drawn and exhausted from all of the night's emotion. 'It was a choice,' she said flatly, wiping away her tears with the back of a glove.

'What do you mean, 'It was a choice'?'

'He had to choose. Between me . . . and God.' A sarcastic chuckle escaped. 'Not exactly a fair fight, is it?'

'The address, in Yonkers, it's a church?'

'St. Joseph's Seminary, of Dunwoodie.' She relayed her trip on the bus, about the woman with the dog who had given her directions. 'As soon as I found out, I felt so stupid. I mean, it was so *obvious*. The unexplained absences, the mystery about his studies, where he lived, his shyness, the way he could sometimes just look so *tortured*. He was torn.'

'You talked to him?'

She shook her head. 'I knew it wouldn't do any good. After the woman at the bus stop told me what it was, I still had to go and see it, because I hadn't punished myself quite enough. It's actually very beautiful. I stood by the fence for a while, watched some of the seminarians passing by, but I didn't see him. Thankfully. I couldn't have been certain I wouldn't have made a huge scene, and that wasn't going to benefit anybody. He'd said everything he needed to say in Central Park. I know he feels guilty, feels he led me on.'

'Because he did.'

Dolly shrugged. 'No, not really. Not when you really look at it, plain and true. I've had a month to stew about this. When you take off your rose-colored glasses, you see the world as it is. The truth is I pushed him. I was always pushing. Because that's what I do. I'm pushy.'

Laura looked at the pain in Dolly's face, so

raw you could almost touch it. Somehow, Dolly's calm, workmanlike recitation of the events of the past month was more unnerving than if she had been telling the story in hysterics. There was something profoundly defeatist in her entire body language. Laura couldn't risk Vivian climbing aboard that bandwagon. 'Dolly, don't do this to yourself again,' she said. 'You're always beating yourself up. You *must* stop it. It'll destroy you.'

Vivian had been standing, immobile, the entire time, surveying the scene with the calm reserve she'd displayed all evening. Finally, she spoke. 'Laura is right, Dolores.'

Laura took in a deep breath, slowly exhaled it. *Good, good. Vivian is focused on something else. Let's keep her focused on something else.* Laura spun around on her knees to face Dolly. 'Honey, listen to me. You are a special, special girl. You're funny, and pretty, and smart, and the best friend a girl could ever ask for. Isn't she, Vivian?'

Vivian nodded. 'Yes.'

'You need to take this as a learning experience on the road in life. Look at me: I had two great guys, and now I have none. I betrayed one, only to be betrayed by the other. But I'll learn from it. I'll know better for the next time.'

Dolly smiled ruefully. 'That's because you know there will *be* a next time.'

It took all of Laura's strength not to lose her patience. She could almost hear the voice coming from inside Vivian's head: *You don't know problems, sweetie.*

But Dolly did know. 'I'm sorry,' Dolly was saying, looking up at Vivian. 'I know this must all seem so silly to you, when you have it so much worse. But that's life, isn't it? We all want someone else's life, someone else's problems, because they always seem so much better than our own. Vivian, I want you to know I have always admired you. Honest. Even when I was being nasty. Because you never lie. Ever. You always say what you think, and not many people do that. At least not many people I know. So I want to be honest with you back. This isn't as impossible as it looks. I know it probably feels impossible, and for a girl like you, with so much pizzazz, it must feel like you're going crazy inside. But you're not the first girl to ever be in this situation, to be having a baby, to have a jealous boyfriend. You don't believe it, but you have friends. You have Laura. And you also have me. For sure. I might not be the most swell girl you'll ever meet, but I bet I'm one of the most loyal. We won't let you down if you just let us help. Deep inside, you know we won't let you down.'

Laura had never felt so proud of anyone in her life.

She slid her arm back around Dolly. All of their eyes were watering from the cold; Laura had lost the feeling in her feet. She glanced up at Vivian's face, still placid and knowing. Standing there hovering above them, she looked almost beatific. 'How about it, Vivian? Look at us: three girls, with three broken hearts, surrounded on all sides by the big city four days before Christmas,

342

wondering what happened. But we're still here. We know we can deal with whatever comes our way.' She leaned forward, stretched out her hand. 'Please, Vivian. *Please.*'

For the first time, Laura saw small droplets of uncertainty seep into the resignation in Vivian's face. 'I . . . I don't know. It's so utterly hopeless.'

It was time to go for broke. 'Don't you see? Don't you *see?!*' Laura said, leaping up to her feet. 'That's it! Right there! It *seems* that way. But it *isn't* that way. You can't see it, because you're too far in it. But we can. We can see it. Let us see it for you. You have no hope. You must let us carry your hope for you. I swear, Vivian, I can have you in Connecticut in ninety minutes. And from there we can get you anywhere. He'll never find you. Nicky may have muscles, but my father has brains and money. You have to trust me.'

Laura took one tentative step closer, thrust her arm out again. 'Take my hand, honey. Come on. It's okay. It's going to be okay.'

Vivian's face had turned wary, childlike, and Laura was surprised how much the metamorphosis of her expression jarred her. Vivian was the dame, the broad, the siren. Now all of that had been stripped away, revealing the frightened girl underneath. Dolly remained on her knees next to Laura, no doubt afraid to move a muscle, to interrupt the spell Laura had been casting. Laura could see Vivian's white-gloved hand balling into a fist, then opening again, over and over, as if by itself her hand itself was waging a war over which path to take.

They simply stood, looking at one another,

343

saying nothing, their faces stinging in the frigid temperatures, Laura's arm beginning to shake from being extended so long. But she was winning. She could feel the tide turning, feel Vivian's resistance waning. She just had to be patient, wait it out. She would stand here with her arm extended all night if she had to.

'I left Nicky a card, too,' Vivian said quietly.

Laura tried not to show any reaction. But suddenly, the window of time for saving Vivian had just gotten a lot shorter. *Damn! Why did she have to leave* him *a note?* If Nicky had done what Laura had done, opened his card early, he could be on his way to the Barbizon this very minute. And there was no telling what he would do when he got here. They had to get Vivian off the terrace and out of the hotel. Now.

'Honey,' Laura said gently, 'it's time to come now. Let us take care of you. It's okay. Come.' She thrust her arm out once more.

All of the anguish and conflict and doubt crisscrossed Vivian's face, until she haltingly took a step toward Laura.

She began to raise her hand.

A gust of wind whooshed in from behind Dolly and Laura, and they turned to watch the door to the terrace swing wildly open.

Laura whirled back around. 'Vivian, it's nothing! No one's there! It's just the wind! Vivian!!'

But Vivian's mind crashed under the weight of the moment, of the stark, ugly reminder it provided, that no matter where she went, no matter who she became, no matter how much

344

she tried to start over, Nicola Accardi would always be there, taunting her, haunting her, around every dark street corner, lurking underneath every sinister lamppost shadow. Even if he never found her, he would always be there, the threat that she would think about the first thing when she woke up every morning and before she closed her eyes at night. He would be the ghost who would follow her, and her child, forever. She couldn't live like that. She wouldn't live like that.

Vivian looked at Laura, her eyes brimming with tears. 'I'm sorry,' she whispered.

Laura couldn't even hear her own screaming, even as she bolted toward the terrace ledge, Dolly yelling, wailing, scrambling to her feet behind her, as they watched Vivian, in one swift, fluid, brutal motion, swing her legs over the railing and drop away on the other side.

Epilogue

May 1956

They'd picked a diner in Chelsea to meet, primarily because Chelsea was a neighborhood with no shared memories between them. In all the months she'd lived in New York, Laura couldn't remember once being in Chelsea.

When she walked into the diner, she spied Dolly immediately, sitting at a back table by the window, sipping tea. As she headed toward her, Laura could see Dolly had lost a good deal of additional weight and immediately felt a pinch of guilt. During those periods when she'd thought of Dolly in these past few months, she'd invariably pictured her gorging on a tray of sweets. Clearly, quite the opposite had happened. Dolly looked positively gorgeous.

Dolly stood and they hugged. 'It's so nice to see you,' Laura said. 'You look absolutely wonderful.'

'It's okay to say you're surprised,' Dolly replied, settling back behind her tea. 'I sure am.'

'What have you been doing?'

'Not eating,' Dolly said dryly. 'As you know, I have always been the girl who turned to the bakery for support when the going got rough. But it turns out when the going gets downright catastrophic, I can't eat at all.' She looked up, artificially cheery. 'And how are you?'

346

'Better,' Laura said. 'At least I think better.'

It was hard to believe it had been only five months; it felt like years. Vivian's had not been the first jump in the history of the Barbizon, but it was the first in a long time, and beyond that it had all of the elements of high drama: the Stork Club profession (several papers had incorrectly identified Vivian as a showgirl, presumably because dead showgirls sold more papers), the gangster boyfriend, the city's chic dormitory for girls as the backdrop. The story had been all over the papers for weeks. Nicky had gone to jail on an unrelated matter, something to do with a shady deal in Hoboken, albeit briefly. He was now out on bail pending additional charges, which Laura hoped would include murder, but she doubted it. Vivian had been right about one thing: Guys like Nicky were always getting away with it.

The police had questioned Laura for hours. She had told them absolutely everything she could think of — about how scared Vivian had been, the pregnancy, how Nicky had evidently killed one of Vivian's friends — until Marmy and Dad had swooped into the police station, whisking her back to Connecticut. Marmy had actually been . . . warm. Of course, she'd also been living off of all the drama over canasta and mai tais ever since.

Dolly, fragile to begin with as that long night had unwound, had come completely unglued by the time it was over. After Vivian had plunged over the side, she'd disintegrated into utter hysteria, which didn't subside until the ambulance men had come and injected something into

347

her arm, right there on the terrace. Laura was herded to the police station, Dolly driven to the hospital. It had taken weeks for Laura to track her down back in Utica. They'd sent a few letters, talked briefly on the phone to set up this little reunion. Dolly was en route to her aunt's in Brooklyn, where the Barbizon had sent her things. 'I can't step foot back in that place,' Dolly had told her on the phone.

After Laura ordered a coffee, they began updating one another in greater detail. Laura relayed that she had returned to Smith, where the semester had just ended, and how nice it had been to be back in Northampton. Dolly talked about how she was finishing her Katie Gibbs certification at a local college near Syracuse, and how she had met a nice guy at the library she'd gone out with once and who 'seems blissfully normal,' as she put it. Dolly asked Laura if she'd heard from Box and, because she could not help being Dolly, shared the unsolicited news that she'd recently seen a gossip column photo of Box and a shapely blonde, walking into a premiere at the Ziegfeld. Laura wondered how Agnes Ford felt about that. And was glad to note that she herself felt . . . nothing.

An awkward silence descended over the table once the preliminary catch-ups were over. Dolly was absently stirring her tea, looking out onto Twenty-Third Street, when she said, 'Do you think about her much?'

'Every day,' Laura said.

Dolly sighed. 'It's so strange, really. It comes on me at the oddest times. Like, I'll be on a bus looking out the window, or buying apple juice, or soaking in the tub, and she'll just come into my brain. That whole, horrible night comes into my brain.

'Do you think,' Dolly went on, 'that it will ever stop hurting? Because I would like to believe there will be a day when I will be able to think about her without it hurting.'

'I'm not sure it will ever not hurt,' Laura said softly. 'But I can only hope that, over time, it will hurt less. And the good memories will outweigh . . . ' She trailed off.

Dolly was shaking her head. 'I know it doesn't do any good to go over it anymore. I mean, I even went to see a shrink about it. Did I tell you that? I did. Just once, but I was so desperate I was willing to try anything. But basically he said what everyone says: 'Time heals all wounds.' Sometimes I worry that I have no right to feel this way at all. I mean, it wasn't like she really even liked me.'

'She loved you.' Dolly's head jerked to attention, and their eyes met. 'She wasn't good at showing it,' Laura continued. 'Who knows why. Maybe because of her family. Or maybe that's just the way the British are. I don't know. But I do know she cared about you — about both of us — very deeply.'

'She didn't tell you the whole truth about Box and Agnes.'

'She didn't know the whole truth. I think she didn't say anything not to be cruel, but because she truly felt there are some things you have to learn for yourself. Which I did.'

'I don't know. I just keep thinking the same thought, over and over, that we should have been able to help her. Should have seen the signs. Should have done *something* — '

Laura cut her off. 'You can't do this. It isn't like I haven't had those same internal monologues, over and over and over. I have. But you can't hold yourself responsible for other people's choices, even tragic ones. Vivian was nothing if not strong-willed. She was always going to live on her terms. And she was going to . . . ' The remainder went unspoken. *She was going to die on her own terms, too.*

Out on the sidewalk, their goodbye felt stilted, awkward. They hugged again tightly, promised to call, promised to write. But as Laura watched Dolly walk up toward Eighth Avenue, she felt sadness creep into her heart. Because something told her she would never see Dolly again. Their unlikely friendship had been a summer romance of a different sort. And had, like hers with Box, been irreparably damaged by the actions of another woman. Tragedy may bring people closer together. But once it's over, the only thing anyone wants to do is forget.

* * *

MacDougal Books & Letters looked different in the light of spring. Laura couldn't put her finger on it at first, then realized, as she stepped out of the cab and walked down the few steps, that the door had been freshly painted in a shiny coat of black.

She pushed it open, heard the familiar tinkle of the gold bell that had welcomed her on so many prior visits. *A lifetime ago.*

Why did she think it would look radically different? It had been a little over six months since her last visit. The shelves were still crammed with books of all shapes and sizes, the schoolhouse pendant lights hung from the ceiling, and the worn wooden counter remained stationed at the left, complete with the old rusty cash register. No one was browsing. Laura knew the shop would be quiet on a Tuesday morning. *Connie must be in the back. He's far too trusting leaving the place unattended like this.*

She walked around, glancing at some of the new fiction, took a minute to step to the magazine rack and flip through the current issue of *Mademoiselle*, at its ironic motto: 'The magazine for smart young women.' On the cover there was a photograph of a beautiful model in a flowered swimsuit standing on a tropical beach, and along with teasers for stories on the new cottons and new swimwear there was one that declared, 'What's new in suburbia.'

'If you want to buy it, it's thirty-five cents.'

Laura looked up into the face not of Connie Offing, but Pete Kelly. He was leaning against the counter, nestling a push broom. His hair was still a messy tangle of competing angles, some going one way, another patch the next, but it appeared he'd gained a few pounds, which actually filled him out, made him appear a few years older. They'd all grown up in the last year.

Laura was glad she'd worn a pretty outfit, a

slightly flouncy blue-and-white California dress with cap sleeves and matching white flats. She didn't care what *Mademoiselle* or any other fashion magazine said; it was warm out, and she was wearing her new white shoes, Memorial Day be damned. *What was that saying Vivian had always been quoting?* 'Fashion can be bought. Style one must possess.'

It was nice to think about her and smile.

'Don't tell me you've traded in your bartender's apron for sweeping the floors,' Laura said.

'Temporary reassignment,' Pete replied. 'Just looking after the place while Connie's in the hospital.'

'Oh no. What happened?'

'No, no, don't worry, he's going to be fine. He just decided he'd had enough trouble with the foot, so he had some surgery to alleviate the pain. He'll be up and about in no time.'

'Thank God.' She was going to add something and stopped.

He studied her, so intently that Laura was forced to look away and out the window, onto MacDougal Street. 'The window is sparkling,' she remarked. 'You've been busy. Connie should have had an operation ages ago.' She glanced around. 'It looks nice.'

Pete set the push broom aside. 'Ah, it's nothing.' He took in a deep breath. 'So . . . what brings you back to town?'

'Well, final exams were last week. I'm mulling whether to take a job as a nanny on the Cape for the month of August, believe it or not. Can you imagine that? Me as a governess?'

His quiet intensity, the one she had never completely been able to put out of her head, returned in full force to greet her. 'I've imagined a lot of things about you.'

She had to look away again. She didn't know what to do with her arms, now fidgety and rubbery and flailing, crossed, then uncrossed, at her sides, then hands clasped behind her back, then back to the front, hands now rubbing together. 'And you? What have you been up to, other than sweeping floors and polishing windows?'

'Still at the bar a few nights. Writing's gone well, though. I finished the book.'

'*Wonderland*?'

'The very same.'

'Tell me,' she said, laughing, 'does she get a happy ending?'

'You'll have to buy the book to find out.' His smile, warm and inviting, jarred her. She had thought that if she ever saw him again, all of that would be gone, vanished, like so much about her time living in New York already was. Vivian's face appeared again in her brain, and she fought to shake it out. 'It's nice to see you,' he said.

'You, too.' *Say something.* 'I got your letter,' she continued. 'That was very kind. It meant a lot to me.'

He shrugged. 'You didn't reply. I didn't know how you'd reacted to it. But I just wanted you to know . . . Well, you know.'

'No, no, I'm sorry. It's just been so . . . ' She shrugged. 'I couldn't even be sure how I would feel once I came back to the city. I haven't been here since everything happened. And back then I couldn't ever imagine coming back.'

'Have you spoken to Dolly? How is she?'

Laura told him about their coffee. He asked if she'd heard from others. She'd gotten a few cards and notes, the most surprising being one from Metzger, on a pale blue note card embossed simply, THE BARBIZON HOTEL. 'Hope you are doing well and readjusting,' it read. 'I wish you every good thing.' It was signed, simply, 'Your friend, Anne Metzger.'

Pete was now directly in front of her, searching her eyes. 'I'm sorry. We don't have to keep talking about this. I was just asking . . . Actually, I have to be honest: I don't know what to say.'

'I know what to say to *you*,' she said. 'I'm sorry.'

He kept looking at her.

'I need you to understand,' she continued. 'Sometimes in life, we pick the wrong door. The one real thing in my life in all my months here in New York was the one thing I let slip away. And I cannot tell you how often I have thought of that and regretted it. I didn't answer your letter not because I didn't want to, but because I was afraid to. I owed you an honest response, and I was afraid if I did that — if I allowed myself to do that, all the way through — and you weren't receptive . . . ' She trailed off. 'I know that's cowardly. But I'm not as strong as you are. Or as brave.'

'I think you're incredibly brave,' he muttered quietly. He pulled her into him and hugged her,

354

pressed the side of his face against hers. 'I'm here.'

'I don't . . . I can't . . . '

'Yes, you can. Don't be afraid. Let it out. I'm here. I've got you. For once, Laura, for once — don't take what you think you should. Take what you really *need*.'

And so she did. She wept, and clung to him, and wept more, quietly at first, then forcefully, her body shaking in his grip, until no more tears would come.

Neither of them moved to break the embrace. They stood, not quite standing still, not quite swaying, as if dancing in place. She allowed herself the liberating freedom of nuzzling into his chest, her eyes once again glancing out of the sparkling window. He kissed her temple.

She didn't ever want to be anywhere else.

'It's so sunny and warm outside,' she said.

'Summer's coming.'

'Yes, summer,' she said. She looked up at him. 'Will you take me back to Atlantic City?'

He leaned down and kissed her gently on the lips. 'Of course,' he said, his face a portrait of pure, unfiltered joy. 'But this time, I'm making sure you bring a notebook.'

Acknowledgements

Writing a novel is like driving a car at night. You can only see as far as your headlights, but you can make the whole trip that way.

E. L. Doctorow

I may have driven the car, but I had a lot of help with directions.

First and foremost, my deepest gratitude to the incredible members of my writing group, Philomena Papirnik and Manuel Moreno. Your unfailing dedication, incisive critiques, and throaty cheerleading saw me through many an 'I can't write another word' night. I owe this book to you.

My agent, the fabulous Jane Dystel, believed in this project from the start, and she and her partner, Miriam Goderich, provided invaluable counsel navigating these new waters. My editor at Houghton Mifflin Harcourt, Nicole Angeloro, not only dove passionately into the story, but resurfaced with thoughtful edits that took the book across the finish line.

Novels may be stories of imagination, but they require thorough research in order to ring true. My editor at *Vanity Fair*, David Friend, immediately seized on my pitch for a magazine piece about the Barbizon, and the story I wrote put me on the road to this novel. To him and the esteemed Graydon Carter, I express my sincere appreciation for their continual indulgence in letting me roam around the glamorous past for stories.

My researcher, Christine Wei, spent hours combing through microfiche and dusty documents; Shawn Waldron of the Condé Nast Archives was instrumental in recommending resources about *Mademoiselle*. Betsy Israel, the author of *Bachelor Girl*, served up key insights into the lives of the Barbizon doyennes, as did food critic extraordinaire Gael Greene, whose 1957 *New York Post* series remains one of the definitive accounts of life inside the hotel's walls. Modeling legend Eileen Ford was both gracious and deliciously blunt in detailing the lives of the Ford models. And *molte grazie* to all of the former Barbizon girls who took the time to share their stories with me: Jaclyn Smith, Cloris Leachman, Cybill Shepherd, Shelley Hack, Betsey Johnson, Carmen Dell'Orefice, Joyce Schwartz, Barbara Cloud, Mary Ann Powers, Kathleen Mickey, and Judith Sherven.

Three books were integral to my research: *The New York Chronology*, by James Trager; *The Fiction Factory*, by Quentin Reynolds; and *New York Fashion: The Evolution of American Style*, by Caroline Reynolds Milbank. I have made every effort to re-create the New York of 1955 as authentically as possible, except in a few places where the story demanded otherwise; any mistakes are strictly my own. Likewise, although characters such as Sherman Billingsley and Betsy Blackwell were, in fact, real people, their stories here are strictly a work of fiction.

I could never properly thank all of the friends and family who encouraged and supported me during this process, but a few deserve shout-outs: my brother, Pat, and his wife, Jean, the best friends a guy could hope for, who cleared out of our shared beach house regularly so I could write; and Cheryl Della Pietra, Piper Kerman, Larry Smith, and the gang at Philly Mag, who routinely dispatched my nerves and doubts with their encouragement and wit.

Finally, the most special thank-you of all to my wonderful parents, Jack and Eileen Callahan, whose never-ebbing generosity of spirit and faith in me has been a constant for far longer than the time it takes to write a novel. I cannot find the words to express what your love and encouragement have meant to my life. If I have one regret, it is that my father did not live to see this book published. But he will always be very much alive — along with everyone who helped me on this incredible journey — in my heart.

We do hope that you have enjoyed reading this large print book.

Did you know that all of our titles are available for purchase?

We publish a wide range of high quality large print books including:
Romances, Mysteries, Classics
General Fiction
Non Fiction and Westerns

Special interest titles available in large print are:
The Little Oxford Dictionary
Music Book
Song Book
Hymn Book
Service Book

Also available from us courtesy of Oxford University Press:
Young Readers' Dictionary
(large print edition)
Young Readers' Thesaurus
(large print edition)

For further information or a free brochure, please contact us at:
Ulverscroft Large Print Books Ltd.,
The Green, Bradgate Road, Anstey,
Leicester, LE7 7FU, England.
Tel: (00 44) **0116 236 4325**
Fax: (00 44) **0116 234 0205**

Other titles published by Ulverscroft:

THE ARTIFICIAL ANATOMY OF PARKS

Kat Gordon

At twenty-one, Tallulah Park lives alone in a grimy bedsit, where a strange damp smell causes her to wake up wheezing. When she finds out her estranged father has had a heart attack and arranges to visit him, she isn't looking forward to seeing her relatives again. Years before, she was being tossed around her difficult family: a world of sniping aunts, precocious cousins, emigrant pianists and lots of gin, all presided over by an unconventional grandmother. But no one was answering Tallie's questions: why did Aunt Vivienne loathe Tallie's mother? Who was Uncle Jack, and why would no one talk about him? And why was everyone making excuses for her absent father? As Tallie grows up, she learns the hard way that in the end, the worst betrayals are those we inflict on ourselves . . .